The Vatican Protocol

Brian Gallagher

For more information about the controversial subjects in Vatican Protocol visit:
www.vaticanprotocol.com
Twitter@GallagherAuthor
www.facebook.com/BrianGallagherAuthor/

ISBN 978-1-61225-334-3

Published by Mirror Publishing
Fort Payne, AL 35967
www.pagesofwonder.com

Printed in the USA

This book is dedicated to Rose Sadoski. Your unending enthusiasm and belief in this work provided the inspiration to persevere. You're a true Guardian Angel..........

Thanks Rose, this one's for you.

Acknowledgements

I could never have written this book without the support of my family. Their unending confidence and encouragement helped take this project from conception to print and kept me moving forward. My brother Dan was a tough critic and offered ideas that made for a better book. My social media maven and friend, Alice Martin at shroomsocial.com, did the social media dirty work that I would have never done on my own. Thank you Alice, for developing my Facebook and Twitter following and providing terrific advice that helped me navigated through the whole process.

A thank you to the cover folks:

Wewelsburg cover artwork from videogame Lost Horizon.
©2010-2016 Animation Arts Creative GmbH. Published 2010-2016 by Deep Silver, a division of Koch Media GmbH, Austria.

I would also like to thank Michael Garrett, my editor, for not only doing a great edit, but for providing insight as to how I could become a better writer. His advice made Vatican Protocol a better novel.

Prologue

The Black Forest, near Freiburg Germany, 1936

Gerhard Wagner stepped from his warm living room onto a freezing front porch. He filled his lungs with frosty air and watched as the darkness became white from his exhale. The only intrusion into the night came from three lanterns flickering through two large windows and from an impressive three-quarter moon over the tops of the imposing pines.

He lived in the same small log home located deep in the Black Forest for sixty years. His grandfather built it by hand, and Gerhard took ownership when his grandfather passed away. He never married, and his family consisted of three large Bouvier des Flandres.

The weather-beaten porch provided a front row seat to the sparkling diamonds set in the ebony sky and the long dark shadows from the surrounding forest. He took another deep breath and appreciated the sweet scent of pines in the light breeze. He debated how long he'd remain in the brisk air when the dogs became agitated. This was not unusual given the abundance of wildlife found in the woods, and it was typically the scent of wolves that aggravated the dogs. Gerhard watched as their pacing increased.

Glancing skyward, he saw it. Streaking across the sky was a silent fireball. He'd never seen an airplane, and the lack of formal education meant the possibility of a meteor never occurred to him. The flaming object came closer and lost altitude as time stood still. He didn't move until the object disappeared below the silhouettes of primeval evergreens. Seconds later there was an explosion, and for a moment daylight replaced the night. Soon a distasteful odor filled the air, a combination of burning rubber and sulfur. It was the same sort of rotten egg smell produced by paper mills, but with a burning scent thrown in for good measure.

He went into his house and slipped into a worn woolen plaid coat, grabbed a leather hat complete with ear-flaps, put a pistol in his belt, and picked up his shotgun along with additional shells.

Gerhard entered the primitive barn, lifted a battered leather saddle, and placed it on the muscular back of the *Schwarzalder Kaltblut*, better known as the Black Forest Cold Blood. The workhorse breed was Gerhard's pride and joy, and he rode it everywhere. Its stunning dark chestnut coat was offset by a flaxen mane and tail. Gerhard finished tightening the saddle and mounted his steed.

The combination of a clear night with an assist from the moonlight provided a shimmering semblance of visibility, but he brought along a kerosene lantern for additional light. He guided his mount slowly into the woods with the Bouviers following close. Gerhard knew the forest topography like most people knew the inside of their homes. He could navigate blindfolded through the many game trails and his own pathways sculpted over the last fifty years. He was comfortable in the woods, but his awareness was heightened at night. Having the Bouviers along reduced his anxiety given their famous sense of protection.

Once he entered the forest, its blackness increased, but the lantern provided enough light to maneuver on the path. It took about ten minutes to find his way to the site of the explosion. As he got closer, the odor became stronger, and an eerie glow shown through a myriad of branches and evergreens. The horse slowed to a walk and resisted as he closed in on the clearing and the dogs stopped short and moved abnormally. Gerhard dismounted and tied the reins to a branch so his transportation wouldn't decide to bolt.

He came to the edge of the impact area and was astonished by its appearance. The thick forest had been flattened to an oval shape, where trees and undergrowth seemed to have vaporized. He gingerly tiptoed into the midst of smoldering fires, carefully avoiding anything burning. The ground was devoid of organic material as something burned in the middle of the newly created clearing. Gerhard, wary with each step, slowly sauntered to the remnants of the craft. It was in the shape of a German Helmet, was silver in color, and even though the fires had been burning for some time, the exterior of the craft looked smooth with none of the soot residue one would expect.

A hatch appeared to be open at the top of the craft, and as Gerhard walked around he was stunned to see three small bodies in shiny metal suits. His heart pounded as he went from spooked to afraid. The size of the bodies were those of small children, but the uneducated man from the Black Forest knew these were not children.

Gerhard was a product of an environment where werewolves and vampires were regarded as real, and stories like Hansel and Gretel and Little Red Riding Hood were believed throughout these woods. He noticed the metal was thin, and curiosity got the best of him as he removed his glove and picked up a piece of something shiny. It was light weight and cool to the touch, despite its proximity to the fire. He didn't want to go near the bodies, but he felt somehow compelled to stay.

He dropped the remnant from the craft when he heard voices from the edge of the forest and stepped back toward his tethered horse. Gerhard wasn't a social character and preferred to see who it was before he made them aware of his presence. The woods parted, and four of his neighbors stepped into the clearing.

"Good evening," Gerhard said, stepping out from the woods."

"*Herr* Wagner, what do you make of this?" the burly neighbor asked.

"I have no idea. All I know is it stinks and my dogs won't come close. Wait till you see this," he said pointing to the bodies.

"Oh my, they're so small," another neighbor said.

"Yes, but two of them are much larger," Gerhard said.

"And what happened to the forest. The trees have disappeared," the neighbor said.

"I know. This place is making me uncomfortable. I came over to check it out, but now I wish I'd stayed home. I don't want to think about what this could be. I've seen enough, I'm leaving," Gerhard said and stepped into the woods.

When he reached his restrained horse, the hyperactive Bouviers surged to him with unbridled frenzy. Gerhard swung his leg over the saddle and his entourage retraced their earlier steps.

Gerhard crawled into bed that night and was unsuccessful at clearing his mind, with childhood superstitions appearing and reappearing all night long. This rather simple man of the Black Forest couldn't process what he'd seen.

He awoke before sunrise, and by mid-morning could no longer ignore whatever was grounded ten minutes away. He decided to return to the site and again assembled his weapons and went to the barn.

Moments later he was on his way with the Bouviers once again in tow. Gerhard was curious how the dogs would react to the site in the light of day. This trip was easier, and as they approached the clearing the animal's behavior once again showed nervousness. As he dismounted he noticed the silence of the previous night was replaced by odd noises coming from the defoliated area. He tied his horse to the same branch as the night before, stepped out of the woods, and couldn't believe his eyes. The entire oval was roped off and guarded by *Heer* Troops. There were uniformed men milling everywhere, inspecting the craft and bagging scattered objects. The inspectors wore either Nazi or SS uniforms while those guarding the perimeter were *Heer* troops, the regular Germany army.

Gerhard approached the closest soldier, whom he recognized as Hans Fuhrmann, an acquaintance from Freiburg.

"Halt, come no closer," Fuhrmann said.

"Hans, it's Gerhard," he said.

"Gerhard, what are you doing here? It's not safe to be seen," Fuhrmann said, "the Nazis are running the show and they like to make people disappear."

"What are they doing?" Gerhard asked.

"They're packing everything and I overheard they're taking it to Wewelsburg Castle," he said.

"Who is the big guy in the light blue uniform?" Gerhard asked.

"Have you heard of Hermann Goering? That's him. The little guy next to him is Heinrich Himmler, he's the head of the SS. This thing brought Nazis out of the woodwork," he said.

"I've heard of both of them. Who's the guy in the suit? It looks like he's the one in charge," Gerhard asked.

"He's Wernher von Braun and he is in charge," Fuhrmann said, "look, you've got to get out of here. You don't want them coming to your front door."

"I think you're right. See you," Gerhard said, and returned to his tethered horse.

He returned to his cabin and felt it best to forget everything he'd seen. He didn't trust the Nazis and maintained a well-founded fear of who they were.

For two days Gerhard's anxiety gradually dissipated. As the sun was getting lower in the sky on the third day there was a rap on his front door. An official looking man in a black SS uniform stood on the porch.

"Good afternoon, *Herr* Wagner. My name is Captain Diederich and I am here about a crash not far from here. Are you familiar with it?"

Gerhard hesitated. He knew the SS was dangerous and would only say enough to stay out of trouble.

"I saw a flame in the air and heard an explosion the other night. The next morning I went to see what it was and a guard told me to leave and I did," Wagner said.

"I see. Did you observe anything?"

"I saw people picking up things, and I saw things sitting on the ground, but I left when instructed to do so."

"Well, *Herr* Wagner, this event is of the highest secrecy. I need to know anything else you know about this incident. Have you spoken with your neighbors or anyone about it?"

"I didn't see anything and haven't had discussion with anyone. As you can see, I keep to myself and prefer living alone with my dogs."

The SS captain was silent for a moment, which made him even more menacing.

"What was the name of the guard you spoke with?" Diederich asked.

"I don't know. I never saw him before, and he didn't give his name. He sent me away."

"Very well, *Herr* Wagner. Please remember this conversation. It is a capital offense, which means, if you ever discuss it, you will be executed. You do not want the SS coming back to visit you, *Herr* Wagner."

"I will never speak of what I saw," Gerhard said as he relaxed for a moment. That was a mistake.

The SS officer removed his Luger and pointed it at Wagner's face.

"Goodbye *Herr* Wagner," Diederich said as his finger pulled the trigger and sent a bullet propelling through the woodsman's skull. Gerhard crumbled to the ground without knowing the same fate had already befallen his neighbors.

In 1938 another UFO crashed outside the villages of Czernica and Kopaniec in occupied Poland, and the Nazis handled the craft recovery in much the same fashion as the Freiburg recovery. The same group of military officers and scientists, under von Braun's direction, removed the craft to Wewelsburg Castle.

Gerard Wagner wouldn't be the only individual to meet an unfortunate fate for living in the wrong place at the wrong time. The unfortunate inhabitants living near the Polish crash site also met the same end.

Bend Oregon, USA   2014
Chapter 1)

Sean O'Shea nestled into his weathered leather recliner and turned on the television. The "UFO Files" were on the screen and claimed to have new details regarding the Roswell event. Sean relished the History Channel, because much of its programming related to UFOs, the unexplained and unexplainable. He felt escapism was underrated.

He had owned a home in Scottsdale, Arizona during the well documented UFO sightings during the 1990s. He never had the good fortune to see a UFO, but conversed with many who had.

Sean closed his eyes and let his mind wander through the last few years. He was an unwilling participant in the housing meltdown in 2009 and journeyed from being financially set for life to losing everything. Sean was forced to start over and created a web site selling organic products which did well enough to pay the bills. Cat, his raw foodist wife, had taken over the business so he'd have time to focus on other ways to rebuild the family fortune.

Life had been good to Sean, with successes in sports and business, and while the financial issues hurt the pocketbook, truth be told, the damage to his ego was even more devastating. He longed for the days like Short Round told Indiana Jones, "You do it for fortune and glory." His motivation was to not only regain financial independence, but also to restore his self-esteem.

He had an idea of how to accomplish the goal, but knew a full commitment was required. He always wanted to become a writer, but to date, every attempt ended with an unfinished manuscript. At one time he started writing a book attempting to prove the existence of Shape-shifters, better known as Vampires, but it sat untouched for the past six years. He had written ninety pages before his enthusiasm waned, but always expected to pick up where he left off. He had other false starts, but attributed those failures to the lack of passion for his chosen subjects. Sean thought he might be categorized as a failed writer, but preferred to think of himself as a struggling writer. He knew he could create a great book if he could find subject matter worthy of holding his interest.

The History Channel was at fault for his newest obsession. He was toying with the idea of trying to prove Wright Patterson Air Force Base and Area Fifty-one held multiple alien spacecraft. Taking on this project would be an interesting and entertaining journey, even if turned out to be a dead end. He would love to write a book exposing the truth of how the American public had been kept in the dark about alien visitation.

His daydreaming was jolted back to reality when Cat called to him.

"Sean, Liam just texted and he's ready to be picked up. Can you get him?"

"Sure, I'll be up in a second," he said.

He climbed the stairs as Cat walked by in a tight t-shirt and jeans.

"You're looking great, no one would ever guess you're forty-five," he said. "You're a walking wet dream."

"Would you get out of here, he's waiting," she said.

"Ahhhh, what stinks? It smells like Boo crapped on the floor," he said.

"Yeah, it does smell a little. I'm making a vegan soup with cabbage and broccoli. My mom swears by it."

"Where's Boo?" he said, looking for their eight pound Norwich terrier.

"I put him in the back yard. He didn't like the smell either. You've got to get going, Liam's waiting."

They had a close family with Liam, in his senior year in high school, and Cassie, a college sophomore at Heidelberg University in Heidelberg Germany. It was Liam who needed to be picked up after a day of snow-boarding at Mount Bachelor. Sean pulled the SUV out of the garage and proceeded toward the mountain.

His thoughts turned to Cassie and his two older daughters. Both older daughters lived in Wisconsin, his favorite state. Claire Bear, her nick-name, lived in Wauwatosa with her husband and two-year-old son Moose, and Amie lived in Madison with her twelve-year-old son. Sean missed all his girls. He hadn't seen Claire Bear and Amie in a year and a half and Cassie had stayed in Europe over Christmas break, so he hadn't seen her for seven months. This was causing acute separation anxiety.

His attention returned to the road. The drive to pick up Liam wasn't a chore because of the spectacular scenery. Mount Bachelor, a ten thousand foot extinct volcano, offered the best skiing/snowboarding on the West Coast. Driving from Bend, which was bone dry, to Mount Bachelor was like entering a winter wonderland in twenty minutes.

As he drove, he thought back to his book idea. How would he be able to start the process of proving what so many ufologists tried and failed to do? It occurred to him that an old friend, Alan Rockenbach, once had security clearance with the state department and connecting with him could be a place to start. They'd known each other since grade school when Alan had moved from Germany to the U.S. Alan owned a software company in Strasbourg, France, and they recently discussed starting a new venture together. Sean thought Alan might be helpful in getting inside information and made a mental note to give him a call.

Sean was three-quarters of the way to the mountain when he exited a thick section of pine forest, and there it was. Mount Bachelor loomed above as a white spherical spike penetrating the brilliant peacock blue sky. The verdant forest extended in every direction, heavy with snow, with sections of evergreens peeking out. It reminded him of one of those glass balls, that when tipped upside down, fake snow fell onto the plastic green trees held captive inside.

Sean rolled up to the entrance of the Pine Marten Lodge, proceeded to the pick-up area, parked the car and got out to open the back of the vehicle. The icy breath of the cold mountain air on his face, was the first thing he noticed.

"Hey dad, I'm over here," Liam said, picking up his snowboard.

"Hey bud, it's a lot colder up here than at home. How was it?" Sean asked.

"The snow was good, but it's not the same when you're by yourself. I miss doing this with Cassie," he said.

"I know, I miss her too," Sean said.

His son was eighteen, tall and muscular befitting the fact he all he did was work out. He was in the midst of investigating college options for the following year and dealing with the associated anxiety.

Sean slammed the rear hatch and eased their way down the snow covered mountain road.

"Why do you think Cassie chose to go to Heidelberg University of all places?" Liam asked.

"For as long as I can remember she seemed fixated on it. I can understand it because I find it fascinating. It was founded over sixty years before Joan of Arc was executed, the Medicis came to power in Florence and Gutenberg invented the printing press. I think she was enamored by its historical relevance."

"I get that, but it's so far away. I just miss her nasty sense of humor," he said. "When's she coming home?"

"She's not due back until the end of May, we've got another three months before her sweet face can spew all her gross comments," Sean said.

"I think she should be a stand-up comedian. You know, pretty and innocent looking like Sarah Silverman until she opens her mouth and shocks everyone," Liam said.

The terrain changed from five feet of snow at the top of the mountain to bare ground in less than fifteen minutes. Sean turned onto his street and pulled into the garage.

Sean resumed his position in the overstuffed recliner and turned on the hockey game between the Chicago Blackhawks and the Anaheim Ducks. As the game played in the background, Sean pulled up Alan Rockenbach's phone number and hit the send button on his cell phone. Alan answered on the third ring, and after a brief discussion regarding their joint venture, Sean got to the real reason for his call.

"So I want to shift gears. I have a little project I'm dreaming up and have a question. Do you still have your security clearance?" he asked.

"No, that lapsed a few years ago. We shifted to more commercial work and there was no reason to keep it up. Why do you ask?"

"I'm thinking of researching and trying to prove the government has covered up UFO evidence at Wright Patterson or Area Fifty-one," he said.

"How'd you come up with that idea?"

"First, I've always found the whole UFO thing intriguing and second, I really believe there's something to all the rumors."

"So how would you go about finding out what so many others have tried and failed to do?" Alan asked.

"That's why I asked about your security clearance. I must find a different approach than others have taken."

"I've always had a similar fascination about your subject matter. You know, I grew up in the Black Forest in Germany, and there were rumors about UFOs when I was a kid. I'd be interested in collaborating with you if you wanted a sidekick," Alan said.

"I'd love to work with you on this. I'm just glad you didn't think I was a kook," Sean said. "Let's think about how we can do this together." They agreed to think about a next step and signed off.

Sean stood, bounded the ten steps to the living room, and repeated Alan's comments to Cat. He could see her mental wheels turning.

She looked at him kind of funny and said, "Sean, have you thought about speaking with Wolfe?"

He looked at her and shook his head.

"How didn't I think of Wolfe? He would be the perfect guy to speak with about this idea."

Wilhelm Wolfe was the caretaker for their summer home located on the Lac Du Flambeau Indian Reservation in the north woods of Wisconsin. The home was a charming ninety-four-year-old log home and was on the Historic Registry. It had a wet boathouse, and sat on a peninsula stretching along two thousand feet of Long Interlaken Lake, part of the Fence Lake chain. Sean and Cat purchased it twelve years earlier when they were in far better financial shape. Now they were in a holding pattern trying to sell it before the bank started knocking on the door.

When they bought it, they inherited the caretaker. Since it was a seasonal home and getting close to one hundred years old, it required a fair amount of maintenance. Wolfe was quite the character. He was like a real life Santa Claus standing about five feet six inches and was as round as he was tall. He had white hair, a white beard, and spoke with a lingering German accent.

Sean and Wolfe became friends over the years, and Sean started finding out fascinating things about his roly poly caretaker. Wolfe emigrated from Germany in 1947 as an eighteen-year-old. When he came off the boat he was pulled into a room with no windows and was met by a representative of the State Department. The gist was, if Wolfe wanted entry into the US, he had to agree to work for the Central Intelligence Agency, better known as the CIA.

Wilhelm agreed and became what some would call a spook, and he was the most unlikely of secret agents. All these years he maintained both his German and US citizenship. His special area of expertise was the Middle East, with most of his time spent in Europe.

14

His wife Ada was a short, spry woman with white hair, and together they looked like an elderly couple on a Currier and Ives print. Over the years Sean and Cat had entertained the Wolfes with numerous dinners. Sean took these opportunities to get Wolfe to talk about his CIA activities, and Wolfe's response was he would only discuss the secrets if he was drunk. In a running joke, Sean would offer him a drink, and Wolfe would inform him he didn't drink. This banter had gone on for thirteen years.

In the early part of 2002 and again in 2003, Wolfe called Sean to inform him he would be out of the country for a few months and any required maintenance would have to be scheduled accordingly. When pressed, Wolfe was evasive and would only say he would be seeing the Eiffel Tower in Paris and the tulips in Amsterdam. It was clear he was being called back into some sort of active duty because of his European and Middle East expertise. All he would say is nine-eleven changed the landscape. To think of a seventies-something Santa Claus acting as a reconstituted secret agent was beyond comprehension.

Sean considered the likelihood of getting Wolfe to engage in a discussion and thought it was fifty-fifty. Since the topic wasn't about national defense, the Middle East, or assassinations, Sean surmised he might have a better chance to pry something meaningful from his caretaker. He didn't have a trip scheduled to Lac Du Flambeau until May, but he was always looking for an excuse to take a trip to the lake. Now he had a legitimate reason, or at least a semi-legitimate reason to try and convince Cat this trip was necessary.

"Cat, what a great idea. I wasn't going to Flambeau this early, but if I'm going to get Wolfe to help with this, I need to do it face to face."

"I'm not crazy about you traveling, but it does make sense to speak with Wolfe in person. Since it was my idea, I can't complain too much," she said.

Lac Du Flambeau would be cold and semi-barren this early, but he knew the conversation with Wolfe could be a catalyst. He grabbed his ever-present lap top and searched Kayak.com. Within fifteen minutes he was booked on a flight the next day from Redmond, Oregon to Rhinelander, Wisconsin. Leaving the house in Bend at seven in the morning would get him into Rhinelander at seven-thirty that night.

He then called Alamo and rented an SUV for the week.

Next he placed a call to Wolfe. It only took one ring and he was

15

greeted with a sweet old lady's German accent.

"Ada, this is Sean; is Wilhelm hanging around?"

Seconds later Wolfe's friendly voice boomed through the phone.

"Sean, how are you?"

"I'm great. I wanted to give you a heads up. I'm coming to the house tomorrow. I should roll in around eight or nine tomorrow night. Can you get to the house and get the water started and the heat turned on?"

"Certainly, I'll do it first thing in the morning. The house should be toasty by the time you get here."

"Perfect. One more thing, can you come over the day after tomorrow? I have something to run by you."

"Absolutely, what time should I come by?"

"How is mid-morning?"

"I'll call before I come. Have the coffee on."

"I will." Sean said, and disconnected the call.

Sean finished his whirlwind of phone calls with one to his brother. Deagan lived a half mile from Sean's home in Lac Du Flambeau, and he and his wife Zoey lived in the north woods year-round. He let Deagan know he would be in for a week, and they made plans for dinner later in the week.

"Okay, Cat, all done. I leave at seven tomorrow morning, and I'll get to the house about nine tomorrow night. Are you okay with taking me to the airport?"

"Of course. Besides, I'll need the car since Liam has taken over the Mini Cooper," she said.

"We're set then. It'll be a good trip. I can get the house open for the year, spend time with Deagan, and see if I can get anywhere with Wolfe," he said.

As he finished the sentence, his cell phone rang. It was Alan Rockenbach.

"Sean, I've been thinking about our discussion. I didn't say much when we spoke, but I've been thinking about your comments about UFOs and cover-ups and I have something to share with you. My family was from Freiburg, and UFOs were always a major topic in my family. Whenever we would get together it would become the primary subject. My father and his brothers weren't Nazis, but fought in the war. They were in the *Heer*, which was part of the Wehrmacht, and was the equivalent of the US Army.

16

Before the war they were stationed at a base near our home.

"In 1936 there was an unusual incident which never received the kind of press you would've expected. A burning disc-shaped object flew low through the sky, emitting an odd smell, and crashed into the Black Forest not far from our home in Freiburg. My father and his brothers were part of the detail sent to secure the area. They never got close enough to see it, but fellow soldiers told them it was some kind of a round object, the likes of which they had never seen before. They also claimed several bodies were taken from the crash site. These bodies were only about four feet tall, and discussions about the encounter became the main topic at any family gathering.

"Within hours, Hitler's SS troops took over and several luminaries showed up to inspect the crash site. Get this; Wernher von Braun, Hermann Goering, Max Von Laue, Otto Hahn, the guy who discovered nuclear fusion, Werner Heisenberg, and Himmler himself were there. This group was the who's who of the German scientific and military community. My father was on duty when they showed up and they spent a full day at the site. Rumor has it, the object was taken to Wewelsburg Castle, headquarters for Himmler's SS. We never heard another word about it, and there was never any mention about what seemed like the German version of Roswell.

"Two years later, in 1938, there were rumors of another disc going down in occupied Poland, and again the SS was there in short order. Supposedly the same group of scientists visited this site, and again the object was shipped out in two days. Everything about this site was hearsay, but it was supposedly quite similar to the Freiburg crash site.

"Now you know where the conversation went every Christmas when the Rockenbach clan gathered. My father and two of his four brothers survived the war, and they've always debated what happened, what it was, and why no one has ever heard about it. I didn't want to say anything when you brought up aliens because we've always kept it in the family."

"Alan, this story is fantastic. I wanted to investigate the U.S. cover-ups, but this may be better. Is anyone still alive we could speak with?"

"My father and uncle are still alive. They're ninety-four and ninety-six, and I would guess they may know others still living."

"In my wildest dreams I couldn't have expected this. Keep thinking about anything else which might come to you. I'm headed to Wisconsin tomorrow to open my summer home. I plan to have a conversation with my caretaker, and it might be quite interesting. He's from Germany and was, or is, connected to the CIA in Europe. I'll let you know if it goes anywhere."

"Okay, I'll let you know if I think of anything else. Give me a call and let me know what he has to say," Alan said.

"Will do; talk to you soon."

Sean clicked off his phone and was left to ponder what Alan had shared. This was an incredible stroke of luck, and he was curious why he never heard of the German UFO incident. This kind of Germanic Roswell should have been all over the news, books, and movies. The ramifications of alien technology in Hitler's hands in 1936 were mind-blowing. This would provide the foundation for his discussion with Wolfe. If this story was real, Wolfe should know, and maybe Sean could read his reaction.

The next morning came early. Sean awoke with his mind moving fast, and he knew he couldn't get back to sleep. His original idea for contacting Alan was to determine if he still had security clearance, but he may have hit on an intriguing story.

At six fifty-five Sean hugged Liam.

"You're the man when I'm not here. Stay safe." Sean said.

"You too dad," Liam said.

***

It was seven-thirty when Cat dropped him off and after a warm hug and kiss, plus an admonishment to stay out of harm's way, he entered the airport in Redmond, Oregon.

It was five degrees below zero when the plane touched down in Rhinelander, Wisconsin. It took only fifteen minutes to be on his way in an ice cold Tahoe SUV. The cold, crisp air felt good, and he loved being back in the north woods. He would make it his permanent home in a heartbeat, but the small towns in the north woods weren't big enough for the rest of the family. Sean was satisfied shopping at Loon Land and the Twisted Root Emporium and didn't need a Nordstrom, but he was in the minority.

In twenty-five minutes he rolled into Minocqua and pulled into Trig's parking lot. He picked groceries for the week and was back on the road. The terrain was thick with pines, shimmering in the amber glow of his headlights, due to an earlier snowfall.

He wondered about the condition of the house and whether the driveway would be passable. Forgotten in the haste of the trip was a call to his neighbor, who doubled as his snow removal service. When Sean arrived at the driveway he was relieved to find it had been plowed within the week. The four wheel drive Tahoe easily climbed the uphill slope, and as he approached the house he could see Deagan had been over.

The inside and outside lights were on, and as he had done in the past, his brother built a fire, needing only a match to get it started. Sean snapped his thumbnail on the phosphorus tip of an old fashioned match stick and it sprung to life. He lit the fire and began bringing in the groceries.

The house looked great. Built in 1923, it gained its Historic Register designation because it was the finest example of Piece De Sur construction in the Midwest. Built as a three season Swedish hunting and fishing lodge, it wasn't meant for habitation when the temperature dipped below twenty degrees. The living room was up to about sixty degrees, but Sean knew once the fire burned for a half hour it would warm to a comfortable temperature while the bedrooms would be lucky to get up to fifty-five degrees. It would be nippy in the morning, but it felt like he was home.

He looked forward to speaking with Wolfe and discovering where the discussion would take them.

After getting everything put away, and with the house warmed sufficiently, he called Cat, then packed it in. The bed was cold, but it felt good to close his eyes.

***

The next morning was bright, sunny, and cold. It reached fifteen below the previous night and would be slow to rise. Temperatures were expected to reach fifty degrees in a couple of days, and it couldn't come too soon. It was hard to believe Minocqua Country Club would be open for play in thirty-two days. Welcome to life in the north woods.

His thoughts went to Cassie and how she was doing a half a world away. He and Cat were overprotective with their kids, and having his youngest daughter across an ocean was something he found unsettling. Sean built a new fire and worked for an hour to warm the house. He cranked up the thermostat, turned the oven to four hundred degrees, opened the oven door, and fired up the space heaters.

The house started to get comfortable, and Sean made blueberry pancakes and bacon. There was something about bacon sizzling in the pan and the associated aromas he remembered as a child that evoked comfort. Pancakes, bacon, and pure maple syrup seemed to be perfect in the woods. He remembered Deagan once stated bacon should be its own food group, and he agreed.

Chapter 2)

At ten o'clock his cell phone rang; it was Wolfe. They agreed to meet in an hour.

Before he knew it, there was pounding on his front door. Sean jumped from his down stuffed sofa. He moved into the entryway as the door swung open and Wolfe stepped into the foyer. After a welcoming embrace, Sean offered fresh coffee, something Cat cut out at home, and Wolfe accepted. Sean poured a slightly burnt French roast into two heavy mugs and they drifted toward the living room. The logs in the over-sized fireplace had been ablaze for over two hours, and the room was comfortable. A scent of pine char filled the room, joining the thousands of fires which had burned in the same place for over ninety years. The field-stone exterior was complete with charcoal stains from blazes either getting out of control or, more likely, from the flue remaining closed by the rocket scientist attempting to start the fire. Four sets of antique French Doors merged indoors and out as Sean looked toward the lake and noticed flakes beginning to drift through the trees.

His attention turned back to Wolfe as they each eased into cushioned log-framed chairs. After the normal family updates Sean got to the point.

"Wilhelm, I want to bounce something off you. I'm researching a potential book, and I think you may be able to point me in the right direction. Don't think I'm crazy, but I believe the government has been covering up UFO visitations forever. I believe there may be alien spacecraft at Wright Patterson Air Force Base or Area Fifty-one and I'd like to investigate. Since this is far from your responsibilities in the CIA, I thought you might be open to sharing any rumors you've heard."

"Ha Ha. I'll tell you everything I know when I get drunk. But you know I don't drink, ha," Wolfe said.

"I know I can't get you to drink, but I thought there may be areas you'd be comfortable discussing."

"Well, I never had any first-hand contact with UFO's," he said, then hesitated and looked away. "I can't talk about anything regarding the CIA."

Sean knew the longer the conversation lasted, the more would come from Wolfe's loose lips. Several months before, prior to nine-eleven, Wolfe predicted George W. was going into Iraq to get Saddam as payback for the assassination attempt on his father. The conversation happened at least a year before the war to "liberate" Iraq. Wolfe's prophesy had been an eye opener.

"Wilhelm, you were in Germany until 1947, long before you became part of the CIA. Do you remember any Nazi-related UFO rumors?"

Again Wolfe hesitated. This wasn't like him because there was never a silent moment with Wilhelm. He would've been great on the radio because there was never a threat of dead air. He was struggling with what he was willing to reveal. This was good. His nature was to talk, so Sean knew he needed to prolong the conversation.

"Where did you grow up?" Sean asked.

"I grew up about halfway between Heidelberg and Strasbourg," Wolfe said.

"I've been all through that area. I think it would've been a great place to grow up except for a little thing called the war," Sean said.

"It was such a beautiful place before Hitler's idiocy. I was three when the Nazis came to power, and all I knew growing up was the bullshit from Nazi propaganda. We were fortunate because we were in the hinterlands and didn't have the bombing and destruction the cities had. The misguided thinking was Strasbourg and Freiburg escaped the bombing. This was true until 1944, but then they both had the shit bombed out of them. The city that escaped unscathed was Heidelberg.

"Yes, back to your original question, it was and still is a beautiful area, but what a strange time to grow up," he said.

"Did you get back there often?" Sean asked.

"Oh yes, because of my profession I spent a great deal of time in Germany. My family was scattered throughout the western portion of the country so I was able to maintain family connections."

Sean realized this was the perfect time to push.

"Two days ago I had an interesting discussion with an old colleague. His family is from Freiburg, and when I told him of my interest in UFOs, he had some interesting insights," Sean said, then recounted his discussion with Alan. When he finished, he knew it was time and asked, "So, have you ever heard of such a thing?"

He could see the wheels turning in Wolfe's head. He also felt, since this was prior to his CIA involvement, Wolfe would reveal what he knew. Sean was right.

"Yes, I remember hearing discussions about something found outside Freiburg. I was only about six so I was oblivious at the time. The SS arrived almost immediately, put a tight lid on everything, and the story is, everything was taken to Wewelsburg Castle."

"Why was it taken to a castle?" Sean asked.

"The castle was Himmler's SS headquarters and was the center of all the crazy Nazi occult activity. I didn't learn about the second crash in Poland until I got older."

"What did you hear when you got older?" Sean asked.

"The area was odd. Everything around the crash site was dead and nothing would grow. Animals would no longer go near it, and it became a barren area. This was similar to what happened with the Freiburg site.

"So the entire area was devoid of anything living?" Sean asked.

"Nothing at all,' Wolfe said. "Frozen tundra in the winter and bare dirt and rocks the rest of the year."

"Did you ever learn more about the area?"

"I did, but only later. When I accepted the State Department's take it or leave it offer, I went into a period of schooling and training. For three years I learned English, coding, and a bunch of things I can't talk about. It was in the fall of 1950.

"For the last six months of my training I was based at Wright Patterson. I was being groomed to work in Europe and to focus on countries occupied by the Soviet Union. When I was at Wright Patterson I started making some interesting friendships. Guess where most of the ex-Nazi scientists were working and living?"

"I think that's a rhetorical question, but my guess is Wright Patterson," Sean said.

"It was and you're right. Many of the higher echelon were at Wright Patterson and their records had been expunged. Since these were top German scientists, and there were about twenty-five of them, they had their own little culture club. They still spoke in German and kept to their clique. I was nineteen going on twenty at the time. I was sort of viewed as a surrogate son and was more or less adopted by the group.

"We all had significant security clearances, so no one worried about

23

what was said within our group. It was during that time I learned many secrets of the war and beyond. I can rationalize telling you about this because it had nothing to do with my assignments in Europe."

Sean was right about Wolfe. It was almost like priming a pump. It had three stages. At first there was no water, next the trickling started, then followed by the fire hose. Wolfe was about to go full force.

"Let's start with the beginning in Germany. These scientists, Wernher von Braun, Max Von Laue, Otto Hahn, and Werner Heisenberg, were all members of the Nazi party. Some joined against their beliefs and some endorsed the Fuehrer.

"Wernher von Braun was a commissioned officer in the SS and a visible party supporter. He appeared in many photos with Nazi leaders. Once he came to the United States, the U.S. government rewrote history and he became one of the key figures in creating NASA. In fact, I think they called him the father of NASA, and his Nazi past wouldn't have looked good on his resume. He was in charge of the German rocketry program and was responsible for developing the V1 and V2 rockets," Wolfe said.

"Didn't Hitler think he had some super weapon?" Sean asked.

"He did. The scientists at Wright Patterson, were the driving force in the German Atomic program. By 1945 it was apparent to all the Third Reich wouldn't prevail. The Nazi atomic program had been shut down, so the hope of a super weapon was gone. The program was curtailed because the German scientists couldn't make it work. It was revealed to me that a number of key scientists sabotaged the results so Hitler wouldn't have the atomic bomb. Von Braun was always candid after a few too many pints, and he claimed he and his fellow scientists saved the world from mass destruction. They felt Hitler was out of control and unpredictable," Wolfe said.

"I think he may have been right. Was there any repercussions from Hitler?" Sean asked.

"No, by then the war was lost and Hitler's health was failing. He had too many other issues to worry about.

"The scientists' biggest concern at the end of the war was how to save their skins. They knew anyone in the Nazi party was going to be a target for retribution, and their community included the likes of Joseph Mengele and many like him. The scientists were aware of the human extermination and the unconscionable experiments done on human guinea pigs.

"Arthur Rudolph was chief engineer of the V-2 rocket factory at Peenemunde and supported the idea of using concentration camp prisoners as slave labor when a labor shortage developed. The scientists knew what was going on and were active in the worst kept secrets of the Reich," Wolfe said.

"Did they think they could do whatever they wanted?" Sean asked.

"No, they knew they wouldn't survive scrutiny from the rest of the civilized world. They just thought Germany was invincible in the early years of the war.

"Their leader was von Braun, and he built a great escape plan. As the war was grinding down in the spring of 1945, von Braun brought his team together and discussed whether they should surrender to the Americans or the Russians. They picked the Americans because the Russians were renowned for their atrocities and brutality to prisoners.

"In May of 1945, von Braun, along with his brother, managed to find a group of American soldiers and surrendered. They were taken for debriefing, and the Americans had to figure out what to do with them. Von Braun was at the top of the list the Americans wanted to interrogate, but because of his notoriety, membership in the Nazi party and being an SS officer, he was viewed as problematic. According to von Braun, his situation had the highest visibility to the Allied command headed by Dwight Eisenhower," Wolfe said.

Sean saw the white flakes were coming down at a faster rate and the windows vibrated from gusty winds. He stood to add two new logs to the crackling embers.

"Wasn't there a law specifically meant to keep Nazis out of America?" Sean asked.

"There was, and it gets worse. As von Braun was held in protective custody, the horrors in the concentration camps were coming to light. This put pressure on the Allied Command to move von Braun and many of his cohorts to the prison set up for Nazi war criminals in Nuremberg.

"Von Braun attempted to play the atomic card, but the American leadership was aware the German program was considered a failure. They weren't buying the sabotage explanation since it seemed too convenient and appeared concocted."

"What did he do then?" Sean asked.

25

"He was forced to play his wild card. He insisted on speaking with only the highest in command and in the strictest of secrecy. He claimed he had world-changing information, and the Allied command agreed to meet with him. None other than Dwight Eisenhower, who at the time was the Military Governor of the Occupied Zone, would meet with von Braun. Eisenhower was based in Frankfurt, and this was such a sensitive issue he took personal control.

In early June, 1945, Dwight Eisenhower met with von Braun and the secret was revealed. He told Eisenhower of an alien spacecraft crash outside Freiburg Germany where he was on site within hours. There were eight dead crew members, and in short order the SS removed the craft and the bodies to Wewelsburg Castle. It was there, he and his team set about reverse engineering the technology, and this became the basis for how the German weapons and technology programs leaped ahead of the rest of the world," Wolfe said.

"That had to blow Eisenhower's mind," Sean said.

"For sure, he must have had Eisenhower's full attention. When von Braun told Eisenhower he could produce the alien craft, the bodies, and duplicate the reverse engineering within American technology, he had guaranteed his safety and his future. He then told Eisenhower of a second crash in Poland where he had also been present. He accomplished what he set out to do. Within days the Americans launched a secret program called Operation Paperclip. It wasn't announced until August, 1945, but it was created as soon as Eisenhower figured out what he had in his hands," Wolfe said.

"Okay, I thought there was some sort of law against Nazis working for the government," Sean said.

"There was, and Operation Paperclip replaced Operation Overcast because the Americans decided to expand the program to include as many of the Reich scientists as they could find. America was still at war with Japan, and the Russians were aggressive in their search for the same German scientists. When the prospect of gaining an unexpected technological advantage surfaced, the American hierarchy felt an urgency to act.

"I need to take a break, visit the bathroom, and get more coffee. I can smell it from here," Wolfe said.

Sean took Wolfe's mug and refilled it as Wolfe came into the Kitchen.

"I needed that, I thought I was going to explode. Wait until you're my age and you have to pee ten times a day." Wolfe said.

"I can't wait," Sean said.

They reentered the living room and Sean added fresh logs.

"Back to our discussion. I thought there were laws about Nazis coming into this country and working for the government," Sean said.

"You're correct about the law. Prior to President Truman signing off on Operation Paperclip, all members of the Nazi party were prohibited from working for the United States government. Arthur Rudolf, von Braun, and Hubertus Strughold would've been ineligible at best and deported for war crimes at worst. The US government handled the sticky issue by expunging their war records. It was as if their Nazi military record never existed. This enabled them to work for the U.S. government, even with pictures of von Braun wearing his SS uniform and his Nazi swastika lapel pin," Wolfe said.

"Didn't anyone question Operation Paperclip?" Sean asked.

"No, remember the U.S. was still at war. Plus, the press coverage was far different in those days, so many questionable things were never reported.

"The US added the German scientists to its atomic program in June. In August the U.S. dropped the first atomic bomb on Japan. Von Braun took credit for his team providing the missing pieces to the American atomic program. On August tenth, 1945, World War Two ended, and the focus for the U.S. scientific community changed. Von Braun continued to build the same V-One and V-Two rockets he developed in Germany, but they were now the beginnings of the U.S. space program.

"In 1947 another major event took place. Roswell happened. The well-documented fake weather balloon story was in reality the third alien spacecraft von Braun had the opportunity to work on. This time he didn't have go to the crash site because all the debris was brought to him at Wright Patterson. He continued to work on reverse engineering, and it's no coincidence that the last sixty years provided the greatest technological advancements in the history of mankind," Wolfe said.

"Back to the crash in the Black Forest. What was the Nazi reaction when they realized what they had?" Sean asked.

"At first it was shock. Hitler was interested in the occult, and after the crash those activities accelerated. Indiana Jones was close to reality.

27

The Nazis were looking for everything from the Arc of the Covenant to the Holy Grail. They created an underground base in Tibet and used psychics. When the craft was discovered, Hitler put the Vril Society on the case. The Vril Society was an occult group headed by a woman named Maria Orsitch. She was a famous German medium, and Himmler, Goering, and Bormann were all members of her little group. The Vril Society all disappeared at the end of the war, and there's always been speculation as to where they went," Wolfe said.

"I know Hitler was into the occult. Did von Braun share his occult vision?" Sean asked.

"I don't think so. He didn't view the UFOs as occult. Prior to and during the war, von Braun worked on a variety of reverse engineering projects, and every time he was successful, Hitler's confidence grew.

"The scientists at Wright Patterson were unanimous in thinking Hitler came to power by focusing on domestic issues, but after the UFO crash he became obsessed with ruling the world. He always felt the scientists would develop a super weapon from the alien technology and he couldn't be defeated. The addition of the second crash put Hitler's confidence over the top. Some of the group thought the discovery of the second crash led to Hitler's decision to invade Russia when all his generals were warning him about the dangers of a two front war," Wolfe said.

"How did this stay secret?" Sean asked.

Wolfe looked up and said, "Denial and misinformation. There was so much confusion in the immediate aftermath of the German surrender one hand didn't know what the other hand was doing.

"The Roswell situation was a perfect example of denial and misinformation. Many witnesses came forward, and it continued to be, denial, denial, denial. There was another crash site in a different area of New Mexico a year after Roswell and the German scientists said several aliens survived. They didn't live long after they arrived at Wright Patterson, but again, how does this stay quiet? Threats and denials."

"Did these guys just sit there and tell you all this?" Sean asked.

"No, over a six month period we had constant contact, and after a long day we'd have pork schnitzel, dumplings with sauerkraut and the German beer would flow. It was more like a German holiday and overindulgence was common. I would simply listen to their conversation and sometimes ask a question. The information was almost indirect, but after

28

so much time together it all kind of came out."

"How can I ever get proof?" Sean asked.

"Good question. The government has, and continues, to suppress this information. The CIA knew more about what was going on than the FBI. There were rumors J. Edgar Hoover wanted to know more about Roswell and he was told, in no uncertain terms by the military, the information was on a need to know basis. What a shot to the jaw? There's also rumors some Presidents have been kept in the dark with the same explanation," Wolfe said.

Sean sat for a moment. Goose bumps tingled on his skin. He had just received the most unbelievable information, but didn't know what to do with it. There was no doubt he now knew the truth about UFO's.

"Wilhelm, thank you so much for sharing this with me. If you were me and wanted to have some proof, what would you do?"

"I would think you need some sort of documents or something irrefutable. Eye witnesses have been discredited over the years, and pictures can be dismissed as doctored, so you would need some kind of official documents, physical evidence, videotape, or something beyond reproach," Wolfe said.

Sean offered Wolfe a coffee refill, but he declined. His errands were waiting, and he hadn't planned to stay this long.

"Wilhelm, I'm sure I'll have thoughts and questions. Would you be able to stop back in a couple of days?" Sean asked.

"Sure, I'm always around. Call me."

Wolfe departed, and Sean walked back into the kitchen, grabbed another cup of coffee, and re-entered the living room. What was his next step?

Sean considered how a revelation of this nature would shake the foundations of the world's belief systems. Talk about creating a new world dynamic. How would true believers react to their religions? Would governments be able to control their people, would the financial markets crash, or what other disasters would occur?

As he thought about these questions, the one jumping at him was the religious issue. Governments would have no issues controlling their populace, the markets would be fine, but how would religions survive when Adam and Eve might have been Mr. and Mrs. ET? He smiled while considering the possibilities. It would be a rude awakening for those who followed religious leaders preaching the flock must have faith and their religion was the only religion.

It occurred to him, religion was at the root of most of the world-wide conflicts for at least the last two thousand years. The advent of Christianity, Judaism, and Islam put the world in conflict for artificial reasons, while Buddhism, Hinduism, and other ancient religions didn't seem to create the same my *God is better than your God* attitude. Christians, Jews and Muslims have been killing each other over whose God was better since before the Crusades. How do those religions handle the revelation we are not alone? They could spin the message to say their God was above the aliens, but the basis of the conflicting religions was earth-based origins of life.

What happens to control over their flock? How many suicide bombers would still believe they'd get one hundred virgins if they blew themselves up trying to kill the infidel? The flock would soon wise up and the contributions to the churches, synagogues and mosques could dry up overnight. Bill Maher might have to do a sequel to *Religulous*. This was starting to sound like a subject worthy of a book. Sean contemplated how the religious world would react and the ramifications of the resultant shake out.

Sean's eyes leveled at the dwindling flames and he knew it was time to trek to the woodpile. He put on his boots and winter coat and took a broom to the stacked firewood. The snow was fluffy, and he easily brushed off more than eight inches of the frozen powder and retrieved enough wood for two days. The sun now shone brightly, and he thought about descending the fifty stairs to the boathouse. He looked down the steps and saw they were covered with a foot and a half of snow and made the wise decision to admire the lake from afar.

It was time to get Alan in the loop, he thought, dialing his friend's number. Alan answered on the second ring, and Sean recounted Wolfe's incredible story. Alan was astounded his account was so thoroughly corroborated by a third party. They discussed the next step and the possibility of connecting with the folks in Freiburg.

He spent the remainder of the evening searching the Internet.

***

It was already bright outside when Sean opened his eyes. He threw the heavy down comforter to the side and swung his bare feet onto the floor. The house was warmer, but the floor was still cold, getting Sean's full attention. He went into the kitchen to check the time on the antique-looking red Elmira stove. The clock stared back at him with an eight, a three, and a zero, surprising him because he never slept this late. He trudged upstairs as the ninety-one-year-old staircase creaked and groaned with each step.

The house was designed as a three season home and the second story had no heating ducts. He felt the increased chill as his feet hit the landing on the upper floor. Sean had planned ahead, and when he swung open the bathroom door, a warm rush of air from an oil-filled space heater enveloped him like a warm blanket. He showered, shaved, and was ready for the day.

Returning to the kitchen, Sean brewed a large pot of coffee and opened the refrigerator door to remove one of his guilty pleasures, a Racine Cherry Kringle. After munching on a couple of the slivers, he made a cheese and mushroom omelet, fried potatoes with onions and green peppers, and stepped into the living room to finish his breakfast. He started to consider what he would do for the day as his cell phone rang.

"Hi hon, I just wanted to see how you were doing," Cat said.

"I'm great, but this house was not made for winter. Still, it feels good to be here," he said.

"Put Liam on, and then grab a chair and I'll tell you what Wolfe had to say."

"Okay, here's Liam."

Liam answered, and they went through the ritual of finding out about each other's day as Sean tried to connect with his son from long distance.

When finished with Liam, Cat got back on the phone and Sean recounted Wolfe's entire story. They signed off with a promise to talk again in the evening.

Fifteen minutes later the phone rang again. He anticipated it was Cat, but was surprised to hear Alan's voice.

"Hey, Sean," Alan said, "I've been burning up the long distance lines to my family since we spoke, and they're excited. I talked to my cousins, and they've heard all the stories, but what you've uncovered has everyone buzzing. My father and uncle are both in good health and lucid, so they should be a good source of information.

"I've been thinking about this. I'm going to Europe in three days to meet with my developers and do quarterly planning. Why don't you come with me? We could fly into Strasbourg, and once I'm done with my meetings, we can head over to Freiburg. We can spend some time with my family and do some snooping to see where it goes. What do you say?"

Sean didn't have to think twice, but he had a different idea. "Alan, my daughter's at Heidelberg University and I haven't seen her since August so this would be perfect. It would give me an excuse to see her, then meet your family. I could go to Heidelberg for a couple of days and meet you in Strasbourg," Sean said.

"Excellent. I'll meet with my team, you can see your daughter, and we can spend a couple of days in Freiburg."

"Count me in. I'll go to work on it right now. Send me your itinerary and I'll coordinate our schedules," Sean said.

They agreed to start making their preparations.

Sean knew he needed to get Cat's agreement. She wouldn't be thrilled, but the fact he could spend time with Cassie, and at the same time pursue his project, made it a no brainer. He called her.

"You know I don't like those long flights to Europe, but I love the fact you can see Cassie. I'd love to go with you, but I don't think we can leave Liam by himself. How long will you be gone?" Cat asked.

"I think it'll be at least a week. Two days of travel, two days with Cassie, and two or three days in Freiburg at a minimum. I want to take full advantage of being over there. If things are going well I'll stay as long as it's productive."

Cat was on board and Sean told her he would call later.

Forty-five minutes later Sean finished his travel schedule and emailed the itinerary to Alan.

He then dialed the phone.

"Hello, this is Cassie O'Shea," she answered.

"*Hello Cassie O'Shea, this is your father,*" he said, in a fake Darth Vadar voice.

"*Daddy, how are you?*" she asked.

"I'm terrific, and I have some good news. I've just scheduled a trip to Strasbourg and I planned it so I could spend a day or two with you," he said.

"That's great, when are you coming?"

"I'm in Flambeau and leave in the morning. By the time I make my connections I'll be flying all night and get into Frankfort sometime around five in the morning the day after tomorrow."

"*Wow, that's quick. I can't wait to see you.*"

"Me too. Check your classes, I don't want you to miss anything important, but let's spend as much time together as we can."

"*What a nice surprise, travel safe.*"

***

Sean thought about his next step. He had to let Wolfe know he was leaving early. He picked up the phone and called him. After providing a quick recap, he told Wolfe he was headed to Europe. He was greeted by an odd response. Instead of the excitement Sean anticipated, he was greeted by hesitancy.

"Sean, are you sure about this?"

Sean paused, surprised by the question.

"Wilhelm, you of anyone should appreciate why I want to go. You're the one who fueled my interest," he said.

"I want to come over and talk about this. What are you up to in the next hour?" Wolfe asked.

"I'm here, come on over. I'll start a new pot of coffee."

"I'll be there in twenty minutes."

Sean looked at his phone. What the heck was that about? He didn't have to ask Wolfe to come over; he was coming on his own. What had him on edge?

Sean started a new pot of a strong French Roast and soon heard the clang of the wolf's head door knocker. His caretaker let himself in, and Sean handed him steaming coffee in a heavy loon-themed mug. They headed into the living room in silence.

"Sean, I'm concerned. I shouldn't have been as forthcoming as I was yesterday. I shared confidential and classified information with you, and I'm afraid investigating this will put you in harm's way," Wolfe said.

"What caused you to change your mind? You were all in on this yesterday, and this is an about face."

"You're right, yesterday, it was fun to let you in on an inside story. It's fun to reveal secrets and see the surprise from the person who's just learned something new. I don't get to do it often, and I don't do it with anyone other than Ada. You hit me at the right moment and I felt good about sharing it. Now I don't feel so good."

"Okay, why is that?" Sean asked.

"After we spoke yesterday, I did my errands and went home. I spoke to an old friend in Europe, someone I worked with in the CIA. I got around to talking about the events in Germany and Roswell and mentioned wouldn't it be interesting if those events saw the light of day. It was small talk and I guess it was my way of justifying what I'd told you. He was more serious about the subject than I would have ever thought. He's still in the CIA, and he's privy to current information.

"He said as interest in UFOs increased during the last few years, the aggressiveness of UFO enthusiasts also increased, and odd things have happened," Wolfe said.

"Okay, you've got me intrigued. What are those odd things?" Sean asked.

"I didn't know this, but in the late sixties, a French UFO researcher named Philip Robert heard about the events outside Freiburg. He started investigating and appeared to be making progress. He showed up on their radar screen because he started asking questions from people in our network. Our agents had no issue with him and kept track of his progress out of general interest.

"Even if he uncovered something substantial about a UFO, it was doubtful he would get traction. He kept digging and was fairly high profile about what he was doing. He did an interview with a reporter on June third, 1968 and revealed he was being followed, and stated he was about to drop a world- changing bombshell. There was a reference to religious ramifications, but he didn't elaborate," Wolfe said.

"Keep talking, I'm going to open the door, the fire getting too hot," Sean said, and opened the antique French door a crack.

"So our friend Robert had a news conference scheduled for June fifth, where he was set to reveal his bombshell, but sometime before midnight on June fourth, Philip Robert, from Lyon France, was found dead with his throat slit and a bullet in his brain.

"Sometime after midnight on June fifth, 1968 another event took precedence. Robert F. Kennedy was assassinated in Los Angeles, California and no one ever paid attention to the demise of a little known UFO researcher from Lyon, France," Wolfe said, pausing, maybe for effect or maybe for the fact he hadn't taken a breath in five minutes.

"In 1986, a Dutchman named Hans Gusdorf began his own quest on the subject. He had a relative from the Black Forest and heard the story over the years. He started asking questions and visited the site outside Freiburg and then visited the site of the second crash in Poland. He was gathering evidence about what took place in both locations and started giving interviews with his thoughts and speculation.

"He was found dead in the Black Forest between Freiburg and Villingen. His throat was slit, and he had a bullet in his brain. Do we see a pattern here? He had hashish and marijuana on him, so it was reported as a drug thing."

Sean was getting the drift and wasn't sure what to say.

"Wilhelm, you can't think they were killed because of the UFO investigations."

"Sean, I'm not done yet. There's been two other murders associated with people investigating the UFO crashes. I don't think you should go to Europe, and I don't think you should pursue this. Remember, I know where bodies are buried. I know things you don't, and I'm saying this is not safe. I don't want Cat to be a widow and Liam and Cassie to grow up without their dad."

"Come on, Wilhelm, you can't be serious. I can't believe this can be dangerous."

"Sean, one death is an accident, two is a coincidence, and four deaths are way beyond any statistical anomaly. Something is going on here. Someone is eliminating anyone looking at these crashes. The question is why? I don't see a government going to these extremes. They do all right with their denials and misinformation so they don't need to kill anyone.

"My contact had no real explanation. Their focus is on terrorism, and if something falls outside a threat to the U.S. they make a note and move on. This hasn't been high on their radar screen, but I can tell you one thing for certain. Something sinister is at work, and I'm concerned you're about to step into the middle of it."

"Why would someone kill these folks? It doesn't make sense. Did your guy have any theories?" Sean asked.

"The only insight he had was someone was suppressing something at all costs. But who and why? The Nazis are long gone except for a few loser skin heads. The governments keep control over their sheep with mis-information, so who's left?" Wolfe said. He looked up, hesitated, and then said, "The Catholic Church."

Sean sat back. How did Wolfe just make the leap from governmental UFO cover ups to a religious murder conspiracy? This wasn't making sense, but at the very least he knew he had to exert caution as he moved forward. Sean was certain the victims had no idea they were in danger. He at least had the advantage of being forewarned.

"Wolfe, I'm not going to give up, because this is the kind of story I've been searching for. Knowing I'm not going to be dissuaded, what do you think I should do?" Sean said.

"The first thing I'll do is set you up with my old contacts. I have a certain responsibility because I introduced you to this whole thing. I also care about your family so I'll do what I can to protect you. Don't expect me to ride in and save your ass, but I still have a network over there."

"I thank you for that. What do you suggest?"

"You'll need to keep as low a profile as you can. When you're asking questions, try to know who you're asking and keep your eyes open," Wolfe said.

"You said the church; what did you mean?"

"The intelligence community recognizes the power hierarchy in the world. You have a handful of governments that are always in the mix and considered. For example, let's look at European influence. Once you get past Germany, Russia, Great Britain, and France, who's the next most powerful entity in Europe? The intelligence community would tell you it's the Vatican. They're more powerful than any other European, African, or South American country. Are you getting the picture? And who can move with impunity and do whatever they like without consequence? The Vatican.

"There are unseen forces influencing and sometimes dictating what happens in the world. Beyond the wealth of the Vatican, it's their unseen power controlling the mass minds of their followers. If you took the major religions in the world, I'd make a case they're more powerful than any single government in the world. Their power can't be discounted.

"By the way, could you shut that door? I'm getting cold in my old age."

Sean stood and closed the door. This was going in a direction he wasn't prepared for.

"So you think I could be in danger from the Catholic Church just by asking questions?" he asked. "That seems farfetched."

"Only if you're getting close to whatever they fear. Whoever has taken out those investigating the crashes didn't silence them until they became a perceived threat. I just know you need to be careful. I'm going to give you a contact in Germany and one in France. I'll let them know our concerns and leave it up to them as to what you should do. Do you have experience with firearms?" Wolfe asked.

Sean was taken aback, "Do you think it's necessary?" he asked.

"Given the fates of your predecessors it's a prudent skill you should possess. I'll make sure you're taken care of. You never answered my question. Do you know what you're doing with a firearm?"

"I've had only limited experience and never with a handgun. The last time I shot an over-under I almost blew my foot off at the Bull Valley Hunt Club. I think I could figure it out as long as I know where the safety is."

"Get a piece of paper. I don't want to use email for this," Wolfe said and proceeded to give Sean names and phone numbers for his contacts in Germany and France.

"Sean, this is off the record. These are long-time associates and friends whom I trust and are dependable allies. They'll take care of anything you need, but I again remind you to keep a low profile and be careful."

The discussion was over. Sean had a lot to consider and was grateful for Wolfe's involvement, but still couldn't get a grip on why this would be a hazardous endeavor. He didn't get the connection between the Catholic Church and a couple of alien crash sites in the thirties. Why had four people connected to this story been murdered? He made a decision to say nothing of this to Cat.

Wolfe stood.

"Sean, this isn't kids play and isn't a game. It might have started that way, but given what we now know, it's deadly serious to someone. You have to be careful and stay on your toes at all times. Agents are lost because they get complacent. You aren't an agent, you have no training, you don't speak the language, and you don't know how to protect yourself.

"Sean, remember what Churchill said in World War Two. 'The truth

37

is so precious; it must be protected by a bodyguard of lies.' It would serve you well to consider those words as this plays out. My specialty was disinformation, but I never told you that. If someone becomes aware of you, and I have every reason to believe they will, you need to anticipate and be ahead of the curve.

"They've taken out at least four unsuspecting amateurs, and it must have been like shooting fish in a barrel. They'll think you're cut from the same cloth and won't expect you to be ready for them. You'll have an initial edge, but only for a short time, because they're likely professionals."

Before they parted, Wolfe reached into his pocket and pulled out a piece of paper with a phone number scrawled on it. "Here's my satellite phone number. It doesn't get much use anymore, but if you run into trouble, call me," he said.

They shook hands and both sensed this project was about to get serious. It was apparent they just entered into a different relationship, and at some point they might be communicating during a dangerous time.

Wolfe moved down the snow-packed flagstone steps one at a time. He sure didn't look like a secret agent. Sean went to his favorite intelligence device, his lap top, and found the web site for The Minocqua Gun Club. The home page announced they would open on April first. How appropriate, April Fool's Day. It was also the next day.

Sean always felt he "knew" things. He related to Clint Eastwood's character in *The Line of Fire* when Eastwood looked at Rene Rousseau and said, "I know things about people, Lilly." That's how Sean had always felt. When he was in touch and moving through life with vitality and purpose, he could always see several steps ahead. When he retired, he checked out, stopped paying attention to his intuition, and lost his ability to know what was coming next. He paid a high price for that apathetic period in his life and now he was back in the game and functioning better than ever.

The rest of the evening was spent doing Internet searches on Nazis, alien crash sites, and related controversial subjects. The content on Nazi occultism provided all the reading material he could handle. Sean learned Himmler was the driving force behind the Nazi quest for anything occult, but he wasn't alone. Many like-minded Nazis such as Alfred Rosenberg, Joseph Goebbels, and Rudolf Hess were all part of the Nazi inner circle, and all believed in everything from astrology, to the Arc of the Covenant, to the Holy Grail. It was evident Hitler believed forces in nature, if found, would give the Reich an advantage, and he spared no expense trying to find his potential super weapon.

Sean was surprised to learn as early as 1930, Hitler was sending expeditions into the Himalayan Mountains looking for proof of the origins of the Aryan Gods. O'Shea was getting a little side-tracked, but he wanted to read everything he could relating to his subject matter.

As he bounced around the Internet he found something called the hollow earth theory. What bullshit, he thought; then he recognized he was about to spin a tale about UFOs so he knew not to cast aspersions on someone else's theory. He found the Nazis occult focus to be fascinating, but was aware it wasn't the target of his research. He was trying to figure out how to prove UFO's crashed and the Nazis reverse engineered their technology. In his mind this wasn't mysticism or rumor, but rather unproven truth. By eleven o'clock he was ready to hit the sack, checked to make sure the fire had died down, and walked to the bedroom.

Sleep came easier as he was getting more comfortable with the incredible discoveries of the last few days.

Sean awoke at seven-forty-five to the warmth of the sun. His internal clock was getting adjusted just in time to leave for Germany and throw his body back into confusion.

He showered, had a light breakfast, headed to the Minocqua Gun Club, and at ten o'clock pulled into its parking lot. Sean walked up several steps into the impressive old hunting lodge. The heads of several animals stared ahead with unseeing glass eyes suspended from the dark brown wormwood. He knew Cat would hate this place, and he was pretty sure PETA wouldn't be a fan. The crunching of heavy steps caused him to turn as a Grizzly Adams looking guy came down the hall carrying a large pot of coffee.

"Good morning, you're the first customer of the new year," the man said.

"Good morning to you. I'm in need of a quick pistol lesson. I used to shoot skeet years ago, but I need to learn the basics of a hand gun."

"Well, you've come to the right place, bud."

"Can you teach me everything I need to know in an hour?"

"You bet," said the large hairy man.

"Ready when you are," Sean said.

Two hours later, Sean clicked his blinker as he pulled out of the gun club parking lot. He had received a crash course in hand gun operation. He was now confident, possessing the basics of how to operate the safety, add a new clip and other things that could make him dangerous to himself and everyone else. Sean asked many questions, and when he got around to shooting at a target was surprised to find he had some skill.

He was reviewing his just completed experience as he navigated his car north on Highway 51 toward Minocqua. Rolling down the window, he felt the bite of frosty air on his face and the perfume of pines in his nostrils. The sunshine warmed him even though the temperature was far from balmy, and he wondered when he would next return to this sleepy northern Wisconsin town.

Sean stopped, bought a Chicago Tribune, and drove to the Hunan Inn where he ordered chicken with black beans and hot and sour soup. In many ways Sean was a creature of habit. He had favorite recipes, favorite restaurants, and tended to order from a small group of proven items. After finishing his garlic-laden lunch he was back on the road, and five minutes later turned right onto Highway 70 West, passed Trigs and Jim Peck's Wildwood, and twelve minutes later pulled into his long uphill driveway.

He immediately started planning for a seven-day trip and thought about what he'd need from underwear and socks to shirts and pants. He finished the mental checklist and realized he was at his summer home where he had fewer clothes.

It took about twenty minutes to pack and he was relieved to find everything he would need. He stoked the fire and heated water for hot chocolate when he was startled by a banging at the front door.

Sean pulled it open, and there was Wolfe looking back at him without expression.

"Willhem, what's going on?"

"I wanted to come over before you left. I spoke to my guys and have them sniffing around. Everyone is up to speed and on the same page. Not much happens in Europe they don't know about, and they're going to dig a little deeper. We need to determine the enemy and what they're trying to protect. By the time you get there they may know something," Wolfe said.

"That's wonderful news. By the way, I took your advice and spent some time at the gun club this morning. I now have a feel for using a pistol."

Wolfe looked at him with some distain. "You're more dangerous to yourself than anyone else, just remember that. But it's good you have a little knowledge about using a weapon," he said.

Sean appreciated Wolfe's concern and detected a different mode. The normal jovial attitude was replaced with an intensity and focus Sean had never seen from his caretaker. Maybe that's what it took to do what he did and survive. Sean felt the seriousness and made note.

"Make sure you contact my guys when you get into their territory. They'll have something for you when you get together. This is important; you have to listen to them. If they tell you something, do it and it may save your life. I don't like how this whole thing feels. Someone is hunting and killing people who were doing what you're about to do. I don't like it at all."

"Wilhelm, I can't tell you how much I appreciate your concern and your efforts. I look forward to meeting your guys and I'll listen to them. Believe me, I'm more apprehensive than you think," Sean said. He hadn't completely bought into Wolfe's paranoia, but had to admit it was starting to get to him. They said goodbyes for the third day in a row, and Wolfe waddled down the slippery flagstone steps.

Sean watched him leave and stood at the open door for some time. He knew he was getting into something, but what? His energy level was way up, but now his anxiety levels were also increasing.

Chapter 3)

The alarm sounded at six-fifteen, and Sean jumped out of bed ignoring the chill on the floor. He showered, and at one minute after seven closed the ancient door behind him. Sean spent so many years traveling he was expert at getting to places on time, and today would be no exception.

He rolled into Mosinee's Central Wisconsin Airport at eight forty-five. It took ten minutes to return the rental and he was then standing at United's ticket counter. He checked his luggage and was ticketed all the way to Frankfurt, but his efforts to sweet talk his way into first class fell on deaf ears.

Once in Chicago he again tried and failed to upgrade to first class, but at least secured a business class seat in a row where he was the only passenger. The gate agent said it wasn't a full flight and had a good chance it would remain open, so like Bill Murray in *Caddyshack*, he had that going for him. Since business class seats on international flights were the same as domestic first class it would make for a nice flight if he had no seat mate. As luck would have it, the seat remained empty, and he was thankful. Once they were airborne, he pulled out his carry-on, removed his head phones, eye mask, ear plugs, and the *Chicago Sun Times* he had picked up at the airport. He would see what was on the dinner menu, have a glass of wine, and do his best to grab a little sleep.

He was somewhere in the grey twilight of semi-sleep when he awoke to the unmistakable scent of burnt, dark roasted coffee. The aromas were enticing and convinced Sean additional attempts at sleep were futile. The attendant pushed the breakfast cart to his row where he chose an omelet over the fruit plate. An hour later the captain announced the final approach, and Sean moved to the seat by the window. He hadn't been to Frankfurt in twelve years and wanted to see it again from the air.

Once on the ground, it became hurry up and wait, as he stood in the customs line for forty-five minutes. He exited the airport with growing anticipation of seeing Cassie and was soon tooling down the Autobahn toward Heidelberg.

His youngest daughter left for school in August, and it had been tough on everyone. He wondered if this whole UFO story was just an excuse so he could come to Europe to spend time with her.

Sean had enjoyed past visits to Heidelberg with its legendary castle, and he admired her decision to attend the university with its wealth of history. The comparison of Heidelberg to Frankfurt was stark. Where Frankfurt had been bombed into the Middle Ages, Heidelberg had been spared, because it was to become the Allied headquarters. Heidelberg wasn't bombed at all and was still one of the most visited tourist destinations in Europe.

An hour later, Heidelberg Castle, sitting high on a craggy hill above the city, came into view. The thirteenth century castle was in partial ruins, but that made it even more interesting. Sean couldn't pry his eyes away as he drove around and past it. Sitting on the highest point in the entire area, it could be seen from the entire countryside and city. Sean entered the town of Heidelberg and appreciated its Disneyesque feel. It was like a giant exhibit at Epcot except it was real. He turned into the University of Heidelberg and found his way to the residence hall where Cassie lived.

Sean shut his door and heard a squeal to his left.

"DADDY."

Sean beamed and opened his arms as Cassie ran into him.

"It's so good to see you!" Sean said.

"I've been waiting and watching for you. I couldn't wait till you got here. I saw you pull up and couldn't get to you fast enough," Cassie said.

"Where can we go to catch up?" Sean asked.

"I've got just the place. It's a café, and I think you'll love it. Let's go," she said.

Cassie directed Sean through Heidelberg to Cafe Gundel.

"Dad, you'll like it. They have the best German bakery, great coffee, and it's a cute place."

"Sounds good to me. I'm hungry from the long trip, and I know how you like your cafes. If you like it, I'm sure I'll like it," Sean said.

They spent the next two hours enjoying the bakery delicacies and talking.

"Cas, before it gets too late, I've got to find a hotel, and I'd like to get one close to the castle. How about I find a hotel and check in. Then we'll hang out at the castle and find a nice restaurant for dinner."

"That's perfect. I haven't gone to the castle since last year. I had an early class this morning, and I'm skipping the English Lit class this afternoon so I can spend time with my Pops," she said.

"Great. The last time I was here I liked that boutique hotel, what was it, the Heidelberg Suites? I think that's it. Do you know how to get there from here?"

"Sure, I know my way around Heidelberg."

Sean paid their check, and ten minutes later they were at the Heidelberg Suites. There was plenty availability since the tourist season was still two months away, and he was given a charming suite with a river view, two bedrooms, and a large sitting room. It would be a good place for he and Cassie to relax and far more comfortable than Cassie's dorm room with her three roommates.

They spent three hours hanging out at the castle and then returned to the hotel. After being on their feet for most of the afternoon, lethargy enveloped them, and the overstuffed chairs of Sean's room were a welcomed relief.

"Do you feel like some wine and cheese?" Sean asked.

"Oh, that'd be perfect. I'm starting to develop my wine palette instead of rum and Coke," Cassie said, and smiled. "Like father like daughter."

Sean picked up the phone and called room service. After ordering a cheese plate with some type of crackers and a combination of sausages, he got around to the wine choices. They offered a nice Barbera and he ordered two bottles. Twenty minutes later room service arrived, and for the next hour Sean and Cassie enjoyed their pre-dinner snack. They discussed Sean's project, and Sean was careful not to include any of Wolfe's concerns since Cat and Cassie Skyped almost every day.

"Dad, what time are you planning to head to Strasbourg tomorrow?"

"That sort of depends on you. What does your schedule look like?"

"I've got several classes I can't miss. The first is at ten."

"I thought we'd spend time together tomorrow, but I don't want you to miss anything important. Let's do this. Why don't we stop by your place so you can get an overnight bag and stay here tonight? We got lucky to get a suite with two bedrooms, so why not use them? We'll have tonight and breakfast together in the morning. Then I can drop you off at class and I'll leave for Strasbourg. That'll give us more time together."

"I like that. Let's figure out where we're going for dinner and we can get my stuff before we go to the restaurant. I've got a suggestion that everyone talks about. It's called Qube and it features Mediterranean cuisine."

"Sold. I'll get a reservation."

Sean was thrilled to spend quality time with his youngest daughter. Her goal was to be a writer or screenwriter, and she was pursuing it with a passion. He admired her single-mindedness, her sense of humor, and who she had become as a person.

They had a great dinner, talked well into the night, and enjoyed breakfast together at the hotel restaurant. As breakfast wound down, Sean started having a familiar empty feeling in the pit of his stomach. He knew he'd have a strong sense of loss when he drove away.

They hugged for a long time, but the feeling wasn't as bad as when she left in August. Sean promised he would stop and see her again if he flew out of Frankfurt, but at this point he thought he might fly from Strasbourg or Freiberg.

As Sean pulled away he was conflicted with missing Cassie offset by the anticipation of the next few days. He decided to focus on what was coming. It was easier. He looked at the clock and it was nine forty-five.

***

He called Alan's cell phone, and it was answered on the second ring.

"Alan, on my way from Heidelberg and should get there by eleven-thirty," Sean said.

"I've got a new idea. My meetings have gone well, and I can wrap up this afternoon. Instead of coming to Strasbourg, why don't you head over to Freiburg? Find the Colombi hotel and I'll meet you there. I'll call and add a day to our reservation, and I'll cancel the hotel reservations in Strasbourg. We can get a head start on your little project," Alan said.

"I love the idea," Sean said. "There's a new development I haven't had the chance to share with you.

Sean spent the next twenty minutes telling Alan about Wolfe's concerns and the link to the murders. "Wolfe went so far as to ask if I'd had experience with firearms," Sean said.

"Alan, with this new information, I'd understand if you'd want to distance yourself from this whole thing. I'm not worried about the initial discussions with your family, but as visibility increases you may want to back away."

"Not on your life. I wasn't quiet because I was afraid; I was trying to sort out why someone would want to bury the truth. It doesn't make sense. The German people have known for years Nazi sects were still active and for all I know they may still be fooling around. Even if they were the culprit, they'd have no reason to care if the truth was exposed. It has to be something else," Alan said.

"When I asked that question, Wolfe had a short response. He said the church. When I pressed him, he said after Germany, Great Britain, Russia, and France, the Vatican was the most powerful entity effecting Europe. He had plenty to say about the church and tried to dissuade me from coming here. He also gave me the names and phone numbers of two CIA agents he used to work with and told me to call them. He said they'd give updates on anything they might discover and would keep an eye on me."

"It sounds like Wolfe has taken a personal interest in your well-being. For him to involve active agents seems unusual. Why would active agents get involved?"

"I think we've become an extension of Wolfe's family. I'm not sure how active his guys are, but as Wolfe told me, they know where the bodies are buried. I think their involvement is a combination of a personal relationship with Wolfe and the fact they want to know what's going on. They'd dismissed several murders which now appear to be linked, and it might give them pause. Someone is going to great lengths to keep something hidden, and I think they're interested in what it might be."

"I think you might be right. Once the conspiracy element enters the picture their radar has to kick in. It's also nice to know we have someone watching our backs," Alan said.

"When I get to Freiburg, I'll reach out to both of them. By the time you arrive I may have a better picture of what's going on," he said.

"Perfect. Call me when you've checked in. Drive safe."

Chapter 4)

At four o'clock Sean's cell phone rang.

"Hello," Sean said.

"Sean, it's Alan, I've just arrived. Let's meet in the bar in ten minutes," he said.

"Perfect. I'll see you then."

Sean was sitting at the bar nursing a cold, crisp Kabinett when Alan walked in.

"Hello my friend," Alan said extending his hand. "It's great to see you and you look great."

"The same to you, what's it been, eight years?"

"It doesn't seem that long, but I think you're right," he said.

"What would you like to drink, I'm buying," Sean said.

"I'll have a Becks," Alan said.

"This was a great idea, I would've enjoyed seeing Strasbourg again, but I'd much rather get started," Sean said.

"That's what I was thinking. I've spoken with my cousins and they're excited to meet you. They're scrambling to get everyone together tonight and we'll head over in a few minutes.

"Let me give you some background on everyone," Alan said.

"Gola's the Freiburg Police Chief. He's married with two kids. He's a smart guy and the most serious of the brothers. He gets focused and can become intense and a bit abrupt.

"Max is a Freiburg inspector and works with Gola. He's married and has no kids. He's more fun than Gola and more laid back. He has a logical mind, and I think the two you will hit it off. We'll be gathering at his house tonight, and his wife Marta is sort of the matriarch these days and keeps everything organized.

"That brings us to Alfred. I guess every family has one, but he's the black sheep. You'll find the Rockenbachs to be generous and engaging; everyone, that is, except Alfred. Anytime there's a free meal he'll be first in line, but ask him to contribute and he disappears. He's the kind of guy who, if he's buying dinner, he'll only order an appetizer, but if someone else is buying he'll order drinks, appetizers and lobster. He's always trying to take advantage of everyone else's generosity. It's been wearing thin on the family for years. Now you have a snap shot and you can make your own observations."

"Thanks, that'll help to have context around each person. Alfred sounds like a real winner, but I'll withhold judgment."

***

Twenty minutes later they turned into a pleasant neighborhood and pulled to a stop in front of a home that could have been on any American street. For some reason Sean expected every home to be old, but the opposite was true.

Alan took the steps two at a time, as Sean followed close. As they approached, the door opened, and a tall, attractive, forty-something blonde greeted them.

"Alan, you made it," she said.

They embraced, and Alan stepped back to introduce Sean.

"Marta, this is Sean. Sean, meet Marta," Alan said.

Sean took her outstretched hand, and it was warm and firm. They entered the house, and it felt like home, with wood accents, beamed ceilings, and several of the famous Freiburg cuckoo clocks perched on the walls. They followed Marta to the back room where Max was building a fire in a large stone fireplace. Sean was six foot two and he was looking up at Max as he put out his hand. It was accepted with bone crushing enthusiasm.

"I'm Sean, and it's nice to meet you."

"Sean, great to meet you. I'm Max, and I've been excited to meet you since Alan told me about your little project."

Alan came into the room and they hugged. Max motioned to the comfortable looking plaid chairs as Sean took in the view. They were in the middle of a city of over 200,000 people, yet it felt like they were in the woods based on the density of the trees in the back yard.

"Max, who's coming over tonight?" Alan asked.

"Gola and Alfred will be here, but I'm not sure about their wives. They view this as a guy's thing and don't have much interest. Our fathers are not coming, but we'll meet with them tomorrow. They don't like the

48

commotion of everyone getting together anymore and aren't too flexible with impromptu gatherings."

Alan turned to Sean and said, "As I mentioned, Gola, Max, and Alfred are all brothers and my cousins. Their father is Richard and Tomas is my dad. They were the soldiers assigned to guard the perimeter of the crash site years ago." Alan turned back to Max and said, "How much noise have you all been making about this, and how many people know we're having these discussions?"

Max looked a little surprised at the question, which sounded like an interrogation.

"Well, we've been excited about the subject and we talked among ourselves. I can tell from the look on your face there's a reason you asked. I don't know what other conversations my brothers have had, but we can ask tonight."

Again Alan looked at Sean. It was clear he was measuring what he wanted to say. He chose to say nothing.

Sean recognized Alan's thought process and let him take the lead. When he didn't say anything, Sean decided to stay mute as Marta entered the room.

"What can I get you boys to drink? We have some wonderful white wines from our local vineyards," Marta said.

Sean looked up and smiled. "If you have a Kabinett, I'd love it. Otherwise I'll take your recommendation."

"Sean, you have excellent taste. Kabinetts are a mainstay in this part of Germany. Alan, what can I get you?"

"I'll have the same as Sean, thank you."

Marta left the room, and they all looked at each other with an uncomfortable silence.

"Alan, since word will likely get out of our immediate circle, we need to make sure everyone knows the concerns Wolfe expressed," Sean said.

"I agree," Alan said. "Go ahead."

Sean nodded and spent ten minutes describing the warnings issued by the ex-CIA agent. When Sean recounted the four murders, Max whistled, and when the recap was finished there was silence.

Max looked up and shook his head from side to side.

"That puts a different slant on how we should proceed. We'll have to take inventory of what's been said. We do have one huge advantage. Gola is chief of police, and I'm an inspector, so we can check out what is known about these murders," Max said.

Having two members of law enforcement as part of his inner circle was more than Sean could have ever hoped for.

Marta entered with their wines and handed Max a tall glass of dark beer. She placed a selection of cheeses, crackers and sausages on a little round table and moved it to the middle of the room. They thanked her, and Sean took a substantial mouthful of the cold Kabinett. It was clean and crisp and it occurred to him that a good Kabinett was one of the most under-appreciated wines on the planet.

"This knowledge changes everything. Instead of an adventure, the whole thing takes on a different persona," Max said.

***

Four hundred and seventy-eight miles from Freiburg, in an old building, a tall man in a long black robe descended a wooden staircase. At the last step he was greeted by another man, also in a black robe.

"It appears to be happening again. I had a call from Freiburg and questions were asked about the 1936 event. We know nothing more," the man at the bottom of the stairs said.

"Stay close to it. It may be general interest and may not amount to anything. Let's hope it goes away," the tall man with white hair said.

The other man nodded. He said, "We'll keep our eyes on it."

***

In Max's sitting room, Sean enjoyed the tartness of the Kabinett.

Turning to Max, he said, "Has there ever been much talk about the UFO incident, given what we've discovered?"

"There hasn't been as much as you'd think. We've discussed it because of our family's involvement, but it's never been a real topic of discussion in the town. When I think about it, I'm surprised it's been such a non-subject. Wouldn't you think it would be like your Roswell? I've seen pictures where the entire town embraces the idea of being the site of an alien visitation, yet here it's as if it never happened," Max said.

"How do you know about Roswell?" Sean asked.

"When your father was directly involved in a UFO incident, you read everything you can. It doesn't mean you broadcast it, but you're certainly more aware."

Sean realized he might have more resources than he counted on.

"Max, are you saying you've always stayed up on this or is it something new because of what I shared with you?" Alan asked.

"Alan, you probably weren't involved in the discussions because you're only here for short visits, but you'll see I'm not the only avid follower of UFO lore. When your father and uncles were involved, you grow up with family discussions and can't help but become interested."

Alan looked at Sean and only had a one word response.

"Excellent," he said.

Marta came back into the room with a new bottle of Kabinett in one hand and a beer for Max in the other. Without speaking she handed Max his drink and filled the visitor's glasses.

"Come on, boys, I brought all these Deutsch delicacies and they haven't been touched," she said.

They looked at the tray, then at each other and kind of shrugged. They'd been so engrossed in the discussion they hadn't thought about the food in front of them.

"We'll make short work of your fancy little tray. Give us a few minutes," Max said.

They heard a commotion behind Marta and in walked another large fellow.

"Sean, meet my brother Gola," Max said.

Sean stood and shook Gola's hand, then Gola turned to embrace Alan.

"I couldn't wait to meet you, Sean, and hear more about this fantastic story," Gola said.

"The usual for you, Gola?" Marta asked.

He nodded, and within moments Marta handed Gola what appeared to be the same brew Max was drinking.

Gola sat down, but before he could speak another guest was greeted by Marta. The new arrival took longer to join the group, and when he did, he had drink in hand. It was obvious this group enjoyed their libations.

Alfred entered the room and went straight to Sean.

51

"You must be Sean. I'm Alfred. I didn't want to miss anything. When Gola said you were on the way I hopped into the car and here I am," he said.

"Marta, what feast do you have planned for us? There are wonderful smells coming from your kitchen," Alfred asked.

"In honor of our guests I'm preparing duck, dumplings and sauerkraut. It will be done in about two hours," Marta said.

"You gentlemen need to come here more often," Alfred said.

Gola, acting like the chief of police he was, took charge.

"Alan filled us in on your caretaker's story, but we've been waiting to hear it from you. Please let us have it first-hand," he said.

Sean enjoyed the direct approach and spent the next half hour recounting the story with as much detail as he could remember. When finished, he asked a question that had been on his mind. "Did your uncles and father ever talk about what went on during those two days?" he asked.

Gola replied before the others had a chance and said, "As we grew up there was always discussion and speculation. They didn't see the craft themselves, but spoke with friends who had, and they did see Himmler and von Braun coming and going," he said.

"We've gone to the site a number of times. It's barren and nothing grows there. It has the shape of a large oval and animals avoid the area. It's kind of a given that something unnatural crashed there," Max said.

Sean looked at them both. "How has this stayed so quiet? Do the locals ever speculate or talk about it?" he asked.

They all looked at each other, and there was a pregnant pause before Gola spoke.

"Stories are told among the town elders about how the crash was the main topic of conversation when it happened. Soon after the craft was removed, the SS came to Freiburg and made it clear the crash was not to be spoken about. Between 1936 and 1939 several people disappeared after talking about what was then called the incident, and it was apparent the SS was monitoring local speculation. The disappearances, and later on, the disastrous results Hitler was producing, managed to squelch conversation.

"After the war, there was so much rebuilding to be done the focus was on the practical. Many Freiburg residents were lost in the war, so idle speculation for entertainment purposes wasn't done. The culture has kept conversation behind closed doors and within families. This remained the norm until the eighties when things started to loosen up and the topic returned to public discussion.

"Sometime in the mid-eighties a fellow came to town and started asking questions. He interviewed everyone with first-hand knowledge and was revving up local interest. His open discussion caused the greatest increase in public interest since the incident happened. He was going to write a book or some such thing, then one day he was found in the woods with a bullet in his head.

"This happened before I became chief of police. The investigation yielded nothing, and it has gone unsolved. When I became chief, I looked at the file, but it contained little information.

"Over the years other individuals have come into town and asked questions, done interviews, and looked like they were doing research on the subject. Rumor has it that at least two or three of these folks were murdered, and discussions have again gone behind closed doors."

Alfred reacted with surprise.

"Gola, are you saying you knew about several murders connected with the incident in the last few years?" Alfred asked.

"We all knew about a murder, but it was never connected with investigating the incident. The other alleged murders were nothing more than rumor and didn't happen here. There was never any connection other than gossip, and there was never confirmation. Again, this was before I took office and my predecessor never paid attention to it. I'll pull some records tomorrow and see what we have."

"Back to the UFO crash. What haven't we talked about?" Sean asked.

Max scanned his brothers and said, "I don't know of any stories, but there is one thing. Our father's best friend was a guy by the name of Helmut Clausen, and he was one of the first on the scene. He inspected the craft and was assigned to guard the immediate area. He told my dad he didn't know what it was, but said debris was scattered everywhere."

Max looked at Gola, almost as if he was waiting to see if there was an objection, then he continued, "Clausen told our father he had a piece of whatever crashed and pulled it out of his pocket. Dad said it was light and they tried to crease and cut it, but it was immune to damage. They agreed to say nothing about it, which turned out to be a good idea.

"Once the craft was removed, the SS gathered the soldiers and warned them they were now involved in a state secret, and any release of information would result in a firing squad without trial. That got their attention. Clausen knew he couldn't reveal his prized possession and, other than telling our father, he kept it quiet for years."

"Did you ever see it?" Sean asked.

They all broke out with grins.

"We have it. Clausen and my father remained best friends. Ten years ago Clausen was on his death bed from cancer and asked my father to take the piece. He felt it should be made public at some point, but left that decision up to dad. We never agreed upon what to do with it, so it's remained a silent treasure."

"Where is it and can I see it?" Sean asked.

"Yes, of course. It's at my dad's and we'll be there tomorrow. We hadn't planned on your arrival today and have dinner scheduled tomorrow night as our big get together. When Alan called and said you could come over this afternoon, we scrambled to open our schedules and never thought about bringing it along," Max said.

"Does anyone outside the family know of its existence and have you ever thought of getting it tested?" Alan asked.

"This has been a family secret, and we don't think Clausen ever revealed anything," Gola said.

"I was hoping you would say that," Alan said.

It occurred to Sean they had been effective at keeping it quiet since Alan never heard the story.

"We need to get the piece tested and get the information documented, but given what we know, we need to be discreet," Sean said.

"Sean, you'll find no fear in this family. This secret wasn't kept quiet because we were afraid. You've uncovered incredible information. We have proof, and we want to be part of whatever happens," Gola said.

Sean looked around the room and every set of eyes looked back and heads nodded.

"Okay, it looks like we're on the same page. The next question is what do we do first and how do we protect ourselves from this malevolent sentry," Sean said.

"We've started," Gola said. "First thing tomorrow, Max and I will pull everything we have regarding our unsolved homicide. We'll re-open the investigation and see where it goes."

"That's prefect. I'll call the two contacts Wolfe gave me," Sean said.

He didn't mention they were CIA agents. He thought it best to keep that to himself and Alan at this point.

"Gola, do you have a local trustworthy lab that can test your item? People have been killed for doing research and asking questions, think what would happen if this artifact became known," Sean said.

"We have labs, but I'm not sure they have the capability to do the extensive sort of testing this will require. I'll check around."

Sean understood, at that moment, he had a team. Everyone was eager to take a role and run with it. Everyone except Alfred, who interrupted the energy by asking when dinner would be served. At least almost everyone was ready to jump in with both feet. By now almost two hours had flown by and Marta made Alfred happy by announcing dinner was ready. Everyone stood at once.

The group adjourned to a dining room for a true German dinner. The room was more formal than the family room, and natural light shone through large French windows on three walls. The rectangular distressed pine table was set for ten and could have handled a larger group. Marta and Max started bringing large platters of food, and Sean felt like he joined the Rockenbach clan for a European style Christmas dinner, except it was April. The only thing missing was the tree and the presents.

Conversation slowed as everyone filled their plates and respective mouths.

"Sean, did your friend Wolfe ever discuss what happened to the alien crafts?" Max asked.

"Nothing more than what I mentioned earlier. He said Himmler had them taken to Wewelsburg Castle, but where they ended up is anyone's guess," Sean said.

"So he didn't speculate where they might have journeyed from there?" Max asked.

"No, he said he didn't know what happened after they arrived at Wewelsburg. He said the Nazis reverse engineered the alien technology, and it may have resulted in the significant technological advantage Germany experienced over the rest of the world. The V-1 and V-2 rockets were way beyond anything the rest of the world possessed, and Hitler always contended he had a super weapon.

In retrospect, his arrogance could have been the result of this technological advantage. This could have been a deciding factor in his decision to open a two front war. At least that was Wolfe's speculation," Sean said.

"His theory has merit," Max said. "History has questioned why he opened a two front war against the counsel of his generals. He had support from the Deutsch people and was given everything he wanted when the Munich Accords handed him the Sudetenland. England and France caved to what Hitler demanded. Old-timers here still believe he wasn't delusional, but rather overconfident because he had knowledge that no one else possessed. It would also make it easier to understand why he believed he could achieve world domination."

Sean took in the aromas emanating from his plate. His fork speared a chunk of dumpling covered with sauerkraut and delivered it to his waiting mouth. He was instantly transported and was once again an eight-year-old in his great-grandmother's kitchen. The sharp bite of the kraut against the soft texture of the bread dumpling was exquisite.

"Marta, this is wonderful. You've picked the perfect meal for my first dinner with the Rockenbachs," Sean said.

"I'm so glad you like it," she said.

"Marta, it's great as usual, but I have to bring us back to the topic at hand. Has there ever been discussion or even awareness about the Polish crash?" Alan asked.

Everyone shook their heads indicating it was unknown to them.

"I never heard a word," Gola said. "The craft would've been removed and the locals threatened, so little would be known. I'll make the call tomorrow, but it may be a challenge. I don't know how much information a Polish police chief will share with the police in Deutschland."

"Gola, is there some kind of unspoken relationship between the chiefs of police in different cities where special consideration is given?" Sean asked.

"Sometimes there's a professional courtesy, but everyone is an individual and you never know about someone until you start a discussion," Gola said.

"Okay, we have several areas where we can focus. Now what do we do about the threat issue? We can't ignore it. We have the advantage of having a team looking at this instead of one guy who never knew what hit him. Any ideas?" Alan asked.

"We need to be aware of anything unusual," Gola said. "Let's not bring attention to what we're doing. Once we start asking questions, we can't help but create noise. It's evident there's an information leak alerting someone when certain questions are asked. Vigilance starts tomorrow."

Heads nodded around the table. Dinner was finished, and both Alan and Sean were running on fumes. Sean had been functioning on pure adrenaline, and after a deep breath, his eyelids felt like lead weights as jet lag envelop him.

"Alan, I'm crashing. How are you feeling?" Sean asked.

"I'm beat," Alan said. "Hey, guys, this has been fantastic, but we're still on U.S. time. I think we need to get some rest. We'll be more refreshed tomorrow."

Sean started shaking hands and Alan was giving hugs. Everyone looked forward to the next evening, and the group seemed united with a purpose. They said their final goodbyes and headed toward the car.

"Now that was something. I loved your family. Can you believe where we're at? We have physical evidence and we have a team that includes law enforcement," Sean said.

Alan gave a low whistle.

"This is about to get very interesting," Alan said.

***

Sean stirred as the early sun came through his window. He glanced at the clock, it was six-thirty and he jumped out of bed with an energy he hadn't felt in years.

At six-fifty he entered the hotel's breakfast area. He grabbed a to-go plate from the buffet, found a large mug, filled it with hot strong coffee, and returned to his room. It was now five minutes after seven.

He fired up his laptop and, using the hotel Internet, was able to connect without a problem. He checked his email and realized he forgot to call Cat. He picked up his cell phone and dialed.

"Hello," Cat said in a sleepy voice.

"Hi hon, I'm sorry, I can tell I woke you."

"That's okay, I'm just glad to hear your voice. How's it going over there?"

"It's been terrific so far. I spent time with Cassie and that's been the highlight. She's doing so well, you'd be proud. I wish you could be here."

"I know, I wish I was too. What'd you do with her?"

"We ate well, we talked, visited the castle, and just hung out. I was lucky enough to get a two bedroom suite so she stayed over and it gave us more time together."

"That sounds wonderful. How's Alan doing?"

"He's been great and I love his family. They've been welcoming and want to be involved in this whole thing. Two of them are cops so that's an advantage."

"How long until you come home?"

"I'm just getting started so that's impossible to know."

"I know, I just miss you."

"Me too. Why don't you get back to sleep and I'll call you tomorrow."

"Okay, love you."

"Love you too."

***

At eight he made his first call.

"*Bonjour,*" Philipe Laflamme said.

"*Bonjour, Monsieur* Laflamme, this is Sean O'Shea. Wilhelm Wolfe gave me your phone number and suggested I call you when I arrived."

"*Bonjour, Monsieur* O'Shea. I have been awaiting your call. Where are you staying?"

"I'm at the Colombi in Freiburg," Sean said.

"Good, you're not too far from me. I live in Vendenheim. I can be there in just over an hour. Would you be available, say, in an hour and a half?"

Sean was surprised, while both pleased and concerned.

"Yes I am."

"Good. I've been to your hotel several times. I'll meet you in the lobby. I'm sixty years old and have black and white hair. I think you Americans call it salt and pepper. I'll be wearing a dark brown leather overcoat. I'll see you in a little while."

They signed off, and Sean was pleased.

58

Chapter 5)

Sean was sitting in the lobby when a thin man fitting Laflamme's description walked through the hotel's double door entrance. His features were thin and sharp. Sean stood as he approached.

"*Monsieur* O'Shea?" he asked.

"Yes, it's nice to meet you, Philipe. Please call me Sean."

They sat down and Laflamme removed his leather coat. The coat reminded Sean of the old pictures of the Nazi Storm Troopers, and Sean thought it was an odd choice for a Frenchman.

"Thank you so much for coming to see me," Sean said. "Would you like something to drink?"

"*Oui*, it would be appreciated," Laflamme said.

They stood and walked to the long coffee bar. Sean picked the French roast, Philipe the expresso, and they returned to the beige sofa.

"Are you okay talking here?" Sean asked.

"This is fine. No one is around, so this will work for us," Laflamme said.

"I'm surprised you wanted to get together so soon. Wolfe said I should check in and you'd be a resource if I needed help."

"Your friend Wolfe has a warm spot for you. He called and told me about your project and he's concerned for your safety. He asked me to sniff around and see what I could find out. I might add he and I have been friends for thirty-five years and worked on many, er, activities together. I was saddened when he decided to, as you say, ride off into the sunset. I knew I'd miss him, we were more like brothers than colleagues. I would do anything for him, and when he called, I told him I'd watch your back. I can justify my involvement because something odd has been going on for years and I'd like to know what it is."

"Wolfe is a great guy and I welcome your interest. Can I ask just how active you are in your profession these days?"

"Let's just say I have no profession, but I am active in everything I do," Laflamme said, and a slight smile crossed his face.

Sean didn't need to ask another question and thought how those same words could have come out of Wolfe's mouth.

"I was surprised by what Wilhelm revealed to you. He said you knew a great deal of the story, or at least you had an accurate theory, but it was uncharacteristic for him to provide the sort of detail he gave to you. I'm still puzzled, but it doesn't matter because here we sit. I just want you to know you have a guardian angel in Wilhelm," Laflamme said.

"I have a special relationship with him and, believe me, I appreciate it. He sort of adopted my family as his own, and I think he feels like my kids' grandfather."

Laflamme nodded.

"Since Wilhelm opened the door I have no choice but to walk through it. I am not comfortable with what I am about to share, but I believe I must at this point," Laflamme said. "Our community of agents has long been aware of the crashes you plan to investigate. The crashes at Freiburg, Poland, and Roswell have changed life on earth. There have been others, and there have been bodies and survivors," Laflamme said.

Sean was startled. Wolfe never told him anything about survivors. He decided not to let on because Philipe didn't know what Wolfe did or didn't tell him.

"It isn't a question of if UFOs are real. We know they are. The question is, who is trying to keep information about the Black Forest crash from coming out. One might think of governments, but we know that is not the case. If it was, I would know. Second, there is no reason for governments to do this. They have a program of denial, denial, denial, and it has been effective.

"When Wilhelm told me he shared the crash information with you, I asked if he remembered the case of Philip Robert. He did not. I asked if he knew of three subsequent murders tied to crash research. He didn't know of those either. It was then I realized, during that time, his focus was on the Middle East and he didn't have visibility to lower level European issues. I knew of them because I'm based in France and the murders took place in France and Germany.

"When I told Wolfe, he became concerned for you. He is afraid you will become a target by whoever took out your four dead predecessors. He asked me to see what I could find out," Laflamme said.

"Do you have any theories about who's responsible?" Sean asked.

"We never conducted a detailed investigation. We always look into these kinds of events, and every situation is evaluated as to whether it presents a security risk. We knew the subject of the victim's investigation, but there didn't appear to be a terrorist risk, so we did not look any further. Wilhelm and I had an extensive discussion about this last night. We considered the most logical source and our conclusion was the same; the Vatican," Laflamme said.

"Why would the church care about a UFO crash over seventy years ago? And if they did, they're the church. Why would they kill people? They're about religion, God, and following Jesus' word," Sean said.

Philipe leaned forward and put his face into his hands. Sean recognized, if he was adept in reading body language, the act before him would carry a definite meaning.

"What I am about to tell you will give you knowledge known to only an elite few and almost all are contained within the intelligence community. It will change how you think about many subjects. Did you ever read The Da Vinci Code?" he asked.

"Yes, I thought it was great," Sean said.

"The book was surprisingly accurate when it focused on The Vatican and Opus Dei, but it stopped short of all the other factions that complicate church activities. The gist of secret groups within the Vatican was right on the money."

"Is that why Wolfe suggested religion as the likely culprit behind the murders?" Sean asked.

"Let us set down some basic facts. What is the Vatican and the Catholic Church?" he asked and continued, "It is the greatest financial power in the world and the world's largest property owner. With its ability to raise money, it is the world's largest wealth creator. The church possesses more material riches than any other entity, institution, bank, government, corporation, or country in the world," Laflamme said.

"Are you saying there are no checks and balances on the Vatican?" Sean asked.

"They have none. The Vatican is its own sovereign micro-state. It has a head of state, a cabinet, and its own bank.

"It is interesting to look at the structure within the Vatican. The Jesuit Order has been the control arm of the Vatican for 500 years. It controls covert operations, geographical and political operations and is structured like a military organization. Its leader is the Superior General, but he is better known as the Black Pope.

"The Vatican is made up of a number of groups. The U.S. government has the CIA, DIA, FBI, and Homeland Security. The Vatican has the Sovereign Military Order of Malta, the Brotherhood, which is a segment of Freemasonry, Opus Dei, the Illuminati, the Prieure' de Sion, and numerous other groups that have secret rituals and odd beliefs."

"So you're comparing the U.S. Government to the Vatican?"

"Not in size, but they have a similar structure, having multiple groups with covert operations which sometimes overlap," Laflamme took a breath and continued. "The Military Order of Malta is also known as the Knights of Malta. Its membership used to be limited to Italians and heads of state, but in recent years opened its membership to attract the wealthy and powerful. The plan has been to have these high profile members serve as cover.

"The newer members are now involved in both business operations and in military operations. The MOM, as it is known, is all about investing, protecting their assets, and destroying or stealing what they do not own. Control of money is their main focus. It is our guess the Military Order of Malta is the group responsible for the acts of violence directed at the UFO investigators," Laflamme said.

"I appreciate the background, and I understand there are dark forces within the Vatican, but I still ask the same question. Why would they care about an unsubstantiated UFO crash from over seventy years ago?" Sean asked.

"We have seen it before. Whenever the Vatican feels a threat, they will kill to protect themselves without a second thought. You might find this interesting. There are over thirteen thousand priests in the Jesuit Order, and many have taken the *fourth vow secret oath* in which the killing of a heretic is not considered a crime. So it appears the Vatican feels they can create their own amendment to the Ten Commandments, allowing them to ignore the commandment of 'thou shall not kill." By the way, the *fourth vow secret oath* is endorsed by the Order of Malta," Laflamme said.

"Curious how that oath mirrors the Muslim belief in killing infidels," Sean said. "What I still question is why both you and Wolfe have gone to the church theory without an investigation taking place."

"I was afraid of this. Wilhelm and I have been open with you because it did not compromise our professional responsibilities. UFOs from over seventy years ago and German scientists going to America under a secret program did not put us in a compromising position. Now we are moving into an area that is starting to make me uncomfortable."

There was silence as Philipe considered his dilemma and he said, "You have a general idea of what Wilhelm and I did for the last forty or so years. You cannot be in this business, in this area of the world, and not know the many clandestine activities that have taken place.

"I'm not going to be specific with you, but suffice to say if fanatical and ruthless regimes in this part of the world were ranked, the Vatican would fall right behind Nazi Germany and Stalin's Russia. I'm not comparing the purges and outright slaughter of people in the war, but I am talking about how these organizations protect their interests and how easily they will eliminate a perceived threat."

Laflamme stopped and took a long swallow of his now lukewarm coffee.

"If you think about the history of the church you will recognize the signs. Who kept orchestrating the Holy Wars and the Crusades? It was the Holy Roman Empire headed by the Vatican. The first Crusade was called for by Pope Urban the second, and subsequent Crusades were driven by Pope Gregory the seventh, then Pope Gregory the eighth and so on.

"Throughout Europe, there have been countless assassinations, disappearances, and intimidation done by unseen forces for the benefit only one entity; the Vatican. So when Wolfe and I say this feels like the church, it is not guess work. We've seen it over and over, and it has their signature all over it. Now we have to determine their motivation."

Chapter 6)

Gola dialed the phone and it was answered by the Czernica Police Department receptionist. He introduced himself and asked for the chief of police.

"Hello, this is Chief Barinski," he said.

"Good morning Chief, this is Gola Rockenbach. I'm the chief of police in Freiburg, Germany."

"Good morning, Chief Rockenbach. What can I do for you?" Barinski asked.

"I'm investigating a murder we think has some relationship to an alleged UFO crash in 1936 outside of Freiburg. It appears, at different points in time, new UFO investigations took place, and in each case the person asking about the events turned up dead in what seems to be a professional hit. I believe your area had a similar event in the late 1930's, and I'm looking for any connection or unusual activities you may be aware of," Gola said.

"You have an interesting matter, Chief Rockenbach; far more so than a teenager stealing one of our farmer's goats. I haven't thought about that old story in a long time. Legend has it something crashed in the woods and Nazis were all over the site. The Germans removed everything, and I'm surprised you even know about it. I've been chief since 1967 and few outsiders ever heard of it," Barinski said.

"Since we had our own crash we're a little more aware of any similarities, and my relatives were part of the guard detail. Our family has discussed this matter many times over the years," Gola said.

"There have been rumors, and the fact that nothing will grow in the area is all the proof the locals need to believe the crash happened. I did have a guy come here years ago when I was new on the force, and he asked a lot of questions. He was investigating the UFO rumors and was going to write a book or something. He was a Dutchman, Gus something or other, but I don't remember his name. I spent about an hour with him, and I know he was going out to the site. I think he spoke with someone who was somehow involved, but who it was doesn't come to me either. If I think of anything I'll give you a call. What's your phone number?" Barinski asked.

"Could his name have been Gusdorf by chance?" Gola asked.

"That's it. Very good, chief. How did you know?"

"He's the homicide victim I mentioned earlier. The case has been in our cold case files for some time and we've reopened it."

"Are you making any progress?"

"Not yet, but new facts have emerged, and we're following up. By the way, did you ever have contact from a Frenchman named Philipe Robert around 1968?" Gola asked.

"No, never heard of him. Who is he?" Barinski asked.

"He was another homicide victim who was investigating the same story as Gusdorf and was researching the UFO crash sites in Freiburg and in your area. He seemed to be far along in his research and was killed in Lyon. I'm surprised he never contacted you," Gola said.

"No, I would remember. No Frenchman named Robert ever contacted me," Barinski said.

Gola thanked him, they exchanged contact information, and Gola replaced the phone. He was disappointed the call was a dead end, but at least he made contact. Barinski told him to call at any time, but also made Gola aware that he was retiring in two months. He said at seventy years old he had enough excitement to last the rest of his life.

Gola looked up as Max walked through the door.

"Find out anything?" Max asked.

"I didn't get anything worth following up. The chief in Czernica spoke with someone doing research, but didn't remember his name and didn't know much of anything else. I suggested the name Gusdorf and he said that's who he spoke with. He said he would call if he remembered anything else," Gola said.

"Have you looked into the other murder victims yet?" Max asked.

"Not yet. My first call was to Czernica," Gola said.

"Okay, let's continue to dig and see what we can find," Max said.

Chapter 7)

As Gola and Max had their discussion, Chief Barinski of the Czernica Police Department dialed a number with an area code for Rome, Italy.

"*Hallo?*" the man in a long black robe said.

"This is Barinski in Poland. I believe it's happening again."

There was momentary silence.

"We have also had another report. Who was asking questions?" the man in a black robe said.

"His name is Gola Rockenbach, and he's the chief of police in Freiburg. He was sniffing around. He didn't share much and said he was looking into an old murder and new information has come to light. He asked if we ever had any murders or issues related to our UFO crash," Barinski said.

"What did you tell him?"

"I said we hadn't, but I had spoken to someone who was asking questions. I told him I never heard back from the guy."

"Okay, let me know if he calls back. Don't contact him, and let's see if you hear from him again."

"Will do," Barinski said.

Chapter 8)

Sean thought about the previous evening with the Rockenbachs and was ready to share the information with Philipe.

"I appreciate the religious history lesson. I was a history major, and I've long believed organized religion was, and is, the root of most conflicts in the world. It's all about my God is better than your God. It's nothing more than religious dick measuring," Sean said.

Laflamme smiled. He said, "I like the analogy, and you are right."

"I want to bring you up to date. I'm traveling with an old friend named Alan Rockenbach. He was the first person I spoke to about my premise, even before I talked to Wolfe. This is an unbelievable coincidence, but his father and uncles were assigned to guard the crash site. Alan was born in Freiburg and moved to America when he was small, but the rest of his family stayed in Germany. During World War Two, his father and uncles were in the German Army, and when the crash was discovered they were sent to the site. It was my conversation with Alan that propelled me to talk with Wolfe.

"Last evening Alan and I met with his cousins. The information that came out was remarkable. His cousin is chief of police in Freiburg, and another cousin is the chief inspector. We talked for hours, and they want to participate in the investigation. The most exciting thing is they have an artifact from the crash. There's another dinner tonight, and they promised to show me the item, I'll need to find a secure lab to have it tested and analyzed," Sean said.

Sean expected excitement from Laflamme. He didn't get it.

"That's interesting, but also quite dangerous. The more people you involve, the less control we have. Your little project now risks a greater likelihood of being discovered.

"See if you can get the artifact tonight, and I'll take it to a secure lab. I know how to navigate under the radar. At this point you've involved a number of amateurs, and it'll have the same effect as tracking a wild animal while walking on gravel. It makes a lot of noise," Laflamme said.

Sean understood the point, but it didn't diminish his enthusiasm for his new team. It was nice to know he wasn't the Lone Ranger. Laflamme seemed less interested in the significance of the artifact and more concerned about maintaining secrecy. Sean guessed it came with the territory.

Chapter 9)

The man in the black robe dialed his phone. Instantaneously, a discolored beige telephone came to life in a seedy third floor apartment in the famous Red Light district of Amsterdam.

The phone was answered by a stocky man with short blond hair and pock-marked skin. "Yes?" he said.

"It has started again. We may need your special skills. What is your availability?" the man in a black robe asked.

"I'm available. Where is the target?"

"We don't know if there is a target, but there may be multiple targets. It appears they are around Freiburg, Germany."

"What's the timeframe?"

"We don't know yet. We are waiting to see if it will be necessary."

"Keep me informed," he said, as the man with bad skin didn't wait for a response and replaced the receiver. He looked out the window at the scene below. It was just before noon, and the cobblestone walking paths had sparse foot traffic. He could see the display windows on the first floors had opened for business. The B team was in place, and he was puzzled why men would pay women for sex when they looked like their night job was at the circus. It was even odder since once the sun went down, the A team took over, and they looked like a parade of playmates of the month. Amsterdam; what a place, he thought.

Chapter 10)

Max walked into Gola's office.

"I think I have a little something," Max said. "We know one victim was Philip Robert. I checked him out and he was found dead in Lyon on June fifth, 1968. His throat was slit, and he had a bullet in his brain. I checked the news reports, and he had a press conference scheduled for the following day. The article indicated it was related to his UFO research.

"Gusdorf was killed in 1986, and he was found fifteen miles from here with his throat slit and a bullet in his head. His death was attributed to a drug deal gone badly because he had hash and marijuana in his pockets. I'll follow up on Robert and dig a little deeper, but I haven't been able to tie the other murders to the right names. I'll keep on it," Max said.

"I told you the chief in Poland confirmed Gusdorf was the name of the guy asking questions about UFOs. Our files reveal nothing memorable about the Gusdorf murder, but the drug motive seems too convenient and it sounds like the same thing with Robert. If they were killed over drugs, the hash and weed found on their bodies would have been taken. The motive attributed to Gusdorf's murder always bothered me," Gola said.

Max nodded and turned to leave, then stopped. He craned his head toward Gola.

"What time are you coming tonight?" Max asked.

"I'll come early, sometime around five. That's when we told Alan and Sean to arrive," Gola said.

***

At the same time Gola and Max were chatting, Sean was wrapping up with Laflamme. Sean knew Laflamme and Wolfe shared the same concern about his welfare, and it was apparent they could ascertain when danger was at hand. Sean and Philipe agreed to talk in the morning and set up an exchange of the artifact.

Sean's phone vibrated in his pocket and caller I.D. showed Alan's name.

"Alan, your timing is perfect, I just finished meeting with Philipe

Laflamme. Both he and Wolfe seem confident the church is the responsible party. When I asked why, he went off on the Vatican's position of influence since the Middle Ages and seemed convinced of their power," Sean said.

"How curious. We can discuss this tonight at dinner." Alan said.

***

In Freiburg Max sat at his desk and felt he was at a dead end. He knew there had been four murders and only had scant information on the Gusdorf matter, then the light bulb went off. Philip Robert had a news conference scheduled the day after he was killed. He was going to announce something and may have had some type of evidence. Maybe it still existed, but 1968 was over forty years ago. He considered the odds if something could be found? Robert was from Lyon, which was only two hundred miles from Freiburg, and he could be there in three and a half hours. He had his starting point.

Chapter 11)

Max turned to his computer screen and searched the Lyon Police Department phone number. Thirty seconds later he was dialing the phone in his left hand.

"*Bonjour, un commissariat de police.*"

"*Bonjour,* this is Chief Inspector Max Rockenbach from the Freiburg, Germany Police Department. I'm conducting an investigation and I think it can be linked to a murder in Lyon in 1968. The victim's name was Philip Robert, and I'm inquiring as to how I can review any information about this matter."

"*Un moment, s'il vous plait.*"

"*Bonjour,* this is Chief Inspector Acord, can I help you?"

"Chief Inspector Acord, this is Inspector Rockenbach in Freiburg, Germany. I'm conducting a homicide investigation and we think it's connected to a murder in Lyon in 1968. The Lyon victim was a Philip Robert, and I was hoping to review old case files if they still exist."

"Nineteen sixty-eight is long time ago. The inspector who trained me, worked that case. He talked about it all the time. There is no one on the force who was here in 1968, but I'm sure we have those files. They would be stored in the catacombs and you're welcomed to have look."

"Thank you, Inspector Acord. I'd like that very much. Do you know if there was any talk about it, you know rumors, strange things, the kind of stories that people talk about over the years?" Max asked.

"I'd have to think about that. Chief Inspector Lemieux would talk about odd things, but I don't remember specifics. He was unhappy the case went unsolved. He would say Lyon was the home to forensic science so we should be able to solve the crime. Lyon has had its share of high profile criminals over the years."

"You mentioned your ex-chief inspector, is he still around?" Max asked.

"*Oui*, he retired around seven years ago and now mostly reads and hunts. He will talk your head off."

Acord found Lemieux's phone number and gave it to Max, "Tell him I gave you his number and I said *bonjour* and he owes me a call," he said.

"Thank you very much. You just saved me great deal of time. I'll call you when I'm coming to Lyon so we can coordinate our schedules," Max said.

Max glanced at his watch. There wasn't enough time to get to Lyon and back in time for tonight's dinner. He would go to Lyon as soon as the retired Inspector would agree to see him. He dialed the phone number of ex-Chief Inspector Lemieux.

It took three rings and a strong loud voice boomed, *"Bonjour."*

Max introduced himself and explained his discussion with Inspector Acord and how he came to have Lemieux's phone number. Max told him he was coming to Lyon to review the case files and asked if they could get together. Lemieux agreed and set a lunch date for the following day. Max was thrilled with Lemieux's responsiveness and called Acord. Lyon's Chief Inspector agreed to have the files ready for him the next morning.

Chapter 12)

As Sean and Alan drove to Max's home, Sean repeated the discussion he had with Laflamme.

"We have interesting theories about the UFOs; Hitler's overconfidence, Operation Paperclip, the American space program getting their kick start from the re-engineering of UFOs, but how does it all tie together and why is the Vatican killing people? Whatever they're hiding would have to be so dramatic it couldn't be spun and made to go away," Sean said.

Sean asked Alan to find a liquor store so he could bring a small contribution for dinner. They pulled into GH Strecker, and Sean bought four bottles of a high end Kabinett and was checking out when Alan put down a bottle of Port and another of Remy Martin VSOP Cognac.

"I was thinking the same thing. We can drink yours before dinner and mine after," Alan said.

Five minutes later they pulled into an older neighborhood with mature trees and vintage homes. The houses were cottage- like with stone with dark wood, peaked slate roofs, and walls covered by ivy.

Alan stopped in front of a home appearing to be from the pages of a travel magazine. The ivy was dormant, but Sean envisioned its look at the height of the summer. He thought Cat would love this, then he realized he hadn't spoken with her today. She wouldn't be happy. He was so preoccupied with his quest it slipped his mind and would need to call in the morning.

They were greeted at the door by Marta. Sean entered and fell in love with the house. It reminded him of a famous old German restaurant in Milwaukee named Karl Ratzsch's, and he wondered if it was still in business. It also took him back to his great-grandparents' home in Fox River Grove, Illinois. They came from Bohemia near the German border, spoke broken English, and created a similar looking home. He knew he would appreciate this evening.

Marta greeted him with a hug, and Sean handed her the wine as she led him into a large dark room where flames danced and shimmered inside a huge field-stone fireplace. Max stood and greeted Sean like he was one of his brothers. It was obvious Sean had already become part of the family.

Turning to two smaller men sitting in massive leather chairs, Max introduced them.

"Sean, meet my father, Richard, and my Uncle Tomas," he said.

Sean bent over the elderly men, extended a hand to each and was surprised by the firmness of their handshakes. Alan, who had disappeared with Marta, came into the room and went to Tomas. Tomas stood and was taller than Sean had expected. The size of the chairs and the apparent frailty of the ancient men made them appear smaller than they were.

Tomas and Alan held a long affectionate embrace as fathers and sons often do after an extended absence. Alan turned to Richard and hugged him as well. These were the actions of a family appreciative of their patriarchs and aware they wouldn't be around forever.

Before they could sit down there was a commotion behind them. Sean turned to see Alfred and Gola come in together, and for five minutes chaos reigned. Bodies were going in every direction, and Alfred and Gola went into, what Sean guessed, was the kitchen. Minutes later they returned with large glasses of white wine as others grabbed choice seats.

Sean found an unoccupied rocker with a comfortable looking cushion and planted himself as Marta came into the room to take drink orders. She again appeared to have assumed the role of Grande Dame of the family, and although not quite old enough for that designation, she seemed comfortable in the role.

Max added another log on the blaze and became the de facto keeper of the fire. Everyone seemed to have a defined role, which Sean thought, might be indicative of the German mentality.

"Well, did anyone make progress today?" Gola asked.

"I called Philipe Laflamme this morning. He's the French contact Wolfe gave me, and within ninety minutes he was at my hotel. We had an enlightening meeting, and I haven't mentioned this, but he's a CIA agent," Sean said.

"What is CIA?" Alfred asked.

"The CIA is the Central Intelligence Agency." Sean said. "It's the primary and most visible intelligence agency for the United States."

"Alfred, you've never heard of the CIA?" Max asked.

"Oh yes, I was just making sure," he said.

"Now that we've cleared that up, what else did the Frenchman have

75

to say?" Max asked.

"Laflamme spent a great deal of time talking about the Vatican. He went on a little tirade of how they're the world's wealthiest and most powerful entity, are ruthless, and will kill without a second thought to protect themselves.

"The interesting thing is Wolfe also mentioned the Vatican as a likely culprit early in our discussions. Laflamme maintained his concern regarding the danger associated with this project. These guys don't give up. My next call is to the German contact, and I expect to hear the same from him. Alan and I have explored several theories, and I'll share those a little later. I'm interested in progress everyone else made," Sean said.

"I spoke with the chief of police in Czernica, Poland, but he wasn't helpful. He was aware of the crash, but didn't offer anything useful. He said he would call if he thought of anything," Gola said.

"I did a little better than you," Max said. "I decided to follow up on the first murder victim, Philip Robert. My thinking was, he had scheduled a press conference and was killed the day before it could take place. I figured he must have had something concrete to announce. I spoke with a police inspector in Lyon, and he told me no one remained on the staff from 1968, but I was welcome to review the file. He shared that the retired chief detective on the case was also his mentor and remains interested in the homicide. He gave me his phone number, and guess what? I called him, and he and I are having lunch tomorrow. I'm reviewing the files at nine-thirty, then I meet with him."

"Well done," Gola said. "You may have created our best lead."

"I'm excited to see what tomorrow brings," Max said.

Sean turned to Gola. "Have you had the chance to fill in your dad and uncle about our discussion last night?" he asked.

"Yes, we reviewed everything," Gola said.

"I wish we could add something, but we talked at length and can't think of anything to help," Richard said.

"Is there anyone still around who had contact with the craft?" Sean asked.

"There aren't many of us left. We think a couple of men from our detail may still be alive, and Gola is going to contact their families tomorrow," Richard said.

Sean was disappointed, but progress was being made, so he didn't dwell on any negatives.

"Oh, one other thing. When I spoke with Laflamme, he said he had a trusted lab to analyze the artifact. This reduces the chance for a leak, and he's used to functioning in those grey areas," Sean said.

This was Sean's not so subtle signal to see the artifact without having to ask. It worked. Max stood and walked to the table where a single shoe box rested.

"I think you'll need this," he said and handed the box to Sean.

Sean felt his hands start to sweat, or at least that's what he imagined, and opened the box. He was surprised to see a piece of silvery metal that looked like aluminum foil. It was shiny and smooth, and when he removed it from the box had a sensation he was holding something not of this world. It was light, almost weightless, and he tried to put a crease in the metal. It would bend, but it wouldn't fold. He handed it to Alan without saying a word. Alan accepted the item and looked at it without comment. The room was silent but for the tick tock of the antique Bavarian clock.

Alan looked up and offered the item to anyone, and there were no takers. Sean guessed their many years of examining the non-descript piece led to some indifference.

Marta came into the room and announced dinner was ready.

"What do we have to look forward to?" Alfred asked.

His brothers exchanged glances, and it was evident in the pecking order Alfred was at the bottom, even when he made innocent comments.

"I made Pop's favorite, Hungarian Goulash and Spaetzle," she said, and dinner was served, followed with cherry strudel. Everyone was satiated as plates were cleared.

During dinner Sean asked about the wives who were absent.

Gola said, "They're out together. To be honest, they're tired of years of UFO talk, and sometime ago told us whenever we get together to discuss the subject they were going out for a nice dinner. That's okay with us because when everyone is together we run out of room."

"I think my wife would be right there with them," Sean said. "It seems Max and I have specific to do's for tomorrow, is there anything to be done here?"

"I'll call the families of the two guys we talked about earlier and see if they're still alive and kicking. I'm at a dead end with the Polish chief, so there's nothing more to be done there. I can look into the Gusdorf homicide and see if anything was missed. Max, did you have a chance to take another look yesterday?" Gola asked.

"I glanced at it, but not in detail. I reviewed the write up, but nothing more," Max said.

"I'll make it a priority tomorrow," Gola said.

Sean asked the two old UFO guards more questions, but they couldn't add anything. Small talk ensued, and after another forty-five minutes Sean could feel jet lag creeping back.

For the second night in a row, they said their goodbyes with promises to get together and compare notes the following night. Alan suggested they meet in the restaurant at the hotel and it would be his treat. Alfred jumped at the offer, but the rest of the family said no, and they would split the bill. Alfred looked annoyed, but everyone else was jovial as Alan and Sean headed out the door.

***

Once Sean entered his room he called Cat. She had already begun her worrying routine, and he spent the first three minutes calming her down and the next five giving her the play by play of their progress, omitting anything related to Wolfe's concerns. He spoke with Liam, then signed off with a promise to call the next day.

He picked up his day planner, looked up Rudolf Weiler's number, and dialed the sixties-style beige phone.

Rudolf Weiler answered, and Sean introduced himself.

"Good evening, Mr. O'Shea. I've been expecting your call," Rudolf said.

"It's good to meet you," Sean said.

"I spoke with Wilhelm and Philipe today and know what's been discussed. Philipe said you had an interesting item to give him," Rudolf said.

"I do. I picked it up tonight and have to call him to arrange a hand off," Sean said.

"That's good. It will be intriguing to find out what it is. I know you've heard this, but I want you to also hear it from me. You're involved in a dangerous game," Rudolf said.

"That seems to be all I'm hearing. Why is everyone so nervous? We haven't even gotten started?" Sean asked.

"First, we know what happened to people who were doing the things you're about to do. Second, we suspect we know who is behind these murders and, let's say this; they're bad people and won't stop until they succeed. As this escalates, the vulnerability factor will increase," the CIA agent said.

"Okay, you guys just don't let up. Wolfe scared me to the point I even brushed up on my hand gun skills."

"I understand you're coming to Freiburg. Have you arrived yet?" Rudolf asked.

"I have. I'm staying at the Colombi Hotel," Sean said.

"Good. I'll come to see you tomorrow afternoon. I have a package for you, courtesy of Wilhelm," Rudolf said.

Sean chose not to ask what it might be.

"I'll make sure to be here. Tomorrow evening we're reconvening our group around six, so any time before will work," Sean said.

"I'll have a four-hour drive, so I should arrive by mid-afternoon. Your little group is one reason we think this could become visible sooner rather than later. You do realize the more people involved, the greater the likelihood of word getting out?" Rudolf asked.

Sean started to ask more questions, but Rudolf cut him off.

"We'll talk tomorrow. There are some things I've been checking and I'll know more in the morning. Let's wait until then," he said.

They signed off, and Sean was surprised by the small army now assembled.

***

At eight the next morning Sean walked into the breakfast room where Alan was already seated. O'Shea recapped the conversation with the agent and his expected arrival later in the day.

"What do you think he meant when he said he had a package for you?" Alan asked.

"I'm not sure, but I wouldn't be surprised if it was a gun. These folks live in that world," Sean said.

"What are you going to do if he gives you one?" Alan asked.

"These guys are the pros, and if they think I need it, I should listen."

"If you get a weapon, make sure you don't go all Dick Cheney on

79

me," Alan said.

"I give you no guarantees," Sean said with a smirk, "but I do have an idea for you today. Gola is going to try to track down the two old guys, and he's also going to take another look at the Gusdorf case. Maybe you could do something with him because we're still in discovery mode."

Alan agreed. He would go to the police station and see if he could help Gola review the files. When breakfast was finished, Alan left to see Gola and Sean went back to his room.

Sean called Laflamme. "*Bonjour*," he said.

"*Bonjour*, Philipe, this is Sean. I have a little something for you and want to get it into your hands."

"*Tres bon*, Sean. I have a thought. I know Rudolf is coming to see you this afternoon. Why don't I come to Freiburg and we can all talk and I can get the artifact."

Sean was amazed at how these guys seemed to know everything going on and had a plan for what to do next.

"That would be fantastic. It'd be perfect for the three of us to meet, and I want to get this analyzed as soon as possible," he said. They agreed to meet at two in the afternoon, and Philipe said he would call Rudolf.

***

Alan walked into the Freiburg police station and was greeted by a hefty woman wearing a uniform and sitting behind a large raised desk. He had to look up at her, and Alan understood the design was not by accident.

"Chief Rockenbach please," Alan said.

"Can I have your name and the nature of your business?" she asked.

Before he could answer he heard a familiar voice.

"The nature of his business is to come here and disrupt my day," Gola said. "Hilda, meet my Cousin Alan Rockenbach."

Hilda's grimace changed to a smile as she extended her hand. Alan took it and had to squeeze hard to keep the bones in his hands from being crushed, then followed Gola as he retreated down the corridor.

"I'm glad you came by. What are you up to today?" Gola asked.

"I had breakfast with Sean this morning and we were trying to figure out how I could help. He's meeting with the German agent, Max is on his way to Lyon, and I knew you were going to follow up on a couple things. I don't want to be out of the loop, so I thought I'd see if you needed any help," Alan said.

"Great idea. I'm about to start calling the families of the two old guys. How about taking a look at the Gusdorf files? I just had everything brought up to my office, and maybe your eyes will see something the original investigators didn't see," Gola said.

"That's perfect," Alan said, "I can finally feel like I'm contributing. I'd be happy to go through whatever you have."

The Freiburg Police Chief's office was nicer than Alan anticipated. It was a large room with Gola's desk sitting in front of two large picture windows and a large circular table and four chairs in the corner. On top of the round table were several boxes.

"There you go, Alan," Gola said, pointing to files. "Have at it."

Alan felt a surge of enthusiasm. He was ready to dive into the detail of someone's murder, and he was excited. He wondered, did that make him insensitive?

Chapter 13)

Many miles away a man in a black robe dialed a gold phone. After four rings it was answered.

"*Hallo?*" Battalini said.

"It is I. Have you heard anything about Freiburg or Poland?" the man in the black robe said.

"I've heard nothing. Why, do you think we have another situation?" Battalini asked.

"We had a call from Czernica. Questions were being asked by a police chief from Freiburg. Have all potential information sources been eliminated?" the man in the black robe asked.

"No, we thought we were in the clear after the last termination. After all, the last guard is ninety-six years old and we were waiting for nature to do its thing," he said.

"Do you know where he is?" The black robed man asked.

"No, we stopped tracking after the last elimination," Battalini said, "He's an old man, let him die in peace."

"I suggest you start looking again." the man in the black robe said. "He doesn't get the luxury of dying in peace."

"When we find him, then what?" Battalini asked, obviously irritated.

"Do you have to ask? You eliminate the threat," the man said with sarcasm.

Chapter 14)

Max rolled into Lyon, navigated to the police station, and went to a sharp featured woman at the front desk.

"Inspector Rockenbach to see Inspector Acord," he said.

"*Un moment, s'il vous plait,*" she said.

Max recognized the voice and the words as the woman who had answered his first phone call. She looked up.

"He'll be out *un instant,*" she said.

Moments later a large friendly-looking man came to greet him.

"*Bonjour Monsieur* Rockenbach," Acord said with a big smile and extended a meat hook of a hand.

"*Bonjour Monsieur* Acord," Max said.

They looked at each other and smiled. Max took an immediate liking to Acord.

Max followed the inspector into a large room. There were about twenty well-worn dark brown desks occupying the space, and most were quite messy. Inspector Acord moved to the last row and sat at a desk in the corner.

"So, *Monsieur* Rockenbach, you would like to see the Philip Robert file. How do you think it will help?" he asked.

"I'm working on another murder which may be related and am looking for anything that may provide a motive. Before I forget, when we're done here, I'm meeting Monsieur Lemieux for lunch," Max said.

"Well done *Monsieur* Rockenbach. You'll enjoy Lemieux. Tell him I said *bonjour.*"

"I will."

"The file for the Robert homicide is waiting for you down stairs."

"I'm ready when you are."

"Follow me."

They descended an old stairway, and Max considered this is what the Bastille would have looked and smelled like. As they continued their downward trek, the stairs got narrower and the stones in the walls grew bigger. They reached the last step as the mold-laden mustiness reached its thickest point. Max looked around as darkness played with shadows against the damp thick walls. Acord turned to his left and went into a small room with a single flickering light bulb dangling from the ceiling. An old square table sat in the middle of room, and three stained cardboard boxes were piled on one another in the corner.

Acord gestured to the boxes and said, "Here you have it. These are all the files concerning the Robert matter."

Max nodded and said, "*Merci beaucoup*, I appreciate your generosity with the files and information."

Acord nodded, smiled, and started up the stairs as Max lifted the first box onto the table. The file box was the standard square, eighteen by eighteen, at least a foot tall and contained folders along with loose leaf papers. Max began by taking everything out and making piles on the square table. He had no idea of what he was looking for and wanted to get a feel for the amount of information at hand. He started reading and when finished with a document would return it to its damp repository.

The reading was not so different from other homicide reports other than they were written in *Francais*. Most everything Max looked at was mundane, and there was a lack of tangible evidence.

He finished the first box, placed it on the floor, and lifted the second box onto the table.

He went through the same process of taking out all the items, stacking them onto the table and began reading. This box was far more interesting. It contained many documents Robert had been accumulating and illustrated how he was building a case proving a UFO had crashed outside Freiburg. It told of eye witness reports and included interviews with a number of soldiers. Most of the information was written on loose leaf paper and wasn't in any kind of a binder. Max wondered if anyone ever bothered to read the content written on these pages.

As he reviewed the new documents, he started finding some nuggets. Two of Robert's eye witnesses talked about two types of bodies. One was the standard three to four foot aliens popular in Ufology, but Max found it odd to read human sized bodies were also identified as being from the spacecraft. This was something he'd never encountered in any UFO speculation.

Robert's notes indicated one of the soldiers gave him a crash remnant along with a book written in some type of hieroglyphics, and both were attributed to the craft. A note stated knowledge from this book would change the world. The handwriting matched other documents signed by Robert.

Max wondered if he would be lucky enough to come across the artifact or the book in Roberts' belongings as he continued to search. The rest of the second box was a series of random thoughts and some interviews that seemed unrelated.

Toward the bottom of the box he came across an interview titled *Chief Barinski of the Czernica Police Department*. It was two pages long, and he thought Robert had been more successful gathering information from the chief than Gola. There were other names on the loose sheets, so he decided to help himself to the evidence of this long dead investigation. You never know when you might stumble upon something of importance, he thought.

Max moved to box three and found nothing else of value. He looked at his watch and realized time was getting short. He also realized Lemieux had agreed to meet for lunch, but hadn't picked a location. He popped open his cell phone, but there was no signal from the depths of the catacombs. He closed box three, put it on top of box two, and moved up the steps two at a time. When he got to the top of the stairs he again tried to get a signal and was successful.

"*Bonjour*, Chief Inspector Rockenbach," Lemieux said.

Max realized that Lemieux must have caller ID or at least recognized his number.

"*Bonjour Monsieur*, Lemieux. I'm just finishing up at the station, and I realized we haven't picked a spot for lunch."

"There's a restaurant near my home called Alize. It is excellent and I think you'll approve," Lemieux said.

"Sounds great. I'll see you there."

Lemieux gave Max the address and directions, and they agreed to meet in thirty minutes. Max went into the bullpen area to look for Acord and found him hovering over the coffee machine.

"Well, Inspector, did you discover anything of interest?"

"That remains to be determined. I did get names I didn't have and some information about Robert's activities. As you know, this is all about the accumulation of information, then putting the big puzzle together," Max said.

Acord nodded and said, "I'm glad you were able to get something of value. If you need to look at the files again you are welcome *mon ami.*"

"I appreciate your hospitality. I'm meeting your old friend Lemieux in twenty minutes."

"Fantastic. Tell *Monsieur* Lemieux I send my regards," Acord said.

"I'll be happy to," Max said.

Max put out his hand, they shook, and Max headed out the door.

As Max steered his car toward the rendezvous with Lemieux he thought of the various notes, and the two pages he had commandeered. He wondered if there was anything of value in the old documents.

Twenty minutes later he pulled in front of Alize and parked on the street. He entered the restaurant with the realization he had never asked Lemieux what he looked like. He didn't have long to wait. He walked through the doors, and before he could say a word he was greeted.

"Inspector Rockenbach, *bonjour,*" Lemieux said.

He turned, and a short man with white hair greeted him with an open hand.

"*Monsieur* Lemieux, how did you know it was me?" Max asked.

"Easy. I pride myself in keeping sharp. I saw you park in front of the restaurant in a police car with German license plates. With the time, the car, the plates and the fact that you look the part, who else could it be?" Lemieux said.

"I'm impressed, *Monsieur* Lemieux."

The hostess interrupted and asked if they were ready to be seated, to which they replied in the affirmative.

"Inspector Acord sends his regards."

"I haven't seen him in a month. How is he?"

"He was terrific and couldn't have been more helpful."

"Acord is a good man. I taught him everything he knows."

"That's what he said you'd say," Max said with a laugh.

"What'd you find?"

"I got a couple of names I didn't have and found a few additional details Robert had discovered. It appeared he was conducting a thorough investigation and was ready to make a significant revelation," Max said.

"You're correct. I spent many hours on this investigation. Robert uncovered compelling information and it's disappointing his discoveries have never seen the light of day. He had material on two UFO crash sites, interviews with eye witnesses, artifacts from the vehicle and a book written in some hieroglyphics from the UFO. He also had some interesting theories. None of his work was ever released," Lemieux said.

They looked up to see the waiter hovering.

"Are you ready to order?" he asked.

"I'm ready if you are," Max said.

"Okay then," said Lemieux, "I'll have the *Croque Monsieur.*"

"How is their *bolognese*? I saw it being served when we came in, and it smelled wonderful." Max said.

"It is. It's heavy on the red wine, and is unique. If you like red wine you'll love it," Lemieux said.

"I'll have the *bolognese*, and an iced tea," Max said, and the waiter departed.

"Where were we? Did you determine if he was working alone?" Max asked.

"We always believed that. No one ever came forward with information. Someone attempted to claim his belongings, but they couldn't produce the necessary identification so they were denied. They never came back, so we thought they may have been involved somehow."

"What was your take on this whole thing?"

"Someone wanted to silence him and bury the information he was about to release in the press conference. It's a shame."

"Did you ever have a suspect?"

"No, we never had one. It appeared to be a professional job. We never had a clue."

"Did you ever have a theory of who was responsible?" Max asked.

"We never put that together. We only considered who might be affected by his revelations. Our list included governments and organized religion. Who else would object to the release of information about UFOs on earth? We couldn't think of anyone else who would have an issue with this sort of evidence.

"We were certain the Vatican would have knowledge of these two UFO incidents because they had closer relationship with Nazi Germany than people realized. We were aware they were supportive of Nazi attempts to find the Holy Grail, the Arc of the Covenant, and a number of other occult activities. The Vatican has always been leading the quest for truth because it needed to know what they had to cover up, so their version of truth was the only version of the truth," Lemieux said.

Max was surprised to hear the retired ex-inspector's insight, which was now a reoccurring theme.

As Lemieux finished, the waiter reappeared with their lunch. He placed a steaming bowl of dark red *bolgnese* over *bucatini* pasta in front of Max, and the *Croque Monsieur*, with herbed red potatoes in front of Lemieux. It not only looked like the cover of *Bon Appetit Magazine*, but their olfactory senses screamed "feed me."

Max thought about certain details uncovered in his review of the files. Between bites, he said, "I have another question. I came across a reference to an artifact Robert had at one time along with a small book he also had from the crash site and you mentioned them. Did you ever come across those items?"

There was silence. Max waited. There was more silence.

"I've never told this to anyone, but I don't want to take it to my grave. When we found Robert's body, it had no identification. It took several days before we received a missing person report leading to the identity of our homicide victim.

"I was at Roberts' residence soon after we determined he was our victim. It had been searched by someone and was a real mess. I looked and found nothing of help. At that time we had no motive and no idea of what he'd been doing. It wasn't until days later that we started putting pieces together.

"Three boxes appeared from a delivery service, addressed to the Inspector of the Philipe Robert case. They were delivered to my desk. The first box contained a letter from Robert. It described the project he was working on and stated he was close to making a major revelation. It also indicated he was been getting anonymous warnings to abandon the project and his residence had been robbed twice. His letter finished by stating he was protecting his research and the contents of the boxes contained the details of his investigation. He also said if a police officer was reading this material, he was likely dead."

"Were those the three boxes I looked through this morning?" Max asked.

"They were," Lemieux said.

"The files didn't yield a great deal of information. I didn't see the letter from Robert you referenced, and I was a little disappointed there wasn't more detail. There were notes indicating Robert had real physical evidence, yet there was nothing in the boxes to support the claim."

"There's a reason you didn't get the information you were seeking. I removed it long ago."

Max jerked his head, from his bowl of half eaten pasta, and peered at Lemieux with a stunned expression. "Did you just say what I thought you said?" Max asked.

"Yes. Given the contents, I felt it best to put it somewhere safe. I never returned it to the evidence boxes because I was afraid it would disappear. So in an opposite way, I made them disappear so they wouldn't disappear, if you comprehend."

"So you still have them?" Max asked.

"I've kept the items and notes in a safe deposit box for many years."

"You do realize if anything happened to you, this evidence would have been lost forever?"

"Yes. I took precautions, and in my will I designated my safe deposit box to go to the Lyon Police Department."

Max felt better, but was still concerned about the unorthodox way in which Lemieux handled the evidence. He then realized Lemieux most likely saved the evidence by doing what he had done.

"Is there any way I can see what you have?" Max asked.

"I thought you would ask, so I removed the contents this morning and everything is at my house."

Excitement welled up in Max's stomach, and suddenly he was no longer hungry.

"Let's get the check and go," Max said. "Lunch is on me."

Lemieux didn't argue for the check. It must have been a retirement thing.

Max followed Lemieux, and five minutes later they stopped in front of a modest, but immaculate single story home. They entered, and Lemieux motioned toward the living room. The home had no feminine touches, and it was evident Lemieux lived alone. The living room had the bare essentials. It contained only a sofa and two chairs, a coffee table, an end table with a lamp, and a TV. There were no knick knacks, as Max's wife called them, and it was devoid of pictures, artwork, or anything meant to warm a room. Max thought a retired police inspector in his seventies and living alone would likely live in a home with this lack of decor.

Lemieux entered the room holding a large rectangular box. "Here's everything," he said

The retired copper handed the box to Max, who was oblivious to the threadbare sofa, and placed the box on the scratched worn coffee table. He removed the box top and began spreading its contents across the table's surface. Max created a mental inventory and lifted a circular object wrapped in muslin.

"I placed fabric around the object to protect it from getting scratched," Lemieux said.

Max unwrapped the featherweight artifact, and he thought if this was extra-terrestrial, it didn't need the muslin to protect it. The object was about the size of a shooter marble, was shiny, dark gray, and had odd etchings. He was struck by how cold and light it felt in his hand.

"You didn't have this in the refrigerator, did you?" Max asked.

"No I didn't, but it always seems to be cold."

Max put it back into its wrap and continued to go through Roberts' long hidden evidence. He came to a larger object wrapped in the same type of muslin, and as he removed the wrap he recognized it as the book he had hoped to find at the police station. It contained an unrecognizable writing similar to Egyptian hieroglyphics, was about six inched long and about two inches thick. He realized what he held in his hands could be one of the greatest finds in the history of mankind. He turned his attention to the loose leaf papers in the box.

"I understand why you removed the objects, but why did you also take these notes?"

"I felt it was important for two reasons. There are names mentioned, and I felt they could be at risk if discovered. There is also Roberts' conjecture that I thought should be protected," Lemieux said.

Max glanced through the papers and saw references to family names he recognized from Freiburg.

"How would you feel if I borrowed this evidence and was able to study it? I would also like to have the metal object analyzed and have an expert to look at the book. Would you object?" Max asked.

"I don't object. This case needed someone like you to dig in and understand what it means. I'm not going to do it, and I was afraid to give this to the station. I'm happy to give it to you. You're looking at the big picture, and that's what's needed. These are now yours," Lemieux said.

A shocked Max couldn't believe what he heard. Not only had he seen the missing objects, but he could take them.

"Thank you for your faith and trust. Of course, if our investigation leads to a suspect in the Robert matter, I'll keep you appraised of our progress."

"I think we both know that's not likely to happen. There's bigger issue here, and it's why I protected this evidence over the years. You're on the right path, and the Robert matter is a clue in a bigger picture."

"I think you're right, Inspector Lemieux, and I thank you so much for this. I'll keep in touch so you know of our progress. If you think of anything else, please contact me. I have the feeling we're just getting started," Max said.

They both nodded, and Max put everything back into the box. They exchanged a hand shake and eye contact of purpose and trust.

As Max drove away from Lemieux's home he had a hard time believing what he now possessed. He was excited to share this with the team.

Chapter 15)

About the time Max departed from Lemieux's home, Sean was sitting down with Rudolf Weiler and Philipe Laflamme. They met in the deserted lobby of Sean's hotel. Philipe and Rudolf greeted each other like old friends, and it was obvious they had been speaking about Sean's activities. Sean was meeting Rudolf for the first time, so he turned his attention toward him.

After their initial hellos, Rudolf produced a satchel and handed it to Sean.

"Here's your package. I trust you know how to use it," Rudolf said.

Sean looked into the satchel and saw a black handgun with a number of clips.

"It's a Beretta ninety-two, in case you were wondering. I included twenty clips," Rudolf said.

"What if I run out of clips?" Sean asked.

"If you've gone through twenty clips, you better have called me or Philipe," Rudolf said, exchanging a quick glance with Philipe. "Wilhelm is quite fond of you, so we have the responsibility to get you home in one piece," Rudolf said.

"I'm with you, and I'll take direction from both of you. Let me bring you up to speed," Sean said, and gave them a quick update.

"Today Max Rockenbach is in Lyon to review the Robert homicide files, and he has a lunch set up with the former inspector on the case. It'll be interesting to see what he discovers. Have either of you uncovered anything new?" Sean asked.

Laflamme said, "Yes, I have. I looked into Robert's background and found he was a respected journalist in Paris. He was working on the same thing you are and was getting close to making an announcement. His scheduled press conference may have been the reason for his demise."

"So he wasn't just a guy sniffing around," Sean said.

"Far from it, he was an established reporter. His death was big news and the reason why more is known about him than the other victims. If the Gusdorf murder was not in Freiburg's back yard, you would have never heard of him. Think about it. Gusdorf was found here, yet there is little known about him, except that he was making inquiries into the UFO crash just before his death. The other murders are even more obscure," Laflamme said.

"I've looked into the other two murders. They were both committed in Poland. There's almost nothing known about them, which I find unusual. Someone is taking great care to not only eliminate these people, but also everything about them. This is professional and organized," Rudolf said.

"The fact so little information is available makes me wonder what's going on and who's behind it," Laflamme said.

"How did you determine the other two victims were associated with the Poland site?" Sean asked.

The two agents looked at each other.

"We know when things happen in Europe. We may not have all the answers, but we look at anything of interest. We determine if we need to know more about any given situation. When the homicides took place, our operatives investigated. Our people uncovered the victims were interviewing anyone connected with the crash site and were far from low profile.

"We concluded there was no threat to our interests, so our investigation ended, but we did keep records of what the operatives found. I looked at the reports yesterday. In each case our people spoke with Police Chief Barinski in Czernica. He could add nothing and was of no assistance. They did not, however, hit a total dead end.

"It was determined the investigation by the Czernica Police was stopped before it began. When investigators were interviewed, it was apparent no one was assigned to either case. This raised a red flag. They kept digging and came away convinced in both cases these homicides weren't investigated. Our people didn't dig further because there was no clear and present danger to the United States. So the big issue, as I see it, is we hit a dead end with the police chief, and he didn't assign anyone to investigate two murders. Behavior of this type indicates some sort of involvement," Rudolf said.

Rudolf finished and looked at Philipe as if he expected some additional comment.

Philipe shrugged and said, "When law enforcement does not investigate the most significant of all crimes, there would appear to be something amiss."

"Oh, before I forget, I have something you'll find interesting," Sean said, removing the spacecraft artifact and handing it to Laflamme.

They took turns studying the piece. Both were amazed at the strength and lightness of the object. Laflamme put it into his briefcase.

"I will take care of this. I placed my lab on alert, and they are waiting for it. I'm looking forward to what they have to say and if it's from this earth," Laflamme said.

Rudolf brought the conversation back to the immediate danger.

"Sean, I don't want to harp on this, but someone is watching and reacting. Philipe and I have to be on high alert, because those same people will soon have us on their radar. We have an educated guess, but there's no clear picture as to why or who is doing this," Rudolf said.

After another forty minutes of discussion they agreed to reconnect as soon as they had results from the lab. Philipe took the lead and said he would let them both know when he had something to share, and Sean should brief them on any new developments. They all shook hands and headed in their separate directions.

Chapter 16)

Alan was growing bored after reading file after file and finding nothing of value. The first two boxes were put on the floor as he opened the third hoping, but not expecting, to find a nugget. This box was filled with interviews from anyone and everyone living in a three-mile radius from where the body was discovered.

He hadn't found anything of interest until he came to notes describing an interview with a priest. The interview was conducted with a Father Schmidt from Freiburg. It wasn't that the good father knew anything about the victim or the actual murder, but his comments about the rumored UFO crash and the church were insightful. He said he didn't know Gusdorf, but offered an observation.

"Whoever killed Gusdorf was focused on silencing the story of the UFO crash. The church would have taken a deep sigh of relief, because it wouldn't have to defend itself from the Alien Theory," Father Schmidt said.

The comment from Father Schmidt must have emphasized the last two words because the interviewer followed up by asking for a definition of the 'Alien Theory.'

Father Schmidt offered a reply.

"Within the Vatican there are protocols dealing with how to handle different threats. For example, if an archaeologist discovered a crucified body which was carbon dated to Jesus's time, there's an entire protocol dealing with how to discredit the possibility it could be Christ. The concept is, even if they knew it was the body of Jesus, they would go to any lengths to prove it wasn't and to make it disappear.

"Likewise, there are protocols for discrediting people with the Stigmata, the history of the Wickens, the importance of women in the history of the church, multiple ancient texts and manuscripts contradicting the Bible, the possibility Jesus married Mary Magdalene and fathered a child, and that aliens visited Earth and altered human DNA. The protocols are to be put into action if any of these events gain visibility. The Alien Theory is an actual protocol to activate if and when investigators got close to uncovering details of the Black Forest UFO crash," Schmidt said.

The interviewer was obviously stunned by these revelations.

"Why haven't we ever heard about these protocols?" he asked.

"You have. All of the possibilities I just mentioned have come to light, and in each case the protocols went into action and the noise about the subject disappeared," Father Schmidt said.

"How has the church's response to perceived threats gone unnoticed?" the interviewer asked.

"Priests take an oath of silence. Just like there's an oath of silence regarding confessions, it pertains to all church business," Father Schmidt said.

"Since there's an oath of silence, why do you feel comfortable talking about this today?" the interviewer asked.

"I've reached my breaking point with Vatican hypocrisy and have struggled with the likelihood of becoming an ex-priest. I've not lost my faith in God, but I've lost it in the church. You caught me in a weak moment, and that's why I've been this open. I'm not sure I want all this on the record, but it's time for the lies to stop," Father Schmidt said.

There were no notes asking what constituted the lies he referred to, but Father Schmidt was someone they needed to speak with, thought Alan. His comments about the Vatican were startling, and he seemed to have been anxious to reveal the other protocols.

Alan's review of the remaining documents proved uneventful, and he could understand why the people who read these files put them away without noticing the significance of the good father's comments. The investigators were looking for clues to the murder and for anything related to Gusdorf. Little or no attention would have been paid to the ramblings of a priest who had no connection to the murder.

Gola walked back into his office and sat in a creaking wooded swivel chair.

"Alan, good news. I've tracked down Hans Bauer. He was one of the guys we needed to find. He may be the last person still alive who actually saw the craft. He lives in Baden-Baden, so it's only an hour drive, and he's agreed to see me tomorrow. You're welcome to come if you'd like," Gola said.

"Count me in. I'll enjoy the ride and the company. I haven't been to Baden-Baden in years," Alan said.

"Okay then, we'll leave at nine tomorrow. Did you find anything of value in those old files?" Gola asked.

"There was no information about Gusdorf or his murder, but I found something intriguing," Alan said.

He told Gola about the investigators' notes and Father Schmidt's comments. Gola leaned back, his chair whining its discomfort, and gazed out the window as the wheels in his head were spinning.

"Our dinner tonight should be lively. Have you made reservations?" Gola asked.

"Not yet. Let me check to see if we can get a private room at the hotel. I think we need to be as private as possible," Alan said.

"Good, I agree. I wonder how Sean did with the CIA guys and how Max did in Lyon," Gola said.

"I'm sure we'll have plenty to talk about. I'll set the reservation for six so we have all evening. I should get back to the Colombi and make the arrangements. Can you call your brothers and let them know the time?"

"Consider it done."

***

Upon returning to the hotel Alan called Sean, and they agreed to meet in a half hour to discuss their findings. Once they connected in the hotel bar, Sean recounted how Rudolf discovered there was never a formal investigation of the Polish murders. He also confided in Alan that Rudolf had given him a Beretta and asked if he should tell Gola.

"That's a tough question. I'd feel better if he knew, but I think we should hold off a little while. He may feel obligated to take it from you and, if things get dicey, you'll be glad you have it. The bigger issue is whether you'll shoot me by accident or shoot off your dick," Alan said and laughed.

He then proceeded to tell Sean about the investigators' notes about Father Schmidt.

"Your priest is one conflicted guy. This will be another interesting topic tonight," Sean said.

The bartender came to take their drink order, and Sean ordered the local Kabinett. Alan predicted Alfred would be the first to arrive and would be early. He didn't disappoint, arriving at five-thirty.

"It's kind of a family joke. Like I've told you, if something is free,

Alfred is the first to arrive. If it's time for a contribution, he disappears," Alan said.

It was close to six when Gola and Max arrived. Drinks were ordered and served, and soon they were shown to the private dining room. Seats were chosen, and Alan, acting as host, led the discussion.

"I trust we've all had a stimulating day. I suggest we go around the table and share what we've learned. Does that sound like a plan?" Alan asked. Heads nodded and Alan continued, "I went to the station this morning and Gola gave me the files of the Gusdorf murder. I didn't find specific evidence about Gusdorf or the murder, but I did find something quite interesting.

"It was an interview conducted with a disgruntled priest named Father Schmidt. It sounded like he was deciding if he wanted to remain a priest, and he made some rather unusual statements. He talked about protocols developed and in place to protect the church if certain events took place. One he spoke about was the Alien Theory. Others were the Stigmata, the Wickens, women's place in the early church, ancient texts like the Dead Sea Scrolls, Jesus marrying Mary Magdalene and fathering a child, all things in conflict with Bible teachings. He commented the church would do anything to protect itself."

"What do you suppose the Alien Theory is?" Max asked.

"Finding Schmidt should be a priority so we can find out what he meant. Let's see what he has to say," Sean said. "Gola how about you."

"This morning I found Hans Bauer, and he's living in Baden-Baden. Alan and I are meeting with him at ten tomorrow morning," Gola said.

"Max, did you get anything useful in Lyon?" Alan asked.

"I think I did. I spent the first couple of hours going over the Robert homicide files, and it turns out he was a respected journalist freelancing for the International Herald Tribune. He wasn't just some guy sniffing around, and he had compiled a good bit of information. He had a news conference scheduled and was killed before it could take place. There can be no coincidence on the timing. Much of the evidence was missing, so I thought we were at a dead end. By the way, I pulled two pages from the evidence box for you," Max said, looking at Gola. "Don't let me forget to give it to you."

"Great. I'll remind you. Please continue," Gola said.

"After reviewing the files I had lunch with the original investigator on the case. His name is Inspector Lemieux, and although he's retired he was a wealth of information. He and I hit it off, and he was forthcoming," Max said.

Max provided an overview of the discussion with Lemieux and continued.

"The retired inspector speculated the executioner was connected to a government or the church. He said he always believed the church was the most likely perpetrator, but there was never direct evidence. He then went off on the Vatican and how powerful and ruthless they were when facing any perceived threat. This seems to be a growing theme with everyone we speak with," Max said.

"Max, it's too bad we can't get our hands on the items you mentioned. Did you find out what happened to them?" Gola asked.

Max got the question he hoped for and reached into his pocket.

"I don't know what happened to them," he said, smiled and paused for effect, "Oh, could you mean these?" he asked.

He placed the book and the round piece on the table. The sides of his mouth curled into a grin as he perused the faces with satisfaction and amusement.

Eyes darted from the items, to each other, then back to Max. Everyone stood to come for a closer look, and there was silence.

Just then the waiter came into the room, and Gola turned and asked him to come back in a few minutes. Their focus wasn't on their stomachs, well, except for Alfred.

"Could I have a menu?" he asked

Gola looked at him and shook his head.

"So this is what I should remind you about?" Gola asked.

Max didn't get it at first, then the light bulb went on.

"Oh no, I have something else for you. It's much less dramatic than these items," he said.

"I hated to remove evidence, but their investigation is dead. I knew you spoke with the police chief in Poland, and I thought you might find this helpful. There are two pages of notes from Robert's interview with the chief, and it contains several names of other people Robert spoke with in Poland," Max said.

Gola glanced at the papers in the baggie, but didn't open it.

"I thought you would be excited by this?" Max said.

99

"I am more than you realize," Gola said. "The police chief in Czernica told me he never heard of Robert and had never spoken to him. This is a huge find. Why would he lie to my direct question and state he neither heard of nor spoken to Robert?" Gola asked.

The others around the table stopped looking at the object and turned to Gola. It was clear something significant just happened.

"It's my turn," Sean said. "I met with the two agents today. When the murders of Robert, Gusdorf, and the two victims in Poland occurred, they investigated each homicide. They were surprised to find out that no formal investigation was ever conducted in Poland. Their operatives were asking questions and got little information. The agent felt the lack of an official investigation was both inexplicable and unacceptable. The exact comment was when you're in law enforcement and the most heinous of all crimes takes place and there's no investigation, something is amiss."

Looks were again exchanged around the table.

"I think we've just learned something important. It's evident the chief lied to me and, at the very least, is guilty of a cover-up by omission. The question is why and who is he in bed with?" Gola asked.

Chapter 17)

The gold phone rang once again.

"*Bonjour*," the man in the black robe said.

"A police inspector from Freiburg visited the Lyon Police Station this morning and spent two hours reviewing the Robert file," the Lyon-based cardinal said.

"Is there anything in the file to worry about?" the black robed man asked.

"No, it was cleansed of anything of importance and didn't have much to begin with. The key pieces have never been located," the cardinal said.

"So no harm has been done."

There was a hesitation.

"We don't know for sure. The man from Freiburg first met with an Inspector Acord, then for a couple of hours with a retired inspector named Lemieux. Prior to the meeting, Lemieux went to the safe deposit box area in his bank," the cardinal said.

"This is not good. Do we need to eliminate Lemieux?"

"I believe it's too late. Lemieux told him whatever he knew. If we eliminated him now it would just draw more attention, which we don't want," the cardinal said.

"What about any of the others? Hans Bauer may be the only living person who guarded the craft. Could they know of him?" the Black Pope asked.

"It's possible. Bauer's name wasn't in any documents, but he's from Freiburg. They may be aware of him."

The man in the black robe thought for a moment.

"I'll call Amsterdam and instruct our man to get to Freiburg post-haste. I've alerted him to the possibility, and he'll eliminate Bauer. How close are these policemen to linking this to Wewelsburg?" the Black Pope asked.

"Difficult to say. They got nothing from our man in Poland, so they only have the Robert and Gusdorf matters. They learned everything they could from Lemieux, and there was never much information about Gusdorf. They should be at a dead end."

"We will eliminate anyone connected. I don't know where else they can go but to Bauer. We should have eliminated Lemieux a long time ago, but I didn't think we would face this again. This is a more dangerous situation since the police are involved and not just a journalist. If we move on them it will create greater visibility and invite more scrutiny. Do you know what prompted their interest?" the Black Pope asked.

"I do not. I first heard of this when you told me about the call from our Polish contact. The next thing I heard was of the Freiburg police visit. I don't know what has caused this interest. You should also know the Freiburg chief and the inspector are brothers?" the Frenchman said.

"I did not know. That makes it even more difficult. It is likely their families will know of the investigation. This could get messy. If we need to take out one of them we may need to take out their entire family. We don't want that much attention unless it is our last resort. I will call Amsterdam," the Black Pope said.

"Do we know for sure if anything remains buried at Wewelsburg?" the Frenchman asked.

"We do not know for sure. The Black Pope who preceded my predecessor thought the contents were to be moved. Things happened so fast at the end of the war he never received verification. He should have sent agents to substantiate, but by then the castle had been destroyed, and the Allies controlled the area. Had he tried to determine if anything was in the underground labs, he would have risked exposing what he wanted to hide."

"What about when the museum was restored?" the Frenchman asked.

"When the museum was rebuilt, we exerted some influence and only the north tower restored. When they poured new concrete on top of the existing floor, we thought we were secure. My predecessor felt it was safer to do watchful waiting. We've been successful at removing threats, until now, but I regret not finding some way to make sure. We hope we will never find out if our fears were justified." the Black Pope said.

Chapter 18)

The phone rang in the sleazy, third floor apartment in Amsterdam's Red Light district.

"Yes?" a pocked-faced man said.

"Time to move. The target is Hans Bauer. He lives in Baden-Baden," the man in the black robe said.

"How soon?"

"Immediate."

As the conversation was unfolding, the man with bad skin opened his computer and entered Amsterdam to Freiburg for flight options.

"I can leave on a seven-fifteen flight and get to Freiburg at ten fifty-five. I would get to Baden-Baden between twelve and one. I'm better off driving. It'll take four to five hours to drive, and I won't have to deal with airport security. How do you want it to appear? I can make it look like an accident, but that will take longer."

"Time is of the essence. It is best to make it look like an accident, but it needs to be done by tomorrow afternoon. I do not want Bauer to see the sun go down."

"It'll be done."

"When you finish, go to Freiburg and await further instructions. There may be more work to be done."

"I'll eliminate Bauer and be in Freiburg by late afternoon."

The man with pock-marked skin didn't wait for a response and terminated the call. He reached under his bed and pulled out a large faded duffle bag and scratched leather case. He opened it and looked at his array of weapons. He was going to take selected items, but as he looked at his options, he decided to take the entire case. He also packed a large bag of hashish along with an assortment of drug paraphernalia.

He was amused as he put together his weaponry and drugs. Here he was, supporting his decadent lifestyle by killing people for the Vatican. He lived in the Red Light district because people here didn't ask questions, he had access to legal drugs, and could fuck women more beautiful than he could ever attract as long as he had fifty euros.

It was perfect since he didn't have the wiring to create the kind of emotional bond necessary for a real relationship. He just wanted his biological drives satisfied, and if he didn't have to speak to the women, so much the better.

He went to his closet and removed a few ratty looking shirts along with dirty pants. He couldn't care less what he looked like, how he smelled, or what people thought of him.

He felt fortunate to make a living at something he enjoyed. He'd been killing things since he was six-years-old and first came to the attention of the Vatican when he was eighteen. They needed some wet work done and he was recommended by a fellow degenerate who had worked for them for years. Together, they eliminated several potential problems, including a couple of pregnant fourteen-year-old girls who did more than confess to their priests and were threatening exposure.

When his associate met a rather violent end, the man with bad skin became the go-to guy for Vatican messes. He loved the irony of the Vatican paying him to do what he did for them. He knew he was what some people considered a low life, but it was his opinion that he was smarter than the people who paid him. Intelligence and morals didn't go hand in hand. Before he left for Germany he would eat, go down to the street and window shop until he found the right woman to satisfy him. Fifty euros for fifteen minutes would be all he required.

Chapter 19)

The waiter was removing dinner plates when Alfred asked for a dessert menu. Looks were exchanged, as always. If it was anyone else no one would have thought anything about it, but when it was Alfred it seemed like he was afraid of being gypped out of a free dessert.

"We need to be careful. The CIA guys have been pounding away at me, and I'm starting to believe it. With what we've discovered about the police chief in Poland, I submit we're known. Likewise, with Max's visit to Lyon, it's likely those guarding whatever it is they're guarding are aware of our efforts. It's safe to say they're thinking of implementing their silencing program," Sean said.

"I think you're correct in your assessment. We should start to think about doing everything in pairs. We need to check our backs and always be aware," Gola said.

"I have an idea. We need to investigate what's going on with the police chief in Poland, and I don't think it can come from us because he's already told Gola he never spoke with Robert. I'm thinking I should approach Rudolf Weiler and see what he can do. They investigated the Polish homicides on two occasions and felt something wasn't right. They should have the wherewithal to operate in Poland," Sean said.

"Great idea. I agree, for us to engage the police chief would be a mistake, and this would be a way to get intelligence on the subject," Gola said.

"I'll also need to get Max's new discoveries to Laflamme so he can get them analyzed," Sean said.

"Excellent. Let's plan our next steps. Tomorrow Alan and I go to Baden-Baden to see Hans Bauer. Why don't we have Max and Sean try to find Father Schmidt? I have a feeling we should see these people as soon as we can. If we're asking questions, it's fair to assume the people we want to talk with could also be in the cross hairs of our antagonist, whoever it may be," Gola said.

"That sounds like a plan," Max said.

Just then the waiter reappeared, and before he said anything, Alfred shouted that he would have the cherry cobbler with vanilla ice cream. Everyone else declined dessert and continued the animated discussion.

Soon the waiter delivered Alfred's dessert, and he wasted no time dribbling it onto his chin and shirt. Sean recognized the dessert eater never asked if he could participate in any way. Without doubt he was the black sheep, thought O'Shea.

"Let's talk about long-term. Right now we're still gathering clues and following leads. Is there anything else we can do?" Sean asked.

"During an investigation we're trained to keep following the clues and keep asking questions. I see no reason to deviate from that strategy," Max said.

"I agree. We're getting more branches to follow with every meeting. The bigger question may be what we do if the Vatican is behind this, because all signs point toward Rome," Gola said.

It was the first time anyone stated what everyone was thinking. Or at least everyone but Alfred, who had his face buried in his cherry cobbler.

"My initial plan was to write a book about the UFO crashes and how the Nazis re-engineered the technology. I wanted to show the link to Operation Paperclip and the connection to NASA, all this with the help of ex-Nazis. This whole Vatican connection was never in the equation. Maybe I should make it an expose' on the Vatican's use of assassination as a means to silence anyone perceived to be a threat to their power," Sean said.

"You may be right," Gola said. "The real answer is we don't know where this is going and we shouldn't spend our time with supposition. More often than not it's a waste of time. Let's just keep following the clues. The longer we follow the leads, the closer we get to the source. They've been successful eliminating a single researcher, but they haven't encountered a team like ours. How fast can you put your contact on the trail of our friend the Polish chief of police?" Gola asked.

"As soon as we conclude our discussion tonight, I'll call him," Sean said.

"I'm all done," Alfred said.

Everyone at the table turned and looked at him in silent semi-contempt. Was it Sean's imagination, or was Alfred getting more annoying by the minute?

"I have an idea. Why don't I go to my room and call Rudolf. I'll come right back and update everyone," Sean said.

106

"That's perfect. Let's get some coffee and we'll wait," Gola said.

"Well, I have to get going, so I'm not going to wait around," Alfred said.

No one responded, and Sean departed to his room.

Moments later Rudolf answered his phone.

"Rudolf, this is Sean. We're in the midst of our dinner meeting and a few things have come to light. Inspector Rockenbach found notes of an extensive interview Robert conducted with the Polish Police Chief Barinski.

"Gola Rockenbach spoke with Barinski yesterday, and the chief denied ever speaking with Robert. He lied to Gola about Robert and never investigated the two murders connected to the Polish UFO crash. That puts Chief Barinski in the center of a cover-up.

"We can't barge into Poland without raising a large red flag and think your people will be far more effective in checking him out," Sean said.

"You guys are doing good work. Yes, I agree, there's no way for you to pursue this without bringing unwanted attention. This is right up our alley, as you Americans would say. I'll speak to the operatives who conducted the initial investigations and they can focus on the chief. We have means not available to normal law enforcement, and we'll start tomorrow," Rudolf said.

"That's great. We have more interviews set for tomorrow, and I'll give you an update tomorrow night," Sean said.

He returned to the private room and noticed Alfred's chair was empty. He chose not to comment.

"Great news. Tomorrow Rudolf is going to unleash his people and see what they can find out about the chief," Sean said.

"Perfect. We'll continue to move forward and take one step at a time. Starting tomorrow, everyone needs to be armed. I suggest automatic weapons in the trunk and hand guns on your person. Alan, I'll bring you a little something when I pick you up in the morning. Max, will you make sure Sean is taken care of before you set out to find Father Schmidt?" Gola said.

Sean put up his hand, but before he could speak Gola reacted.

"Sean, you may not think it is necessary, but at some point we'll be visited in an unfriendly way, and we need to be prepared," Gola said.

"I wasn't objecting. I just wanted you to know I'm all set with the hand gun, but I could use an automatic weapon."

Gola looked stunned.

"How did you pull that off?"

"The CIA guys feel the same as you do. Rudolf brought a Beretta and twenty clips to our meeting this afternoon. They harped on the dangers and told me I had to have it with me at all times."

"Where is it?" Gola asked.

"It's in my room," Sean said.

"Then it's not on you at all times is it?"

Sean thought for a moment, then smiled.

"*Touché*, you made your point. I'll keep it on me. I was concerned how you'd feel about it," Sean said.

"We're a team, and the welfare of everyone is my primary concern," Gola said.

"Does Alfred need a weapon?" Sean asked.

"Why would he need one, so he could eat it?" Max said.

Gola nodded.

"Shouldn't he be alerted as to your concerns?" Sean asked.

"Yes, I'll call him on my way home tonight," Gola said. "He isn't much help, but he could find himself in harm's way because of what we're doing," Gola said as he departed.

"I guess we didn't have to worry about telling Gola about your Beretta," Alan said.

"What do you think?" Sean asked.

"We're hearing the same message from every direction. I think we'd be stupid to disregard the professionals," Alan said.

"We're on the same page. I just wanted your take. I look forward to tomorrow; it should be interesting."

Five minutes later Sean was talking with Cat. She was pissed off he wasn't staying in touch, but she missed him. He apologized and changed the subject. Liam was doing great and Sean was happy to know everything at home was copacetic. He told her how hospitable the Rockenbach's had been and how they were making positive progress. He neglected to mention murders, concealed weapons, and warnings from CIA agents. They talked for a half hour and were comforted to hear each other's voice. Sean promised to call tomorrow and signed off.

Morning came early, and Sean was up before the sun rose. He showered and had breakfast at the hotel's buffet. He took a strong coffee to go, returned to his room, and at eight called Max to ask how they should go about finding Father Schmidt.

"I'm way ahead of you. I called the Archdiocese of Freiburg in Baden-Wurttemberg. I figured I'd start with them. At first they wouldn't release any information, but when I told them he was a potential witness in a murder investigation they relented. He's no longer a priest, and they didn't seem to want much to do with him. He's now living in Villinge which isn't far from here. I was about to call him when you called," Max said.

"My, the efficiency of the German police. You have your man," Sean said.

Max laughed. "Not yet. It's a little early, but let me call him and I'll call you back," he said.

Max was on the phone moments later, and ex-Priest Schmidt answered.

"*Hallo?*" Schmidt said.

"Father Schmidt, this is Inspector Rockenbach from the Freiburg Police Department. We're investigating a murder from a number of years ago, and I wondered if we could speak with you?"

"First, I'm no longer Father Schmidt, I'm *Herr* Schmidt. I'm no longer a priest nor associated with the church. Why do you think I can help?"

"We're investigating a murder of a man named Gusdorf. You were interviewed about the murder and you stated you didn't know him or anything about the murder, but you did offer some unique thoughts about a potential motive. We'd like to speak with you today if you're available," Max said.

"I don't know how I can help, but I'm happy to meet with you," *Herr* Schmidt said.

"Would you be available around eleven?" Max asked.

"Eleven would be fine," Schmidt said.

"I may have an associate with me if it's okay with you?" Max asked.

"It's fine with me; the more the merrier. I don't see as many people as I used to. I'll have the tea on."

"We'll see you then," Max said.

He then called Sean. "We're on for eleven with *Herr* Schmidt. I'll pick you up at ten," he said.

Sean stood, opened his suitcase, and dug to the bottom. Underneath his socks and Fruit of the Looms he removed the hidden Beretta. He also removed four clips and wondered what good twenty clips would do if he didn't have the means to carry them. He stuffed the Beretta into his belt and clips into his pockets. He made sure the barrel wasn't aimed at his most important attribute, and he wondered how many people had experienced that particular misfortune. He didn't like the visualization.

***

Gola stopped in front of the Colombi Hotel at eight forty-five. He came early to review a couple of things with his cousin. Alan had been waiting outside for five minutes when Gola pulled up. The chief stopped, got out of the car, and moved to its rear.

"Alan, come back here for a moment."

Gola opened the trunk to its full height, and Alan stared at a full blown arsenal.

Are we going to invade Strasbourg and take it back for Germany?" Alan asked.

"We need to equip you. Do you know how to use one of these?"

"I do. I thought you knew I used to shoot," Alan said.

"Okay, do you have a preference for your hand gun?"

"I don't know, what do you recommend?"

"Here, see if you like this. It's a Smith and Wesson. It should be a good fit."

Alan picked it up and felt the weight in his hand. Gola next handed him several clips, pulled out a shoulder holster, and handed them to Alan.

"You've been wearing a jacket every day so this will work. One caution; this model of the Smith and Wesson doesn't have a safety. Make sure you never have a round in the chamber.

"I need you to sign this. I'm appointing you to temporary deputy status so you can carry the weapon. If we have any issues and you use the weapon, we want to be covered so we don't violate any laws," Gola said.

Chapter 20)

Gola and Alan made good time and rolled into the outskirts of Baden-Baden a little early. Moments later Gola pulled in front of a small stone home with a thatched roof and spotless yard. Gola clanged a heavy wolf's head iron knocker, and the door swung open. A stooped old man stood in the doorway and greeted them with a friendly smile.

"*Herr* Bauer, I'm Chief Rockenbach, and this is Alan Rockenbach, my cousin and one of my deputies."

Alan shot Gola a look, then turned his attention back to Hans Bauer.

"*Guten Morgen*, gentlemen. This may surprise you, but I've been looking forward to your arrival. I have water on for tea; can I get you some?" Bauer asked.

"Yes, thank you," Gola said.

"Follow me," he said, and the little old man turned and trudged through an archway into his ancient kitchen.

"What type of tea do you prefer? I have black or licorice tea," Bauer said.

Gola opted for the black tea, and Alan chose the Licorice. Neither took anything in their tea.

"Let's go into the sitting room," Hans said.

He motioned to chairs for his visitors, and everyone took a seat. Alan sank into a faded, creased leather chair. The touch of the leather was soft, befitting its age and care. He looked around the room and admired the décor of dark wood and structural beamed ceiling. The walls were adorned by three different types of cuckoo clocks, and family pictures cluttered the table. The low level lighting along with the large picture window behind Bauer cause a bit of a glare. Alan noticed there was no TV in sight. Good for Hans, he thought.

"Are you boys related to the Rockenbach brothers?" Hans asked.

"We are," Gola said. "Richard is my father and Tomas is Alan's father."

"They were both friends of mine. I haven't seen them for years. How are they?" Bauer asked.

"They're doing well for two old guys. They've just moved in together and are trying out a new live-in caretaker, but we're skeptical as to how that will work out. Do you live alone?" Gola asked.

"I still live alone, but my son lives next door, so it's a perfect arrangement. I get to see my son, grandkids and great grandkids, but always next door. If there's too much commotion I just say *auf wiedersehen* and come home. Plus, I don't have to do the junk stuff like mow the lawn and yard clean up," Bauer said.

"That's a perfect setup," Alan said. "I hope I end up so lucky."

"So what do you think I can help with?" Bauer asked.

"Our fathers told us everything they knew about the UFO crash, but they were on the outskirts and didn't see it. They remembered you were on site early and were assigned to protect the craft. We thought you might remember something we haven't heard," Gola said.

"That was long ago. What was it, around eighty years ago? I was just a kid, but I remember like it was yesterday. I think of it almost every day. If the world only knew what we saw," Hans said.

"How would you describe it?" Alan asked.

"The whole thing was crazy. The aircraft was different than anything I've seen before or since," Bauer said.

"We heard rumors about bodies. Did you see any?" Alan asked.

"There were bodies all over. There were these small, three or four foot tall bodies, and the oddest thing was there were two human size corpses. They were all wearing the same suits and helmets so they all had to be on the craft. The small bodies had three fingers on each hand, and the larger bodies had five fingers like us. There was scattered wreckage, and a couple of my friends took several pieces.

I didn't want to touch anything, because I knew the Nazis, and I didn't want to give them a reason to make me disappear. I did look at some of the pieces and they were unlike anything I've ever seen. Very strong, very light, and you couldn't crease them.

"We were assigned to guard the crash site, and were sworn to secrecy for the Fatherland with a threat of death if we spoke about it. This wasn't something we talked about until after the war and even then not so much.

"Everything was gone so fast we didn't have to guard it long. The day after the crash, Nazis were coming out of the woodwork. Himmler was there, along with von Braun and many others. The craft, bodies, and anything and everything was boxed up and gone within thirty-six hours."

Gola was listening to Bauer, when his attention was drawn to the window behind his host. He noticed the same vehicle pass the house three times in a short time and his radar clicked on. He stood and made a stretching motion.

"Hans, I need to stretch and use your bathroom. Could you point me in the right direction?" Gola asked.

"It's right down that hall."

Gola followed Bauer's directions and went into the bathroom where he looked for a window. There was a small privacy window, but it didn't provide visibility. He re-entered the hallway and turned away from the discussion taking place in the sitting room and stepped into what appeared to be a guest bedroom. The room had a larger window facing the street similar to the window in the sitting room. He looked up and down the street and saw nothing. He moved across the hall into another bedroom which had a large window overlooking a modest back yard and alley beyond.

Gola looked for movement, then he saw it. Someone was walking down the alley. He seemed to be studying the house while walking past it. Gola couldn't tell if he was the same person who passed in front of the house, but he guessed it was. He continued to watch as the man disappeared around the corner as adrenalin began to flood his body.

Gola removed the Walther PPK/S from its holster and took off the safety. His gut told him this was a real threat. He moved back into the sitting room with his gun hidden under his arm pit.

Hans was still speaking, as Alan glanced toward Gola. He watched Gola go to the picture window, then saw the gun butt in Gola's hand. Alan's instincts took over, and he reached into his jacket and opened the strap to his shoulder holster.

Gola moved to the side of the front window and stood motionless. Hans was oblivious and continued talking about Himmler, the crash victims and the craft being removed to Wewelsburg Castle.

Gola was now standing behind Hans and put his finger to his lips in the universal signal.

Alan continued to ask questions, but wasn't listening to Hans's answers as his body was getting ready to react.

"Mr. Bauer, I don't want to alarm you, but I think someone seems

113

to be watching your home with unusual interest. We're concerned you could be a target, so please move out of view from the window," Gola said.

A surprised Hans Bauer turned to face Gola just as the window shattered and Hans crumbled to the floor.

Alan jumped to Hans's aid and pulled him away from the window. He could see the old soldier was bleeding from somewhere on his upper body. Guilt flashed through his mind about his part in ending the life of a late nineties ex-soldier who had been through so much. He didn't have any idea of the extent of Hans's injuries as he rolled him onto his back.

Hans was awake and in obvious discomfort as Alan saw blood pumping from his shoulder. A wound to the shoulder was good news as long as it hadn't hit an artery. Alan jumped up and withdrew his pistol in the same motion.

"Have you seen anything?" Alan asked.

"Someone walked through the alley and seemed to be casing the back of the house, but I didn't see where he ended up. You stay here and call for an ambulance. I'm going out the back and will circle around. Whatever you do, don't shoot me," Gola said.

Gola moved with speed to the door next to the kitchen and exited into the back yard. He crept in the same direction the would-be assassin had moments earlier.

Gola peered around the house next to Bauer's and saw movement. Between two houses across from the Bauer home, he could see a man crouching. The man had short blond hair, but Gola was unable to discern any other detail. The man wasn't moving.

The shot through the window told Gola the attacker knew of their presence and felt he needed to act immediately. This wasn't the same level of professionalism shown in the previous murders, but the appearance of the squad car in front of the Bauer residence might have created a sense of urgency.

Gola decided to flush out the assassin. He pressed two, hit send on his cell phone, and was connected to his station in Freiburg.

"This is Gola. We're at *Herr* Bauer's and we're under attack. Call the Baden-Baden Police and get them over here."

He gave the address and hung up. He knew when the police arrived it would force the gunman's hand. The man across the street began to move. When he stood, Gola could see he was holding a rifle. The blond stocky man ran in a crouch to two parked cars, and seemed to be going in for the kill. Gola had no shot and waited. The man dashed across to the rear of the Freiburg squad car and was directly in front of Han's house. Gola wondered what Alan was doing.

Gola was about to move when patrol cars turned the corner and approached from opposite ends of the street. He hoped they wouldn't mistake him for the perpetrator.

He didn't have to worry for long as a series of shots rang out from behind Gola's parked car and one of the oncoming police cruisers veered off, went over the curb, and slowly collided with a house across the street. There was no movement from inside the now still squad car.

The other driver turned his car at a forty-five degree angle in the middle of the street, and two uniformed officers jumped out behind open doors. Shots were fired at the assassin and were penetrating Gola's car. From behind the perforated police cruiser, fire was returned and took out the windows on the Baden-Baden squad car.

Gola doubled back to attack from the rear, but before he could complete the journey gunfire erupted from inside Hans' house. He aborted his plan and darted into the house where Hans was on the floor bleeding and moaning.

"I heard shots and came back in case you needed help," Gola said.

"I saw what was happening and it looked like a standoff. I had a shot and I took a couple, but I think I missed," Alan said.

"I'm going around the side and come up from behind," Gola said.

Before he could get outside, an old Audi rolled slowly down the street from the same direction as the crashed police vehicle. It slowed almost to a stop as it came to the cruiser.

That was all the man with the bad skin needed as he moved the ten feet in a flash. The officers couldn't shoot because the driver of the Audi was in the line of fire as the assailant ripped open the driver's door and pushed the motorist across the seat. He stomped on the gas and did a U turn as he continued firing at the huddled officers. The assassin shot out the tires of the police vehicle, and Gola couldn't believe what he was seeing. This guy was getting away just as it appeared they had him cold.

He thought of giving chase, but he didn't want to be mistaken and shot by the patrolmen who would be rattled. He chose not to take the chance and could hear sirens on the way. The ambulance would arrive soon.

Gola returned to the sitting room and checked to see where Hans was hit. It appeared to be a non-fatal shoulder wound. Hans should survive providing that a mid-nineties man could handle the trauma of being shot.

***

The man with the bad skin drove the short distance to where he parked his car. He left it there thirty minutes earlier and walked to Bauer's house, not anticipating the complications he just encountered. Moving as fast as possible, he knew he had gotten lucky with a guardian angel showing up at just the right time. The thirty-something in the shotgun seat was terrified and with good reason. The assassin didn't think, didn't make moral judgments, but just acted. Before the car came to a complete stop he put a bullet into the forehead of his unwitting getaway accomplice. The Audi came to an abrupt halt next to the beat-up reddish Volvo.

***

The ambulance pulled away with Hans as the guest of honor while Gola was being interviewed by an inspector and the two officers who waged the gun battle. They spoke with Alan first, and Gola was grateful he had deputized his American cousin. The inspector knew Gola was chief of police in Freiburg, and Gola explained he and his deputy were conducting an interview regarding a murder investigation when *Herr* Bauer was shot. The two officers in the other police vehicle were shot and killed instantly, and it was clear their adversary was quite proficient.

The paramedic told Gola Hans's injuries weren't life-threatening, but given his age there was added complexity. Gola made a mental note to visit Hans.

Alan turned to Gola.

"I feel we're to blame for Hans being shot. If it wasn't for us this wouldn't have happened," he said.

"Nonsense, I disagree. Think of it this way. The wheels were set in motion several days ago. Max going to Lyon, me speaking with the chief in Poland, questions being asked throughout southern Germany, and calls being made to Hans and Father Schmidt. Somewhere the wrong people

116

woke up. The only reason this wasn't an assassination is because we were here to stop it. They didn't know we'd be here. They were coming to kill Hans and silence him forever. We saved Hans' life; we're not responsible for his being shot," Gola said firmly.

"You're right. Thank you for putting it in perspective. Let's get word to Max and Sean and let them know it's started. Whoever's responsible won't back away at this point," Alan said.

Gola called Max, but there was no answer, and left an urgent message.

He then called the station and was told Max and Sean were meeting Father Schmidt.

"It looks like Max found Schmidt, and he and Sean are meeting with him as we speak. I wish he would answer his phone. I'd like to let him know what happened here," Gola said.

"I think you need to call Alfred. I know he isn't involved, but he could be in danger. Let him know he has to keep his eyes open. We need to get everyone together tonight to review what's happened. Sean told me this morning he wanted to take care of dinner tonight, and given what we'll discuss, we need a another private dining room," Alan said.

"We'll handle it when we get back to Freiburg," Gola said.

He turned his attention to the inspector who was just finishing with the two surviving officers.

"Are we done here?" Gola asked.

"Yes, for now. I'll have more questions, but this was a clear attempt on *Herr* Bauer's life. We'll speak with him, then we should speak again. I know you said you were investigating an older homicide in Freiburg, but we need to try to establish the link of why someone would want to silence *Herr* Bauer. Until we figure out why this happened, *Herr* Bauer will remain in danger," the inspector said.

"I'm at your disposal. You know where to find me, and I'll assist in any way. We believe Bauer isn't the only person in danger with this investigation. The murder we're investigating is connected to at least four other unsolved homicides, and we think this is just the start," Gola said.

The inspector seemed to receive a little jolt to his blood pressure.

"Do you think there's a serial killer?" he asked.

Gola shook his head.

"No, on the contrary. We think this is an attempt at a cover-up, and the offending party is eliminating anyone who could provide insight into events from long ago. We have some theories, but they're rather far-fetched, and I want to wait until there's proof before we discuss them," Gola said.

The young inspector accepted the explanation.

"Okay, Chief Rockenbach, please let me know when you can share your findings. I'll call if I need to speak with you again."

They shook hands, and Gola and Alan went to inspect Gola's bullet-riddled squad car. They hadn't considered whether the cruiser would still drive. Gola saw the tires were intact and hoped the gas tank wasn't leaking. He checked and, despite the bullet holes, it appeared it might function. When he turned the key he was surprised it started and hoped it would operate well enough to get them back to Freiburg.

Both Gola and Alan shared the same physiological oddity when one faced a prolonged adrenaline rush. They were shaky and their bodies felt heavy and tired.

Alan broke the silence.

"You'll get everyone's attention when they see this car. It appears you were in a big-time shoot out. They won't know you were hiding in the house out of harm's way," Alan said.

"Oh, and you were out there with guns blazing?" Gola said.

"If I remember, I was the only one to have used my weapon and didn't just carry it around like a slab of bacon."

"I may never live it down. My Americanized cousin saw more action than I. How am I supposed to deal with that?"

Alan looked at his cousin, and his smile turned to a frown.

"We're fortunate. We didn't lose Hans, and we came out of this unscathed while two officers, and most likely, a passer-by died. It looks like Sean's CIA buddies are on the money," Alan said.

"I'm willing to bet we've just met the same guy who was responsible for Gusdorf's demise," Gola said.

Chapter 21)

The gold phone sprang to life and gave a slight shake as the ringer banged against its old metal cylinder.

"*Hallo?*" the Black Pope said.

"I had some trouble this afternoon. When I arrived at Bauer's house he had company. I drove past a few times and could tell he was speaking with someone. The car in front of his house was a police cruiser, so it was some cop speaking with him. There were stickers on the car indicating it was from Freiburg. There was no clear way to get in considering there was a cop in the house.

"I ended up in the front with a clear shot at Bauer and decided to take it. I thought I had him in my cross-hairs and took the shot, but he moved just as I pulled the trigger. I know I hit him, but I don't know if he's dead.

"Then all hell broke loose, no disrespect," he said, chuckling to himself. "Cop cars came from both ends of the street. I sent two of them to their maker and shot it out with the other two. To my good fortune a Good Samaritan happened to be coming by, and he gave me a lift away from my police friends. It was too bad my new buddy only lived another few minutes.

"I then drove to Freiburg, and I'm now in a low rent motel which suits me fine. The cops have no idea who I am, so I'm still free to get the job done. What do you want me to do next?" the assassin said.

The Black Pope considered his response.

"Sit tight. I need to assess what comes out of your encounter today. Before I plot the next move I would like to know the fallout and reaction from today's events. Call me tomorrow and we will figure out what we do next," the Black Pope said.

"Okay, I'll kill some time and will call tomorrow."

The man with the bad skin hung up. The man with the golden phone did not. He pressed down the white button atop the phone and a new dial tone buzzed into his ear. He turned the circular dial and the phone began ringing.

"*Hallo?*" Battalini said.

"It is I."

There was silence at the other end.

"What is it?" Battalini asked.

"We may have a problem. Our man from Amsterdam has encountered complications. He may become a liability. How long would it take you to get someone to Freiburg?" the Black Pope said.

"Ten hours' drive time, plus packing whatever might be needed," Battalini said.

"Be forewarned, I may be calling back, so be prepared," he said.

"I will," Battalini said and terminated the call.

The man holding the gold phone replaced the hand set in its worn cradle and put his face into both hands. He rubbed his face and his head remained in his hands for a few moments.

On the other end of the phone, Father Battalini stood holding the receiver. Battalini was the man in charge of the "Customer Relations" group of the Vatican. That was the ironic name for black operations within SMOM, or its more formal name of the Sovereign Military Order of Malta. His mentor had been a Jesuit named Michael Serafian, who gained fame with a well-known quote, stating "Pope Pius twelve's closest advisers regarded Hitler's armored divisions as the right hand of God."

Battalini learned politics and covert operations from a man of the church who was also in bed with the Nazis. As World War Two continued, it became obvious the Nazis would be defeated, and Serafian decided to play the dangerous game of also cooperating with the Allies.

His mentor was instrumental in creating an air of legitimacy for the SMOM by changing it from an Italian-only organization, to one of global membership made up of the powerful and influential. The original front was as a global charity organization. After World War Two, knighthood was bestowed on many CIA agents by the SMOM, and the organization morphed into a front for intelligence operations.

The Sovereign Military Order of Malta became the most effective covert military group in the world. The Vatican was the world's only landless sovereignty, and all Vatican diplomats were entitled to diplomatic immunity. Agents and materials could pass through customs without inspection, and they could operate in a foreign country without the laws of that host country being applicable to the agent. For an intelligence organization

120

it didn't get any better.

Father Battalini operated in the twilight world of clandestine operations, and one day the man in the Black Pope requested his presence. That was twenty-one years ago. He was asked to create a secret group within the SMOM to handle all the dirty and wet work with the sole purpose of protecting the positions of the church. There were other organizations within the Vatican with groups preforming similar functions, but the Black Pope wanted his own secret team he could direct as he saw fit. Battalini wished he had never received the Black Pope's call.

He never had a problem working in the interesting dark world of covert intelligence, but moving into the wet world in the name of God and Jesus, was too much of an oxymoron.

Putting together operations to eliminate an eighteen-year-old because she had become the victim of real Stigmata was outside his moral compass.

Killing war veterans because they had once guarded a rumored UFO was unacceptable, but that was his world and what he was asked to do. He would have preferred these directives were carried out by the organization within Opus Dei, as had been done for centuries, but the Black Pope's distaste for Opus Dei led to his desire to create a covert group under his direct control.

Battalini disliked the Black Pope, and bile rose in his esophagus every time the man in the black robe called from his cheesy gold phone.

When Battalini went into the priesthood, then became a Jesuit, he had done it for all the right reasons. How had he gotten so far off track? He realized he was having a major moral dilemma, and he knew he had to get over it.

The Black Pope called the shots on almost all issues and told the elected Pope what to do. Why would a man of his position and power maintain a relationship with a pervert like the man from Amsterdam? Battalini wanted that scumbag gone long ago. He was a moral degenerate, yet the most powerful man in the Vatican continued to view him as a direct report.

Battalini was now being told to ready his people to clean up an operation where he had no involvement. He wouldn't mind taking out the man from Amsterdam, but he also fantasized about including the Black Pope in his little daydream. Well, he knew he couldn't go there. He would start to prepare his team.

Chapter 22)

As Gola and Alan were in the midst of a shootout with an unknown assailant, Max and Sean were knocking on the door of a modest bungalow in Villingen, Germany. The door creaked open, and a robust man in his late fifties or early sixties appeared.

"*Guten Morgen* Chief Rockenbach," *Herr* Schmidt said and extended his hand.

Max was impressed since he had only stated his name once during their initial conversation.

"Nice to meet you, *Herr* Schmidt. Please meet Sean O'Shea," Max said.

Turning toward Sean, his hand was again extended. "Nice to meet you, Sean," he said.

"It's nice to meet you, *Herr* Schmidt," Sean said.

"Follow me and we'll get something to drink," Schmidt said.

They entered Schmidt's home and followed the ex-priest to a table featuring a pot of hot water with an assortment of teas, a pot of coffee, a bottle of cognac, and a bottle of port. It struck Sean as an unusual grouping of drink options.

"Please help yourself," Schmidt said.

They all selected a drink, and Sean was surprised to see Schmidt choose the Port.

"I don't know how I can be of help, but I'm happy to have someone to talk with," Schmidt said.

Sean thought this seemed to be a common refrain from older men living alone. He could be happy living alone in a log cabin and could care less if he had someone to talk with as long as he had his family around, then he realized Schmidt had been a priest and in all likelihood had no family.

"Thank you for seeing us on such short notice. We're investigating a cold case murder of a victim named Gusdorf, and we've been trying to figure out a motive. We found an old interview with you, and your comments about the church provided some interesting insights and led us to a potential motive. We wanted to share our thoughts and hear yours," Max said.

"I remember discussing some murder, but I couldn't help the investigator, and I don't remember what I would have said. I think the only reason they wanted to speak with me was because our church was near where the victim was discovered," Schmidt said.

"You're correct. Standard operating procedure would be to speak with everyone who might have stumbled across something useful," Max said.

Sean raised his hand as if he were in school trying to get the teacher's attention.

"The comments Max is referring to were related to your feelings about church hypocrisy. You mentioned something you called the Alien Theory and certain protocols, and it was obvious you were struggling with whether you'd remain in the church. We're trying to determine if there could be a link to the victim and these protocols," Sean said.

Herr Schmidt looked at Sean with new recognition.

"The Alien Theory; I haven't heard those words in a long time," Schmidt said.

"Why haven't we heard about any of this?" Sean asked.

"I'm no longer part of the church. The Alien Theory was a hot topic in the church and often discussed by the good fathers, but these discussions were frowned upon by the church hierarchy. Talking about this gets me a little worked up."

"Could you discuss what issues caused your disillusionment?" Sean asked.

"Let me tell you about my problems with the church. I have a number of friends, including my best friend, who rose faster in the church than I did. They weren't as opinionated and argumentative as I and were able to navigate the incessant politics of the Vatican," he said and took a long swallow of his ruby red port, and continued. "Because of their proximity to Rome, they were promoted and eventually became part of the inner circle. As such, my friends were privy to secret information and discovered the church has long known about the existence of extra-terrestrials," Schmidt said.

"Did I just hear you correctly? The church has known of extra-terrestrials?" Sean asked.

"Yes, my best friend became the head of a group in charge of sup-

123

pressing this information. He shared knowledge with me which would blow the top off the church. The Vatican maintains the position that the flock doesn't have the intelligence nor emotional stability to deal with certain realities. The church higher-ups, view true believers as sheep, and feel they wouldn't or couldn't accept the truth had it become known," Schmidt said.

"It's hard to believe the church would suppress this knowledge," Sean said.

"The Vatican is full of hypocrisy. If the church was open and honest we would have a better world. Had its leaders trusted their followers to make their own assessment of the truth, the church would have been dealing from honesty, not from the constant cover-ups that now define it," the ex-father said.

Sean shifted his body toward Schmidt.

"What do you mean, constant cover-ups?" Sean asked.

"Let's start with scriptures which lay down the basic tenants of Christianity. They've been manipulated. There are many hidden scriptures buried in the secret Vatican archives. A number of leaks have occurred over the years, but while noise was generated, nothing concrete was ever released to the public," Schmidt said.

"Can you provide an example?" Sean asked.

"In the early days of the church, women had a prominent and influential role. You can go back to the relationship between Jesus and Mary Magdalene. There was jealousy directed toward Mary, and writings in the hidden scriptures are downright bitter about her influence with Jesus. Those writings have been suppressed because of the potential backlash if the flock recognized the pettiness and envy directed toward Mary.

These writings weren't complimentary to the apostle's behavior as women fought for their place in the early church. From the earliest times there was manipulation of 'the word of God,'" Schmidt said.

"How can you be certain their goal was to undermine women's role in the church?" Sean asked.

"The hidden scriptures illustrated the apostle's negative view so a different tact was taken. A concerted effort was made to eliminate the influence of women, and words were added to the scriptures to accomplish this. There are many examples such as, *'in the Word of God under which women are not to discipline men, not to stand in authority over men, and women are not to teach men.*' This language was added so males in power could point to the word of God as their guiding force. What bullshit? Who would believe this nonsense, but it was adopted and now is part of the dogma," Schmidt said.

"This is the opposite of how most people view church doctrine. Do you have other examples?" Sean asked.

"Do you know there are large gaps of time where there are no scriptures? Why do you think that is? There were scriptures written, but they reside in the secure room in the Vatican. The reason they don't exist to the outside world is the Vatican would lose its credibility.

"Do you know some of those years were filled with writings called '*The Apocrypha*' or '*The Old Testament Apocryphal Writings.*' These books appeared in the Bible until the end of the nineteenth century, then fifteen books and two sections disappeared from the Bible.

"This is just an example of how individuals have edited what people are reading as the word of God. It is more like the word of the editors who have something to gain. *The Dead Sea Scrolls* and *Book of Enoch* are other examples of missing books that have come to light," Schmidt said.

"You mentioned something called the Alien Theory. How do you define the Alien Theory?" Sean asked.

"The Alien Theory is the real bombshell held under lock and key and relates to a scripture detailing encounters with extra-terrestrials and their influence and involvement with the human race. It's been speculated that human life as we know it came from outside the earth or possibly life forms on earth were altered," Schmidt said.

"Are you saying there's some proof of this contact?" Sean asked.

"There's an apparent amount of detail making this theory more than a theory. These writings have been hidden forever, and the rumor among the inner circle is the Old Testament was modified from alien involvement to Moses getting the Ten Commandments from God.

Don't you find it interesting that the description of Moses prior to receiving the Ten Commandments, then afterwards, describes someone who has been exposed to radiation poisoning? The Alien Theory is the supposition the human race came from elsewhere. Many of the stories in the Old Testament could relate to alien involvement instead of God. The Moses description is just that sort of story," Schmidt said.

"What do you think proof of alien involvement would do to the Bible and church's credibility?" Sean asked.

"Before you answer *Herr* Schmidt let me add. If they really had been hiding the proof, it would make the Vatican nothing but con men. If they knew this to be fact, or at least suspected it to be fact, and their efforts from the beginning of the church were to sell the concepts in the Bible as the word of God, they perpetrated the single biggest con in the history of the world," Max said.

"*Voila*, I haven't always been anti-church; I became a priest, for heaven's sake. The world has bought into the concept of religion, and those of us who went into the priesthood did it with all good intentions and belief. The key word is belief. We were long subjected to the concept of faith. The doctrine is you must have faith in those things which can't be proven. This is code for we'll tell you what to believe and how you should think. And by the way, we want you to give us minimum of ten percent of what you earn every week and never ask how we use those funds. What a racket. This was my life for almost my entire existence," Schmidt said.

"Unbelievable," Sean said, "Can anything be documented?"

"Any proof would be controlled by the Vatican and impossible to obtain, but just look at history. When women attempted to regain their rightful position of influence and began the Wicken and Goddess movements, what happened? What did organized religion do to the early Wickens? They burned them at the stake in Europe, then again in Salem, Massachusetts.

"What did the Vatican do to the Knights Templar when they could no longer be controlled because of their wealth and power? They created the infamy of Friday the 13th with the torture and mass murder of every Templar they could find.

"What was the Spanish Inquisition designed to do? Eliminate any and all opposition to the church and rule by intimidation.

"What do you think the Crusades were about? It was nothing more than a giant land grab. The inner circle of the Vatican knew about the details of the Alien Theory. Therefore, they knew the holy city of Jerusalem was a sham, but on the excuse of regaining the Holy Land, they mounted repeated attempts to grab more land. Why, you ask? More land equals more potential converts, and that generates more weekly donations, which results in their ultimate goal of greater wealth.

"The Vatican was the world's first major corporation and did it by having the morals of the Mafia. They used force, intimidation, and murder to accomplish their goals of ultimate power and wealth. Who does that sound like?"

"*Herr* Schmidt, you paint a disturbing picture. Can you tell us more about the Alien Theory?" Max asked.

"I don't know. The theory is one of the main topics of conversation among Vatican priests when they're sharing a bottle of port late at night. I wouldn't have known about it except for my best friend. He and I grew up together, went through the priesthood with one another, and are as close as brothers. When he learned hidden information he would share it with me. I may be the only outsider aware of these secrets.

"Priests outside the Vatican walls know nothing of the Alien Theory. Priests joining the inner circle know nothing of this until they become indoctrinated, then over time they find out the realities of the church. Once they're in the inner circle they become privy to the Vatican secrets.

"Priests around the world do their work without any idea of any of this, and their work done on behalf of the church is still admirable. The problem is, the whole empire is built on a foundation of lies, and the Vatican will do anything to protect itself. It's a ruthless organization," Schmidt said.

"Did you ever hear about the UFO crash outside Freiburg?" Sean asked.

"I heard of it as a kid growing up. Rumor was all I knew, at least until I became aware of the Alien Theory. During conversations with my friend a number of things came out. Prior to the war, the Vatican and Hitler were in lock step, or should I say goosestep. Sorry for my feeble attempt at humor. The Vatican had many Nazi sympathizers and joined them at the crash site in the Black Forest, then again at the Poland crash site.

"The church maintained the Nazi relationship, even after the Vatican cozied up to the Allies. At the end of the war Bishop Alois Hudal assisted a number of high ranking Nazis to escape from Deutschland using churches along the Catholic ratline. This was part of the Vatican teaming with *ODESSA*," Schmidt said.

Sean and Max exchanged looks. They had never mentioned the UFO event in Poland with Schmidt.

Schmidt continued, "I know it's hard to believe, but the same day the Nazi hierarchy and Wernher von Braun were at the Freiburg crash site, so were representatives from the Vatican. The Vatican interest focused on the dead aliens, which included human-sized bodies, along with the small sized bodies we've come to expect. The human-sized bodies made the Vatican nervous."

Sean stood and filled his cup with more hot water and a new tea bag.

"Is there any way to get evidence proving any of this?" he asked.

"Much of what we've talked about is documented. The missing books of the Bible, the atrocities done by the church in the name of God, the relationship with Hitler, and the Vatican, the UFO crash sites in Freiburg and Poland, those are all documented, just hushed up. They're easy to find if one is looking," Schmidt said.

"No, I'm referring to the Alien Theory," Sean said.

"I can't think of a way to get evidence, and I don't think my friend would ever come forward. I don't know how you could prove anything about the Alien Theory unless you got your hands on something tangible. Remember, this is not America. If the Vatican suspected someone would leak this sort of information, they would be eliminated without hesitation. When I say they're ruthless, I mean it."

"*Herr* Schmidt, you mentioned something you called protocols in your police report interview. Could you tell us what those are?" Sean asked.

"The protocols are set up for many different situations. If a particular threat would arise, the appropriate protocol would be implemented. The protocols are pre-planned responses to any perceived threat.

"Excuse me for a moment, I'm getting a dry throat from all this talking. I need a refill of port, can I get you anything?

Schmidt stood and stepped to the table of assorted drinks and filled his glass from the bottle of ruby red port.

"I'll have something cold, do you have ice-water?" Max asked.

"Certainly, here you go," Schmidt said, handing him a tall glass.

"Thank you," Max said. "You were about to tell us about the protocols."

"Oh yes, for example, if a Stigmata is reported, a priest is sent to investigate. Since the priest is sent from the Vatican, the process has an authoritative aura and the priest receives complete cooperation. The public perception is the Vatican is neutral and would like to prove the Stigmata is real, but in reality the priest's job is to discredit or find a reason for the purported Stigmata. When the priest hasn't been able to discredit the Stigmata, he arranges for other dark forces within the Vatican to create an 'accident' to the Stigmata victim.

"The protocol related to UFOs focuses on discrediting the witnesses, but they usually don't have to get involved because governments do it for them."

"What are other protocols?" Sean asked.

"There's a protocol to address the discovery of ancient documents. There's a team in place, including archaeologists, linguistic experts, and para military among others, who would be on site within twenty hours of a discovery anywhere in the world. Their job would be to control the situation, determine what they had, and what would be released to the media and local government. They'll go to any extent to control the release of information. This has happened several times in the last sixty years, with the most prominent discovery being the *Dead Sea Scrolls*. New protocols were developed, because the find became known.

"The protocols are controlled within a secret group in the Military Order of Malta. This is the same organization where my best friend works, and he's been the source of everything I've learned. I'm sure he would be at great personal risk if it was known he revealed these secrets to me."

"Can I ask the name of your friend?" Max asked.

"I'll give it to you, but please don't try to speak with him. Any contact could put him under scrutiny, and he's my only true friend. His name is Father Edwardo Battalini," Schmidt said.

***

As *Herr* Schmidt was revealing Battalini's name, Gola pulled into the Freiburg Police Station parking lot. After exiting the car he gave it another inspection, and his head moved side to side as he perused the damage. He recognized they survived a close call, and had they arrived at Bauer's later in the day, they would have discovered his dead body.

"Gola, we need to get to Sean and Max. They need to know what happened, and I'm concerned they aren't answering their phones," Alan said.

"They should be okay. They were going to see Schmidt and probably turned their phones off. I don't believe anyone would know we have interest in him, so I wouldn't expect the same sort of welcoming committee," Gola said.

In Villingen, Max asked another question of the ex-father.

"*Herr* Schmidt, what's your take on the church's motive to silence everyone having anything to do with the 1936 UFO crash? It doesn't make sense they would worry about covering up something taking place so long ago," Max asked.

"I don't have an answer. If it was a recent event I would understand. They eliminate threats or perceived threats; why eliminate people related to an event over eighty years ago? The only thing I can think of, there is, as you would say, a smoking gun. They're afraid of something becoming public and being harmful to them in some way. Remember, if they're hiding proof of a connection between aliens and the human race, they would be aggressive in keeping it quiet," Schmidt said.

"That makes sense," Sean said.

They spoke for another forty-five minutes, and Sean felt he was developing a great connection with the ex-priest in a short time. They'd been with *Herr* Schmidt for almost two and a half hours when Max glanced at his cell phone. The ringer was turned off, and he hadn't been aware of the frantic calls from Gola. He checked his text message and read with alarm about the attack on *Herr* Bauer.

He turned to Sean.

"I think it's time to head back. *Herr* Schmidt, it's been a real pleasure and, if it's okay, we may want to speak with you again," Max said.

"I'd be happy to. I enjoyed talking with both of you," Schmidt said.

Sean stood, somewhat surprised by the abruptness with which Max curtailed the conversation. He offered his hand to *Herr* Schmidt and it was accepted with enthusiasm.

"If anything else comes to mind, please call us. We'd love to talk with Father Battalini if there would be any way to do so," Sean said.

Schmidt continued shaking Sean's hand. "I doubt that will happen. He's in too deep and, if he were to speak with you, I think it would bring unwanted attention to him, but you never know. I'll be speaking with him this evening, and I'll tell him of our discussion," Schmidt said.

Chapter 23)

Sean turned to Max as they walked to the car.

"What do you make of *Herr* Schmidt?" Sean asked.

"He's an interesting gentleman. I start to get a little concerned when he talks about mentioning us to people inside the Vatican. I have a feeling he could be a key person in figuring this out. He's ex-church and is still connected, but on the other hand doesn't buy into their bullshit. I think we'll be talking with him again.

"We have another issue. I ended the meeting as I did because I read a text from Gola. They ran into some kind of trouble at *Herr* Bauer's house. There was an attempt on *Herr* Bauer's life and he was wounded. Gola and Alan are okay," Max said.

Sean and Max retrieved their respective voice mails at the same time. They drove in silence, exchanging glances as they each listened to details of the shoot-out in Baden-Baden.

Max spoke first and said, "We're way past the point of no return. No stepping back at this point. We've created sufficient attention and are liable to be the next target."

"We need to alert Schmidt. They were trying to take out Bauer, not our guys. They're cleaning up loose ends, so we have nowhere to go. They wouldn't know about Schmidt, but that will change once he talks to his friend," Sean said.

Sean dialed the phone. "*Herr* Schmidt, its Sean O'Shea. I wanted to thank you for the time today and also alert you to a new development. Today, as we were meeting, our chief of police was meeting with a gentleman who was in the guard detail at the UFO site. While they were interviewing him an attempt was made on his life. This was a ninety-six or ninety-seven-year-old man who didn't have an enemy in the world. Someone was trying to take him out for what he might reveal. I wanted to make you aware of this, because if the wrong people think you're helping us or you know something, you could be in danger," Sean said.

There was hesitation on the other end of the phone.

"You fellows know how to make friends, don't you? I guess I need to be careful who I talk to about this," Schmidt said.

"That would be wise. Let's stay in touch, and I'd like to know if you encounter anything unusual," Sean said.

"I will. I think I'll limit my conversation to Father Battalini so I don't say something to the wrong person," Schmidt said.

"I agree with your thinking," Sean said.

Max called Gola.

"Hey, where are you? I've been trying to get you," Gola said.

"We've been with *Herr* Schmidt for the last couple of hours. I just got your message. What the hell happened?" Max asked.

"Alan and I were in the midst of our interview with Bauer and a single assassin tried to take him out. He was shot from across the street, but we think he'll be okay. The local police arrived, and within moments a shoot-out was happening in the middle of the street. Two Baden-Baden officers were killed, a passerby was killed, and the gunman got away. It's obvious our actions have provoked a response, so we're all in danger," Gola said.

"Agreed. We'll be in Freiburg in a half hour. Where are we getting together?" Max asked.

"Come to the station and we'll decide. Keep your eyes open," Gola said.

"I will. See you in a little while," Max said.

Max told Sean about the events in Baden-Baden, and they were silent for most of the ride. Twenty-five minutes later they pulled into the Freiburg Police Station and walked into Gola's office.

"You boys know how to have a good time," Max said as a wry smile crossed his face. He was grateful his brother was safe, but anxiety was now attached to his emotions like a remora to a shark.

"Better than my sibling who takes all the cushy interviews," Gola said, then their smiles disappeared as they realized this could get worse before it got better.

"We should debrief everyone at once so we don't need to repeat our stories. Do we have a spot picked out?" Max asked.

"Alan set us up at Leaf Thaikhe. We can go there now and get an early start. I think we could all use a drink," Gola said.

"It sounds like the two of you have something to share as well," Alan said.

132

"We aren't as exciting as our cohorts, but we had an interesting discussion. Let's go; I'm ready for something stronger than a beer," Max said.

They stood and headed to the restaurant with more trepidation than at any time in their quest.

Sean's phone went off. He answered and was surprised to hear Rudolf's voice come though the earpiece.

"Sean, this is Rudolf. How are you?" he said.

"Rudolf, you have good timing. We're heading to a restaurant to debrief. Gola and Alan were involved in a shoot-out in Baden-Baden and one of our interviewees was almost assassinated. Max and I had the chance to interview an ex-priest who had some strong opinions about the Vatican. To say the least, it's been an interesting day," Sean said.

"I would say so. Tell me what happened," Rudolf said.

Sean proceeded to describe what he knew of the Baden-Baden shoot-out and the discussion with ex-priest Schmidt.

"You're now up to speed, including the theories laid out by *Herr* Schmidt. What do you have?" Sean asked.

"I wanted to brief you on where we are and what we've done in Poland. I have two operatives in Czernica, and they're sniffing around. They managed to place phone bugs in the chief's office and his home. We'll monitor calls coming in and out. We accessed phone records from his office and have found something of interest. There's an outgoing call from his phone to a Vatican area code three days ago, and it was made two minutes after an incoming call from a Freiburg area code. Would you check with your chief and see if this is his number?" Rudolf asked.

Sean wrote down the number and promised to check.

"I don't think this is a coincidence. I think you've found the direct link and how they found out about us so quickly," Sean said.

"That's my take. We're also in the process of trying to check numbers dialed from the Vatican number, but it's a trickier business. They have some of the strongest security on the planet, but we should be able to get the records; it'll just take longer. Bugging their phones will be next to impossible. We have people on the inside, and it's still difficult because they always sweep for bugging devices," Rudolf said.

"This is outstanding information; please call me if you get anything else. I'll call you when I verify the phone number. No, wait, I'm with Max. He'll know," Sean said.

133

Sean gave Max the number supplied by Rudolf.

"Sean, that's Gola's cell number," Max said.

"Did you hear that, Rudolf?" Sean asked.

"Yes, I did. We now have verification of what we suspected. The chief in Poland is dirty and connected to the Vatican. Now we know why investigations were never conducted. It also explains why he gave Robert an interview about the murder, then told your chief he never spoke with Robert. He wouldn't know he was mentioned in Robert's notes or they would ever be read by someone investigating this matter and he'll be in the dark about our knowledge of his involvement. I'll inform our people of the verification, and they'll start turning over his background and private life. I'd expect we'll uncover deeper connections, and I'll call you when I know more. Keep that little present with you at all times and trust your gut," Rudolf said.

"I will. I'm learning quickly," Sean said.

They signed off, and Sean turned to Max and said, "My, my, we'll have plenty to talk about tonight. Information is just flying at us from every direction, and we'll have to try to make sense of it all."

Max brought the car to a stop in front of Leaf Thaikhe. They entered and were led to the private room Alan requested. Sean entered the room and noticed Alfred wasn't in attendance.

"Gola, is Alfred coming?" Sean asked.

"No, I didn't call him. I guess maybe I should have, given what we now know. Max, what do you think?" Gola said.

"Since you didn't call him, it's no big deal. We can brief him. He would've come for the free dinner and wouldn't want to get involved, so I don't think we worry about it as long as we let him know the threat level has been upgraded," Max said.

Everyone nodded.

"Just so everyone knows up front, I can't thank you all enough for your support, help, and hospitality. Dinner tonight is on me," Sean said. "Now let's bring this meeting to order. We have much to talk about tonight. Gola, why don't you tell us about your picnic in Baden Baden."

"Yes, it was a picnic alright. As you all know, Alan and I met with Hans Bauer. We were in the early stages of the interview when Bauer revealed an important piece of information. He was one of the first to the crash site and while he didn't take any crash debris, he did confirm the scattered items were light and strong.

His most important revelation were the bodies strewn all over the site. He saw the typical three to four foot bodies we've heard about in UFO lore, but he also observed two full-sized bodies appearing to be human. The smaller bodies had three fingers on each hand while the larger bodies had five. He told us this rather startling information when I noticed the same beat-up Volvo drive by the house for a third time," Gola said and continued to review and concluded his recap.

"He drove to wherever he stashed his car, killed the civilian, and escaped without leaving a clue to his identity. It appears Bauer will recover, but we have no idea what hole our assassin has crawled into. That's it," Gola said.

"It sounds like the most important detail was his statement about the bodies. We now have corroboration for the comments I found in Robert's notes. Robert also had references to bodies, but there was no detail. Do you think this is the information someone is trying to hide?" Max said.

"We didn't get to finish our conversation with Bauer, but my guess is the revelation of the bodies could be the smoking gun," Alan said.

"It could be, but it's unsubstantiated. Let's continue with all the updates, then we can go back and see what makes sense. Max and Sean, what did you learn from Herr Schmidt?" Gola asked.

"We had a great conversation, and Schmidt is a wealth of information. He's now anti-church, and he's starved for people to talk to. If we need to talk with him again, I'm sure he would be happy to do so." Sean said.

They spent the next ten minutes providing an overview of Schmidt's comments and reasons for his viewpoint.

"Sean, it seems Schmidt has corroborated some of our theories," Gola said.

"One thing is now evident. The fact they attempted to silence Bauer is an indication they aren't in possession of the bodies or the craft. If they knew what happened to the hard evidence, it would have been destroyed and they wouldn't care about the investigations. I think they fear discovery of something they consider a threat. I believe the motive is becoming clearer," Max said.

Sean said, "You could be right. As Max and I were on the way here, I got a call from Rudolf Weiler. He put his operatives to work in Poland

135

and discovered something. They were able to obtain the phone records from the police station. Two minutes after Gola hung up from his call to Chief Barinski, a call was placed from Barinski to a number in the Vatican. They've bugged Barinski's office and home phones and are trying to get phone records for the numbers in the Vatican. They suspected all along the chief was involved because of the lack of any investigation, and now it's been verified," Sean said.

Gola looked at the faces around the table. He asked "Are there any other updates before we go further into motive?"

No one spoke.

"Okay, let's try to poke holes into Max's theory. If the information we've spoken about tonight is true and could be proved, it would destroy not only the Vatican, but probably all Christian, Islamic, and Jewish beliefs. Given the power and financial resources of the Vatican, it's obvious they would go to any length to control this knowledge," Gola said.

Alan shifted in his chair, then said, "Let's suppose this were to come out. Let's think about the fallout. The church would deny and deflect and claim the documents were fabricated. Governments and the church have done it forever whenever faced with a threat. Some followers would accept their story no matter what proof was put in front of their faces, but the church would lose huge numbers of its members and would certainly lose the well informed, who are the wealthiest of the flock.

"There's also a huge downside for the church with their relationship with governments. How long do you think it would take for governments around the world to take away the tax exempt status the church enjoys? The church is the largest land holder in the world. Their taxes alone would be gigantic. So think of this. The church is reeling in disgrace, they lose what, eighty percent of their followers, so their cash flow drops to almost zero, and their expenses go through the roof.

"Because of their wealth, they won't go away overnight, but their influence and power would be gone, and they'd be like a corporation going into bankruptcy.

"They would also face a great deal of hostility from those who contributed their hard earned money all these years. Imagine realizing you'd been played for a fool and you had donated thousands so the church could perpetuate a lie. Think how outraged you would feel. Multiply that by millions and millions of embittered ex-followers. I would venture to say being a member of the Vatican and clergy might become hazardous to one's health.

"In essence, the Vatican would be finished and would have no option but to liquidate their assets to fuel their continued expenses," Alan said.

"Well said. There can be no doubt this is a life and death issue for the church if it was true, and became known. Does anyone disagree?" Sean asked.

Heads nodded in agreement around the table. Before Sean could speak again, the waiter came into the room and asked for drink orders. The group ordered stronger drinks than in any of their previous dinners. Vodka, in a variety of combinations, was the popular choice, but Sean stayed with the local Kabinett.

Sean continued, "Okay, so I think we're confident we've identified a motive and we know the responsible party. Before we continue, I want to ask a philosophical question. Are we prepared to continue forward on this path, given the potential worldwide chaos and upheaval, if this knowledge comes to light? Are we willing to be the vessel to unleash a change in the worldwide psyche and stability?" Sean asked.

"I for one believe it would be a good thing. The church should be exposed, and I think I have a higher regard for how people would react than you've indicated. I'm not convinced we would have anarchy. The Vatican would be thrown into chaos, but forgive me when I say this, who cares? Will any of us lose sleep over what happens to the Vatican?" Gola asked.

Sean said, "You know most wars fought in this world had religious motivation. Sometimes all based on religion, other times less evident, but still an underlying reason. Just think, would the Muslims and Christians still want to kill each other, would Islamic fundamentalist terrorist organizations still want to kill the infidel, and would they want to blow themselves up if their fantasies of 100 virgins was out the window?

"Gola, I think you're correct; it might not be a bad thing. The world has been led down a path of faith as a method to deal with an unknown future, and there's more conflict than ever. Wouldn't it be better to have knowledge of our origins and eliminate artificial reasons to kill each other?" Sean said.

"Don't lose track of one thing. Today's religions would try to spin this. The Ten Commandments and Bible, supposedly the word of God, would have been discredited; however, God himself or herself would still be the focus of what would be left of organized religion. After all, who created the aliens? I can envision the Vatican saying, never mind what we've been preaching for two thousand years, God is still what we worship, so keep those collection plates full. That's how they would try to save face and keep their power. The Muslims would still say Allah is great," Max said.

"You're right, Max," Sean said, "but we would be exposing a corrupt, ruthless organization. People would now be free to worship God and not a false organization. So far I haven't heard an argument against exposing the church."

Again there was silence.

"I'm shocked no one is taking a position that we should consider not exposing the truth to protect people from themselves," Sean said.

Gola had a quizzical look.

"Do you realize if we argued from that perspective, we would be taking a similar position as the governments around the world? The church has been deceitful, but world governments have covered up UFOs because their view is the populace couldn't handle reality. I hate to think we would align with their thinking," Gola said.

"That's it then. We won't look back, and we move forward doing everything we can to prove what we now believe to be true. We need to look at our options of how we go about getting evidence. What do we do next?" Sean asked.

Alan perked up.

"We'll need concrete proof if we want anyone believe to us. We need to decide where to start looking. We have the Vatican, but we'll get nowhere with them. The crafts and bodies were taken to Wewelsburg Castle. What do we know about the castle?" Alan said.

"Let me answer that. Sean, you probably don't know this, but I have a history degree from Freiburg University. The focus of my expertise is German History, and I was a professor of history at the university for ten years. That's where I met Marta, who was an art professor. I happen to know a great deal about the Nazis and Wewelsburg Castle," Max said.

"You guys never fail to surprise me," Sean said.

"Wewelsburg Castle could be an interesting option for evidence.

Here's a quick castle history lesson. I won't take you to the beginning, but it was sitting unused and in ruins when Himmler was looking for a castle to use as his SS Center of the World showpiece. He looked at several possibilities and chose Wewelsburg the day he laid eyes on it.

"He started a surface restoration in the early thirties and by 1933 started using Wewelsburg in an unofficial capacity. He took a one hundred year lease and started doing excavation and transformation work on the castle.

"There was a strong occult bias in the Nazi Party and he was using all sorts of symbolism in the construction efforts. Certain things are well documented, such as building his famous crypt in the north tower and his own quarters in the south tower.

"Historians focus on the north tower, where much of the construction was centered, but local rumor has it there was an underground command headquarters complete with laboratories, experimental facilities and Himmler's ultimate bunker all built beneath the south tower. When the crash took place in 1936, Himmler came to Freiburg, and within hours everything was removed to the castle.

"Von Braun was a Nazi officer and part of the SS, so he had full access to study and work on the craft in secret. By the time of the 1938 crash, Himmler is purported to have expanded the lab's footprint, and the remnants of the Polish craft were also brought to Wewelsburg. Now fast forward to the end of the war. As Germany was about to fall, Himmler ordered one of his officers, Heinz Macher, to go to Wewelsburg and blow up, then burn the castle to the ground. Why would he do that unless there were secrets he was trying to hide?

"When Macher arrived at the castle he didn't have enough gasoline nor explosive material to blow up the entire castle. What did he do? He took all of his explosives to the south tower, detonated it, and set fire to the entire castle. The next day a U.S. infantry division came upon the remains of the still smoldering castle, which by then consisted only of its exterior walls.

"In 1948 a restoration was undertaken and the castle was partially rebuilt. For some reason the south tower didn't receive a full rebuild. Today the castle is a museum and has been criticized for glorifying Nazi memorabilia. I think Wewelsburg Castle may be our best bet to find something.

"Why do you suppose the south tower, which was the only part of the castle destroyed by explosives, never had a full restoration? The south tower laboratory could contain records, spacecraft, bodies, you name it. My suggestion is to look there first, and it would be far easier than trying to penetrate the Vatican," Max said.

"Great idea. Where's this castle?" Sean asked.

"It's about three hundred sixty kilometers north of us, a little over a three-hour drive," Max said.

"Does anyone have connections to the castle?" Sean asked.

"I know the curator and he owes me one," Max said.

"And I have a casual acquaintance with the Paderborn Police Chief. We spent a couple of evenings over a few *Doppelbochs* about three years ago," Gola said.

"I think it's a great place to start. I'll also contact my CIA friends and see if they have any ideas. Do we have any other starting points worth considering?" Sean asked.

"I don't see one," Gola said.

"We may want to revisit *Herr* Schmidt. If we lay out our theories, he may be able to point us in the right direction. He still has a close contact inside the Vatican, and maybe his friend could become sympathetic to our quest," Sean said.

"It makes sense to revisit Schmidt, but don't expect help from inside the Vatican, given we could bring down the church," Gola said.

Max stood and walked to the one window that allowed natural light to enter their private dining room.

"Okay, let's look at our options. First we have the castle and whatever could be buried under the south tower. Second, we can explore the possibility that locals may have looted evidence. Third, I'll see if our CIA guys have any ideas, and fourth, we'll check with Schmidt and see if there's an opportunity to speak with his Vatican contact. Does that sum up the options as we know them?" Sean asked.

"I believe you've summarized it very well. As we uncover information, we'll go down different paths. You never know where it will lead," Gola said.

Chapter 24)

The man in the Vatican dialed his gold phone.

"*Hallo?*" the man with pock-marked skin said.

"It is I. It is time to start surveillance. Do not engage, but I want to know more about who these guys are and to whom they have spoken. We do not know about anyone other than the two policemen from Freiburg. I want to know who else is involved and why they are interested. Then we can decide what further action is required. I want to know the scope of this before we start to eliminate people," the Black Pope said.

"Understood."

"Since law enforcement is involved, whenever we move on them we will draw scrutiny. Call me as soon as you have something," the Black Pope said.

"Okay," he said.

The man with the bad skin looked at the phone in his hand. He just had a conversation in which he said three words. Interesting. Tomorrow he would stake out the police station.

Chapter 25)

"Let's determine who does what," said Sean. "I'll contact the CIA guys. Max, can you contact the museum people, Gola likewise with the police chief you know in Paderborn, and Max, and I'll meet with Schmidt again. Does that cover everything?"

Everyone nodded.

The waiter came into the room and asked for dinner orders. The special of Atlantic salmon seemed to be popular around the table, although Sean ordered Beef Wellington. After taking the order for the wine, the waiter left.

Conversations were intense, and when Gola tapped the water glass with his knife he had everyone's attention.

"Before I forget, I managed to get a good look at the car driven by Bauer's would-be assassin. It was an older Volvo with badly oxidized paint. I'm not sure of the color, but I'm guessing it was a red or maroon and should be easy to identify. We have an advantage because he doesn't know how many of us were in the house. He knew there was a police cruiser in front, but I doubt he knew there were two of us. He knows of me because of the chief of police in Poland, but he may not be aware of Sean or Alan. We can use that to our advantage," Gola said.

The waiter returned with their dinners and all conversation ceased. The dinner discussion turned to wives, small talk, health, and firearms. It was a lighter discussion and served as an oasis from the constant stress. Sean hadn't recognized the effects of never-ending tension until he realized how his body felt after a few glasses of wine. He liked the feeling of weight dissipating from his shoulders. As dinner came to an end, Sean returned their focus to the tasks at hand.

"We all have to do's, but for the most part we should finish early tomorrow. Max, let's try to see Schmidt again in the afternoon. I'm sure he'll welcome us back," Sean said.

"I'll call him first thing. Let's plan on it," Max said.

"I'm not sure if we can get all this done on short notice, but depending on what we encounter tomorrow, I would suggest we should plan a trip to Wewelsburg Castle the day after tomorrow. Who wants to go?" Gola asked.

"I'm in for sure," Sean said.

"Me, too," Alan said.

"I also want to go. Gola, do you think we can both be gone for the entire day?" Max asked.

"Yes, we have plenty of people to hold down the fort. We can take two cars and cover a lot of territory. I want to see the chief in Paderborn, and I have another thought. Max, let's see if we can find out who did the original architectural drawings for Himmler and see if we can uncover who was contracted to do the work. Himmler would most likely have used local talent. I'd be interested to see the architectural drawings and if they show anything built underneath the castle," Gola said.

"I'll ask those questions of the curator tomorrow. I agree, it is likely locals were used, and there wouldn't have been many architects and builders in the area in 1933. Since the castle is now a museum, the detailed history should be a matter of record," Max said.

"Yes, this is still a murder investigation and is official business. We may be going down a different path, but we're still trying to find those responsible for killing Gusdorf. We'll drive and cover the expenses," Gola said.

Dinner ended, and they adjourned to their cars and personal reflection.

***

Sean chose to wait until morning to call the agents. Instead, he called Cat as she was getting Liam ready for school. They couldn't talk long because of the normal chaos, but he felt better after making the connection.

"Once they hung up he fired up his computer and did more searches on the castle, Nazis and Himmler. The more he could educate himself, the better. At midnight he turned off the laptop, the lights, and tried to sleep. It didn't go well. He couldn't quiet his mind, and in the morning awoke groggy, wondering how much sleep he actually achieved. He showered and before breakfast, started making calls. His first was to Laflamme.

"*Bonjour*," Laflamme said.

"*Bonjour, Monsieur* Laflamme, this is Sean O'Shea."

"Bonjour Sean, comment allez-vous?"

Sean brought Laflamme up on the latest events, the attempted assassination of Bauer, and their church theories. Sean then gave him an overview of their plan for the next couple of days.

"Well, you have stirred the pot," Laflamme said. "I am guessing they don't know of your entire team, but when you show up in Paderborn, you all will become known. Don't get complacent and think they won't find out about you. They are moving into action again, and you will end up in their sights."

"I believe you're correct, but we're determined to move forward. I was wondering if you knew anything about Wewelsburg Castle," Sean asked.

"I do. What did you want to know?" Laflamme asked.

"We believe two UFOs crashed and the wreckage and associated bodies were taken there under the direction of Himmler and von Braun, and they conducted reverse engineering. Since the castle wasn't designed for those activities, our supposition is when Himmler did the reconstruction of the castle, he had secret labs built underground.

"Our best guess is these labs were built under the south tower, which, coincidentally, was the only part of the castle to be blown up under Himmler's directive. I wondered if you could corroborate our theory and if you had access to any architectural or construction information about the castle," Sean said.

"I'm quite impressed with your theories. We know of the UFO situation, and you're correct, everything was taken to Wewelsburg Castle. We know Himmler built an entire underground laboratory and had the walls and ceilings reinforced so it doubled as a giant bomb shelter. Himmler's intent was for the castle to become the headquarters for the SS and his personal bomb-proof safe house. It was said to be built better than the Fuehrer Bunker, but I don't know of any plans or drawings.   I have to say your team is developing an intriguing hypothesis," Laflamme said.

"Did the Allies investigate the castle after the war?" Sean asked.

"It wasn't investigated at all because the laboratory had been kept secret. Germany was in such devastation all efforts were focused on finding Nazis and reconstruction. Operation Paperclip was created to round up Nazi scientists and get them to America, so the very people who would have had an interest were removed from the country.

144

"To the uninitiated, the castle looked like any of the other burned out buildings in post war Germany. By the time von Braun and company could have returned to Germany, they had their own UFO with the Roswell event. I know von Braun wanted to come back to the castle right after the war, but the American State Department refused. He was a high profile Nazi officer and a member of the SS, and with the Nuremberg trials underway, the politicians didn't want the potential controversy.

"The Roswell event happened prior to the end of the Nuremberg trials so he no longer needed to go to the castle. He had a new UFO to work on," Laflamme said.

"What happened to the castle after the war?" Sean asked.

"It was restored as a tourist site, not an archeological site. It's now a museum, and the south tower was given an exterior cosmetic renovation, but there was never an attempt to excavate below ground level," Laflamme said.

Sean was quiet for a few moments.

"Do you realize the importance of what you just said? You've not only agreed with our premise, but expanded our hypothesis to include bomb-proof walls and a bomb-proof ceiling. What you've described is an underground building, possibly in the same condition it was in 1945," Sean said.

This time the other end of the phone was silent.

"I think you could be right. The castle was never a focus and I don't remember ever having a discussion about it. I don't know why, but when you state it as you have, it seems important.

"I think anyone examining Wewelsburg Castle would have felt it was totally destroyed. Until you pointed out Himmler's reconstruction was built to withstand Allied bombs, I never considered the possibility of whatever was down there is still there. The only individuals who would have known of the contents were the scientists who were extracted, and they couldn't return. Himmler and other high ranking SS officers were either dead or on the run," Laflamme said.

"This only gets better and better," Sean said.

"This is your smoking gun. The Vatican has been trying to cut off any investigation by killing anyone investigating the UFO crash. Any successful investigation would lead Wewelsburg Castle and where you are today. If you were to discover an alien UFO and possibly alien bodies in a preserved lab, the Vatican would crumble and the world would become a different place. I think you've just found your motive," Laflamme said.

"How can you help?" Sean asked.

"I'll contact our person in Rome. We need to see what is going on inside the Vatican. This whole operation would fall under the control of the Black Pope. The Black Pope is the equivalent of the Secretary of Defense, the head of the FBI and CIA all rolled up into one person. He has many groups at his disposal. Among them is the Military Order of Malta. Within the SMOM, as it is known, is the 'Customer Relations Group,' which Hollywood would call black operations. This is the group that handles all the wet work for the Black Pope. We have deep cover in SMOM, but not in the 'Customer Relations Group.' I will see what I can find out," Laflamme said.

"What would you suggest as our next step?" Sean asked.

"Have you spoken with Rudolf?"

"No, he's my next call."

"Tell him what we've discussed. He may have some ideas about the castle. Let him know I've contacted Rome and will update him when I get a response," Laflamme said.

"I'll do so right now," Sean said.

"Very good. I'll be in touch," Laflamme said.

Sean next dialed Rudolf Weiler and was updating him within moments. When Sean told him Laflamme was contacting Rome, he interrupted.

"He told you he was contacting our man in deep cover in the SMOM? He's being very open with you, *Herr* O'Shea," Rudolf said.

"Laflamme thought you may have ideas about the castle."

"The castle is near and dear to my heart. I'm a student of Deutsch history and have tried to make sense of what happened in my homeland. I studied old German castles when I was at university, and Heidelberg and Wewelsburg are my favorites. The irony was, Heidelberg became the site of the Allied headquarters and Himmler was setting up Wewelsburg to be his version of the Center Of The World. I know people with a connection to the castle, let me make some calls," he said.

"I'm most interested in any architectural drawings and any contractors who worked on the restoration," Sean said.

"I'll see what I can find out," Rudolf said and hung up.

Sean thought these guys didn't waste any time on saying goodbye. He called Alan, and they agreed to meet for breakfast in ten minutes.

Sean told Alan of his discussions with Laflamme and Rudolf, and Alan agreed it was likely they discovered the motivation driving the Vatican actions. After breakfast they left for the police station to update Gola and Max. Five minutes later they entered the station.

***

Fifty yards away, the man with bad skin sat in his car and watched the Freiburg Police Station. He positioned his car in an inconspicuous spot, partially blocked by a grouping of large white pines. He was semi-obscured, yet he could still observe the comings and goings through the station's front door.

"He reached into a wrinkled, grease spot-stained brown paper bag and pulled out a piece of a foul smelling lukewarm white cheese. It was a cheese meant to be firm and cool, yet this was warm and soft. He also pulled out some sort of warm blood sausage in wrinkled casing and proceeded to eat his breakfast, washing it down with a large strong coffee he purchased from the petrol station. He seemed oblivious to the disgusting nature of what he was putting down his gullet, licked his fingers, wiped his now greasy hands on his shirt and continued to eat.

He observed an Audi with rental license plates pull in front of the police station. Two men got out, one taller with white hair and a white mustache and the other six inches shorter, balding and stocky. Both appeared to be in their late forties. He watched as they entered through the front door and wondered if they could be among his prey. He continued to eat his disgusting decaying combination.

***

Sean walked in and was greeted by the woman at the front desk like he was an old friend. He guessed any friend of the chief was a friend of hers. She motioned for Sean and Alan to come in and didn't bother to announce them. They ambled back to Gola's office and entered without knocking.

"*Guten Morgen.* How did you boys sleep?" Gola asked.

"I can't speak for Alan, but I couldn't get my mind to slow down. I

147

tossed and turned for the longest time," Sean said.

"Same with me. I think we're all afflicted with the same thing," Alan said.

"Having trouble sleeping, eh? I overheard. I think we're all going through the same what ifs and the ramifications of what may take place," Max said.

He turned to Sean.

"We're on for eleven o'clock with *Herr* Schmidt. We need to leave in an hour," Max said.

"Perfect. I want to throw some theories at him and get his reaction," Sean said.

Sean looked out the window and smelled the emerging flowers for the first time in at least a week. It was going to be a beautiful early spring day with the flowers popping up and buds opening.

"I had a couple of fruitful phone calls this morning," Sean said and recounted his conversations with Laflamme and Weiler.

"So the rooms under the south tower could still be intact? That's unbelievable. Now we need the architectural drawings to determine if there's a way into the underground structure. It's all starting to make sense," Max said.

Gola gazed out the window and said, "I'm interested in the SMOM and this black operations group. First, they could be dangerous, and second, they can move with impunity because of diplomatic immunity. They'll be unpredictable because, if they think they're doing the Lord's work, they'll be as fanatical as the Muslim terrorists who strap C-4 to their bodies. They're the worst of all opponents because death isn't an issue to them. Max, when you talk with Schmidt, find out a little more about this group."

"We will," Max said.

"I'm about to call the chief in Paderborn. Give me five minutes and I'll know if he can see me tomorrow," Gola said.

They moved to Max's office, and five minutes later Gola rejoined the group. He said, "I'm set for tomorrow. We'll have to leave early; I'm having lunch with Chief Achen at eleven- thirty. I asked him for ideas regarding the architectural drawings and he's going to see what he can find out."

"Do you know what the critics are calling the museum?" Max asked.

"They call it *Naziland,* and it's catching a lot of heat for glorifying Nazi artifacts. Now they're talking about creating a museum for the Gestapo in their old headquarters in Berlin. Who comes up with this stuff?"

"The so-called historians want to set up these museums, but in a way they're showcasing the Nazis. I don't know what they're thinking. In any case, let's leave from here at seven tomorrow morning. Is everyone good with that?" Gola asked.

Everyone nodded agreement.

"I feel like today is going to be a waste. I don't have anything to do or people to speak with," Alan said.

Gola shifted his weight, looked at Alan and said, "Let's take a drive to Baden-Baden. We could check on the health of *Herr* Bauer and see if he recalled anything."

"I'm game if you are," Alan said.

"Okay, when Max leaves we'll go, too," Gola said.

Forty-five minutes later Max stood and announced it was time to go. The four of them walked out of the front door and split up with Max and Sean heading to one car and Alan and Gola going to Gola's replacement cruiser.

***

Across the street the man with bad skin sat up. He saw the four men come down the steps and divide into two cars. He noticed the two men who had arrived earlier were now paired with different men. He now had four people to eliminate. They drove two separate police cruisers, so he guessed the drivers were police officers, but was unsure about the other two. Since the two passengers showed up in a rented Audi, he guessed they were not of law enforcement.

Now he had to make a choice; who would he follow? He picked the police car that turned left and stayed well behind and wondered where it would take him.

Chapter 26)

Forty minutes later he entered the town of Villingen. He continued to follow at a safe distance through winding medieval streets until the cruiser stopped in front of a small bungalow. He pulled over and watched as the two tall men exited the vehicle and walked to the front door. When the door opened they were greeted like old friends, and it was apparent they weren't meeting for the first time. The man with bad skin may have been a miscreant, but he was good at what he did. He waited until they were inside and drove slowly past the house, made note of the street number, and drove around the block to reconnoiter the rear of the house. As he drove, he entered a number into his cell phone and at the other end the gold phone was answered.

"*Hallo?*" the Black Pope said.

"I need a name and information about the person living at 3911 Tennenbronn in Villingen, Germany," the man with bad skin said.

"I will call you right back."

Five minutes later the cell phone in Villingen chirped to life.

"*Hallo?*"

"The man at 3911 Tennenbronn is an ex-priest. His name is Father Schmidt, or should I say ex-Father Schmidt. He was a priest for a long time, but two years ago he quit. I thought his name was familiar, so I checked further. He had been a dissident and came to the conclusion the priesthood was no longer a noble calling and made a lot of noise before he left.

"I don't know what he may know, and I'm not sure why they would have an interest in talking with him. As soon as they leave I want you to do an in-depth interrogation which you know how to do so well. I think we need to find out what they spoke about. Then eliminate him."

"Understood."

***

"*Herr* Schmidt, it's so nice to see you again and so soon," Sean said.

"The pleasure is all mine," Schmidt said, and they entered Schmidt's home.

"To what do I owe the honor of this visit?" Schmidt asked.

"We have theories coming together, and we want to see if they resonate with you," Sean said.

"By all means, but first, what can I get you to drink?" Schmidt asked.

They both accepted coffee and settled into the comfortable living room chairs.

"I'll get right to the point," Sean said. "The last time we were here we spoke about the UFO crashes and that the crafts and bodies were taken to Wewelsburg Castle, where von Braun and company worked to reverse engineer the alien technology.

"We've taken that theory a step further. Himmler had a full reconstruction done on the castle, and it included a laboratory and bomb-proof bunker built below the south tower. This is the area where von Braun would have conducted his work. These rooms were built to withstand Allied bombing and act as the ultimate bomb shelter. Himmler was in Berlin when he realized all was lost. He gave orders to destroy the castle. The demolition wasn't a complete success due to a lack of explosives and gasoline. The south tower was blown up and the entire castle set on fire, but it wasn't totally destroyed.

"What no one realized was the underground laboratory was built to withstand this type of destruction. The castle was covered with rubble, and when it was restored into the present museum, the focus was on the north tower and main level, with the south tower receiving only a superficial face lift. The restoration didn't include access to the laboratory, because its existence had been kept secret. It is doubtful those in charge ever knew there was anything underground, given the thickness of the floors.

"It's our belief the alien craft and bodies could still be in that lab. If we're correct, it establishes the Vatican's motive for eliminating anyone investigating the UFO crashes. Once an investigator figured out the Wewelsburg connection, the risk to the church increased significantly. If the contents were discovered, the Alien Theory could become known and the church as we know it would change forever. We have motive and we have the perpetrator. That's it in a nutshell; what do you think?" Sean asked.

"I think you lads have nailed it. We kind of talked in circles around these ideas when you were here last, but now I understand why the Vatican would see fit to start killing people. The existence of this sort of evidence would create urgency from the church. They run the risk of ruin if evidence of the UFO crashes was discovered," Schmidt said.

Max took a long sip of coffee and said, "Thank you, *Herr* Schmidt. We wanted to do a sanity check to see if you agreed with our premise."

"*Herr* Rockenbach, I agree. This will fall under the auspices of the Black Pope. I told you last time about the Military Order of Malta, and they're under control of the Black Pope. He's like a Mafia Godfather. It's interesting to note, the Black Pope has always been an Italian, just like the Mafia. I guess you could call it coincidence, but the way they go about their business is similar. Over the years the relationship between the Mafia and the Vatican has been cozy. I just find it so curious," Schmidt said.

"We were hoping we may gain some insight into the SMOM," Sean said.

"My insight was a result of conversations with Father Battalini. He was the one who told me of the Alien Theory and the protocols and has always been the source of my knowledge." Schmidt said,

"I know we asked last time, but do you think he would ever talk to us?" Sean asked.

"No, I don't think so. He's in charge of a group within SMOM, and I gather it's an important position. He's never told me what he does and I haven't asked. I trust him with my life, and he feels the same. You have to remember, we've been best friends since childhood. He's like my brother, and our conversations have been heart to heart. He's related his growing concerns and doubts about the church, and he feels the same about the hypocrisy as I do. Most of my feelings have come from what he's told me, but those discussions are kind of like conversations with a priest or attorney; they're for no one else's ears.

"I only told you because of the subject matter of your investigation and the fact I left the priesthood. I also have a big mouth and like to take shots at the church whenever I can. I did talk with Father Battalini last night and told him of our conversation, and he seemed quite interested. I let him know that I liked you both and that it was nice to speak to a human being face to face," he said.

Sean and Max exchanged a quick glance.

"Can you think of anyone else we can speak with or anything we've missed?" Sean asked.

"I think I've told you everything I can think of. I'll let you know if anything else comes to mind," Schmidt said.

They talked for another forty minutes before Max brought the discussion to an end.

"One more thing," Max said. "I told you about the assassination attempt on *Herr* Bauer. You need to be aware of anything unusual. The perpetrator was driving an old Volvo covered with oxidized paint. The car appears to be red or maroon, but the oxidation is so bad it's difficult to tell the real color. If you see a car fitting the description, dial the emergency number of one one two, go to the nearest police station, and call me," Max said.

"I will, but why do you think they'd connect me to your investigation?" Schmidt said.

"They seem to be a couple steps ahead of us. We don't know how, but they're active, and they're dangerous," Max said.

"Okay, you have me concerned. I'll keep my eyes open," Schmidt said.

Sean stood and offered his hand.

"You've been most helpful again. We wanted your opinion, and you've reinforced the conviction we're on the right track," Sean said.

"I think your theories are creative and have merit," Schmidt said, taking Sean's hand.

They said their goodbyes and moved down the short path. Once in the car, they buckled up and Max started the cruiser.

"Well, we corroborated our theory, and he feels we're on the right path," Max said.

"It's encouraging," Sean said.

Herr Schmidt gave them a final wave as Max pulled the car into the street and started looking for a place to turn around. He didn't find one before he got to the intersection, so he turned right to go around the block. They passed several parked cars along the curb, got to the next intersection, and turned right again, now heading in their desired direction.

"Something is bothering me and I can't tell you what. Did you notice anything?" Max asked.

"I didn't. What are you thinking?" Sean asked.

"I don't know, but I'm getting an uneasy feeling."

"Turn around and let's see if anything looks odd," Sean said.

Max was able to do a u turn since this road was wider than Schmidt's street. They retraced their short route, and as they turned left on the side

153

street they saw it at the same time. Sitting tucked between two cars, with a hedge of evergreens as a backdrop, was an old Volvo with oxidized reddish paint.

"I think our man is here," Max said.

"He must have followed us," Sean said.

Max pulled the cruiser to the curb, and they bolted from the car. Crouching with guns drawn, they moved to the back of Schmidt's house. Max motioned for Sean to stop and put his fingers to his lips. Max hunched low and moved past a large picture window. He rose just enough to peer through the window, but the glare eliminated visibility. Motioning for his partner to stay put, he disappeared around the side of the house. Sean felt helpless, decided not to wait and moved to the other side of the house. Schmidt's bedroom was on his side, and the window was half open. He stopped, listened, and could hear a voice.

"Who were they and what did they want?"

The sound was coming from the same room Sean had been in only minutes before.

"*Who the hell are you?*" Schmidt asked.

He had strength in his voice and no hint of fear.

"This is not going to end well for you, *Herr* Schmidt. You can determine how painful you choose to make it. I need certain information and, make no mistake, *I will* get it. It just depends how hard you'll make me work for it. The harder I have to work, the more painful it will be for you. Now I ask you again, who were they?"

The next reply was less certain. Gone was the initial bravado, replaced with a slight quiver in Schmidt's voice.

"They were police from Freiburg," *Herr* Schmidt said.

"Were they both police?"

"I don't know. I know at least one was."

"What was his name?

"His name was Inspector Rockenbach."

"Who was the other guy?

"His name was Sean something or other. What's this about?" Schmidt said.

Schmidt's question was ignored.

"What did they want?"

Sean waited and wondered what Max was doing. He slowly moved to the front of the house and peered through a smaller side window. He could make out a stocky man in shabby clothes with short blond hair. He could also see Schmidt sitting in the chair he used while hosting Max and Sean. It looked like he was tied to the chair with several wraps of something wide and grey in color. As Sean looked through the window, he saw movement from down the hall. It was Max creeping slowly toward the sitting room.

"Old man, I ask you one more time, then I start to peel some skin. What did they want?" the man with bad skin asked.

"They inquired about a murder some years ago near my old church. It was a gentleman named Gusdorf. I told them I didn't know anything."

"Mr. Gusdorf; ah yes, I remember him. He had the unpleasant fortune to make my acquaintance. So your church was near his final resting place. How convenient. I saw the way you greeted your two guests. It was clear you knew them. Do you expect me to believe they would come to see you if you didn't know anything?"

"I don't know what you're talking about," Schmidt said.

"That's too bad; let me help you remember."

The man with bad skin put his gun, complete with silencer, to Schmidt's knee and pulled the trigger. The retort was muffled, followed by a scream which was not. Schmidt writhed in pain as the stocky man yanked Schmidt's hair straight back and their eyes met.

"Let's try again. Why did they come here?"

"I don't know. They wanted to ask about a theory they had," Schmidt said.

"And what was the theory?"

"That an old UFO wreckage is in the underground laboratory at Wewelsburg Castle."

"Ah, interesting. How much did they know about it?"

Before Schmidt could answer, Max shouted, "Freeze. Move and you're dead," Max said.

Sean entered the front door just as the man with the bad skin put his gun to Schmidt's head.

"I think we have a Mexican standoff," he said.

A smirk corkscrewed from bluish lips as Horst Massier appeared amused.

"I don't think so," Max said and fired. The bullet entered Massier's wrist, disabling the muscles in his right hand. The gun clanged to the floor, but the assassin didn't make a sound as malice flashed in his eyes.

Sean leveled his gun at the wounded man while dialing one- one-two for an ambulance.

"Spin around asshole," Max said, as he slapped handcuffs on both of the wounded man's wrist.

"I'm bleeding you fuck," the wounded man yelled.

"Forgive me, but you mistake me for someone who gives a shit," Max said.

"I'll remember this you prick. We'll meet again."

"Eat shit and die you motherfucker. You'll be meeting Nazi skin heads where you're going and they'll like that sweet mouth of yours," Max said.

"Fuck you pigfucker."

Max turned his attention to Schmidt, who was going into shock as sirens could be heard in the distance. Moments later, large men in white coats streamed through the door. They put Schmidt on a stretcher and rushed him to the rear of the ambulance. His knee was spurting blood, and they concentrated on halting the flow.

A second ambulance came to a halt in front of the Schmidt residence, and more large men in white coats, came through the door. They attended to the bleeding wrist of the assailant under the gaze of Inspector Rockenbach. Max refused to remove the handcuffs, making repairs more difficult, and he also refused to allow a trip to the hospital. Rockenbach was taking his prize to the Freiburg jail.

Within ten minutes the Villingen Police arrived and started questioning everyone. It became evident to Max his prize might not be his after all.

Shortly after the first wave of police arrived, the Villingen Chief of Police, Wilhelm Kreis, appeared. He and Max had a passing acquaintance, and Max greeted him as he stepped into the sitting room.

The Freiburg inspector spent the next five minutes giving an overview of what transpired. He omitted any reference to UFOs or the Alien Theory and gave the reason for the visit as part of the Gusdorf investigation.

When Max attempted to get agreement to take the assailant to Freiburg, he met immediate resistance. Chief Kreis asserted his jurisdictional control and told Max under no circumstances would he relinquish control over a perpetrator who attacked and wounded a citizen in his town. He left Max nowhere to go with his argument, and when Max asked when he could interrogate the suspect, he was greeted with a non-committal answer.

Chief Kreis felt the wounded assailant needed to go to the hospital, and he wasn't accommodating Max's wishes. He appeared miffed his turf had been invaded without a courtesy call. Max recognized this and realized there was nothing he could do and hoped Gola had a better relationship with the chief.

The man with bad skin refused to speak and had no identification. Max knew where the assailant's car was parked, but didn't volunteer the knowledge. He would get the VIN number and see if he could trace the perpetrator's identity. The chief turned to two of his young officers and gave instructions to take the assailant to the local hospital. One would ride with the paramedic and the other would follow in the squad car.

Max turned to the perpetrator, who was staring at Max, and a crooked grin came to his unpleasant mouth. Max was uneasy with the display of arrogance, and it felt as if there was a joke and he wasn't in on it. The prisoner was taken outside to the ambulance, and Max couldn't help but feel something was slipping away.

Sean rejoined Max and they walked out the front door and headed around the block.

"That turned out to be more than we bargained for," Sean said.

"It was, and I didn't like the attitude of the chief. I also find that piece of shit asshole killer to have an interesting attitude. He was smirking the entire time," Max said.

"I have a little surprise for you. While you were talking with your buddy the chief, I was snooping around and managed to find Schmidt's personal address book," Sean said.

Max's head snapped toward Sean. "What did you do with it?" he asked.

"I'm getting good at this stuff. It's in my pocket," Sean said.

Max broke into a big smile.

"You're indeed getting good at this. That could be important," Max said.

"I believe it already is. The first entry I found was the contact information for Edwardo Battalini, complete with his mobile, and direct phone numbers," Sean said.

When they reached the squad car, Max opened the trunk, pulled out a Slim Jim, and walked across the street to the Volvo. Using the tool often used in the act of auto theft, it took all of fifteen seconds to open the Volvo's driver door.

The car stunk of body odor and old food. He checked the glove box and hoped for some identification, but there was none. He felt under the seat and there was nothing but dirty wrappers and the source of some of the nauseating smells. The Volvo stunk like the sickly sweet scent of a full garbage can sitting for days in the hot sun.

He pushed the trunk button and it clicked open. They were shocked when Max lifted the trunk lid. It was a veritable goldmine of automatic weapons, hand guns, and a bag appearing to be marijuana or hashish. In addition, there was food and water bottles. The assailant was prepared for a variety of situations.

"What do we do with this?" Sean said.

"That's a great question. If we take it, we'll have a material effect on an assault and attempted murder case. However, we're also investigating a murder, and in my estimation there's a potential murder weapon in here, wouldn't you agree?" Max asked.

"I would say you're correct in your assessment. It seems we need to impound the car to perform ballistics tests on these weapons," Sean said.

"My, my Sean, aren't you becoming the law enforcement expert?"

"It must be your influence rubbing off," Sean said.

"Okay, we're taking this. The good news is, it'll be easy to hot-wire," Max said.

Max buried his face under the steering column, and within a minute the engine sprung to life.

"Sean, you get to drive this garbage can on wheels. We'll go the speed limit, so just follow me. When we get to the station, I'm going to pull into the back where we have a large over-sized ten car garage. We'll pull both cars into the garage and out of sight," Max said.

"This isn't my idea of a good time. I need a Hazmat suit," Sean said.

"It's one of the advantages of rank. Let's go," Max said.

Sean was disgusted as he got into the stinking vehicle. He squinted, held his breath, and wasn't amused by the smiles coming from his partner.

Chapter 27)

Forty-five minutes later they pulled into the Freiburg police garage.

Max wrote down the VIN number and the license tag registered in Holland. He would now find out the name of the prick who attacked Schmidt.

***

About the time Max and Sean were pulling into the garage, Gola and Alan were on their way back to Freiburg. Their visit to Bauer brought no additional enlightenment, but at least they were able to see him and wish him well. They met his son, who was with the senior Bauer, and they felt some closure.

Gola wondered how Max was doing and called on the police radio. Max was entering the station as he answered the call. He asked Gola to put him on the speaker and proceeded to tell Gola and Alan of their escapades in Villingen.

As he finished the recap, he asked Gola, "What's your impression of Chief Kreis?"

"He's somewhat arrogant and aloof. He has a superiority complex and in the old days would have been the perfect SS candidate. I think that should tell you everything," Gola said.

"It does. I suggested several things, and he did the opposite of everything I asked for," Max said.

"That sounds like him. Don't expect much cooperation. I'm glad you took the car. We may get more from the vehicle than from the perpetrator. We'll see you in twenty minutes," Gola said.

Max next contacted the police in the Amsterdam, gave them the license and VIN number, and asked for the owner's information. Two minutes later he had the name of the assailant.

"The car is registered to a Horst Massier of 324 Sint Annenstraat, apartment three B, Amsterdam, Holland," the Amsterdam Gendarmes said.

"Do you have any idea where that's located?" Max asked.

"Let me check," the officer said. "It's right in the middle of the Red Light district."

"Thank you very much. Can you send through a photo ID so we can verify the suspect in custody?" Max asked.

The response was affirmative. Max hung up and felt good about identifying the perpetrator. He next called the Amsterdam police station closest to the Red Light district and spoke with an inspector responsible for the area. He explained the situation and asked how he could obtain a search warrant for Massier's lair. Max then walked to the Officer on Duty's desk and gave him the notes he'd just taken.

"I need a search warrant for this location as soon as possible. Go ahead and do the paperwork, and let me know how long it will take," Max said.

He returned to his office where Sean was waiting.

"We have a name for this asshole," Max said, "I also have an address in Amsterdam's Red Light district, and we're in the process of getting a search warrant. Are you interested in going to Amsterdam?"

"I am. How long do you think it'll take to get the warrant?" Sean asked.

"Since this is a murder investigation and the assailant is in custody, the warrant will happen fast. I would think by the day after tomorrow.

"Here's what I'm thinking. We're going to the castle tomorrow and will be more than halfway to Amsterdam. Why don't you pack an overnight bag and, if we get the warrant, we'll continue on to Amsterdam when we're done at the castle. It's only three hours from Paderborn, and we can see if Mr. Massier's living quarters shed any light on his employers," Max said.

"I'll plan on it," Sean said.

Gola walked into Max's office.

"You guys just can't stay out of trouble, can you?" Gola said.

"We can't seem to. We just had to catch up to you guys in the action department. We're all building a great track record. Our only two witnesses have been shot and one bad guy is in custody, but not our custody. I think we're making progress. It's a good thing we don't have more witnesses. It would be hazardous to their health," Max said.

Sean laughed out loud.

The phone on Max's desk jumped to life.

Max answered, "Yes, patch him through." Max's eyes met Sean's.

"Hello, Chief Kreis," Max said.

Max was silent with the phone to his ear.

"*HOW COULD THAT HAPPEN?*" Max asked, his face distorted in anger and voice rising.

"*You must be kidding. What kind of police department do you run? This is bullshit and unacceptable,*" Max said.

He listened more.

"Keep me informed," Max said and slammed down the phone. Everyone froze and waited for the news.

"*They're idiots in Villingen.* They took Massier to the hospital, which I told them not to do, and he managed to kill the two officers guarding him, steal their weapons, and he escaped," Max said.

He looked up at Sean.

"Before he left the hospital he found and killed *Herr* Schmidt."

Sean felt an involuntary jerk as if someone punched him in the gut. He liked the irascible Schmidt, and he brought the angel of death to the ex-priest's doorstep. He was stunned and looked into space without seeing. The room was quiet; no one knew what to say. Sean looked at Max, who was resting his face in one hand. It was Gola who spoke.

"We need to stay the course. We'll go to Paderborn tomorrow and continue forward. Massier no longer has his car, but he's armed with the officer's service revolvers. He's also been wounded and will be dangerous. It appears to me he's a professional killer. He killed two police officers in Baden-Baden plus the good Samaritan, and two more officers in Villingen, plus Schmidt," Gola said. "I would say we're all lucky to have survived our encounters with him. I also think this kind of sociopath will want to even the score.

I'm guessing he never fails or he'd be dead." Gola continued, "The logical supposition is that he'll try to take out everyone involved. He's most likely responsible for the murders of a number of people, and he was sent here to stop this investigation. He now knows about the four of us, so make no mistake, he'll be coming to finish the job."

***

Massier was on the move. It was rather simple for him to dispatch the two

161

young officer; the chief made it easy for him. He wondered if it was on purpose and whether the chief had a connection to the Black Pope. He killed both officers before his wrist could be treated, and it now throbbed, but at least it had been cleaned and bandaged by the paramedics.

Armed with the dead officers' service revolvers, he worked his way back to where he left his car, but it was gone. This was a major inconvenience since it contained his weapons, his weed, and his food. He was grateful he left his identification and money in the fleabag motel in Freiburg. Now he needed transportation.

He walked along the road looking for an unlocked inconspicuous car. He found the perfect vehicle, a thirty-year-old Mercedes 300 diesel. He hot-wired it and he was off toward Freiburg in under a minute.

As he drove, he planned his next step. He had eliminated Schmidt and now reconsidered Bauer. Since the old soldier already spoke with the police, they learned whatever he knew. No, it wouldn't be necessary to finish him off. Now, what about the two guys who caused him the problem at Schmidt's? His next step would be to eliminate them, along with the two guys he observed leaving the station this morning. He also needed to steal a cell phone so he could update Rome.

***

Sean picked up his phone.

"I'm calling Laflamme and Weiler to tell them what happened and to see if they have anything for us," Sean said.

They were both surprised how fast events were unfolding. Laflamme hadn't heard from their man in Rome, but Weiler had spoken with the son of Himmler's reconstruction architect. Weiler provided his name and phone number and that he was expecting their call when they arrived at Wewelsburg. When Sean disconnected, he stared at the phone and wondered how these people operated and how they could get this kind of information so fast. He shook his head with appreciation.

He turned back to the group to tell them of the lead for the architectural plans. It occurred to him that what had started as an adventure had dissipated into dread. They would feel far better if they could take Massier out of the picture, but Sean thought about Schmidt and felt awful. He also wondered if he should call Father Battalini to let him know what had hap-

162

pened. He would consider that course in due time.

"We have other news," Sean said. "Weiler has given me the name and phone number of the son of the architect used for the reconstruction. Weiler somehow made contact with him, and he's expecting a call from us when we arrive tomorrow."

"These guys are unbelievable. They seem to be able to do anything," Max said.

"They're impressive," Sean said. "We've been getting together for dinner every night, and I think I need a break. You all should spend the night with your families, we have an early morning coming. After today I need to decompress a bit."

Everyone agreed, and Sean noticed they all looked tired.

Gola cautioned everyone.

"We have a hunter out there. If we're alone, we'll be more vulnerable. Stay diligent," he said.

They agreed to meet at the station at seven the next morning, then went their separate ways. Alan and Sean drove in silence to the hotel and decided to do dinner on their own.

Sean opened the door to his room, walked to the edge of the bed, and fell backwards with his arms spread. He covered his eyes with both arms and withdrew into himself. Despite all the warnings from Wolfe, Laflamme, and Weiler, terrible things happened. He felt like he was watching himself in a movie, except in a movie the actors doesn't get killed. He knew this was no movie. He also knew he was in too deep and could do nothing about it. If he pulled the plug now, he would never be comfortable thinking someone was lurking and waiting to take him out. No, he had to see this through. What should he tell Cat?

He laid still for over an hour and lost track of time as his mind wandered to ex-Father Schmidt. He liked the old guy. He liked his irreverence and that he wasn't afraid to take on the most powerful entity in the world. Sean's role in his death was hard to shake as he continued to lie in a semi-meditative state. He intuitively knew what he was going to do when he started moving, he just wasn't sure how long that would take. After another twenty minutes he was ready.

Chapter 28)

Sean moved with more energy than at any time since finding out about Schmidt. He went to his jacket, which was draped over the desk chair, pulled out Schmidt's black book, and dialed Father Battalini's private cell phone number.

"*Hallo?*" Battalini said.

"Hello, is this Father Battalini?" Sean asked.

"Yes it is. How can I help you?" Battalini asked

"Father Battalini, my name is Sean O'Shea, and I'm afraid I'm the bearer of bad news. Your good friend *Herr* Schmidt has been killed," Sean said, hearing a gasp on the other end of the phone.

"What happened?" Battalini asked.

"We believe he was murdered by an assassin working for the Vatican. It's a complicated story, but I'm happy to share it with you," Sean said.

"I would like that very much."

"I've been investigating two UFO crashes from the 1930s. One was near Freiburg and one in occupied Poland. The Nazis removed the craft and bodies to Wewelsburg Castle. We think the crafts were studied and reverse engineered, which provided the Nazis the large technological lead they enjoyed over the rest of the world.

"As I researched the subject, I discovered four investigators were murdered while doing the same thing I was doing. We uncovered an interview Father Schmidt had given because one of the murder victims was found near his church. He had no knowledge of the murder or the victim, but he had some interesting things to say about the church. He was dealing with a loss of faith and used the word hypocrisy several times.

We were searching for anything that could enlighten us and decided to interview him. He was terrific, and he and I immediately connected. We were at his house twice, each time for over a couple of hours, and several times he mentioned his close relationship with you. He got into a deep discussion about the church and the Alien Theory," Sean said.

"He told you about the Alien Theory?" Battalini asked.

"He talked about it in detail. He also talked about protocols and all

164

the things the church had fabricated and covered up. His exact words were they would do anything to eliminate any perceived threat. I guess he was right," Sean said.

"He also talked about the protocols. Hmmm, he must have felt a strong kinship with you. He had a big mouth and often spouted his anti-church views, but for him to tell you such things meant he trusted you in a short time. That's unusual for him. The fact he told you about me says he trusted you," Battalini said.

"We went back to see him again today and had another great visit. We told him our theories and asked for his thoughts. He felt we were on the right track. We left his house, and as we drove around the block we recognized a parked car belonging to someone wanted in connection with a murder attempt on one of our other witnesses. We ran back to Schmidt's house and observed the assault taking place. The assailant shot *Herr* Schmidt in the knee just as we entered his home. My partner shot the gun out of the perpetrator's hand and he was taken into custody. We wanted to take the assailant back to Freiburg, but were overruled by the chief of police in Villingen. We told him not to take the assailant to the hospital, but the chief ignored us. He put two young officers in charge of guarding this guy and somehow, at the hospital, he killed both officers, then found *Herr* Schmidt and killed him," Sean said.

"Those officers were sacrificed," Battalini said.

"What do you mean by sacrificed?" Sean asked.

"Never mind. What happened then?"

"He escaped and his whereabouts are unknown. We did impound his car and were able to identify him. His name is Horst Massier and he lives in Amsterdam," Sean said.

"What's your next step?" Battalini asked.

"We're going to Wewelsburg Castle tomorrow because we have some theories about what it may contain," Sean said.

"What kind of theories?" Battalini asked.

"Well, the Alien Theory as advanced by Schmidt made us realize whatever was taken to Wewelsburg Castle could still remain in the special laboratory Himmler built under the south tower. We're going there to sniff around," Sean said.

"You're forthcoming, *Herr* O'Shea. Your theories and ideas are original, and your perseverance in the face of an assassin is interesting,"

Battalini said.

"I'm telling you this because of *Herr* Schmidt. I liked him and he was your best friend. I think I owed it to you to be as forthcoming as possible. I'd like to have the kind of relationship with you I was developing with *Herr* Schmidt. I'm writing a book and need a knowledgeable insider with whom I can collaborate on various theories and ideas. I know this is a bad time for you, but I'd like to get your thoughts when you feel the time is appropriate," Sean said.

"*Herr* O'Shea, Father Schmidt was my oldest and dearest friend. He saw something in you, and he told me about your visit and how he liked you. I can offer this; I'll consider the possibilities when I have a chance to digest what has happened. Let me have some alone time and come to grips with this loss. Please call me after you return from the castle and let me know what you've found. We can talk more then," Battalini said.

"Thank you so much, Father. I look forward to speaking with you, and I'll call you upon my return. Again, I offer my sincerest condolences," Sean said.

Father Battalini replaced the hand set and sat back in his chair. He had just lucked into the inner-workings of the very group they were tracking, but at what cost? He had just lost his closest ally and friend. He shared things with Schmidt that he hadn't shared with another human being. Their relationship was irreplaceable.

The man responsible for his death was someone he detested. He loathed the Black Pope and had a major distaste for Massier. Now those feelings had turned into pure hatred. How was he supposed to balance those feelings with the fact the very people threatening the future of his church were treating him as an insider and he would know their every move?

His time in the church had been one of constant questioning, moral testing, and contradiction. Given the events of today those contradictions would never be greater. He was blinded and knew not to make decisions when his emotions were this distressed. In a couple of days he would see this whole situation from a far clearer perspective.

***

Sean felt relieved. After Schmidt's death he knew he was going reach to out to Battalini, but he wasn't sure how it would be accepted. He was satisfied with how the conversation had gone as he replayed it over and over looking for validation he was correct. He did think about the odd comment made by Battalini. What had he meant when he stated the young officers had been sacrificed? It was almost like he knew something. The comment was odd and out of place. He wondered what role Chief Kreis played in this. If the police chief in Poland was in bed with the Vatican, why wouldn't the chief of police in Villingen be there as well? He would bring this to Gola's attention. He was happy he called Battalini.

Chapter 29)

Massier was walking away from a local pub in downtown Freiburg as he pressed numbers into the cell phone he'd just appropriated. What better place to procure a cell phone than in the dim lights of a place where individuals were numbing their senses with each drink. The golden phone gave off its usual ring.

"*Hallo?*" the Black Pope said.

"I had some issues in Villingen. The ex-priest has been eliminated per your instructions. There was a little problem. I had to eliminate two cops and got a hand wound in the process. I've now identified four people involved in this investigation, and at least two are Freiburg cops. When I returned for my car, it was gone, so I have to assume they have it. That's a problem because they'll be able to identify me. What should I do next? Should I take out them out?" Massier asked.

"Yes, but this is getting messy. You've now killed four law enforcement officers in three days, plus two civilians. You are bringing scrutiny to this we do not want. Now you are going after at least two more law enforcement officers and two others, and your body count will rise to at least ten. Why don't you just put up a neon sign advertising what you are doing? Eliminate these four and anyone else they are involved with, then get back to Amsterdam and await further instructions," the Black Pope said.

"I understand and will carry out your orders."

The man holding the gold phone didn't hang up. He pushed down the receiver button and dialed another number.

Chapter 30)

"*Hallo?*" Father Battalini said.

"We have a problem. Massier is creating a mess in Germany. He has killed four law enforcement officers, a bystander, and an ex-priest and is going after at least four more individuals, some of whom are in law enforcement. We may need your team to intervene in Germany. At the very least I want you to eliminate Massier when he returns to Amsterdam. He has become a liability," the Black Pope said.

"Who gave the order to kill the ex-priest?"

"I did. He was talking to the investigators."

"What did he know?"

"It's likely he didn't know anything. I have no reason to think he did. He was a loose end. He was an ex-priest, and he was expendable, so he is gone."

Battalini squeezed the plastic phone so hard his hand turned white. He wanted to reach through the earpiece and rip the throat out of the Black Pope. He hesitated long enough to regain his composure.

"When will you know if we need something done in Germany?"

"Soon. In fact, why don't you send someone to Freiburg and have them ready to go. If there are any more problems, they can eliminate Massier, then it will be up to your team to take out these pests."

There was silence for a moment.

"This is important to get right. I think I'll head over to Freiburg and see first-hand what's happening. I'll be in a better position to react if we're needed," Battalini said.

"Excellent idea. We need to stop this threat. This has become a bigger situation than just eliminating a single snoop as in the past."

"I'll leave tomorrow."

"Very good, keep in touch."

Battalini hung up the receiver. He decided it would be easier to drive to Freiburg given the unique tools of the trade he required. It was an eight to ten hour trip to Freiburg, and he knew O'Shea's team was headed to Wewelsburg Castle in the morning. The drive would give him a chance to think. His life had been dedicated to the church and its survival. A lifetime of work was hard to shake. He didn't know how he felt as he was more conflicted than ever. He would leave first thing in the morning.

Chapter 31)

Massier sat on the bed in his low rent motel eating the blood sausage and head cheese he'd just stolen from a nearby deli. He'd returned to his room without incident, and his money and identification were tucked safely under the filthy mattress. He took off his stained shirt and threw it into the waste basket. He didn't mind stained or even dirty shirts, but blood on a shirt brought unwanted attention.

It had been a strenuous day for Massier as his wrist continued to pulsate. He longed for his weed, which would have helped ease the pain, and decided to see where he could make a buy. He didn't like taking the risk, but since his stash was gone he had no choice. He hoped his hand and wrist would feel better in the morning but he knew better. His plan was to kill the four targeted individuals as quickly as possible and be back in Holland by evening. In Amsterdam he could get medical treatment from people discreet enough keep their mouths shut. He put on one of his other stained shirts, sans dried blood, and left as the blistered wooden door banged behind him.

His first stop was the front desk to ask where certain herbs could be obtained. The sleazy, neck tattooed guy behind the desk was as far as Massier needed to go. He bought a five day supply of hash and papers so he had everything he would need. He re-opened the warped, faded door to his room and in mere moments took a deep harsh drag on his hand- rolled joint. By the time his smoke was reduced to a roach, his hand was feeling better, or at least his brain had gone numb. He lay on top of the thread-bare bedspread oblivious to what an ultra violet light would reveal. Truth be told, even if he had known, he couldn't have cared less. He didn't move the rest of the night.

Chapter 32)

The wake-up call clanged to life and Sean didn't reach consciousness until the third ring. He laid on his back taking deep breaths trying to meditate, but realized it was a losing battle. After about two minutes he gave up, thirty minutes later stood in the lobby as the elevator doors opened and Alan walked out.

"Good morning, Sean. How did you sleep after our over- stimulating day?" Alan asked.

"I slept better than expected, considering yesterday's events. How about you?"

"I slept all right. What'd you do for dinner?" Alan asked.

"I walked down to a Chinese restaurant, and it was pretty good. I knew we'd be hungry this morning, so I stopped on the way back and picked up some snacks for the ride," Sean said.

"I was wondering what we'd do this morning," Alan said.

Sean reached in, grabbed the Kolache having the largest amount of fruit topping, and threw the bag to Alan. They drove to the station where Max and Gola were waiting, and by seven they were headed to the castle. Alan and Gola drove together while Sean went with Max. On the way Sean told Max of his call to Battalini.

"Calling Battalini was high risk. I wish we would have spoken first. We don't know who he is. You do realize the Vatican is behind these murders, and it's the Vatican that we're about to bring down. To spill your guts to someone you don't know who lives among the bad guys is fraught with danger," Max said.

"I considered your very concerns, but all of Schmidt's issues with the church were a result of discussions with Battalini. I felt a responsibility to make him aware of what happened, but at the same time hoped we could connect with him like we did with Schmidt. I weighed it and my gut told me to call him," Sean said.

"I believe in going with your gut, but I'm concerned about who he may be. Just keep it in mind, but it's too late now," Max said.

They rode in silence while Max's comments sunk in.

Sean shifted toward Max. "Battalini did ask me to call him after we got back from Wewelsburg Castle. Do you think the request was just courtesy, or do you think it's something more?" Sean asked.

"Let's not lose any sleep over it. I was just suggesting you need to be careful whom you confide in," Max said.

"Point well taken. Based on what happens today, we'll talk about what I should say to him."

"That sounds like a plan."

"I'll tell the others about the discussion at lunch," Sean said.

***

It was eight o'clock in the morning, and Battalini finished putting his overnight bag into the back seat of his black Mercedes S 550. One of the perks of Battalini's position was having access to luxury for his every possible need. His name might not be on the title, but he got to use the best of everything. He made sure he had a variety of weapons in the trunk, along with communication devices, navigation, satellite telephone, satellite tracking, and enough trickery to make James Bond envious. He designed this car for a variety of requirements. He had changed from the typical Vatican robe to chinos and a sweater and was as incognito as possible. Battalini started the Mercedes, pulled out of the guarded gates, and began his trip to Freiburg. He would use the long drive to figure out what he would do. The next forty-eight hours would shape the rest of his life and he longed for the counsel of Father Schmidt.

***

Massier arose at seven o'clock. He planned to eliminate the threats today and be on his way back to Amsterdam to get treatment on his still throbbing wrist. He got out of bed and put on his crumpled clothes. He picked up the grease-stained bag containing remnants of the head cheese and blood sausage he purloined the previous night, his bag of weed, and left his disgusting home away from home. He started the stolen Mercedes and drove to the surveillance point he had used the previous day and would await the arrival of his prey. There he sat. He would have a long day of sitting.

Chapter 33)

It was mid-morning when they pulled into Wewelsburg Castle. The two Freiberg police cruisers were parked in the visitor lot, and the passengers got out of their respective cars. It felt good to stretch.

"This is an impressive place. I want to let the curator know we're here and we'll be coming back later in the day," Max said.

"Alan, do you want to come with me to have lunch with the chief?" Gola asked.

"Yes, I think we make a good team," Alan said.

"That should work," Sean said. "I'll call the guy Weiler uncovered, and Max and I will pay him a visit."

"Let's give ourselves some leeway and plan on meeting back here at two," Gola said.

They went their separate ways. Sean called the number he'd been given by Weiler, and it was answered on the second ring. Sean introduced himself, and Manfred Lueck extended an invitation to come to his home. Sean accepted, wrote down the directions, and they were on their way. As they drove, Max's phone chirped. It was the Freiburg Police Station verifying the search warrant would be waiting for them in Amsterdam the following day. Things continued to happen fast.

Chapter 34)

The trip to Lueck's had taken less than fifteen minutes as they pulled up to a large old home which reminded Sean of what he thought Bavaria should look like. There was some stone, but the predominant theme was a peaked roof with white stucco and dark wood in straight and angled strips. This home was befitting a family with architectural roots.

They approached the door, and it opened before they got halfway up the steps. Manfred Lueck greeted them like old friends. He was a tall, handsome man with salt and pepper hair, and Sean guessed he was in his sixties. He had a cup of steaming cocoa in his left hand and shook hands with a firm pumping motion with his right hand. They walked into a dark foyer and the walls were covered with stuffed heads of numerous animals. They followed Lueck into a large kitchen featuring large commercial appliances, and it was clear this was a kitchen for a chef or someone who employed a chef.

"Can I get you some cocoa? I just made a large pot, or perhaps coffee or tea?" Manfred said.

Sean observed a large Dutch oven filled with freshly made cocoa with a compelling chocolate aroma. Both Sean and Max accepted the hot chocolate.

"I spoke with Rudolf Weiler, and he mentioned you were interested in my father's drawings of the castle," Manfred said.

Sean gave an affirmative nod and said, "Yes, we're investigating a couple of different things and those drawings would be most helpful."

"*Herr* Weiler is an old friend, and I'm happy to assist. My father was the architect who worked with Himmler's on the castle's restoration. He wasn't a Nazi by choice, but had to join the party to work on the Wewelsburg project. I'm a little sensitive about his membership, and I wanted you to know it was out of necessity," Manfred said.

"There's no need to apologize, *Herr* Lueck. My father was also in the war. All of our fathers were, whether they wanted to or not," Max said.

"Thank you, *Herr* Rockenbach. When *Herr* Weiler called and asked for a favor I was happy to help with anything he might ask. My father has been dead for fifteen years, and I'm happy to give you access to his library and files."

"We most appreciate your generosity," Sean said. He wondered why Weiler hadn't mentioned he had more than a casual relationship with Lueck.

"After *Herr* Weiler called, I checked to see what I could find. I looked in storage and found a whole section dedicated to Wewelsburg Castle. I put those drawings in our working print area and you can peruse at your leisure. If you need any interpretation of the plans, please let me know. I'm also an architect and worked with my father for a number of years. Let me show you to the library," Manfred said.

They followed Lueck down a dark hallway, and at the very end they entered a magnificent, two story room. At the far side was a thirty foot floor-to-ceiling wall of windows, and adjacent to it was a large field stone fireplace.

Every piece of wall space, other than the windows and the fireplace, was covered with shelves and books. A dark brown, ornate wooden ladder provided access to the books on the upper levels and two large mahogany desks along with two drawing tables sat in front of the windows. To the left of the desks was a bank of built-in mahogany file cabinets. It was a beautiful room and a great place to conduct one's business. Lueck moved to one of the large desks where several files were piled on top of each other.

"This is where I think you'll want to start," Manfred said, "and feel free to go through the drawing cabinet. Just let me know if you need anything and I'll keep the cocoa on a low heat so please help yourself."

They thanked Lueck and their eyes met. Sean grinned at Max.

"I think we just hit the mother lode. Let's start here," Sean said.

They started with the top file.

"Check this out. Here's a change order signed by Himmler himself," Max said.

Sean grabbed it. "This is unbelievable," he said. "If there's anything to be found, it should be in this room. Maybe we should look at the drawings first," Sean said.

"You can look for the drawings. I want to read all the change orders, because I think detail about the underground labs will show up on those documents," Max said.

"That sounds perfect. Besides, I can read plans, but you can read German," Sean said.

Max smiled. He pulled out a set of the large blue plans from the bottom of the file and handed them to Sean. He put the plans on one of the drawing tables and began his search. The first few pages had detail on the elevations and restoration of walls.

He flipped to the next page, and this one was the wiring plan. The next was the plumbing. All the drawings were of the main level. He came to the floor plan for the towers and still hadn't found anything below the main floor or any of the hyped SS plan modifications. He guessed this was a restoration plan prior to Himmler's grandiose plan. He checked the first page, and his assumption was verified. At the bottom of the page was the date, October thirteenth, 1932.

Sean folded the drawing set and put it on the floor. He walked to the file cabinet and started looking for more plans but didn't find any.

"Are you having any luck?" Max asked.

"Nothing yet. The plans you handed me were dated 1932. Himmler hadn't added his center of the world detail in those drawings. I can't seem to find anything else. It's almost like someone removed everything dated after 1932. You'd have to think there've been many eyes on these plans, and it would be human nature to take souvenirs. If the 'special' Vatican representative knew about this place, there'd be nothing left, and bodies would be strewn all over the place," Sean said.

Sean was looking around the room, and a light bulb went off.

"Hey, I think I'm looking in the wrong place," he said.

His eyes fell on a large, built-in piece of furniture displaying numerous horizontal drawers. It was what an architect would use for finished drawings. Sean pulled open the first drawer and knew he was right. A large, thick set of plans lay on the pullout. He estimated there were around one hundred of these drawers. Sean believed an architect would be logical, so he guessed the plans would be in alphabetic order. He pulled out the bottom drawer. The name on the plan was William Zenck, Marengo residence, 1982. It appeared to be an active drawing produced by Manfred Lueck. Had Manfred removed his father's work? Sean pulled out the drawer above the Zenck plans. Bingo; Wewelsburg Castle, 1934.

"*I've got it,*" Sean said.

His pulse quickened as he withdrew the rolling plan drawer extending two feet out of the wall. German engineering, he thought somewhat amused. Sean lifted the drawing and was startled by its thickness and weight. He placed the plan on the drafting table and could feel an adrenaline rush as he studied the first page.

Final Draft: Wewelsburg Castle November 1934

Per direction of: Heinrich Himmler

Architect: Wolfgang Lueck.

"This is it, Max. It's the final plan and is signed by Lueck's father and by Himmler himself. This is a museum piece. I'm sure no one has ever looked in the pullouts, or if they did, they found Manfred's work and didn't look any further," Sean said.

Sean opened the first page and could see this plan was far different from the first set he reviewed. He could see references to Death's Head, Himmler's Crypt, and the north tower showed an area called Hall Of The Supreme Leaders and numerous indications where SS and Swastika symbols were to be placed. Sean was struck by the odd triangular shape of the castle. He felt the shape would have had some significance to Himmler, and he kept leafing through the over-sized pages.

Even though these plans were over seventy years old, they had been stored in such a way to maintain their original elasticity, and he could work without fear of them falling apart.

Sean was two thirds of the way through the entire set when he found the plan for the underground laboratory. He turned the page for the upper portion of the south tower, and there it was. The complete layout of Himmler's underground laboratory was on full display.

"*Here it is, Max. Come see this,*" Sean said.

Max jumped up, and Sean could hear him take a deep breath. They were gazing down at what they had hoped to locate, but never dreamed they would find.

The plans showed that the walls and ceiling were eight feet thick. Sean knew this was a foot and a half greater than Hitler's *Fuhrer* Bunker, and the *Fuhrer* Bunker was able to withstand nonstop Allied bombing. This structure never had similar bombardment and received only a half-assed attempt to blow it up. The effort was amateurish at best and only managed to create a pile of rubble lasting several years.

The subsequent reconstruction focused on creating a museum. The north tower received a complete reconstruction, while the south tower received only a cosmetic rebuild. Himmler never publicized anything about the south tower because he didn't want exposure to what was happening underground. He didn't live to know it, but he had succeeded with his goal.

"Max, I'm positive whatever was in the lab is still there. Its existence was known to only a few select Nazis and some scientists. The fact Himmler tried to destroy the castle tells me he didn't have time or capability to remove the contents, so destruction was the only option," Sean said.

"I believe you're correct. Let's find the exterior exits. There have to be a couple," Max said.

They scoured the plans page by page. First electrical, then duct work, and last the foundation. That's where they found the exits. There were three emergency exits with one having a large set of double doors. Sean found a blank piece of paper and noted the exit locations and their exact dimensions. He also documented the entryway from main level of the south tower, but knew it was covered by at least eight feet of concrete, making it next to impossible to access from the inside.

"This is what we were looking for. Let's check the documentation to see if there are any special notes," Max said.

For the next hour they studied the documents. There were many notes from Himmler showing his commitment to create the SS version of Valhalla. It was also evident the labs and the size of the facility were important to him. When finished, Sean folded the last document and closed the file. He replaced the large set of plans to their original resting place, and as they were finishing, Manfred came into the room.

"Can I get you anything?" he asked.

"No thanks, we're just finishing up and replacing everything," Sean said.

"That's not necessary. I'll take care of everything," Manfred said.

"I think we have it all done. We appreciate your hospitality," Sean said.

"Did you find anything helpful?"

"We may have, but we won't know until we look at the grounds. We may be back to ask for your input, but we'll check it out and call you if we need your insight," Sean said.

Manfred continued to be as charming and affable as he was when they arrived. He walked them out and welcomed them back any time.

"He's one friendly guy," Sean said.

"That's an understatement. I can't wait to see the grounds around the buried exits. I know they're not visible, but it'll be interesting to see what we have to do to gain entry," Max said.

"We'll know soon," Sean said.

Chapter 35)

They pulled into the museum parking area, and Max checked the time. It would be an hour before the rest of the team arrived, but his thoughts were focused elsewhere. They moved in double time to the back of the south tower and walked the perimeter of the castle. Some areas were covered by a stone walkway, but most areas were just grass, and on two sides the woods had crept closer to the walls than in the thirties.

Once they finished walking around the castle, they returned to the south tower. Sean examined the paper containing his notes and began calculating the location of the emergency exits. Armed with a tape measure Max carried in his cruiser, it wasn't long before they identified exit locations and used orange cones to mark the spot. Just as they placed the third cone they heard someone behind them. They turned to see the museum security officer approaching with some urgency.

"Can I ask what the two of you are up to?" the security guard asked.

His frumpy body stood as tall as possible while showing a certain authoritarian disdain.

"Good afternoon. I'm Inspector Rockenbach from Freiburg. We're investigating a murder, and it has led us here," Max said.

He handed his identification to the security officer. The security officer looked at it and handed it back to Max.

"Well, this isn't Freiburg, is it? Inspector Rockenbach, I'm afraid I cannot let you continue whatever it is you are doing."

Max gave him a knowing smile.

"I think you should call your curator. You'll find he's an old friend, and I'm sure he'll authorize whatever it is we are doing," Max said, showing unmistakable sarcasm.

The security officer's shoulders slumped an imperceptible amount and seemed to accept defeat. He pulled the two way radio from his belt and called for the curator. A moment later he was explaining about unauthorized personnel doing something, but he didn't know what. The curator told him he would be down in a moment. A smug look returned to the security officer's face as he was about to be bolstered by reinforcements.

"You will have to take those markers and leave the property. If you want to conduct an investigation, you will need to apply in writing and ask for permission. Permission is rarely granted," the security officer said.

Sean thought he just met the German version of Barney Fife. He heard footsteps approaching on the gravel, and the curator appeared around the corner of the tower. The security man straightened and started to say something. He wasn't able to. The curator walked right by him without acknowledgement and offered his hand to Sean.

"Claus, meet my friend, Sean O'Shea," Max said.

"Good to meet you Sean. Max filled me in earlier," the curator said.

The security man cleared his throat and attempted to explain the trespassing he interrupted in progress, but Claus Reihaus raised his hand.

"Officer, you can go now," Claus said.

"But, but,"

"I said you can go Officer Gerd, so please be gone," Claus said.

The security man's shoulders slumped as what little authority he tried to assert had just been crushed. He turned without another word and shuffled off looking at his feet.

"So what do we have here?" Claus asked.

"We had the good fortune to get our hands on the original architectural plans. When we reviewed the plans, we found the evidence that Himmler built a secret lab under the south tower. He had it constructed with eight foot thick walls and reinforced re-bar and built the ceiling same way. We believe he conducted secret experiments with a re-engineering program and whatever was there at war's end is likely still there. The plans identified three exterior emergency exits, and we were mapping where they were located," Sean said.

"Max, you said this was somehow connected to a murder investigation?" Claus asked.

"Yes, we know it's connected to two murders and we think to two others," Max said.

"Max, you and I have known each other for a long time, and I'm indebted to you. If this was anyone else I would require the court directive, but this will get you and me even. You can count on my assistance, and you won't have any more issues with Officer Gerd. I'll keep him off your back. The murder investigation is all the justification I need to give my consent to assist in any way possible," Claus said.

"That's most appreciated," Max said.

"So tell me again about this underground facility. We have a blueprint on display in our lobby, and it doesn't show anything under this tower. It also doesn't show the concentration camp that was located on these grounds, so I understand the art of omission," Claus said.

"Since we just viewed the final plans, could we see what you have on display?" Max asked.

"Let's go. Follow me," Claus said.

The plans on display were yellowed, brittle and an earlier iteration of the drawings they viewed at Manfred Luecks. The date at the bottom reflected June, 1933 and was signed by Wolfgang Lueck. Himmler's name did not appear on the plan. The laboratory was not included in the drawing, but Himmler's vault and plans for other Nazi and SS symbolism were shown.

"I know Himmler attempted to destroy the castle and the south tower was blown up, but can you show us what it looks like today?" Sean asked.

"Of course, let's start at the south tower. This area of the castle had the rubble removed and a surface restoration performed. The south tower was rebuilt only to the extent to give the impression the castle was complete. It wasn't rebuilt to its original specifications, and there's no access to anything below. We never knew there was anything under the floor, and the tower remains locked at all times," Claus said.

They walked to the tower door and Claus unlocked it. They entered and saw the south tower was empty, and there was nothing to indicate there was ever an entrance to rooms below.

"When the rubble was cleared, there was extensive surface damage to the floor. When the restoration was conducted the entire castle floor was covered with six inches of new concrete. If the floor is as you said, eight feet thick with reinforced rebar, we'll never get through it without damaging the entire tower. That isn't something I'm prepared to do," Claus said.

"That's not something we're asking for, and it's precisely why we were investigating our options with the emergency exits. Let's go back outside. We hadn't gotten a chance to see if there were any indications of the entrances when the security guy showed up," Sean said.

They went back to the cones and examined the ground around the markers. There was nothing to indicate anything existed below the surface.

"How sure are you fellows about the location of the emergency exits?" Claus asked.

"I measured using the legend at the bottom of the final blueprints and also verified the distance from the corner of the building. I'm confident in my measurements," Sean said.

"Claus, you said you were willing to help. Would you allow us to excavate and find the exits?" Max asked.

Claus looked at him and hesitated.

"If you give me an official request tied to your murder investigation, I'll approve it, provided you return the landscaping to the way it is today and it doesn't cost the museum a penny. There can be no structural nor visible damage to the museum," Claus said.

"That's all I needed to hear, and yes, we can agree to all your conditions. I think it'll only take a couple of hours to have at least one of the exits uncovered. Do you have a preference of whom we should use to excavate?" Max asked.

"No, just coordinate the timing with me so I know when to expect the work to be done," Claus said.

Sean wanted to look at Max, but was afraid to betray his excitement. They just received the go ahead for everything they could hope for and were one step from uncovering what might be history's most important discovery. Sean looked up and saw Gola and Alan coming toward them.

"Gola and Alan, meet my friend Claus," Max said.

"Nice to meet you," Gola said extending a hand.

"It's nice to meet you Gola," Claus said and turned to Alan, "Alan, It's also nice to meet you," as they shook hands.

"Claus, we must get on the road, but I'll call you as soon as we figure out the logistics," Max said.

"I'll look forward to your call and I'm happy to assist," Claus said.

Max turned to Gola and Alan, "Let's have lunch at Paderschanke Restaurant. We can debrief and hear about your day," he said as they walked toward their cars.

"What just happened?" Gola asked.

"Sean and I found the original castle drawings and discovered the laboratory actually exists. We mapped the exterior exits and returned to the castle. I told Claus we were investigating a murder and he's agreed to let us excavate. We got everything we could hope for and I wanted to get us out of there so we didn't get into more discussion," Max said.

"How did you get him to agree so easily?" Gola asked.

"Claus owes me and I'm cashing in the chit. It was a personal situation from years ago and you probably don't want to know about it," Max said.

"What you two have accomplished is remarkable. We had no luck with the chief. He wasn't as helpful as I hoped, but it doesn't matter now," Gola said. "What do we do next?"

"Sean and I are heading to Amsterdam as soon as we finish lunch. The search warrant has been issued, so we'll see what we can find about this scumbag Massier. Why don't you coordinate the excavation and see how soon we can get it done," Max said.

"This project has a bi-polar personality. One day euphoria and the next the lowest of the lows, and the next excitement again." Sean said, "Let try to stay on the higher end of the scale."

"We have to remember there's a psychopath on the loose in Freiburg. Today's been a great diversion, and we haven't had to worry about protecting our back side, but it's time to switch on the radar. Sean and I will be back in Freiburg tomorrow night," Max said. "In the meantime keep your eyes open."

Chapter 36)

Sean gave a quick wave as he and Max went east and the other car went south. They were soon on A-44 and in three hours would arrive in Amsterdam. Sean suggested he make hotel reservations and proposed the Hotel Sint Nicolaas. He stayed there in the past and knew its location would be convenient since it was near the Red Light district and the Central Train Station. Sean made reservations for two rooms, and they were set for late arrival.

Max then called the Amsterdam police station and requested the search warrant be delivered to their hotel. Max wasn't sure if the Amsterdam Police would insist on accompanying them in the morning.

He was now semi-paranoid about who knew what and if they could be connected to the Vatican. Learning the police chief in Poland and guessing the police chief in Villingen had a direct line to the Vatican indicated a pattern he didn't like. He was beginning to think the Vatican targeted the law enforcement community as a way of always knowing what threats might arise, then eliminate those threats with impunity. In the future he would be careful about what he would share with fellow law enforcement brothers in other cities.

***

It had been a long boring day for Massier. He started the day with the anticipation of the hunt and now, after sitting for ten hours, had seen nothing. He was the duck hunter sitting in the blind after the ducks had gone south for the winter. He couldn't understand why not a single one of these guys had come to the station. He was tired, ornery, and hungry. He went looking for something to eat. He was done for the day.

***

Father Battalini pulled into the parking lot of Hotel Oberkirch in Freiburg. He had driven all day and still hadn't decided how he would play this. He thought the drive would bring clarity, but he was just as uncertain as he had been when he departed Rome. He would check in and take a walk. Somewhere he would find a restaurant and hoped some red wine would help his thinking.

***

Sean and Max motored into Amsterdam. It had been a pleasant drive with pretty countryside and the occasional windmill. They checked into the hotel, and the search warrant was waiting. After getting situated they decided to walk through the Red Light district prior to searching for a restaurant for dinner. They were anxious to see where Massier called home and soon they were walking through one of the most unmistakable places on earth. They walked along the canals, their shoes clattering on the cobblestone walkway, taking in the amazing sights of coffeehouses selling marijuana while the local gendarmes stood around looking relaxed and uninterested.

It also was incredible to see the little eight by twelve foot rooms where the local talent showed off their wares. When the lady of the night was standing in full view she was open for business. When the curtain was closed, she was otherwise occupied.

"What would it be like to live in this environment?" Max asked.

"That's the million dollar question. The last time I was here I saw nuns leading church tours walking these sidewalks. It seemed like such an oddity of opposites. There were also little kids strolling along with their parents, carrying their school books and walking up steps fronted by picture windows with women dressed only in negligees. What goes on in the mind of a six-year-old when they grow up like that?

"Wouldn't it be something if years from now, they did a study and found those kids were among the most well-adjusted and productive? Our decisions and attitudes are shaped using a moral compass designed by people with ulterior motives and their own hang ups. What would people be like if they grew up without dealing with age-old morals and mores? This might be the Petri dish," Sean said.

"I agree," Max said.

They stopped in front of Massier's building, looked up at the third floor and saw the windows were dark. They resisted the temptation to go up the stairs.

"Do you think the apartment will stink as bad as his car?" Max asked.

"If I was a betting man, and I am, I would say it might be worse," Sean said. "It's been closed up for several days with no air flow. We might need gas masks."

"Thanks for building my enthusiasm," Max said.

They continued through the district, and on the other side found a decent looking restaurant. The menu was Dutch and featured a number of casseroles. This wasn't gourmet fare, but it was comfort food.

With dinner finished, Sean and Max made their way back through the Red Light district to their hotel and agreed to meet at seven-thirty for breakfast.

Sean semi-collapsed onto his bed. It had been a long few days, and it didn't appear things would slow down anytime soon. Sean first called Cat to check in, then put a call into Rudolf Weiler. He updated Rudolf and thanked him for setting up the introduction with Manfred Lueck.

"I have to say Lueck's blueprints provided the tool to figure out how we move forward and the curator put us over the top. We're scheduling the excavation, and within a few days we should know what we have," Sean said.

"You're making headway and accomplishing quite a lot in a short time," Rudolf said.

"We feel we're on a fast track. Have you had any luck with your inside man in the Vatican?" Sean asked.

"We haven't been able to make contact. I'll continue to try," Rudolf said.

Sean filled Rudolf in on the murder of *Herr* Schmidt and the attempted murder of *Herr* Bauer.

"You're on their target list for sure. I think you must expect something dramatic. Please let me know when the excavation will take place. I'd like to observe from a distance," Rudolf said.

Sean felt some comfort with Rudolf wanting to come to the excavation.

"I'll let you know as soon as we set the day and time," Sean said.

"I've been thinking of coming to Freiburg, and with what has happened, my decision is easy. I'll drive to Freiburg tomorrow. I think I need to get closer to you, because I think, how you say, the shit is about to hit

188

the fan. I'll get a room at your hotel," Weiler said.

Sean provided his room number and thanked Rudolf.

The next morning started with sunshine for a change, and at seven-thirty Sean walked into the breakfast room. Max was already waiting. Sean ordered a strong coffee and helped himself to another odd buffet, continuing his distaste for European style breakfasts. He had Irish oatmeal and a banger sausage even though he wasn't a fan of the odd tubes of European mystery meat.

"I called the Amsterdam Police, and they said we can do the search by ourselves. I think the deciding factor was the residence is unoccupied. We're to notify any uniformed officer and have him accompany us to gain access," Max said.

"Good. We can get this done and get back to Freiburg earlier. I spoke to Rudolf, and he's planning to come to Freiburg. I think he feels the need to baby sit us a little," Sean said.

They finished breakfast and checked out of the hotel. Max drove the short distance to Massier's and found a parking spot. It wasn't hard to find a police officer. For a place famous for its lack of crime, there were plenty of law enforcement milling around.

Max approached the first Amsterdam policeman he encountered, explained what he doing, and handed him the search warrant. The officer was happy to find something to do resembling police work and accompanied them to Massier's building.

Upon entering the building Sean felt an itching sensation in his nostrils as they meandered the dark worn passageway. The scent was musty with an undercurrent of mold and cannabis, and Sean's sinuses screamed get me *outta* here. The steps were threadbare, and Sean surmised they hadn't had a cleaning since the war ended. The war he was thinking of was World War Two. The second floor looked older than the first, and the third floor looked even older than the second. The floor squeaked and groaned with every step, and the third floor hallway was in dire need of a cleaning and fresh coat of paint.

A wine analogy popped into Sean's head. The bouquet had remnants of piss with a hint of vomit and a nasty finish.

They moved to apartment 3-B and their new Amsterdam Police friend took the lead and knocked on the door. There was no answer, and he knocked again while announcing they were the police and had a search warrant. Again no answer. They did what was necessary to satisfy legal requirements, and Max began to fumble with a large jumble of keys. He had skeleton keys for just about every type of lock, and was confident one of them would work. On the fifth try the lock clicked and they were in. Max pushed the door open and reached around the wall, anticipating the location of the light switch. He found it and flicked it on before entering Massier's lair.

The apartment was warm, smelled like dirty socks, and had the sweet sickly odor of old garbage similar to that of Massier's car. Sean expected it to be rank and wasn't disappointed.

They moved through the spartan apartment looking for anything useful. There was a half-eaten piece of toast on the kitchen counter and some sort of colored liquid in a glass. Max started bagging a few things to get fingerprint verification.

"Look for any papers and anything with writing. You never know what we might find," Max said.

"Maybe this guy had a strategy to be so gross and repugnant no one would touch his stuff so they'll never discover anything about him. This fucker is a board certified slime bag," Sean said.

"That theory only works if he thought he might be discovered. My guess is he's arrogant enough to think this day would never come. Hey, Sean, can you search the shower and toilet area?" Max asked.

"No, I think I should leave that for the professional. I wouldn't want to contaminate a crime scene," Sean said.

Even the Amsterdam cop laughed out loud at that. Sean looked in the closet and was disgusted to find even the hanging clothes were dirty, stained, and smelled of body odor.

"This guy must wear his clothes and just keep hanging them up without ever introducing them to a washing machine," Sean said.

"Did you notice next to the bathroom there's a hook-up for a washer and dryer, but there is none," Max said.

"Why doesn't that surprise me?" Sean said.

"Sean, check the freezer and refrigerator," Max said.

"You must be kidding?"

"No, it's a favored hiding place among many low lives and this guy certainly qualifies," Max said.

Sean went to the refrigerator. He opened it and was hit with the smell of bad milk. It was bare except for the milk, a few beer cans, and some old meat.

"Nothing in the refrigerator." He opened the door to the freezer.

"Max, you better come here," he said.

Max came into the kitchen and peered into the freezer.

"I told you," Max said.

Reaching into the freezer, he removed a half dozen frozen clips and an equal number of passports.

"For someone so sloppy, he's been careful to create many identities. This one's interesting. It's a passport from the Vatican. If he was using this one, he would be covered by diplomatic immunity and we couldn't arrest him no matter what he might do," Max said.

"Remember, that was one of the things Schmidt talked about," Sean said.

"You're right. Let's bag these," Max said.

Max picked up the phone. It had no answering machine, but the phone was a newer model which retained the last ten numbers dialed. Max went one by one and wrote down all the numbers. He looked around for any note pads, but didn't find one. They continued to scour the apartment, touching as little as possible. When they finished their search, they thanked the officer and locked the apartment behind them. Once on the street they took well-deserved and much needed deep breaths.

Max called the Freiburg Police Station and asked for Gola.

"Gola, we just left this creeps apartment and it was more disgusting than you can imagine. I did get the last ten numbers he dialed and I'd like to check who he called. Can you get someone to run the numbers?"

"Sure, as soon as we get something, I'll call you."

Chapter 37)

Gola started his day before the sun came up. His absence the previous day meant work would be piled high on his desk and he knew he had to get an early start. By mid-morning he was happy to hear from Max and went to work on Massier's phone calls.

***

Alan chose to sleep in and spent the day catching up with his software business. As the CEO of his company, he had been out of contact for five days and had to make sure the place was still functioning. He was relieved to find out they hadn't missed him.

***

For the second day in a row, Massier sat in the stolen Mercedes across from the police station waiting for someone to show up. For the second day in a row he was disappointed.

He wondered how these guys could vanish into thin air. They'd been so active, and now had completely disappeared. It didn't make any sense.

Patience had never been his long suit, and now his was wearing thin. He had hoped to take out these jokers and be back to his third floor sanctuary last night. Since it was now four in the afternoon he knew it wouldn't happen today. He was angry because he'd been fantasizing about the little red-head on the first floor for the last three days. Fifteen minutes was all he would pay for, but it was also all he would need.

Massier hadn't planned well and didn't bring anything to eat. He'd been sitting all day and was fed up. He could feel his blood sugar dropping, although if asked he wouldn't have known blood sugar from brown sugar and decided he was done for the day. He started the Mercedes and pulled into the street in search of something cheap and filling.

Chapter 38)

The man in the long black robe felt uneasy. His man from Amsterdam hadn't called in two days. The man in charge of black ops, who uncharacteristically went to Freiburg alone, hadn't checked in. He was starting to feel like a eunuch, full of desire and impulse, but powerless to do anything about it.

He knew what he had to do and decided he couldn't wait any longer. The Black Pope walked out of his office and down the hall, entering a different wing and into a small but ornate office. The assistant at the front desk looked up, and the Black Pope walked right by him without acknowledgement and closed the door behind him. The man sitting in the office was Father Gatto, the man in charge of 'security' for Opus Dei.

"Father Gatto, we have an issue that could be our biggest threat since we confiscated most of the Dead Sea Scrolls," the Black Pope said.

"I'm all ears," Father Gatto said.

"The Alien Theory is close to being exposed as a reality. In the past we have been diligent in removing threats, but we are threatened by a group including several law enforcement officials, and we have not been successful at eliminating them. I have a special representative on site, but I fear he has been compromised. Battalini is also on site, but I am not comfortable with this. He never goes into the field, and he has done so without assistance. I haven't heard from him. I need a backup plan which, in short order, may become the primary plan."

"It's interesting the Jesuits come to Opus Dei for assistance. You may be the Black Pope within the Vatican, but we at Opus Dei don't buy into everything you're selling. Why should I help you clean up a mess of your own making?" Father Gatto asked.

"You are not still fighting those old wars are you? When Pope John Paul Two canonized Escriva, I thought you people would fall in line," the Black Pope said.

"You used to claim Escriva was preaching heretical doctrine. I think you were happy when the Da Vinci Code came out and slammed us, and I didn't hear any support from you. Do you know our membership grew as a result while your membership has dropped? I think the next Black Pope will come out of our ranks and you know it," Father Gatto said.

"Never happened and never will, but I did not come in here looking for a debate about our different philosophies of religious conviction. I am requesting your assistance. I have two choices of potential help within the Vatican; Opus Dei or the Dominicans. You are better equipped to offer the sort of help we need. If you refuse, I will deal with this in a different way, but your refusal will not go unnoticed," the Black Pope said.

"What are you asking for? You said you have Battalini on site. He's a good man. Why do you need our help?" Gatto asked.

"I don't know, call it a gut feel. I'm not comfortable with the way this is unfolding, and we can't take a chance of exposure. I want a backup plan to the backup plan," the Black Pope said.

"I ask again. What are the specifics of what you want from us?"

"I want your best man, and I want everyone connected with this investigation eliminated. Is that clear enough for you?"

"Yes, it is. Where is all this taking place?"

"They are all in the Freiburg, Germany area. I also want you to take out our representative."

"*You don't mean Battalini?*"

"No, it is a man named Massier. We have used him a number of times in the past, but he is now expendable."

"Remind me to never get too close to you. You used him on several important assignments, so he was a trusted and successful representative, and now he's expendable. You Jesuits do things different than we do at Opus Dei."

"I don't make those distinctions like you do. I only think of protecting our church."

"We'll help. Can you get me the names of the individuals we need to terminate and their location? We'll start without haste."

"Thank You. I will get you the information. I so much appreciate your support," the Black Pope said, his sarcasm palpable. He wasn't used to having someone challenge his authority. He would take note, but was realistic enough to know there was little he could do about what happened within Opus Dei. Unless, of course, a random accident took place, similar to others that had happened in the past. Precedence was set, after all. The thought brought a rare smile to his face.

Chapter 39)

Battalini spent the day driving around and evaluating the area. He wasn't sure what he was looking for, but he wanted to be close to where things were about to happen. He hadn't checked in with Rome by design and was flying blind. He knew Massier was on the loose, but didn't know what he looked like and he was still determining the role he would take. The threat to the church and his way of life, the way of life he had always protected, was real. So was the fact the Black Pope had sanctioned the murder of his oldest and dearest friend. Battalini remained in turmoil.

***

Max was making good time returning to Freiburg when his phone rang. It was the station.

"Hello, Inspector Rockenbach."

"Max, I ran your numbers and thought you would like the results," Gola said.

"Great. What did you find out?"

"Of the ten numbers you gave me, seven are to local numbers in Amsterdam. Those belong to drug dealers, pizza joints, and what appear to be prostitutes. The other three calls were to an unpublished number with a Vatican area code.

"That's what we needed, thanks Gola," Max said.

Max looked at Sean. "We have our corroboration. Three of the ten numbers I gave Gola were calls to the Vatican. The number is unpublished, but they can determine it was to a Vatican area code. We knew it, but it's always good to get confirmation," Max said.

***

Rudolf Weiler pulled into the parking lot at the Colombi Hotel, was able to get a room across from Sean's and left Sean a message with his room number.

***

Gola finalized plans with the excavation company, then called the curator and the police chief to let them know the timing. Gola and team would arrive at eleven the day after tomorrow and by sometime in the late afternoon would know what they had. The team had no plans for dinner, and he looked forward to a quiet night with his family.

"Alfred, I wanted to give you a call to make sure you're keeping your eyes open. We've scheduled the excavation at the castle in two days and things may heat up," Gola said.

"Is there a dinner scheduled tonight?"

"No. We're taking a break."

"How about tomorrow?"

"There's nothing scheduled, but I'm guessing we will. Max and Sean are on the way back from Amsterdam, so it's likely we all need to debrief what they found."

"Okay. I'd like to come so can you let me know."

"I'll call you and let you know."

Chapter 40)

Father Gatto hadn't disguised his disdain for the Black Pope. He didn't like him or his organization, but had no choice other than to acquiesce. The Black Pope provided the names of two targets with the caveat there were at least two more. Gatto picked up his phone and called the individual he referred to as the cleaner. John Mercurio would do anything Father Gatto requested. Sometimes the requests weren't churchly.

"*Hallo?*" Mercurio said.

"We have a mess to clean up. The Jesuits have created another problem and they've asked us to fix it. How long will it take you to get to Freiburg, Germany?" Gatto asked.

"I can be there tonight. What do you need me to do?"

"The Jesuits, I should say the Black Pope, sent some guy named Massier to Freiburg. His job was to eliminate a group of people getting close to validating a theory that threatens the future existence of the church. For some reason he lost faith in Massier's ability to get the job done, so he came to us. Now he wants us to save his ass and eliminate all these guys, including Massier. The problem is, the Black Pope only gave me two names, but there seems to be several more."

"What do you suggest?" Mercurio asked.

"I believe you'll need to get close to Massier. It's the only way to find out what he knows in a short time. I'll have the Jesuit inform him you're coming to help. Wear regular clothes and don't be identified with Opus Dei. You decide when to eliminate him. I'll also tell you it's critical we terminate the entire threat," Gatto said.

"I understand, and I'll do whatever is necessary," Mercurio said.

Mercurio would do anything for Father Gatto. He was thirty four years old, never married, never had a girlfriend, and never had sex. He ran away when he was eight years old, tiring of beatings administered by his drunken father and drug addicted mother. He stopped being a human punching bag and while living on the streets tried to rob Father Gatto.

Mercurio's attempted larceny on the good father wasn't successful, but it turned out to be the most fateful act of his life. Gatto took him home, and the Opus Dei priest had been kind to him. Unlike certain Catholic priests who might have viewed the runaway as fresh meat, the good father looked out for Mercurio and put him up at the Opus Dei facility. Mercurio was provided a clean bed, three meals a day, wasn't beaten, and after a few weeks he started attending services.

The priests running the facility provided their version of home schooling, but Mercurio didn't prove to be much of a student. The priests found odd jobs for him as a way to offset his room and board, and as he got older he took on more of the jobs no one wanted. Gatto kept tabs on the former delinquent and from time to time would stop in to see him. Mercurio always cherished those brief encounters, because even though he didn't see the father often, he viewed him as his personal savior.

Mercurio curiously watched the fanaticism of the Opus Dei members and viewed their dedication with the hidden amusement of a non-believer. He was amoral, didn't make value judgments, and acted and reacted almost like an animal using its well-honed instincts instead of any logical thought process.

As Mercurio became a young man, Father Gatto would sometimes call on him for distasteful activities. He likened himself to muscle in the Mafia and didn't mind. He had grown to five feet ten inches tall, was of medium weight, and had jet black hair with a Mediterranean look. In any sea port he would fade into the background, because he looked just like everyone else.

He had lived in the same room at Opus Dei since he was eight-years-old, and if pressed, would admit he never wanted nor had a friend other than Gatto. It never occurred to him that this was a negative thing because he thought the Opus Dei fundamentalism was borderline insanity, although those words were not in his vocabulary.

His muscle jobs started when he had to convince certain individuals to conform to the Opus Dei viewpoints and had evolved into eliminating those deemed to be opposed to certain Opus Dei objectives. He never took satisfaction when terminating someone and viewed it as if he was smacking a mosquito about to sting him.

His meals were made for him, his room was cleaned for him, his clothes were provided although he didn't dig the robes, and he was told what jobs to carry out. It never occurred to him to consider what he would do if he had to think for himself.

***

Father Gatto walked into the Black Pope's office much in the same way the Black Pope walked into his. He ignored the assistant sitting in front of the open door and walked to the Black Pope's desk. The Black Pope looked up, but was silent.

Father Gatto didn't hide his disdain. "I made contact with my cleaner. He's leaving within the hour and will be in Freiburg tonight. Without the names you thought you could produce, there's only one course of action. You need to inform your guy he's getting help. My man will need to learn everything Massier knows before he can be eliminated. Do you think you can do that?" he said.

"Yes, I can. I agree this will be the most prudent course of action," the Black Pope said.

"Tell him John Mercurio is coming and get me a time and place they can meet. Also include your man's cell phone number and I'll relay the information," Gatto said. Before the Black Pope could reply, Gatto turned and strode out of the office.

The Black Pope dialed his man from Amsterdam.

"*Hallo?*" Massier said.

"I haven't heard from you in two days. Have you made any progress?" the Black Pope asked.

"No, these guys have disappeared for the last two days. I'll continue staking out the police station. They have to appear sometime," Massier said.

"Do you have their names?"

"No, I know them by sight, so I don't need their names."

"You do now. You have help coming your way."

"*What does that mean? I work alone.*"

"Not anymore. This is the biggest threat the church has ever faced and the bodies are piling up behind you, but not the right ones. Your help will arrive tonight. I need a spot where the two of you can meet in the morning and you can bring him up to speed."

"*What if I refuse?*"

"Horst, you do not want to go there. This is non-negotiable. I have been forced to deal with the arrogance of Father Gatto and he will soon

199

meet with an untimely demise. You do not want to push back on this."

Massier hesitated, and recognized the obvious threat.

"Have him meet me at Cafe Haas. It's a coffee shop and bar. You can provide a description of what I look like. He can find me. I'll be sitting in a Mercedes in front of the coffee shop. Tell him eight o'clock."

"Where did you get the car?"

"I helped myself to it in Villingen. I changed the tags so I should be okay. Where did you find this guy?"

"He's Opus Dei."

"*You must be kidding; those assholes!*"

"Deal with it. He comes with the highest recommendation."

"I don't like this one bit. Have him find me, I'm not going looking for him. I'll be there at eight."

Massier didn't wait for a response as he clicked off. He was upset. He always worked alone. Yes, there were issues with what was happening here, but he didn't like the inference he wasn't capable of getting the job completed. He also understood he didn't have a choice.

The Black Pope walked back to Gatto's office and this time threw a piece of paper on the assistant's desk. "Here is the name and information about our operative. Make sure he gets this," he said.

He turned and left. He was no longer interested in a witty exchange with a man who, if he had his way, would be a short timer in this world.

Chapter 41)

Max and Sean were tiring of their long drive and decided to create a plan of attack. Max called Gola and suggested they meet at Sean's hotel for breakfast the next morning and asked if Gola would coordinate with the team.

Sean turned to Max. "How do we become the predator and not the prey?" Sean asked.

"There's our topic at breakfast. I agree, we can't wait for one of us to be picked off. This guy is a cop killer and I'm a cop, so I have a strong interest in finding him," Max said.

"How do we do that?"

Max thought for a second.

"It sounds old school, but we need to think like he thinks. He may or may not know how many of us are involved, but he knows it includes law enforcement from Freiburg. His first move would be surveillance of the police station. He would be watching who comes in and out, and he'll assume anyone seen with you and I are involved. I'm guessing he hasn't moved on any of us because he needs to determine who's involved and eliminate everyone.

We have to anticipate he'll act in the next day or two, and we need to start looking for him. You and I are known because we've seen him face to face, and he may have also seen Gola and Alan."

"I have an idea. Rudolf Weiler is in Freiburg, and he's the perfect person to look for this guy," Sean said.

"Great idea, he does this sort of thing for a living. When can you get in touch with him?"

"Let's see," Sean said and dialed his number.

"*Hallo?*" Weiler said.

"Rudolf, are you in Freiburg yet?" Sean asked.

"I am and have just checked into your hotel and have the room across the hall from you."

"Great. We've just called a meeting for breakfast tomorrow morning. Can you attend?" Sean asked.

There was a short pause. "I'm not sure I should. I'm working with you, and I don't know if I want the exposure to everyone else," Rudolf said.

"We think it's important you're there. Max and I have been talking about what to do about Massier. We need to find him before he finds us, and we think you're the guy to find him. We'd like to have you there to discuss it," Sean said.

Again there was prolonged silence.

"Okay, I think there are extenuating circumstances to warrant my attendance. What time?" Rudolf asked.

"We'll meet for breakfast at eight. I'll get the private room," Sean said.

"I'll be there," Rudolf said and clicked off.

"Rudolf will join us. He was reluctant at first, but he's agreed to do so," Sean said.

"Good. He may become an important part of our team," Max said.

Chapter 42)

The long drive was over, and Max stopped in front of Sean's hotel. Sean rose out of the car and felt the stiffness from sitting too long. He stretched as his muscles groaned and started to wake up. It took a good thirty seconds to get rid of the numb feeling of being locked up for the last three and a half hours.

Sean entered his room and lay back on his bed. His hands went to his eyes, and he rubbed even though Cat always yelled at him for doing so. He had growing doubts about why he started this project in the first place. It had been fun at first, then frightening, and now it was both exciting and anxiety-ridden.

They were close to uncovering the truth, but his anxiety level was greater than ever in his life. Sean managed to stay out of Viet Nam, but it occurred to him this might be the kind of unrelenting tension the troops would have felt. Calm on the outside, but with his unconscious mind screaming a bullet could be headed for his cranium at any moment.

He couldn't imagine living with the continuous exposed nerves and stress those troops had to endure. No wonder getting stoned was the number one stress reducer.

He decided to have his own stress reliever, called room service and ordered French Onion Soup, Steak Au Poivre, the potato du jour and a bottle of barbera wine.

Sean finished dinner and called Cat. They talked longer than any time since he left Oregon. Cat was asking a number of questions about how things were going and, while he didn't want to lie, he didn't want her to worry. She didn't do well with stress, and if she knew the whole story, she would make his life miserable if he didn't walk from the project. He gave her the high points without discussing the negatives. After thirty minutes he figured they should end the call because he was making Sprint a small fortune. They hung up with a promise to talk the next day.

***

Battalini wanted to get a feel for the area and decided to take a drive. He knew Massier would stake out the police station, so he wanted to check out where he might find the low life tomorrow. He found one obvious location. It had a clear view of the front of the station, but was behind several large pines. It was a good spot to conduct unnoticed surveillance. Battalini would have chosen it for himself and was sure this was where he would find Massier.

***

That night, in Freiburg, Germany, several beds held occupants unable to sleep due to thoughts of assassination and Alien Theories swirling in their agitated minds. There were a number of different agendas at work and others not yet determined.

Between six-thirty and seven, alarm clocks were going off all over Freiburg. It was morning, and many of Freiburg's two hundred and thirty thousand residents started to rise for the day.

Sean went to the entrance of the private dining room and Rudolf was the first to arrive. They shook hands, and Alan appeared a moment later. Sean made the introductions, then everyone seemed to arrive at once. He was surprised to see Alfred.

"Good morning everyone. I suggest we get coffee and discuss the newest developments prior to getting breakfast. Does that make sense?" Sean asked.

"Great idea. I need some caffeine," Max said.

Everyone moved to the coffee bar, and within a few minutes all returned to the table.

Sean introduced Rudolf and the group took turns bringing everyone up to date. Gola announced they were set for the excavation the next day, Max filled them in on their search of Massier's apartment, and Gola passed out photo copies of Massier's driver's license picture.

Sean got around to the main security issue.

"I thought we needed everyone's updates this morning, but we also have an issue we need to discuss. Massier is a stone cold killer and he's on the loose. He's murdered six people and four were in law enforcement. His focus is to kill anyone connected with this investigation, and we're those people.

We'll need to start thinking like Massier, and that's why I asked Rudolf to join us this morning. Massier has identified some or all of us, but he's never seen Rudolf. We need to find him before he does damage to us," Sean said.

Gola nodded in agreement.

"You're right, he's seen you and Max, and it's likely he's seen Alan and me coming in and out of the station. We need to get him now. I think the only reason he hasn't acted is he wants to identify everyone involved, plus we've been out of town. We're all back, we excavate tomorrow, and I would expect something to happen today or tomorrow. *Herr* Weiler, what are you thinking?" Gola said.

"I'll do surveillance today, and if he's watching the station I'll get him. Everyone here is in play, so you all have to watch for anything out of the ordinary. Everyone should be armed and travel in pairs. Does that make sense?"

Nods took place around the table.

"Okay, on that happy note, I think we better get some food before Alfred starts climbing the walls," Sean said.

Alfred looked shocked at his name being used and his brothers smirking. They stood in unison and went to the buffet table. While everyone worked their way through breakfast they asked Rudolf questions about what he intended to do. He avoided answering, and his main advice remained the same.

Breakfast ended and for a moment everyone looked at each other with reticence.

"I have a suggestion. We know the station will be watched today. We have nothing going on, and tomorrow is the big day, so why doesn't everyone stay away today? Max and I will go in like it's any other day, and Rudolf will see if he can shake Massier loose. We have many officers coming and going so he won't know if any of them are involved.

If any of you come to the station, use the back entrance. It's hidden from view and it's unlikely you'd be seen from the park. Tomorrow we'll plan on departing from here at seven. We'll get to the castle by ten thirty and the excavation starts around eleven. I think it's wise for everyone to take a low profile today. Who's planning on going tomorrow?" Gola asked.

They all said they were in, and Gola was surprised Alfred wanted to be included.

"There will be six of us, including Rudolf. Max, you and I will drive. We'll call everyone if there are any developments; otherwise we'll meet at seven tomorrow morning," Gola said.

"Max, did you drive this morning? I left my briefcase in your car yesterday," Sean said.

"No, the car is at the station. Gola picked me up this morning," Max said.

"Okay, I'll come by and pick it up. I'll come through the back. I won't stay long," Sean said.

Everyone stood and exchanged a sort of uneasy interaction. Max, Gola, and Rudolf headed in the direction of the station, Alfred left for his home, and Alan and Sean went to their rooms.

Chapter 43)

Massier parked the stolen Mercedes in front of the coffee shop and checked the time. It was seven fifty-nine, and he was disturbed. On one hand he was offended the Black Pope felt the need to send help. On the other he was upset because his unwanted help would slow him down. He worked alone. He didn't tell anyone what or how he would get a job done; he just did it.

There was a rap on the driver side window, and Massier jumped. He turned his head and saw a man peering in at him. The man had black hair and an oily Mediterranean look. Massier pressed the window button, and it recessed into the door as he looked at the man.

"Are you *Herr* Massier?" Mercurio asked.

"Yes, who are you?" Massier asked.

"I'm John Mercurio. You didn't know I was coming?" Mercurio asked.

"Yes, I'm here, aren't I?" Massier said sarcastically.

"You seem annoyed, *Herr* Massier," Mercurio said.

"I am," Massier said.

Again silence.

"I'm here to help you, not get in your way, *Herr* Massier," Mercurio said. "Can I come into your car and discuss what we are to do?"

"Yes," Massier said.

Mercurio walked around the car and let himself into the passenger side. He decided to take a different tact to get Massier to talk.

"What can you tell me about our targets?" he asked.

This was a harder question to answer with one word.

"Several are cops. This police station has quite a few coppers, so it's been a little difficult to figure out who's involved. I don't know all their names. I called the station and asked for the chief's name. It's Gola Rockenbach. I'm sure he's one of them. I think there are at least four people involved," Massier said.

"What have you been doing so far?" Mercurio asked.

"I've staked out the police station for the last three days. The first day I saw four of them get into two cars. I followed one of the cars to Villingen, where they spoke to an ex-priest named Schmidt. When they left his house I entered and started to interrogate him. I got the names of Max Rockenbach and a Sean something out of him, but the cocksuckers returned and we had a standoff until this fucking cop puts a bullet through my wrist. I was taken to the hospital, and I was able to get loose and took out the two cops who were supposed to guard me, then I found Schmidt and pulled the plug on him.

"I've been smoking weed for the last three days to kill the pain, but I can function. The last two days I sat here and planned to take the pricks out, but each day I sat for ten hours and the motherfuckers never showed up. Sooner or later the fucks have to come back. I've been waiting to take them all out at once. My plan was to continue to wait until they're all here. Then I got a call telling me I would have company, and here we sit," Massier said.

"That's not a lot to go on. You aren't positive of the number of targets and you don't know their names. This is far from an ideal situation," Mercurio said.

Massier's cell phone went off.

"*Hallo?*" he said.

"Have you made connection with the man from Opus Dei?" the Black Pope asked.

"Yes, he's here," Massier said.

"I just heard from our contact in Paderborn. They're scheduled to excavate Wewelsburg Castle's special rooms tomorrow. That's a problem. There may be things there we don't want found. It would be far better to eliminate the threat before they get to Paderborn, but if that is not possible, you will have them all together in one place tomorrow. With the two of you there should be no problem to terminate all of them. You should also take care of the curator of the museum and the security guard. I don't want anyone left to say what they intended to do and why," he said.

"What will prevent questions being asked and determining what they were doing?" Massier asked.

There was a hesitation on the other end of the phone.

"That is a good question. The man who would do the questioning is the same man who just called me. He is the chief of police in Paderborn. He is our contact. We won't have to worry about the aftermath of your work," the Black Pope said.

Massier was in awe of the Black Pope's network. Everywhere he turned, key people were in the Black Pope's pocket. In Baden-Baden it was the chief of police, in Villingen he suspected it was the chief of police, because he had been taken to the hospital by two, green-behind-the-ears cops, and now in Paderborn he had another chief of police. Too bad his network didn't include the chief of police in Freiburg. This would have been far easier.

"Okay, we'll spend the day watching who goes in and out of the station, and if we can finish it today, we will; otherwise, we'll finish this tomorrow in Paderborn. Can we count on any help from the police chief there?" Massier asked.

"No, he is one of our watchers. He relays information, but he is too valuable to risk exposure. It took us a long time to get him in place so he could watch over Wewelsburg Castle. We don't want to jeopardize his position. That's what you're there for," the Black Pope said.

"I understand. I'll take care of this," Massier said and clicked off.

He looked at Mercurio.

"We have our plan. Everyone will be at Wewelsburg Castle tomorrow. We'll try to take out these shitheads today, but if we can't, we'll kill the pig fuckers tomorrow at the castle. We can spend today watching who comes and goes," Massier said.

He didn't wait for a response and put the car in gear to drive to his previous surveillance spot. He parked and pulled out his standard breakfast of two day old, warm head cheese and warm blood sausage. He didn't offer any to Mercurio, not that his car mate would have touched it, and sat eating the rank combination. Massier chewed in silence and Mercurio was semi-repulsed. The combination of language, attitude, and disgusting dining habits were almost too much for him to take. To be stuck with this animal wasn't something he was prepared for, and he decided much of his surveillance would be done from elsewhere.

***

Battalini saw the Mercedes approach and park in the spot he expected. He was confused because the Mercedes had two occupants, and Battalini only expected to see the man from Amsterdam. Battalini dismissed the occupants of the Mercedes as his potential assassins until an hour went by and they hadn't moved. They were watching and waiting for something. Who was this other person? He removed his cell phone and dialed.

"*Hallo?*" the Black Pope said.

"I'm checking in. I'm in Freiburg, have the police station under surveillance, and have noticed something out of the ordinary. A black Mercedes pulled up and appears to be watching the station as I am. I would think it's your man Massier, but he has company. Do you know anything about this?" Battalini asked.

"So nice of you to call, Father Battalini," the Black Pope said. "Where have you been?"

"I've been in Freiburg as I told you I would be. I've been poking, around but haven't seen anything of significance. Why, am I supposed to call you every day like a little child?" Battalini said, having a hard time concealing his contempt.

"Yes, I expect you to communicate with me and I suggest you remember you work for me. I have enlisted an additional resource. The man with Massier is John Mercurio. He is to Opus Dei what Massier is to me. He is a fixer or as they call him, a cleaner. He is there to make sure this gets done with less mess than Massier has created so far," the Black Pope said.

"*He's Opus Dei?*" Battalini asked. "*I came here to make sure this was a smooth operation. Why in the world would you involve Opus Dei?*"

"Simple; I have not heard from you, and this needs to be finished. Once the threat is eliminated, Massier will be eliminated."

Battalini leaned back and took a deep breath.

"So first you brought in a low life scum bag I've told you not to use, then you ignored the fact I was coming here to oversee this, and then you bring in an assassin from Opus Dei. I'm speechless," he said.

"Get over it, Father Battalini. Don't forget the chain of command and whose organization you are still a part of," the Black Pope said, spitting out the not so veiled threat.

"*I'm part of God's organization. I do God's work. Men who think they're God are dangerous,*" Battalini said.

There was silence. The Black Pope didn't know how to respond. He'd never had such a direct challenge, and this was coming from his head of security.

"Father Battalini, I suggest you choose your next words with great care."

Battalini ignored the comment.

"What do you expect me to do with the two people you now have on site?" Battalini asked.

"You need to make sure this is done and cleaned up. It is good you are there to oversee this."

"I'm not planning to make contact with them. I'll observe and only interact if and when necessary."

"Good, that is what we need from you. When you return to Rome we need to have a serious discussion," the Black Pope said.

Battalini again chose not to acknowledge the comments from the Black Pope. "I will be in touch," he said and didn't wait for a response.

Battalini watched as a squad car pull around and parked in the rear of the station.

He also noticed, even from a distance, the two people in the Mercedes sat up and appeared to be attentive. When the police cruiser was no longer visible, the body language of the two individuals, had again changed. The inhabitants, in the car had slumped back and away from each other. Even from his perch he could tell they weren't friends. He waited to see if they would move.

He then noticed a different car come to a stop and park on a parallel street to that of the Mercedes. A man wearing a navy blue jacket exited the car and walked in a casual but purposeful manner. Battalini could pick up little things about people, and there was something about the man that attracted his attention. He watched as the individual in the blue jacket strolled along, but Battalini noticed he always kept his gaze directed toward the Mercedes. He walked past the street where the Mercedes sat, then circled back.

It became evident to Battalini this man was conducting surveillance on the Mercedes.

***

Rudolf Weiler parked his car one block from the spot he expected Massier to be parked. He walked in a semi-circle that took him well behind the parked car. All the cars were empty with the exception of a black Mercedes where he observed two individuals.

211

Rudolf was puzzled and called Gola.

"Freiburg Police Chief, Gola Rockenbach."

"Gola, it's Rudolf. I'm across the street checking out the vehicles, and there's one that could be our guy except there are two occupants. I didn't think we were dealing with more than one. Can you run the tags?"

"What's the make and model of the car and the tag numbers?" Gola asked.

"Mercedes, black, 300 D, an eighty-five or eighty-six. German tag numbers E three-four-eight-six," Rudolf said.

"Let me run it."

Three minutes later Gola had a result and called Rudolf.

"Those tags belong to a green, 2006 Porsche Cayenne. They've been switched. I think you have the right car. It looks like we have two guys after us. Good work; what do you want to do?"

"I'll continue to watch them and, if they separate, I'll take one of them," Rudolf said.

"Keep me posted. Do you want me to come out?"

"No, not at this point. Let's sit tight and see what they do next."

"Good luck."

"Thanks."

Rudolf looked for a spot to watch the parked car, but there was no place to observe on foot without being obvious. He returned to his car and moved to a spot where he could park and still see the Mercedes. Now he would wait.

***

Father Battalini was fascinated as he watched a surveillance of surveillance and he recognized he was the third surveillance. He smiled and wondered who was watching him?

***

Mercurio was getting more uncomfortable by the moment. He hadn't eaten anything because he thought they would eat at the coffee house. He smelled the rancid garbage the guy next to him was shoving into his mouth, and he could hear him chewing and swallowing. He usually didn't pay attention to those sensory functions, but his distaste for his car mate had exacerbated his personal sensitivities. After an hour he had all he could take.

"I'm getting some air and something to eat," Mercurio said.

"Suit yourself," Massier said without looking at him.

Without additional comment, Mercurio open the door and stepped into clear fresh air. It tasted good. Escaping the confines of Massier's self-created crypt was rejuvenating. Mercurio walked across the emerging grass toward the coffee house where he thought they were meeting for breakfast.

He wasn't concerned about identifying the targets since he knew they would be all together tomorrow at the castle. He was a pragmatist who didn't like to waste time nor energy. To do so and still be subjected to Massier's nasty idiosyncrasies were more than he chose to deal with. He would have breakfast, then decide what he would do for the rest of the day. Tomorrow he would handle the situation.

***

As Mercurio entered the coffee shop, Sean was pulling into a parking slot at the rear of the station. His intent was to get his briefcase and get back to the cover of his hotel. As he walked from the car to the station's rear door he had the same feeling as his first day of junior high gym class, when he was forced to take a shower with the rest of the twelve-year-old boys. He felt insecure, naked and uncomfortable.

Gola was the first person he encountered.

"Sean, what are you doing here? I thought you were staying at the hotel today?" Gola said.

"Maybe you didn't hear what I said to Max at breakfast. I left my briefcase in his squad car yesterday and wanted to get it so today wouldn't be a complete waste," Sean said.

"Well, you're here just in time. This is about to get serious. Rudolf has Massier and another guy under surveillance across the street. He's waiting to see if they split up, then he's going to move on them. I was just going to tell Max," Gola said.

Sean pulled out his Beretta and checked the clip. He realized his extra clips were at the hotel.

"Do you have any clips for a Beretta?" Sean asked.

"I believe we do. Let's get Max and we'll get you fixed up. You might want to get something with more stopping power than the Beretta," Gola said.

They went into Max's office and brought him up to speed. Gola and Max took Sean into the basement to their well-stocked armory. They put on vests and took extra handguns with additional clips. They were ready and knew this could be the confrontation they had been expecting.

***

Rudolf saw the dark haired man get out of the car. He watched as the man seemed to take a deep breath and stretched his arms and legs. He walked off in an unhurried pace which seemed contradictory to Rudolf's expectation of someone on a surveillance mission. The man's body language was one of relaxed disinterest, and he appeared to have an absence of urgency. That puzzled Rudolf.

He dialed Gola's number.

"One of the men got out of the car and has gone into a restaurant across the street. I'm going to move on the remaining one which I think is Massier. It will be easier with the other man out of the car," Rudolf said.

"Give me two minutes and Max, Sean, and I will come around from the back of the station to give you backup," Gola said.

"I'll wait two minutes and I'll move. We need to get this done before the other man returns."

"We'll be there."

"We're on. Massier's alone in a car across the street and Rudolf is moving on him in one minute. Let's spread out so we have every area covered. The two of you go out around the back and to the left and I'll go to the right. Massier is watching the front, so stay out of view and we can loop around from the back," Gola said.

They exited the back door and went in opposite directions around the rear of the station.

***

Battalini noticed the movement. He saw the man in the blue jacket exit his car, remove a pistol, and start to move toward Massier's car. Battalini's

214

instincts took over, and he removed his own pistol and took off the safety. He moved down the stairs and went to the car where the man in the blue jacket had been sitting. He opened the door to look for anything of interest, but found nothing. From here he could watch what would develop.

***

Rudolf walked upright with the gun behind his back, and once he got to the sidewalk, he ducked behind a large pine tree. He wanted to make sure Massier hadn't moved. He had not. Rudolf resumed his walk toward Massier's car.

Massier was relieved his unwelcome visitor was gone. He hated that Mercurio had been sent to help him. He didn't want to know him and wished he would stay gone.

He was taking a bite of almost rancid warm cheese when he saw movement in his side mirror. He was chewing as he reached for his gun. He had no reason to suspect any problem from the person coming down the sidewalk, but in three days of sitting in this spot not one person had walked by the car. He could also see the man's arm wasn't visible, which set off alarms. Massier moved the gun to a position aimed just above the left arm rest, pointing outward but hidden, and cocked it.

***

Rudolf approached and his heart thumped fast in his chest. It had been a few years since he pulled a trigger in anger. He came even with the driver's door, lifted his gun from his back and tapped it against the driver's window.

"Let me see your hands," Rudolf said.

Massier didn't hesitate. Being the animal he was, he acted out of the instinct to a direct threat. He pulled the trigger. The bullet ripped through the door and the jagged remnant entered Rudolf's lower gut. The bullet's force slowed as it made its way through the components making up the Mercedes' door, but it still had enough force to slam into Rudolf Weiler's upper intestine. Rudolf staggered back with searing pain. He'd been shot in the past, but only with flesh wounds and had never taken a bullet like this. He cursed as his back hit the grass beyond the sidewalk.

Massier darted out of the stolen car and stood above Rudolf. He

215

smiled down at the wounded man and wasted little time putting three more bullets into Rudolf's body.

Massier was standing over Rudolf's body as he fired the last shot when Gola opened fire. He was moving as he fired, and the bullets were missing their mark by a wide margin. Massier reacted and started returning the fire as Gola took cover behind a large tree and changed clips. Massier hadn't realized fire was also coming from behind him, which might have been because Max wasn't coming close. Massier was now was on the hunt and Gola was his prey. Sean saw this and also noted Max's marksmanship on the move wasn't his strong suit.

Massier was closing in on the tree providing Gola's only protection. This wasn't a fair fight. Massier was a professional killer stalking Gola, who had never shot a human being. Massier was circling Gola's hiding spot on a site usually reserved for Freiburg's open air fair, not a gun battle. Sean was desperate to get close as Massier maneuvered into position and raised his gun for the kill shot. Sean knew it was now or never, aimed, and fired. Massier started to squeeze the trigger as a spinning bullet entered his right temple and brains, along with bone fragments exploded from the left side of his skull. Down went Horst Massier. He never knew what hit him.

Sean took a deep drag of pine-scented air as a release of adrenaline zapped through his body.

"Gola, are you okay?" he asked.

"I'm okay. How about you?" Gola asked.

He came out from behind the tree as Max arrived.

They stood over Massier's body. Gola felt for a pulse on Massier's neck, but there was no need to do so with half of Massier's cerebral cortex dripping from the dark green needles of the nearby evergreen.

Gola looked up at Sean.

"Thanks, Sean. I think you just saved my ass."

"I think I did, too," Sean said.

He attempted to smile, but didn't get a reaction from the muscles in his face.

"I saw Max's shooting ability, and I knew the only chance you had was me," Sean said.

"Rudolf," Gola said.

They ran to Rudolf as he lay with blood seeping from four bullet wounds. Sean checked for a pulse and laid his dead friend's head back in

216

the grass as he closed Weiler's open blank eyes.

"He's gone," Sean said.

A moment later Gola thought of his last conversation with Rudolf.

"The last thing Rudolf said was there were two people in the car and one had gotten out. That's why he went after Massier when he did," he said.

They instantly crouched, hands tightening around their pistols, and started to scan the park and buildings beyond. They saw nothing unusual, nor would they.

***

Mercurio was in mid-bite of his glazed danish when he heard the unmistakable retort of a Walther PPK. He heard the ensuing gun battle and went to the door to watch it unfold. He saw a body lying on the ground near the driver's door of the Mercedes and saw Massier moving and firing at someone in the park. He could also see a man moving behind Massier with gun drawn. It never occurred to him to enter the fray. He would watch and whatever the outcome, he was pretty sure he would have fewer targets to eliminate the next day.

He watched as a man to Massier's right took aim, and suddenly half of Massier's head exploded into the pine trees. His first reaction was it couldn't have happened to a nicer guy, then realized it was time to leave. He paid for his pastry and walked in the opposite direction from the park. He would get a cab and get back to his car.

***

Battalini felt like a spectator at the Roman Coliseum watching gladiators fight to the death. This was almost like a sporting event, except people were dying. He never felt moved to jump in. He never liked anything about the man from Amsterdam and felt a positive reaction when he witnessed Massier's demise. He also watched as the man with the dark hair took in the events from the restaurant door and didn't engage. He departed as soon as Massier went down, which was interesting. He was letting the Freiburg Police do part of his job for him, and Battalini understood.

He also decided it was time to relocate. The normal procedure

217

would be for the police to interview and question anyone in the area, and he wasn't prepared to participate. He made his way to his car and drove away from the carnage.

***

The assault by Massier happened so fast it was over before there were any witnesses, and the only thing anyone saw was Sean shooting the assailant. Within minutes of the shooting at least twenty police officers were on the scene. The whole crime scene was wrapped in yellow tape as was Massier's stolen car.

Sean called Alan. "We've just had an incident. Rudolf found Massier and tried to take him out, but the prick shot him, then went after Gola. He had him in his sights when I got off a lucky shot. Both Rudolf and the Vatican shithead are dead. I knew you'd want to know right away," Sean said.

"Oh my God, where are you?" Alan said.

"We're in the park across from the police station," Sean said.

"I'll be right there."

Sean turned to Max and said, "I'm just sick. Rudolf was involved because of me, and I feel somehow responsible."

"You can't do that to yourself. He was a professional who knew what he was doing. He wouldn't have been involved if he didn't think it was worth it. Don't blame yourself," Max said.

"I've got to call Wolfe and Laflamme. I don't know what else to do," Sean said.

"We all knew from day one what we were getting into. Everyone has done this by choice, and it's not over. Whoever was with him is still out there. It's curious, when the gunfire started, his partner didn't come to his assistance. I'm glad he didn't, because it would have created quite a problem for us, but it's a big question mark for me," Max said.

"I wonder if we should continue with the excavation tomorrow," Sean said.

"My gut feeling is we should go forward with it before whoever was directing Massier regroups and sends a replacement. If we do the excavation tomorrow, it may be safer than if we wait. Let's ask Gola what he thinks," Max said.

218

"You make a good point. I think we should get it done tomorrow," Sean said.

Max, Sean, Gola, and Alan huddled and discussed their options for the castle and agreed to move forward as planned. They were all calm on the outside, but shaken on the inside. Of everyone, Sean had grown closest to Max. They had become good friends in a short time, and Max put his arm around Sean.

"Are you doing okay? It's said taking a life is difficult on the person who did it. I just want to make sure you're okay," Max said.

"Thanks, Max, I do appreciate your concern. You know, I'm okay. In fact, I still have such a feeling of rage toward the dead guy, I'd kill him again if I could wake him up. I liked Rudolf, and Massier put four bullets into him, then he was about to kill Gola. I feel nothing but elation that I was the one to send him straight to Hell," Sean said.

"Well, I guess I don't have to worry about your mental or emotional health," Max said.

***

The rest of the day was spent on the tedious process of paperwork, working with the coroner, and answering questions. Gola had to do the bulk of the work. Once the German version of CSI had finished, the coroner removed the bodies and took them to the morgue. The team watched in silence as Rudolf Weiler's body was loaded into the coroner's ambulance and Sean tapped the side of the vehicle as they closed its doors. As the ambulance departed, Sean walked alone to the center of the park.

His first call was to Laflamme, then to Wolfe. They were difficult calls, and both took the news hard. Laflamme said he would come to Wewelsburg Castle the next day, and Wolfe said he would fly over, but Sean talked him out of it. Sean felt tomorrow's excavation would be the defining moment, and he agreed to speak to Wolfe after the dig. Sean was relieved to have those calls behind him as he walked back to where everyone was milling around. Conversations were at hush levels reminiscent of a wake.

"I just spoke with Laflamme and Wolfe. They were shocked and upset. Laflamme is joining us tomorrow, and I had to argue with Wolfe to keep him from getting onto a plane. They both made an issue of the other guy and where did he go. They couldn't figure out why he disappeared instead of assisting Massier, and it didn't make sense to anyone. They also agreed we aren't done with these guys," Sean said.

Everyone nodded, but no one replied. There just didn't seem to be much to say.

Chapter 44)

Mercurio returned to his car and drove toward his hotel. He called Father Gatto to give the update and ask for what he should do next. Gatto told him to await instructions and walked down the hall to the Black Pope's office.

"We have developments in Freiburg. Mercurio and Massier were staking out the police station. Mercurio left the car to get something to eat and heard gunfire. He doesn't know how it started, but as he watched it was evident Massier killed someone near his car and he was stalking someone else. Another guy came up on Massier's backside, and blew his brains out. So you've lost your man, and Mercurio is waiting for instructions," Gatto said.

"Battalini is on site and ready to step in if I can ever get a hold of him. Do you have anyone else available you could get there by tomorrow morning? It's imperative to stop this tomorrow," the Black Pope said.

"I may be able to get someone else over there. What were the final instructions to your man?" Gatto asked.

"I spoke with him yesterday and told him to eliminate everyone at the castle tomorrow, including the castle security guard and curator. They're excavating at eleven o'clock, and he was going to wait until the excavators left so there were no witnesses. When will you know if you can get someone else there?" the Black Pope asked.

"I'll commit right now to get someone there. I don't understand why you're coming to me when you have your own security group," Gatto said.

"You've hit on a sensitive subject. You know Father Battalini is on site, but he chose to go into the field by himself and has been out of communication yet again. He and I have been at odds and changes will be made when this is all finished. I don't feel I can rely on him because he is not telling me what he is up to. Therefore, I have come to you," the Black Pope said.

Gatto was surprised the Black Pope would reveal discord in his inner circle. He knew Father Battalini was held in high regard throughout the

Vatican. If Battalini was having problems with the Black Pope, his regard for Battalini just increased.

"Plan on the fact I'll get someone else on site, and I'll relay your instructions," Gatto said.

Gatto turned and left the office without further comment.

He returned to his office and thought about who he could get to Wewelsburg Castle by tomorrow. He picked Mercurio because he took direction and didn't think for himself. He wasn't an Opus Dei advocate, but more like hired muscle, sort of a trained pit bull. No thinking, just reacting. He had to be careful whom he would pair with Mercurio. True believers would take issue with Mercurio. He pulled out a list of names and began looking for the right fit. He wasn't finding one. Mercurio always worked alone, and now Gatto was starting to realize why.

He came to Guillermo Mastro. Mastro was a true believer, a dedicated Opus Dei member, and might have a problem with Mercurio. Gatto would have to address the issue up front. Mastro's grandfather had been part of Mussolini's inner circle and was executed when Mussolini was overthrown. His father had been a sadistic, resentful little man who took out his own failures on his son.

Mastro's avenue away from his abusive father was finding Opus Dei. The Mastro family priest was the conduit leading the battered youngster to Opus Dei. After one particularly brutal beating, the priest took the damaged boy aside and explained he had a way to change his life, and Mastro was all ears. He met with an Opus Dei priest who was more or less a recruiter for the cause, and Mastro was sold. He would have agreed to anything to get away from his father.

Guillermo Mastro never again laid eyes upon his father. He was so grateful to be safe he accepted everything being taught and wasn't perceptive enough to recognize everyone at Opus Dei were damaged souls. Truth be known, few well-adjusted people volunteered to join Opus Dei. Mastro was now forty-two years old and practiced the odd corporal mortification rituals, such as self-flagellation and the wearing of a cilice. Self-flagellation was self-explanatory, but the wearing of the cilice was the practice of stapping a spiked chain around one's upper thigh for two hours a day every day except Sundays and certain special days of the year. The spikes painfully penetrate the skin and is the kind of fanaticism common among Opus Dei devotees.

Mastro was in a special group who would do the bidding of his superiors without asking questions. He lived in an Opus Dei facility where Gatto's phone call found him.

"*Hallo*, this is Guillermo Mastro," he said.

"Guillermo, this is Father Gatto. I have an important assignment for you which is significant to the continued existence of our way of life. Can I count on you?"

"Yes, of course, Father Gatto. Anything you ask," Mastro said.

"One thing we need to discuss, Guillermo," Gatto said, "the person you are going to work with is John Mercurio, and he's an associate of Opus Dei, but he's not a member. He's not a believer like you are. I wanted you to be aware and ask you to overlook those issues in the interest of a successful conclusion to this assignment," Gatto said, and proceeded to give Mastro the details of their dilemma.

"That's not a problem, I'll be fine with him," Mastro said.

Gatto told him he needed to be at Wewelsburg Castle the following day and provided Mercurio's cell phone number so they could connect. Mastro went to his room, changed his clothes, and went to see the Opus Dei Numerarie director. The director took Guillermo into the catacombs of the Opus Dei facility to a room with a large steel door equipped with a heavy lock. This was the Opus Dei armory. Once the two foot thick door was unlocked, the director slid the door to the side and they entered. The director flipped a switch and fluorescent lights flickered and exposed what appeared to be an arsenal equal to that of a small country.

"What will you need?" the director asked.

"I want enough firepower, so let's do two Walther PPKs, a Glock, and a knife. I also need a silencer and several clips," he said.

Mastro loaded up, as he had in the past, since these sorts of assignments were not unknown to him.

"I'll also need a cell phone and a car," he said.

The director moved to a back wall holding more than twenty-five active cell phones. He handed Mastro a phone, a charger, and a carrying case to house all of his weaponry.

The director also handed Mastro keys for a 2002, BMW 325, along with a credit card and a thousand Euros.

Mastro carried his weapon bag to his room, packed for two days, and went to the BMW. He started it and began his trip to Paderborn. He had driven this route a number of times and knew how to get to Wewels-burg Castle.

He called Mercurio and explained Father Gatto had asked him to join in the operation. They agreed to meet in the castle parking lot at nine the next morning, giving them time to reconnoiter the area before the targets arrived.

Chapter 45)

By five o'clock the paperwork had been completed, and the TV reporters had finished their interviews and departed to file their stories. The crowds came and went as the shootout in the park became known.

Sean recognized the team was emotionally spent. The trauma of the day's violence and Rudolf's death touched them and brought home the reality of their situation. They agreed to go their own way for the rest of the day and meet in the morning at the Colombi Hotel. Sean and Alan left together as the Rockenbach brothers remained to clean up loose ends.

Sean and Alan decided to have dinner together at the hotel as soon as they arrived. The first thing Sean did was order a first, then second bottle of barbera wine. Sean didn't feel hungry and ordered the special because he didn't want to think. Most of dinner was spent refilling his glass, and he was quite aware his overconsumption served its purpose of dulling his pain and guilt.

Conversation was minimal, and after finishing the second bottle of wine they decided to pack it in. Sean managed to get to his room in one piece, into his bed without ceremony, and was instantly asleep courtesy of the bottle and a half of barbera.

His wake up call rang at least four times before a little voice in the recesses of his subconscious stirred him awake. He groggily sat up and twisted to put his feet on the floor, but he didn't stand. His head was spinning, and he questioned why they ordered the second bottle.

He stood and made his way to the bathroom. It was dark outside, and part of him wanted to return to bed and shut his eyes for just five minutes, but he knew better. Given his condition, he would be down for the count. Once he stepped out of the shower he felt one hundred percent better, which was still about fifty percent below how he should have felt.

Twenty minutes later he left his room for the breakfast area. He wasn't hungry, but knew he needed strong coffee and something in his stomach to stop the pounding in his head. He nibbled at odds and ends from the buffet table and was doing everything at about fifty percent of normal speed when he heard a voice.

"Good morning, Sean. How are you feeling?" Alan asked.

"Not so swift. How are you doing this not so bright morning?" Sean asked.

"I'm doing great, but I was worried about you. I had two glasses of wine and you had a bottle and a half. I don't know about you, but I couldn't drink that much. I'd be a wounded soldier this morning," Alan said.

"Well said. You're looking at a wounded soldier. I should bandage my head for the ride to the castle."

Alan helped himself to some odd looking meat and cheese, and a few minutes later Rockenbachs started streaming in the front door, with Alfred arriving first.

"Is that buffet available to anyone?" he said.

"Yes it is," Alan said.

Alfred went to the buffet table and Alan's eyes followed him.

"What are the odds he'll pay for his breakfast?" Alan asked.

Alfred returned with more food piled up on his plate than he could possibly eat.

Before Alfred could get a quarter of the way through his breakfast, Gola and Max arrived. Gola could see Sean and Alan were finished eating and looked at Alfred wolfing down the mound of food on his plate.

"Hey, guys, it's time to go," he said.

Alfred looked up with a panic, "Can you just wait until I finish?" he asked.

"Alfred, the four of us are not going to sit here and watch you eat. Finish now or get a doggy bag. Let's go," Gola said.

They all started moving toward the door. Sean and Alan went to the cashier, asked for their respective bills, and signed them to their rooms. They were getting ready to walk out as Alfred appeared to be getting ready to scoot around them.

"Alfred, aren't you going to get a doggie bag to go? Oh, and you'll want to take care of your bill," Alan said.

"Oh yes," he said.

He reversed his field and came to the cashier. Alan gave Sean a wink and they headed out the door.

"I just wasn't going to let him get away with that," Alan said.

"I'm surprised Gola doesn't arrest him twice a week for that kind of stuff," Sean said.

"Imagine your brothers are law enforcement and you're pulling this crap all the time. You can tell the veiled contempt they all direct toward him," Alan said.

Five minutes later they were heading toward the castle. Alan and Sean rode with Max, and he simply shook his head upon hearing of Alfred's latest ploy.

"That's so typical. Are you both armed?" Max asked.

They both answered affirmatively. As they drove, their excitement started to build. What would they find? Would there be an attempt on them? Would there be anything remaining in the hidden labs? Butterflies started beating their wings, and they all felt them.

Chapter 46)

At nine o'clock Gola called the Paderborn Police Chief, then the excavator, and finally the curator. When he finished, he was content everything was lined up.

***

Also at nine, Guillermo Mastro pulled into the Wewelsburg Castle parking lot. He turned the car off and got out of the Opus Dei BMW. He scanned the parking lot, saw three cars, and observed a dark-haired man coming toward him. When they were within ten feet he spoke.

"I'm Guillermo Mastro. Are you John Mercurio?"

"I am," Mercurio said.

There was no handshake as they evaluated each other.

"I walked the perimeter, and the digging equipment is already here. The excavators will need to leave before we can act. We can't add to the body count or this will get even more out of control. We know the local police chief will curtail any investigation, but we don't need additional visibility. Let's walk through the castle to see what it looks like before anyone shows up," Mercurio said.

"What do you understand our instructions to be?" Mastro asked.

"We're to eliminate the entire investigation team, plus the curator and security guard," Mercurio said, "I have an idea of how we can do this. Once the excavation is done and they leave, we take these guys out and put their bodies into the excavated area. I know how to operate the equipment, so I can refill the dirt, and we make the curator and security man look like robbery victims. The police chief will block anything else. The sod is already here so we simply replace it, and the excavators will be more than happy to see their job has been done for them. They'll think it was completed by the people who hired them."

"Okay, that makes sense. It will make our job easier because we won't have body disposal to deal with," Mastro said.

They walked along the cobblestone courtyard and entered the museum through its large front doors. The first thing they encountered was a long counter filled with Nazi memorabilia.

As they walked toward the south tower they passed the security guard, who looked them up and down. His body language seemed to be aggressive with an air of superiority. Mastro noticed because it reminded him of his father, and he made a mental note to a bullet into his fat head. He often fantasized his victims were his father. The image made it easier to do what he did without pangs of conscience.

They decided to leave and return when their prey had gathered. The men sent by Father Gatto entered Mercurio's car and drove down the hill toward the town of Paderborn.

***

Laflamme watched as a man arrived, parked his car, and walked the perimeter of the castle. A few minutes later another car pulled into the lot and the driver exited and walked toward the man who arrived first. They had an odd interaction, but then walked around the castle's perimeter and went into the museum together. The two men seemed to be scouting the entire area. They were dressed like tourists, and their body language indicated an indifference toward each other.

His observations were made from a location high in the north tower. After hearing about yesterday's events, he called Wolfe and they commiserated on the loss of their friend Rudolf. Wolfe knew Laflamme well enough to know revenge would be on his mind and reminded Laflamme his primary focus was protecting Sean. Laflamme agreed, but clearly had additional motivation.

His radar went up as he watched the two men leave the castle and get into one of their cars. They exited the parking lot and drove down the narrow road leading away from the castle. Leaving one of their vehicles meant they would return, and he believed he had just identified the adversaries.

Laflamme had arrived at the castle at four that morning. His first activity was to walk the perimeter and get an understanding of the topography and potential hiding places. This activity would be repeated by several people in the next ten hours. After getting a feel for the grounds, he drove down the hill and hid his car in an out of the way parking lot. He walked back up the long entrance road and used an array of lock opening devices to get into the castle.

His plan was to observe from the north tower, and after negotiating his way through two more sets of locks his mission was accomplished. As he waited, he thought of the irony of using the tower for its originally designed purpose over four hundred years ago. He had a view of anyone approaching the castle, the parking lot, and the city beyond. It would be a chilly several hours, but this was the place to watch whatever may unfold.

From his perch he first observed the two potential adversaries arrive, and then depart around nine-fifteen. At ten-thirty, two pickup trucks pulled into the parking lot and three people with yellow hard hats exited the vehicles. At ten forty-five two squad cars, with Sean's team, pulled into the parking lot. Laflamme scanned the surroundings, but noticed nothing out of the ordinary. He had to watch for an attack at any time so he couldn't get complacent.

***

Gola went to speak with the excavation crew while Max went into the museum to find the curator. The security guard took a few steps toward them before recognizing they were the people responsible for his latest bout of humiliation and did an about face. Max found the curator, and they walked to where Gola was talking with the excavators, while Sean and Alan marked the area where the dig would begin.

Laflamme dialed Sean's cell number.

"Hello, Sean O'Shea."

"Sean, this is Laflamme. Don't look up, but I'm in the north tower. I am watching you guys, and no one is paying attention to the woods. You are vulnerable and must pay closer attention. Don't tell them I am up here, but remind everyone to keep their heads up and post sentries," he said.

"Thank you for coming. You don't know how much I appreciate it. I'll remind everyone to keep watch," Sean said.

Sean clicked off and viewed the surrounding area.

"Hey, guys, let's not forget to keep our eyes open. We're getting wrapped up with the emotion of this, and we aren't watching the woods," Sean said.

They all stopped what they were doing and started scanning their surroundings.

"We need at least two of us on guard and watching at every moment. Let's have Alfred and Alan take watch for the next hour. Just focus outward and watch for anything unusual. I'd be surprised if something doesn't happen while we're here," Gola said.

Gola turned his attention back to the excavators with thumbs up. The space was marked off and they were ready. The power shovel was fired up and the digging began.

***

It was two in the afternoon when Mercurio looked at his watch.

"How long do you think it will take to dig the hole?" he asked.

"I'd think there's at least an hour to go. When we go back we'll have a hard time getting up there without being seen. If they're watching for us, it will be difficult to arrive unnoticed. I have an idea. Let's find a travel agency," Mastro said.

Ten minutes later they walked into the Paderborn Travel Centre.

"Good afternoon, how can I help you?" a plump woman sitting behind a gun metal colored desk said.

"Good afternoon. We're wondering if there are any guided tours of Wewelsburg Castle?" Mastro asked.

"That's a good question. You know you can just drive up there and walk around without a tour," she said.

"We know, but we prefer a guided tour so we can learn from the tour guide," Mastro said, knowing it sounded weak, but plausible.

"There aren't any local guided tours. The only guided tour would be World War Two Tours, and they originate out of Frankfort. I don't think that's what you're looking for because they start in Frankfurt and stop at Wewelsburg Castle the first afternoon, but they go all through Germany and it lasts for seven days," she said.

"Can you check, just for fun, and tell us how often they run?" Mastro asked.

"Sure," she said.

She turned to her computer screen.

"Let's see what we can find out. Here we go. It looks like they run every two days, with a new one starting the day after tomorrow. If you're interested, I could make a reservation for you, but seven days is a long time for a guided tour for boys of your age. You'll find ninety percent of the people on the tour are elderly," she said.

Mastro was quiet for a moment, "What time do they usually get to the castle?" he asked.

"Here's the itinerary. Arrive in the morning at Frankfurt airport, lunch in route; arrive at Wewelsburg Castle late afternoon, dinner and lodging in Paderborn. There you go. There's a tour that stops this afternoon, but there's no way for you to get on it," the plump woman said.

"Thank you very much for your help. By the way, do you know what the buses look like?" Mastro asked.

"I don't know what make they are, but they're large double decker buses and on the side it has World War Two Tours in large letters," she said.

"Thanks again," Mastro said.

They walked out the front door he turned to Mercurio.

"I think we have our way in," Mastro said.

"What are you thinking? We can't just stop the bus and get on," Mercurio said.

"That would be the best, but I have a different idea. We'll wait for the bus, which has to drive right by us on the frontage road, and follow it into the parking lot. If we come up by ourselves we'll be spotted, but following the bus will look like we're with them. We'll pull up next to their door and greet them as if we're with the museum. We'll walk in with them and it'll appear to anyone watching we're part of the tour. We can only take a couple a guns, and we'll have to come back for heavier firepower if we need it," Mastro said.

"That's good," Mercurio said.

Mastro pulled his vehicle into traffic as he looked at his watch. It was two-thirty, and he was concerned the bus may have already passed. He drove to the museum access road and pulled his car to the side of the road. They stopped far down the road and weren't visible from the castle. Mastro turned off the car and waited.

***

The hole was getting deeper. The tops of two of the emergency exists had been exposed as the dig continued. Gola and Max were now on lookout. It had been four hours of digging, and they were three quarters of the way to fully unearth the exit doors.

Sean walked over to Max. "What are you thinking? It's been awfully quiet so far," he said.

"I'm surprised, but we're far from done. We've been fortunate the museum has had no traffic today, and we can see if anyone approaches. I'm not so delusional to think we're home free, but so far, so good," Max said.

As Max got out those words he watched a large double decker bus come up the hill toward the castle. He turned to the curator and pointed to the large vehicle.

"Do you see the bus coming up here? Is that something you're aware of?" Max asked.

"Yes, that's World War Two Tours. They're here every other day about this time. This is normal. They should have twenty-five to thirty people on the bus and they'll be here for an hour to an hour and a half," the curator said.

"*GOLA*," Max shouted over the noise of the power shovel, "There's a bus coming up here. It's a scheduled tour and there will be twenty-five to thirty people wandering around. That adds complexity. We need to be ready," he said.

"Give everyone a heads up," Gola said.

It was difficult to hear over the noise of the power shovel, so Max spoke with everyone one on one. By the time he finished, the bus had come to a stop, as had the car which had closely followed it.

***

Mastro had been sitting and waiting when a glint reflected off his rear view mirror. He glanced at it, and a large shiny silver bus was approaching. He started the car and told Mercurio they were ready to go. They had used the down time to make sure their pistols had full clips and their preparations were complete. The tour bus rolled past them, and Mastro fell in right behind. One minute later the bus pulled into the parking lot, and Mastro pulled in just to the right and close to the tour bus's front door.

The door hissed open, and Mercurio and Mastro were standing at the door acting as greeters. As the tour participants de-bused, Mercurio was shaking their hands or offering assistance to those needing help getting off the bus, all the while thanking them for coming to Wewelsburg Castle. The tour folks were appreciative of this warm welcome and the friendliness of their fake hosts. Everyone was milling around, and Mercurio and Mastro fit in like old friends. Some of the old women started asking Mercurio questions about the castle.

"How old is the castle?" a blue-haired lady asked.

Mercurio stammered and said it was over a thousand years old, missing the real date by more than six hundred years. An old lady with big white hair interrupted and blurted out she read about the castle, "Excuse me, but wasn't it built in the early sixteen hundreds?" she said.

Mercurio recovered, "Yes, that's true, but the original building was built over a thousand years ago. It's been built and destroyed several times," he said.

Mercurio was more accurate than he could have known, and this answer seemed to satisfy the anal interrupter. When everyone was off the bus, the tour guide moved to the front of the group. He looked at Mastro ready to defer to him, but he just nodded so the guide continued.

"Please follow me and we'll go into the castle. It looks like they have some restoration taking place, so please steer clear of the heavy equipment," the real tour guide said.

The large group wandered around and entered the courtyard with small groups going in every conceivable direction. Mercurio and Mastro stayed close to the middle of the largest group. Mercurio was doing a good job interacting with people so he looked like he belonged to the tour.

Mastro wasn't speaking with anyone, but didn't stand out and looked over at the dig. It appeared there were seven or eight people milling around, but he couldn't be sure who they were. He would make sure to take out anyone connected with the dig when the tour bus departed. The group, including Mercurio and Mastro, all went into the north tower and the cobblestone courtyard was once again empty and quiet.

***

From his observation tower Laflamme watched the bus and the following vehicle come up the entrance road and into the parking lot. The vehicle looked like the car with the two guys who left earlier in the day, but it was difficult to tell because the bus was so large and the car followed so close he couldn't be sure. He was unable to get a clear view of the car because it pulled up next to the bus and was obscured even from his high perch.

He waited to see if two men came out from behind the bus, but no one did. A large group of people moved in unison and everyone appeared to be together. One individual with dark hair looked similar to the one who visited earlier, but he was engaged with people, chatting and laughing and appeared to be part of the group. Laflamme knew this large group added an uncomfortable element.

***

Max watched as the group disembarked. He tried to see who exited the vehicle, but it was impossible because the bus blocked his view. He also couldn't see the individuals as they exited the transport, but only saw them as they spilled out from around the backside of the two level silver bus. He watched as the group moved toward the castle, and everyone seemed to be interacting with no one appearing out of place. There were a couple of guys who were younger than most of the group, but one of them was so engaged with conversation and laughter he appeared to be a leader of the group.

Max turned to Alan. "Can you get into the tour group and just sort of hang out? See if anything appears to be out of the ordinary. Take someone with you and stick with the group and see if anyone splits off," he said.

Alan looked for Sean, but he was working his way into the hole and the only one standing around was Alfred.

"Alfred, come with me. We're going to merge with the tour group and look for anything that looks odd. Watch for anyone who breaks away from the group. Do you have your pistol with you?" he asked.

"Yes, what are we looking for?"

"Anything that appears out of place or seems to be odd. One or two people splitting from the group would be a red flag. Keep your eyes open," Alan said.

Alan and Alfred walked toward the cobblestone courtyard and found themselves following the curator. He was on his way to join the group to do his obligatory ten minute history of the castle speech. He would then conduct a thirty minute tour of Himmler's vault, the significance of the various rooms and Himmler's vision of Wewelsburg Castle becoming the SS Center of The World.

The curator wasn't aware of any potential danger.

Chapter 47)

Sean was at the bottom of the just finished crater, face to face with an emergency door exposed to daylight for the first time in close to seventy years. Goose bumps rose on his skin and his breathing became shallow. They were about to find out if their speculation was correct. The excavation company had furnished shovels, picks, and crowbars, per Gola's request, and before attempting to open the door Sean came out of the hole to confer with Gola.

They agreed it was time to send the excavators on their way since they didn't want witnesses to what they might find. They thanked the workers and told them their work was done for the day and they would be in touch. The excavators departed as Gola and Max went to the cruisers to retrieve three battery-powered lanterns and miner type hard hats with small centered headlights.

The excavation had taken longer than anticipated, so the team was satisfied to uncover just two of the three exit doors. Sean and Gola were clearing dirt and pebbles from one door while Max went to work on the other. Sean was getting some movement at the top of the emergency door he worked on, but it was locked from the inside. Using a crowbar, he kept rocking it, hoping the antique bolts would fail, but it was only giving by an inch. He stepped back and looked at Gola.

"Do you have any tricks up your sleeve? This looks as tight as the day it was installed," Sean said.

"No, I don't. We can't shoot it off because it's a steel door. If we had a chain maybe we could use the excavation equipment, but we don't have anything to attach the chain to. The door knob would just break off before the door would give. It appears to be bolted from the inside center," Gola said.

Max brushed away the last bit of dirt from the base and the corners of the door he had been clearing and anticipated the same issue as with the door to his right. He pushed down on the door handle, and to his surprise he heard a click, and it moved. He felt a jump in his heart.

"I think this door will open," Max said.

The three men took a collective deep breath. Hearts raced, breathing changed, and fists clenched. Max felt a quick surge of adrenaline and pulled the door as it scraped open. The sounds mimicked fingernails on a blackboard, but no one seemed to care. The door opened, crunching the dirt and stones littering its base. They expected the lab to be moldy and musty, but to their surprise it was dry with an almost antiseptic scent.

"This appears to be an air tight chamber. The dryness and complete lack of mold after all these years indicates this laboratory was built with the intention of being a self-contained, uncontaminated space," Sean said.

Max passed out the hard hats, and as the mini lights were switched on, Max turned to the group. "Let's see what we have," he said.

They entered the chamber with the lanterns and headgear turned on, casting long, irregularly shaped shadows. The floor underfoot was smooth and clean, and the air tasted like the most arid of deserts.

A nervous energy engulfed them as they entered the first room. It appeared to be an operating room with a table in the center and many instruments lined up on a table to its side. They continued down the hall, and every room was a mirror image of the first. Sean thought the rooms looked like they were occupied that morning with a noticeable lack of dust. They continued deeper into the Himmler-designed, secret SS laboratory and started bypassing rooms that appeared to be the same as what they had seen.

"Why do you think they needed all these operating rooms?" Sean asked.

"Himmler was always trying to prove the Aryan Race was superior. I would guess these rooms were for genetic re-engineering. Remember, they had a concentration camp on these grounds so who knew what went on in here. Did you know Joseph Mengele was a member of Himmler's SS, and it was Himmler who appointed Mengele to Auschwitz? Mengele's experiments were what Himmler chased all over the world. For God's sake, he sent Ernst Scher to the Himalayas to try to find the Yeti and prove it was an ancestor to the Aryan race," Max said.

"There's no way that's true," Gola said.

"It's true," Max said. "Himmler was up to many odd things, but my point is, these rooms would fit with what Himmler was trying to do. He would stop at nothing to prove his theories."

"I want to know more about this Yeti crap," Gola said.

They turned the corner and found a huge angular-shaped room. The hallway was narrow, with numerous rooms jutting off at right angles, but this room reflected the triangular shape of the castle. Shadows bounced off walls, and several metallic objects appeared in the rear of the room. Sean estimated they were almost ninety feet away as his heart pounded in his chest.

"*Have we really found this?*" Sean asked.

"It sure looks like it," Max said.

The visibility increased as their lanterns created flashes reflecting off the mercury-like surface of their find, and there was no doubt as to what these were. They touched the surface of the first object which felt almost cold. Sean noticed several desks and file cabinets lining the nearest wall. He walked to the closest desk and started reading the papers strewn over its top. He opened the drawers and pulled out the file cabinet in the lower portion of the desk, then moved to the two tall file cabinets next to the desk. Bingo; the first file cabinet was labeled *Freiburg* and the next was labeled *Czernica*.

"Hey, guys, this is it. There's an entire file cabinet on Freiburg and another one on Czernica. I'll bet all the records are in these files," Sean said.

"This appears to be the work area, and I would guess the re-engineering would have taken place right here," Max said.

They moved to what looked like a work in process. The lanterns provided some illumination, but they would need more light to determine what they were looking at. Max suggested they continue through the rest of the laboratory to see what else they might find. They agreed and continued to walk around the expansive area. There were various tables last having activity some sixty-nine years ago. The entire lab appeared to have been active right up to the point it was abandoned.

"By the look of everything, the lab workers expected to come back and continue their work. I expect the records are all here and reflect everything they did right up to their departure," Max said.

They made their way to the main hallway, then turned right and continued down the corridor to a different type of solid wood door. It was locked. After a few minutes of futile efforts, Max pulled out his pistol and put two bullets through the latch. They pushed the door, and it slid open. It was evident this room was unlike anything they had seen, as the lanterns revealed an entire wall covered with some sort of refrigerated space. Sean pulled open the door and witnessed a world-changing sight. The dried up remains of a four foot alien body lay on a small table inside the inoperative refrigeration unit. The eyes had long ago turned to dust, but there was no mistaking the shape of the head and size of the eye sockets. The body would have been kept on ice until power was killed to the facility. Sean reached out and touched the petrified skin. It was leathery and almost mummified. They stood in silence, stunned by what was reflecting off their optic nerve.

"Let's see what else we have," Max said.

They moved to another door in the refrigerated area. This one housed two more alien bodies. They continued to open doors until they discovered a grand total of nine alien bodies lying in their respective tombs. Included in the alien body count were two apparent human bodies. One of the small Alien bodies appeared to be in the process of a partial dissection and lay on an operating table with its calcified remains open to the world.

They continued to look through additional rooms and found a variety of electronic devices, blueprints, and a number projects in various stages of development. There was also a room containing nothing but file cabinet after file cabinet. This appeared to be the repository for all the experiments and information.

"This is it," Sean said. "This is everything we hoped for and more. This'll shake the world and will be the single most significant discovery in the history of man. I'm going to call Alan and give him the news."

Sean attempted to dial his cell phone.

"No signal," he said.

"Eight foot walls will block any kind of communication device," Gola said.

"You're right. Let's keep going, then I'll go get him," Sean said.

***

The tour was winding down as Mastro stayed to the rear of the large group. The group went from one room to another with the curator discussing the history and significance of each. The participants were enthralled to learn Himmler had a strong belief in the Holy Grail and the Arc of the Covenant. They were also interested to hear Himmler tried to duplicate King

Arthur's Knights of the Round Table and much of the symbolism of the north tower had been built around those concepts.

As they continued to *The Crypt*, one of the most famous rooms of the castle, Mastro ducked behind one of the large pillars adorning the main hall.

He watched as the last of the tour participants disappeared from sight. The security officer brought up the rear of the group as Mastro moved to a room named *Kig Artus*. He stood in the doorway, grabbed a book from a display table, and dropped it to make the loudest possible thud. He waited for the security guard to stop and turn and let the pompous sentry see him enter the study. He moved to the side of the door and waited.

He could hear the fast-paced, clickity clack of the guard's hard soles hitting the concrete floor. The guard slowed as he approached the door. He stepped into the *Kig Artus* study as a bullet slid through the barrel, and then the silencer of Mastro's pistol. Twisting at high velocity, it entered the security guard's left temple and spun its way through his brain, leaving a jagged bloody hole complete with oozing brain matter on the other side of his skull. Blood spatter hit the wall, and his now limp chubby body crushed the Nazi memorabilia displayed upon the table. Mastro grabbed the feet of the dead guard and dragged him just far enough to be out of the view of anyone strolling down the hall.

He left the room and thirty seconds later caught up with the tour. Mercurio caught his gaze, and Mastro nodded as Mercurio noticed the security guard was nowhere in sight. One down, he surmised. The curator was taking questions as the tour was ending and thanked them for coming. There was a murmur of gratitude as the group split, heading toward both the gift shops and the courtyard. Mercurio could hear the women talking about where they would be eating as he and Mastro hung back. It wasn't long before the room was empty and quiet.

Mercurio turned to Mastro. "Did you take care of the security guard?" he asked.

"Yes, I sent him to Valhalla," Mastro said.

"What do we do with the women in the two gift shops?" Mercurio asked.

"There's only one in each shop. Let's wait until we eliminate the curator and the guys we came for. If they see what's happening, we take

241

them out. If we can get rid of everyone without their knowledge, we let them live. They haven't seen anything and they're just clerks. I'd rather not deal with them if we can avoid it," Mastro said.

***

Alan was in the courtyard when he scanned the faces of the group. He noticed the two younger men were nowhere to be seen. The herd had finished buying Nazi trinkets from the two gift shops and were making their way toward their bus as the curator went through the door to his office.

Alan motioned to Alfred. "Did you notice the two younger guys who were part of the group?" he asked.

"Yes, I've seen them walking around," Alfred said.

"They're no longer with the group and seemed a little out of place because of the age difference. I haven't seen the security guard for a while either, and he was visible for the whole tour. I think something is happening. Get your gun ready," Alan said.

Alfred started losing color in his face. "Yes, I have my gun. Ah, why don't I go get Gola and Max?" he said.

"No, we don't have time. We need to find them ourselves," Alan said.

"What if they set up explosives?" Alfred asked.

"We need to do this ourselves," Alan said and took out his gun.

"I suggest you get out your gun and take off the safety," Alan said.

***

Mercurio and Mastro passed through the hallway as they worked their way toward the curator's office. The tall man in charge of the museum was checking messages as the two assassins entered his office. He looked up.

"Your tour is leaving. Did you forget something?" he asked.

"No, we didn't. We need some information. I need to know how many people from Freiburg are involved in the dig on the side of the castle," Mastro said.

"What do you want with them?" the curator asked.

"I ask you again, how many are there?" Mastro asked.

"You have to leave at once," the curator said.

242

Mastro removed his pistol, complete with silencer, and without another word put a bullet through the curator's arm.

"Now do you feel like cooperating? I'll ask you just once more, how many are there?" he said.

The curator grabbed his trembling, dangling arm and replied with fear, "There are five," he said

"Thank you" Mastro said.

They were the last words the curator would ever hear as a bullet exploded through his forehead. His head snapped backwards and his body slammed against a now bloody map of Wewelsburg Castle.

"Let's get this finished," Mercurio said.

He glanced at the parking lot, and the tour people were still milling around taking pictures and talking. They were in no hurry, and Mercurio was grateful for that. He knew as soon as the bus pulled away, his car would be exposed, creating a major red flag to anyone paying attention.

"You go into the courtyard and walk to the bus while they're still here. If you do it now it won't draw any attention because they're still hanging around taking pictures. Check out what's happening with the diggers. I haven't noticed if they've stopped, but I don't hear anything. I'll look for any windows facing the back and try to see what's going on. Let's meet back here in five minutes," Mastro said.

Mercurio walked out of the curator's courtyard door toward the bus. Mastro walked out of the interior office door and headed down the hall when he saw two men coming his way. He had noticed them mingling with the tour, but hadn't noticed them disembark the bus. He had to think on his feet.

"How is the dig going?" he asked.

The question stopped Alan in his tracks and created a moment of doubt which was what Mastro hoped for. Alan never had a chance to answer as Mastro raised his pistol and pulled the trigger, hitting Alan somewhere in his upper body. Alan spun around and went face-first into the concrete floor, knocking him out cold.

Alfred panicked and jumped behind a pillar. He raised his pistol and started firing without aiming. Mercurio was ten feet away and also moved behind a pillar. There was nowhere for either man to go without being exposed. Alfred dialed Gola, and the phone rang and rang and went into voice mail.

Alfred was hoping someone would hear his gunshot and come to help. It was unfortunate for Alfred that only half of what he hoped for came true.

Mercurio had just gotten to the tour group when he heard a muffled gunshot. Anyone else in the tour group would have thought it was a small firecracker, but Mercurio knew better. He walked as fast as he could without drawing attention.

He opened the door to the corridor and drew his revolver. He tiptoed down the hall until he saw a body, face-down, lying in a growing pool of blood. He crept silently around the same type of pillar protecting Alfred and Mastro from each other and was only ten feet from Alfred. He had a wide open shot, raised his revolver, took aim, and squeezed the trigger. The screaming piece of lead pierced Alfred's spine, and he crumbled with a surprised look. Mercurio casually strolled up to him, looked into Alfred's unblinking eyes, and put another bullet through his head. Alfred's body twitched and went limp and lifeless.

Mercurio called out and said, "Mastro, I got him. Are you alright?"

"Yes, I'm coming out," Mastro said.

Mastro saw Alfred piled in a heap and blood expanding over the concrete, but didn't comment.

"When you were outside, could you tell if the digging had stopped?" Mastro asked.

"It stopped, and I didn't see any of the workmen. There are fewer cars in the lot, so I think they finished and departed," Mercurio said.

"Since we've got bodies lying here and bleeding all over the place we're going to have to terminate the ladies. There are only three of these guys left. Let's take care of them and we'll finish our business with the women. Let's go," Mastro said.

***

Laflamme had been in the north tower since before the sun came up. He was tired and stiff and waiting for something to happen, then he heard what he thought were two gunshots from somewhere below.

He delayed for a moment waiting for the bus to pull out to verify his belief. One minute later as the bus departed he felt a jump in his heart. The car arriving with the bus was still sitting in the parking lot. This set off

244

all of his alarms. Their adversaries had been here all afternoon. He dialed Sean's number, but after ringing several times it went into voice mail.

He sped down the north tower steps and looked into the curator's office at the base of the stairs. He saw a chair on its side, opened the door, and saw a not yet stiffening body staring into space with a small dark red spot in the middle of its forehead.

Laflamme took the safety off his pistol and moved down the hall. He saw a dark object lying motionless in the middle of the hall. His eyes went from Alan lying face-down in a pool of blood to Alfred, whose brains were leaking from a gaping void in his head. He stepped over their bodies, avoiding the still expanding pool of sticky, crimson ooze. He continued down the hall reaching the large French doors leading to the courtyard. From there he stepped onto the cobblestones.

***

Mercurio and Mastro were about two minutes ahead of Laflamme's discovery. They had just gotten to the open door leading into the laboratory and could see a faint light coming from inside.

"I'm going in. Why don't you position yourself behind the bulldozer or whatever that thing is?" Mastro said.

Mercurio looked at the large yellow piece of earth moving equipment and agreed.

"That's a power shovel, and I told you I know how to operate it. Don't be long. Remember, our plan is to make this their permanent living quarters for the next thousand or so years. I think I should entomb them right now," Mercurio said.

"I just want to have a quick look," Mastro said.

"Do it fast," Mercurio said.

Mercurio climbed into the cab of the large piece of equipment and liked his vantage point. He sat behind darkly tinted windows designed to protect the operator from the rays of the day long sun, but also provided a perfect spot to observe without being seen.

He watched as Mastro disappeared into the dark laboratory and checked his clip. He glanced up and saw movement from around the corner of the castle. A tall thin man approached with caution and gun drawn. This was the third guy he encountered outside the laboratory, not counting the curator and security guard, and wondered how many more would appear.

He waited until the man stood in front of the hole with his back to the equipment. This was just like shooting the last guy. He aimed the silencer at the center of Laflamme's back and pulled the trigger. Laflamme recoiled as an ice pick like pain pierced his back. He hit the dirt face-first and his world turned black. Mastro was exiting the darkened lab when he encountered a body tumbling into the hole. He looked up at the giant yellow machine, shrugged, and climbed out of the man-made cavity.

"Let's get the bodies of the two guys in the hallway and put them in the lab. The curator and security guard will look like a robbery as long as the other bodies are nowhere to be seen. Let's move quickly," Mastro said.

"Good thinking. Let's go," Mercurio said.

Four minutes later they dragged both Alan and Alfred through the loose dirt and dumped their bodies into the laboratory. They tossed Laflamme on top of the first two bodies as all three continued to seep body fluids. Mastro peered into the laboratory, but could only make out the same flickering light from some distance away. He retreated and slammed the door shut as Mercurio climbed into the large yellow earth mover.

Mastro waved his arm in a circular motion, and Mercurio recognized the signal to start. He fired up the earth mover and started shoveling large amounts of dirt and rock back into the same hole from which they had emerged only an hour earlier. He was filling the hole at a faster rate than it took to remove the dirt.

Chapter 48)

Sean thought he heard something. They were at the far end of the lab looking through files and acting like little kids at Christmas, then they heard it. A loud thud followed by a louder clang at the other end of the lab.

"That's the second noise I've heard. We should check it out," Sean said.

"It might be Alfred and Alan. Let's make sure," Max said.

As Sean walked toward the emergency exit he noticed it was significantly darker than when they entered, and light ceased from the door. Shadows flickered from their head-mounted lanterns and skipped on the floor. As they got closer to the entrance they could see the silhouette of something piled up just inside the door. Sean stepped rapidly and discovered the bodies of their three cohorts. He bent down and turned over the one on top, and his hands were instantly covered in a warm sticky liquid he immediately knew was blood.

"It's Laflamme," he said.

Gola moved to the agent's side and checked for a pulse. "He's still alive, but we need to stop the bleeding," he said.

Sean moved his headlight and noticed a large hole containing brain matter leaking from Alfred's head. He knew Alfred was dead.

He turned to Alan's body and saw he was saturated in blood as Max put his fingers to his neck. "Alan's got a pulse. He's also still alive," Max said.

Sean neglected to make a comment as to Alfred's well-being.

"Let's get them into the operating room. It might have what we need," Sean said.

"How's Alfred?" Max asked.

"I'm afraid he's gone," Sean said.

"*Fuck*," Gola said.

"God dammit, I'm going to bury these pricks. This *is not* over," Max said.

"We need to focus on Alan and Laflamme and keep them alive," Sean said, hoping to divert attention to the living.

247

"You're right. Let's put our attention to where it can make a difference," Gola said.

Sean and Gola attended to Laflamme and Alan respectively as Max tried to move the door. It wouldn't budge, and every once in a while there was a slight noise against the door. He couldn't tell what it was, since bomb shelter doors don't transmit noise as much as they do vibration.

"I think we have a major problem." Max said, "This door isn't budging. Whoever shot the three of them is filling the hole."

The urgency of their situation was evident. If the hole was being filled, where were the security guard and the curator? This wouldn't be happening if they were okay.

"Do you think this is air tight?" Sean asked.

"It is without a doubt. The lack of dust in here after all these years indicates a lack of oxygen," Gola said.

"We know our cell phones won't work, and I don't think there's any other way out of here. Anyone have any ideas?" Sean asked.

"We need to go through this place again. This time we look for lights, generators, air supplies, and anything we can use. There has to be an emergency area where they would have kept supplies in the event of a bombing. I doubt they ever expected to be trapped down here with no way out, but there should be some supplies. Sean, I'll start looking around while you and Gola attend to Laflamme and Alan," Max said.

"Max, how much battery time do you think we have left on our lights?" Sean asked.

"Good question. Let's start conserving them right now."

They clicked off all the lanterns with the exceptions of the one being used on their injured friends and the one that Max was about to use.

"Can you tell how they're doing?" Max asked.

"They're alive is all I can tell you. Laflamme was shot in the back and the bullet is still in him. I have no way to know if it hit an organ. The bleeding is starting to slow, but there's no way to know if there's internal damage. Alan was shot in the shoulder and wasn't wearing a vest. We need to get them both to a hospital," Gola said.

Max started his search.

Five minutes later he located the emergency supplies. There were blankets, age-old dehydrated foods, lanterns, batteries, paper supplies, water, and many other items. Max inserted the battery into one of the lanterns, but when he turned it on it flickered for a moment, then died. He continued looking. Fifteen minutes later he had uncovered nothing else and returned to the room where Gola and Sean were attending to the wounded.

"We need to get to a hospital soon if they're to have any chance," Gola said.

Sean pulled out his cell phone and walked around watching to see if he could get any signal. He couldn't.

"You won't get a signal; eight foot walls and air tight, no chance," Gola said.

The lights started to fade.

"I think we have less than an hour of lantern light. We better get materials to burn just in case," Max said.

"Now there's irony. We make the discovery of the millennium and we have to burn those very records to create light," Sean said.

"It would be better to burn towels and sheets. Anything with cotton will last longer. If we pull it tight, it will act like a torch. Just be aware, fire will burn up our oxygen and it's anyone's guess how much we have," Max said.

They had been in the tomb for about an hour and knew there was only one way out. The fact the hole was filled in by someone other than the workers told them the curator and the security guard were MIA.

"I just had a bad thought. We know the Vatican's reach included the police chiefs in both Villingen and Poland. If the guy here is in their pocket, we have a major problem. He'll block any investigation just like Barinski did in Czernica. If that happens we'll be in here for a long sleep," Gola said.

"Thanks for the pleasant thought," Sean said.

The three men were now sitting on the floor. They understood the gravity of the situation. The room was silent. No one had words to offer as one of the lanterns quivered and went out. The darkness was an inky black Sean had never experienced, and they sat quietly for a few more moments.

"Do we fire up another lantern?" Gola asked.

"Why not?" Max said.

Sean heard the click and the lantern flickered and went on. It seemed bright, both because they had just come from absolute darkness and the fact that it was a fresh battery.

Chapter 49)

It was Sean who heard it. He didn't say anything, but his alert system switched on. He sat still and strained to listen, then he thought he heard it again. He got up, walked over, and put his hand on the door, but felt nothing.

"What are you doing?" Max asked.

"I thought I heard something," Sean said.

"I'd love to think you're right, but you may be hallucinating," Max said.

He heard it again. "Did you hear that?" Sean asked.

"No, but the fact you think you did is encouraging," Max said, jumping up. He put his hand on the door and felt it, "Someone is digging," he said.

Their excitement turned to concern when Max asked what happens if it's someone from the Vatican.

"I'll take my chances shooting it out in sunlight instead of staying down here for eternity," Gola said. "Besides, the only chance Alan and Laflamme have is to get them to a hospital as soon as possible."

They waited and the sounds stopped. For several tense moments they stood waiting. All of a sudden the door started to move. It swung open and a single man stood in the opening.

"Good evening, I'm Father Edwardo Battalini," he said.

Sean was closest to him. *"Father Battalini, I'm Sean O'Shea, and you have no idea what a welcome sight you are,"* Sean said.

The three captives hurried through the doorway.

"Excuse me Father, but claustrophobia has set in," Gola said, as he brushed by Battalini into the clean air.

***

One and a half hours after the door was first opened, Mercurio was finishing his re-filling of the recently excavated hole. In the woods to the left of the dig, Father Battalini watched the proceedings, as he had since the night before. He had parked far below the castle and walked up the road, bringing a sleeping bag, a large flashlight, food, and weapons. He wanted a full view of events about to unfold.

He watched as Laflamme arrived, the first arrival by Mercurio and Mastro, then again later in the day, the arrival of the investigators, then the arrival of the bus. He had observed much of what took place, although he couldn't see the murders occurring inside the castle.

All night and all day he struggled with what role he would play. His job and logical mind was to support and make sure the Vatican assassins were successful. His conscience and heart pointed him to do the right thing and start the process of change. As the day went along he was feeling stronger and stronger about his choice. When he watched Mercurio shoot Laflamme in the back, drag the bodies of two other victims into the laboratory, and bury the rest alive, he sprang into action.

He moved through the woods and went around the opposite side of the castle. His plan was to wait inside the castle until the two assassins separated. It would only be a matter of time before one of them would need to use the bathroom or would hunt for food. Mercurio was almost done filling the hole when Mastro waved to him.

"I'm going to find the women, take them out and make this look like a robbery," Mastro said.

Mastro entered the castle and stopped in the bathroom to wash off dirt and blood. Battalini waited, felt the weight of the Walther PPK in his right hand, and slowed his breathing. Over the years he had directed his operatives to eliminate threats, but he had never been the trigger-man. That fact did not give him pause, as the man in charge of the Vatican black ops opened the bathroom door. Mastro was sitting on a toilet and hadn't bothered to close the door to the stall. Battalini appeared, took aim, and without saying a word put a bullet into Mastro's gaping mouth. The back of the toilet stall was instantly decorated with blood, skin and bodily fluids as Mastro slipped off the toilet. Battalini didn't bother to check for a pulse and headed back toward Mercurio. He knew he'd be exposed if he tried to cross to the power shovel, so he waited.

Mercurio finished with the last bucketful of dirt, dismounted the power shovel, and walked toward the castle. He came around the corner of timeworn fortress and was startled to see a man standing in the firing position with gun drawn. Battalini didn't stop to have a John Wayne macho moment, and as soon as Mercurio appeared, Battalini fired a chunk of lead through Mercurio's throat and down went Mercurio. The good father stood over the now gurgling Mercurio and delivered the next shot through the assassin's right eye. Battalini went to the power shovel, where Mercurio had been only moments before, and began removing the dirt that had just been replaced. The removal was fast because the dirt was loose, and soon Battalini was pulling open the door to the underground laboratory. The door swung open, and Battalini instantly became the hero to three new friends.

After drinking in fresh air, Max and Sean reentered the laboratory and continued to administer aid to Laflamme and Alan. Battalini followed, watched, and noted how the body count had risen.

***

Gola called for paramedics as he considered the loyalties of the Paderborn Police Chief. He chose to call the hospital emergency number and requested three ambulances instead of calling the police.

It wasn't long before ambulances could be heard wailing in the distance, and three minutes later Gola motioned to them to come into the courtyard. Large paramedics in white coats followed Gola into the laboratory, and within minutes both Alan and Laflamme were on stretchers on their way to the ambulances. The paramedics were working feverishly on both of the wounded men as the third group of paramedics took their time with Alfred's dead body.

Twenty minutes later Gola, Max, and Sean stood in the parking lot, which had degenerated into an assault on the senses. Four squad cars arrived right after the ambulances, and all left their lights pulsating and radios blaring.

Among the arrivals was the Paderborn Chief of Police. Sean observed and was startled as Father Battalini conducted a rather animated discussion with the chief. What had they talked about? Why had the discussion take place, and why had Battalini dominated the conversation?

Sean heard Max say he found the security guard and the curator, and they were both dead. The women in the gift shops were shaken, but alive. Sean started to ask himself if any of this was worth it, but before he could get there he cut off the thought. It was what it was, and there was no way to un-ring the bell. They had to deal with it and go forward; there was no other choice.

The police began interviews with the team as the ambulances with Alan and Laflamme departed to the local hospital. The third ambulance sat quietly with Alfred as its sole occupant and the morgue its destination. Before the paramedics could load the other bodies, the police stopped them to preserve the crime scene as the castle degenerated into chaos. The news organizations had arrived, curiosity seekers were trying to get by the yellow tape blocking the entrance, and many people were milling around.

Sean looked for a quiet spot and walked in the direction of the dig. He had all but forgotten about the incredible contents housed in the subterranean crypt. He turned the corner to where the power shovel was sitting and was shocked to see the laboratory door closed with two large chains connecting one door latch to the other with a large lock protecting the contents. Where had it come from and who put it there? He went into the hole and found it wasn't the best of installations, but it was an effective temporary barrier.

He heard a voice behind him. "Do you like my handiwork?" Father Battalini said. "I thought, given the contents, we should keep out the snoopers. Sean, we need to talk."

"Okay, let's find somewhere quiet," Sean said.

They walked into the castle courtyard and passed yellow crime scene tape placed in strategic areas. Sean stepped around Mercurio's still warm body, complete with blood covered face, and looked back at Battalini.

Sean felt the need to wash his hands and face, opened the bathroom, and found Mastro's stiffening body sprawled on the floor of a stall.

"Don't bother with him. He's no longer a threat," Battalini said.

"I do believe you're correct. We were dead men without your intervention. You saved our asses," Sean said.

"I won't disagree with you. After witnessing what was taking place I couldn't sit by and watch," Battalini said.

"How did you know what was in the laboratory?" Sean asked.

"I didn't know for sure, but had a good idea what might be there. While you were attending to the wounded I had a look to verify my suspicions and felt we needed to lock it up.

"Let's take a stroll through the castle and find a private spot. I think the police interviews will take some time," Battalini said.

They walked into the castle, and the man from the Vatican went into the north tower. He entered a large room used by Himmler as his personal office. It had been fully restored so it was private and comfortable.

A thick burgundy velvet rope sagged across the doorway with a do not enter sign hung from its center. Sean thought, without amusement, there was no longer anyone to tell them not to use the office as he disconnected one side of the rope.

They entered, and Sean had the odd sensation of stepping into the 1930s. Nazi memorabilia and SS symbols were everywhere. Himmler must have been an obsessive compulsive, because SS symbols appeared on everything from pens, pencils, cups, and lamps. Every piece in the room seemed to have the SS symbol on it, including Himmler's desk and chair. It seemed somehow ironic he was about to speak with a man from the Vatican, a priest who just saved their lives, in the special office created by one of the most evil men in history.

This room reinforced Sean's surprise at the entire museum. Not only did it celebrate Nazism, but it appeared to be a shrine to the Third Reich. How this museum could exist in a country having laws against such things was curious at best.

"Sean, I have much to discuss with you. I first want to thank you for being a friend to Father Schmidt. He appreciated your interest and felt a genuine connection with you. He called me after your first visit, and he had taken an instant liking to you. I think it was because you didn't judge or argue about his crazy ideas, and instead you asked questions and were interested in his thoughts. That was important to someone who had to deal with a loss of faith and his subsequent rejection by almost everyone he knew.

"I think I'm responsible for his change of attitude, because I told him of many negative things the church hid over the years. I didn't realize it, but I was giving him the foundation for his tormented feelings toward the Vatican. I was so involved in the internal politics of making the Vatican function and protecting it from threats, I lost sight of what he was seeing. It took his death to jolt me to where I could step back and see the bigger picture, and I didn't like what I saw.

"I'm going to be direct with you and reveal something I never shared with Schmidt. I'm the one in charge of security for the Vatican. It's my job to make sure the church's secrets stay secrets regardless of the means. That's how I learned so much about what Schmidt referred to as the church's hypocrisy. I was the one making sure the threats were eliminated.

"I've been tracking the movements of your team from the time contacts were made with Poland and Lyon. You wouldn't believe the reach of the Vatican's tentacles. The elimination of your group was a directive from the Black Pope. He also brought in a man I've always disapproved of and who answered only to the Black Pope. He was the man you killed in the shootout in front of the Freiburg police station. He was also responsible for the death of my dearest friend," Battalini said.

"I'm glad I was the one to take him out," Sean said.

"I'm glad you did, too. If you didn't, I would have. When I found out the Black Pope gave the order, I reevaluated my future with the Vatican. I was supposed to come here to make sure you all disappeared. I didn't involve my team, because I wasn't sure what I was going to do until last night.

"I've now cast my lot. When word of my role gets back to the Black Pope, he'll have me eliminated. You may have seen me speaking with the police chief in the courtyard. He's on the Vatican payroll, as are about thirty percent of the police chief's in Germany and about fifty percent in Italy. I was buying time so I can get back to the Vatican before word leaks out. I'm not sure what I'll do, but I'm not going to run.

"We still have a major issue, and all of you remain in extreme danger. The Black Pope will send more people to eliminate anyone connected with this discovery. What did you intend to do with what you've uncovered?" Battalini asked.

"First, thank you for sharing all that. I did find *Herr* Schmidt to be a genuine guy. I loved his directness and sense of humor. Also, thank you for saving us instead of burying us. When I started this project I was doing research for a potential novel, and it evolved to where we are today. I haven't thought about what we'd do with what's below us, but I do know it would change the world," Sean said.

"I don't disagree that it would change the world, but do you think it would be for the better? Do you realize, with this revelation comes potential destruction of all Christian, Jewish, and Muslim societies whose teaching is one god and an earth centric belief? This would cause destabilization in parts of the world already unstable. Is the release of this knowledge in the best interest of the world?" Battalini asked.

"I believe it's the right thing from a moral standpoint and I think *Herr* Schmidt would agree," Sean said.

"Ha, you did connect with him. There's no doubt Father Schmidt would agree with you, but it doesn't make it right or wise," Battalini said.

"What do you think we should do?" Sean asked.

"Let's keep it locked up for a couple of days and see what happens next. I have to get back to the Vatican and determine my future. Nothing can happen here because this is now a crime scene, and the museum will be closed for several days. The castle is part of the national museum system so they'll have to grant future access. You had admittance through the curator, but he's dead, and it's likely the museum will stay closed until a new curator is appointed.

"In the meantime, attempts on you and your friends are likely to continue, and if I'm taken out, it'll be my organization sent to eliminate you. One option you have is to go public, but you'll lose all control. I think sitting on this for a few days is in order. I'll get back to the Vatican around day-break, and if I'm able, I'll contact you and help set the course if you'll let me," Battalini said.

"Given everything I know, there's no alternative. I'll put my trust in your hands and wait for your call. Thank you," Sean said.

"Sean, to be honest with you, had the Black Pope not sanctioned the murder of Father Schmidt, I might have been on the other side of this. My eyes are now open, and I'm forever changed, so I thank you as well. I'll arrive at the Vatican between five and six in the morning and evaluate my options on the way. I'll be in touch," Battalini said.

He took Sean's hand and shook it for an extended time.

***

Max and Gola were huddled when Sean came out of the castle. They had informed the family of Alfred's death and were dealing with those emotions.

"What are you going to do tonight?" Sean asked.

"We were just discussing the options. Gola is going back and the family is getting together. You tell me what you want to do. If you want to stay, I'll stay with you," Max said.

"I'd like to check on Alan and Laflamme and see how they're doing. Do you know where they were taken?" Sean asked.

"They were taken to St. Vincenz-Krankenhaus in Paderborn. It's supposed to be a good hospital," Gola said.

"Let's go see them, then we'll make a decision on what to do," Sean said.

"Okay, let's go," Max said.

"One more thing. I had a long talk with Battalini. I have a lot to tell you, but here's the gist. He warned we may still be in danger and not to trust the Paderborn Chief of Police. He's in the pocket of the Vatican. Battalini's going back to the Vatican tonight and will call me to suggest next steps as soon as he's able.

"We're lucky to have made contact with *Herr* Schmidt. In effect, it was Schmidt's death that saved our lives and turned Battalini into our savior. According to Battalini, the Black Pope will keep coming at us until he's succeeded. Battalini was supposed to be the backup for the killers, but for several reasons he took a different path and thinks the Black Pope will try to eliminate him. This isn't over. For all we know there may be more of these guys on the way. I'll fill you in when I hear from him, I should know more tomorrow," Sean said.

"Let us know as soon as he calls. If he goes silent we have to assume the Black Pope has taken him out and has sent people to finish the job," Gola said.

"I'm truly sorry for all of this," Sean said.

"Don't be. This is not your fault. We're dealing with an arrogant, dangerous, out-of-control malevolent entity that we must stop," Gola said.

"By the way, Battalini locked the lower level. It's just as well because we have to figure out how we can obtain legal access to it," Sean said.

"We'll be preoccupied with funeral arrangements and how Alan is doing. We also must hear from Battalini before we know how the next few days will play out," Max said.

Sean was surprised to notice the castle lights were on and darkness had fallen. The illumination from the castle, with its three medieval towers, created unique shadows and made Sean think of Himmler standing in the same spot admiring his new toy. It had to resemble what it looked like in 1936. The only thing missing from the vision was a vintage Mercedes. Sean was lost in the image for a moment, then returned to reality. He was here,

257

it was 2014, and he felt responsible for the deaths of several people. Talk about a wakeup call.

Sean turned to Max. "Are you ready to go?" he asked.

"Yes, let's get the hell out of here," Max said.

Max hugged his brother, and the hug lingered longer than it had in a long time. With moist eyes Max walked across the cobblestone to the parked car. Quite a lot had happened since arriving mid-morning.

Max wound his way back down the hill, and in a few minutes they pulled into the parking lot of St. Vincenz-Krankenhaus Hospital. Max presented his credentials and asked where Alan and Laflamme were being treated. Both were in the emergency center, and Max was able to find the attending physician. Laflamme would recover despite the gunshot to his upper back. Fortunately it had missed his organs. Their efforts to stop his bleeding had been effective, and he was on a faster track to recovery than Alan. He had lost so much blood he was still being pumped full of transfusions. It would be twenty-four hours before they would know if Alan would survive.

"What do you want to do?" Sean asked.

"There's nothing more to be done here, so I think we should head back to Freiburg. There's a number of family things that need to be attended to, and I don't want to leave it all on Gola's shoulders," Max said.

***

The trip to Freiburg was like an intermittent broadcast where the signal would come and go, punctuated by long periods of silence.

Max finally said, "What are we going to do now? We have the greatest find in history, but no longer have access to it. We know who the bad guys are, but we can't get to them. It's likely they'll keep coming, but we can't get to the source to stop this nonsense."

"I think you just summed up what I was thinking. The wild card is Battalini, but he may not survive the night. Otherwise, I'm not sure what our plan should be," Sean said.

Sean's phone rang. It was Cat. He debated whether to answer, then clicked the send/receive button.

"Hi, hon, how are you?" he said.

"I just saw a news piece about a number of violent deaths at a castle in Germany. You said you were working at a castle today, and I just wanted to make sure it didn't have anything to do with you," Cat said.

"As a matter of fact, it took place where we were working. It seemed there were fanatics who didn't want us looking for certain artifacts, and they tried to stop us. Alan was wounded and he's in the hospital. The assailants were killed. I'm fine, so you don't have to worry at all," Sean said.

"Sean, when are you coming home? I want you out of there, now," she said.

"We're wrapping this up. It won't be much longer."

"Can you leave tomorrow?"

"No, there's still more to get done. Don't worry. I'll call you tomorrow and give you an update."

"I want you out of there. *Do you hear me?*"

"Yes I do, but I still have to wrap this up so all my work isn't wasted. I also want to be here if Alan needs me for anything," he said.

He knew the idea of helping Alan would change her view.

"Call me tomorrow and tell me when you'll be home."

"Okay. I love you, and tell Liam I love him. Talk to you tomorrow."

Max turned his head toward Sean. "She doesn't have any idea what you've been up to, does she?" he asked.

"No, she'd worry too much."

"Good luck with that one."

At eleven Max pulled up to the Colombi Hotel and Sean trudged into the hotel. So much had happened since they left early that morning.

Chapter 50)

Battalini drove all night. He needed to get back before the Black Pope became aware of the details of the Wewelsburg shootout. The news reports were vague, and the first accounts indicated five people were killed with two more in critical condition. The Black Pope would likely think the mission was successful because no names had been released and no details had been reported.

Battalini knew he had frightened the police chief to the extent there would be no communication from him. Battalini's position as head of black ops allowed him to strike fear into anyone aware of what his position meant. His window to resolve this dilemma was shrinking, and he needed to get to the Vatican as soon as possible. He stopped for food and coffee, which he consumed as he drove. He did a mental review of his interesting life and how this might play out. He didn't want to focus on a worst case scenario, so he just daydreamed about positive what ifs.

During the trek he thought about Schmidt. He started from his earliest memories from nine years old and went in chronological order through the last time he spoke with him. For most of the process his heart was warmed, and it was only when he recalled his last conversation did he feel the pain of loss. When he recalled the Black Pope's casual reference to the elimination of an ex-priest his rage renewed. He considered countless options until he landed on one that felt right.

At five-seventeen Battalini pulled into the Vatican. He felt a surge of confidence when he drove through security because he wasn't stopped or questioned. He parked and went to his office. Mail was piled on his desk, and his computer showed two hundred thirty-two new messages. He called his second in command to verify the Black Pope hadn't been in contact.

His course was clear. Wasting no time, he picked a large gold key from his center drawer and left the office. He descended a curved staircase leading downward and to the right. Shadows bounced off the walls as the dim lights lining the stone steps created a Gothic effect as Father Battalini continued in silence.

At the bottom of the steps the carpet turned into a dark gray stone floor resembling the walls and ceiling. He turned to the left and continued walking deeper into catacombs, seemingly unchanged since the Middle Ages. The only concession to the twenty-first century was incandescent lighting that replaced ancient oil lamps.

He passed several doors, all with large exterior locks, until he stood in front of his destination. He inserted the gold key and the lock clicked open. This ancient arsenal contained every weapon a small army could need. He went to a large apothecary cabinet where each drawer was labeled with its contents. Father Battalini was a historian before he became involved in the dark side of the Vatican and wanted history, irony, and karma to be with him.

He opened a drawer labeled *Veninum Lupinum*. The poison, developed in the 1300s, was documented in a 'how to make' book in the late fifteenth century. It was a combination of several poisons and included almonds, limes, and honey as taste additives. It could be added to wine, tea, or food, and detection was difficult because of its sweet flavor. *Veninum Lupinum* had become the poison of choice for Vatican eliminations. History teaches that six serving Popes had been poisoned, but the real number was, in fact, much higher. He also chose this particular poison, in part, as retribution. It was this very Black Pope, to whom Battalini hoped to serve this special concoction, who selected this poison to serve to Pope John Paul the first in September of 1978.

Battalini opposed that operation because he admired Pope John Paul. The Pope wanted to strip many influential cardinals, including the freemasons, of their power and planned to investigate and reorganize the Vatican Bank. He had been pope for only thirty-three days when he was murdered. *Veninum Lupinum* had been slipped into the pope's medication in powder form, and the Vatican stepped on its own dick by allowing the release of so many contradictory stories. The cause was attributed to a heart attack, but the number of different accounts led to books exposing the method, the motive and the likely perpetrators. As its own sovereign nation the Vatican was able to say and do whatever it wanted. People who saw the Pope's death mask knew it was not a heart attack, but rather an excruciating poisoning designed to inflict maximum pain.

Battalini always wondered why the Black Pope insisted on this poison instead of newer, quicker, silent killers. He suspected the Black Pope was a freemason, and this was his way to get a little payback. Rumors abounded that it was only with great effort that the embalmers changed the expression on the dead pope's face. The Vatican prevented an autopsy, and his successor, Pope John Paul the second, rescinded everything the dead pope had started. The coup d'état was successful and immediate.

Battalini removed the bottle and placed two tablespoons of the poison into a small vial. He replaced the bottle and shut the drawer, retraced his steps, and soon was back in his office. It was now five minutes after six. He had black and red robes hanging in his office and chose the black one, still wearing his pants so he could put a pistol in his waist band. The good father was committed to make this happen whether it be clean or messy. He left his office and again moved down the darkened hallway. This time he climbed the dark, wine-colored stairs.

At the top of the steps he turned left and walked into the kitchen galley. He filled a metal tea pot with water and placed it on a flaming gas burner. Once boiling he added a single tea bag to a cup, intended for himself, and filled to the brim. Next he added the remaining water to a white china tea pot, added the vial of poison, and five tea bags. He opened the refrigerator and took out milk and a lemon, arranging all on a fancy small china plate. He finished by adding a silver serving bowl of sugar and two small spoons.

It was now six- thirty, and he hoped his timing would be perfect. He carried the tray down the hall and placed it on the vacant desk in front of the Black Pope's office, knowing the assistant wouldn't arrive until eight.

Behind the closed door was the Black Pope's office and his fifteen hundred square feet of luxurious living space. The poor people who scrimped to scrape together their tithing would be thrilled to see how their money was put to use.

Battalini needed to get the Black Pope out of bed. He knocked on the door and there was no response. He had never attempted to get to him without the help of the assistant. He removed his cell phone and called the Black Pope's number. It range four times and was finally answered.

"*Hallo*, Father Battalini. I was hoping I would hear from you," the Black Pope said. It was apparent the Black Pope recognized Battalini's number.

"I wanted to give you the briefing in person and drove all night. It was quite a scene yesterday," Battalini said.

"I gather that from the news reports. Can you see me at eight?"

"I can do better than that. There are things we need to discuss that can't wait. I'm standing outside your office door and have a full pot of tea and am ready to give you all the gory details right now."

"*Bravo*, I'll be right there."

Moments later the door opened.

"Father Battalini, so good to see you."

The hostility which had been present two days ago was nowhere to be found. Battalini knew it was only because the Black Pope felt the mission had been accomplished.

Battalini carried the tray into the office and set it on the Black Pope's desk. He grabbed the tea cup he filled in the pantry and drank from it so the pope wouldn't notice it hadn't been poured from the pot. Battalini didn't offer the tea, not wanting to appear obvious or too anxious. He sat back in a guest chair and was quiet.

The Black Pope sat in his chair with messy uncombed white hair, wearing a black bath robe. He was breathless, and Battalini kept him waiting, trying to create nervous energy.

"Okay, tell me what happened," the Black Pope said expectantly.

"Well, it was a long day. I got to the castle the night before and took a vantage point in the woods. It took a long time for things to start happening," he said.

He was stretching it out and it worked. The Black Pope reached over and poured himself a full cup of the special tea.

"Get to the point. What happened?"

"The two guys from Opus Dei showed up at eight or nine, before anyone else, looked around, and left," Battalini said.

The man behind the desk added sugar and lemon to his tea. He still hadn't had any. His frustration grew. "Continue," he said.

"Then around eleven everyone showed up. The guys from Freiburg were there and the excavators started digging. The digging lasted four to five hours."

That did it. The Black Pope took a large swallow of the tea.

"The Opus Dei guys came back to the castle following a large tour bus, quite ingenious by the way."

Another large swallow was taken.

"They mingled with the folks on the tour and came into the court-

263

yard with about thirty other people so they couldn't be distinguished from the crowd."

Another swallow was taken. It wouldn't be long now.

"When the tour left, the Opus Dei guys wasted no time in executing the security guard and the curator."

Sweat was forming on the Black Pope's forehead, and beading shown on his upper lip. Battalini could see the beginning of general discomfort. He could also tell the Black Pope was enjoying his description, almost as if he was watching the movie, and took another large drink as if that would help his discomfort.

"When the hole was dug and the door pried open, three of the investigators entered the laboratory. That's when your Opus Dei friends shot the remaining three, threw them into the underground chamber, shut the door, and refilled the hole, burying them alive."

"*Bravo. What a smooth operation.*" There was a small pause as he shifted in his leather chair. "I am not feeling so well," he said.

"Here, let me pour you more tea. Maybe it will help," Battalini said.

Another large swallow was taken. "It doesn't seem to be helping. I've got cold sweats, and now I'm getting stomach cramping. What about all the bodies the news reported?" he asked.

"Well, I should tell you how it finished up."

"Please do," he said, barely squeaking it out.

"So we left off with the Opus Dei guys filling the hole. One of them went to look for a bathroom as they were wrapping up, and I followed him and put a bullet through his mouth," Battalini said.

"That wasn't necessary," the Black Pope said, almost hissing.

"Oh, I think it was if I was going to get those guys out of their newly created tomb," Battalini said.

The Black Pope blinked and looked at him, not understanding.

"I waited for a while for the other Opus Dei guy to come into the castle, and I put a bullet through his throat. I know he was dead because I put the second bullet through his right eye."

"Why would you do that?" he said.

"Well, of course, so he wouldn't try to stop me from digging out the hole. It only took me about twenty minutes to dig it out. I then released the targets from their crypt, and ambulances came to treat them."

"What are you talking about? Are you saying you rescued them after we had this all wrapped up?" he said as pain was replaced with confusion.

"That's what I just said. And you know what? Everything you feared could be there was there," Battalini said.

"Oh my God, what have you done?" the Black Pope said, as he tried to raise his voice, but it came out more like a whisper.

Battalini smiled at the Black Pope.

"That's not all I've done. Do you remember the obscure ex-priest you had Massier kill? He was the best friend I had in the world. You had him crushed like a bug and didn't give it a second thought. So I created your special little drink enjoyed by a number of popes over the years. In fact, it's the very same concoction you had ordered up for Pope John Paul. You do remember him, don't you?"

"You didn't," the Black Pope said as he gasped with the realization of his painful and short term future.

"I did, and just so you know, I enjoyed doing it to you before you could do it to me."

The Black Pope fell out of his chair and looked up at Battalini as his body contorted into the fetal position.

"You'll never get away with this," he said, almost wheezing.

"I already have. It's six forty-five and your assistant won't be here for an hour and fifteen minutes. You'll have been stiff for over an hour, and there will be no apparent reason. It must have been a heart attack. When was the last time you heard of an autopsy in the Vatican?" Battalini said as he stood and picked up the tea service. He looked down at the Black Pope, who was now writhing. "Have a nice rest of your life, which I think should last for another minute," he said.

Battalini moved to the office door and turned around.

"Just one more thing. If you believe in such things, you're going straight to hell. *Fuck you*," he said and closed the office door behind him.

Battalini was moving with purpose. He returned to the kitchen and replaced the sugar, threw out the milk, and rinsed the vessel. He replaced each item to its original space, rinsed and put away the spoons, threw out the lemons, put away the tray, and walked away with the tea pot and the Black Pope's tea cup and stirring spoon. He went back to the main level and went into the men's room. The tainted tea went down the toilet. He rinsed the tea pot and took it with him.

He went back to the black ops inventory room, unlocked the door for the second time that morning, and placed the tea pot, cup, and spoon deep in a corner. If anyone would ever have a question about its residue, it's what he did for the church, and he was in charge of cleaning up the church's messes. No one would know he had just cleaned up the church's biggest mess, and it was now lying in a heap two floors above him.

***

Word spread through the Vatican like a wildfire. The Black Pope had many enemies and it was doubtful a single tear was shed. The Vatican Police and the Swiss Guard were on site and investigating. There were suspicions it was something other than natural causes, but no one wanted to go there. He could have had a heart attack, but the contorted look on his face indicated to everyone this was a poisoning. People knew he and Father Gatto had animosity and the Jesuits and Opus Dei didn't like each other.

The next question for the Jesuits' inner circle was who would replace the now decomposing Black Pope. This was considered a more important decision than when a White Pope was chosen, but there would be no white smoke nor public proclamation. The Black Pope was elected by the Jesuit General Congregation, but the inner circle would be making this important decision, and the election by the General Congregation would be a mere formality. Secrecy was the watchword.

***

Sean arose at about the same time the Black Pope was enjoying his first taste of Battalini's special tea and called the hospital. It took some effort, but he found a doctor who was present during the admittance process, and he let Sean know both patients were doing better. They remained in intensive care, but were making progress. The doctor felt they would both make full recoveries, but it would be some time before they would be able to leave the hospital.

Sean was relieved to hear the prognosis, and his thoughts shifted to the undetermined danger that still existed. He also wondered what would become of their discovery, about the funeral for Alfred, what would happen with Battalini, and when would he get to see his wife and kids. All he had were questions and no answers.

266

He called Cat to let her know he would still be a few days. He told her that one of the Rockenbach brothers had been killed at the castle and he would be staying at least until the funeral. They debated when he would come home, and then she agreed he should stay until he was finished. She was like that; she wanted him home and safe, but when she found he was staying longer to help someone else, she agreed.

He went down to breakfast, but just picked at his food. He had an empty feeling, and after a number of days of constant focus and motion forward, he felt like he was treading water.

He killed time until eight-thirty and then called Max. The family was dealing with Alfred's death as well as could be expected. The funeral was going to be in two days, and everyone was in support mode for each other. They agreed to hang loose for the day, and Sean said he would call if he heard from Battalini.

At nine-thirty Sean's phone rang, "Hello, Sean O'Shea," he said.

"Sean, this is Father Battalini. I've had a rather active morning. I thought I could set your mind at ease regarding future threats from the Vatican. The Black Pope, the man who was calling the shots and sending the assassins to kill you is dead. He somehow ingested poisoned tea sometime early this morning. You and your friends can take a deep breath and relax. You're no longer in danger. A new Black Pope will be named, and he'll lean on me for help since I know where all the bodies are buried. I'll call you as soon as I have a suggestion for what you might do with your find."

"Father Battalini, I can't thank you enough. You've been our guardian angel. I'll call the others. This takes a huge weight off our shoulders, and I look forward to your next call," Sean said.

Sean called Max, and a great sense of relief flooded both of them. Max said he would immediately call Gola.

Sean wasn't content to sit, and this bit of good news gave him renewed energy. His adrenaline had been running at a high level for so long he couldn't just sit around in a hotel room and do nothing. The Rockenbachs were in mourning, and Alan was fighting for his life. Sean made his decision. He would go back to the castle, which would give him purpose for the day, and he could stop and check on his wounded friends. He put his phone into his pocket, his jacket over his arm, and was now filled with anticipation. This was a far better feeling than he had all morning. He

267

stopped at the buffet table, added coffee to a large cup, and helped himself to a pastry.

Moments later he was on his way to the castle. On the drive his imagination ran wild. He daydreamed about being interviewed on the *"To-day Show"* about how he and his team made the most significant discovery in recorded history. The feeling was intoxicating. His trip went by quicker because he was lost in positive thoughts. He pulled up to the castle and yellow tape was stretched across the access road. There were TV trucks and people hanging around trying to get a glimpse of what was happening as Sean found a spot to pull off the road and park.

He walked up the steep road and ducked under the police tape. His confident bypass of the yellow tape brought stares from the gathered who were respecting the demarcation line. He noticed the tape was farther down the hill than what he remembered from yesterday. He continued walking toward the castle and was in for his next surprise.

He came over the last rise and his stomach tightened. The exterior of the castle was cordoned off with what looked like a mini wall of orange plastic. The barrier was about four feet tall, and stretched between green supports every fifteen feet, that appeared to have been pounded into the ground. Behind the wall were armed sentries about every thirty feet. Sean approached, got close enough to see over the plastic wall, and beheld large green United States Army vehicles.

Sean was within twenty feet when the nearest sentry confronted him.

"Halt, do not come any closer," the sentry said.

"*What's happening here?*" Sean said, now angered that his great find was compromised and his loss of control was clear. "I demand to see whoever is in charge," he said.

"Sir, you must turn around and go back down the hill. This is a military operation and has classified status. No one is being allowed access. Please leave or you will be arrested," the sentry said.

Sean stood still for a moment. He said, "You better inform whoever is in charge the man who led this operation has returned. I was here yesterday and was involved in everything that took place. I saw everything in the underground laboratory and am the one responsible for this whole thing. I think he'll want to talk with me."

Chapter 51)

The sentry was stopped in his tracks. He hesitated for a moment, turned to the sentry on his left, told him he was leaving for a moment and to watch the man in front of him. Moments later the sentry returned. "Please follow me, sir," he said.

Sean found an entry point and followed the sentry into the courtyard. He was taken to a large man in full uniform who turned as they approached.

"Good afternoon, Mr. O'Shea. I'm General Pendleton. We need to talk," he said.

Sean was speechless. "How do you know who I am?" he asked.

"When something of this magnitude comes to our attention we find out everything as fast as possible. Your police interview made it easy. Please follow me inside so we can talk about this in a more private setting," he said.

Sean followed the general and found himself back in the Himmler office. How strange; less than twenty-four hours ago he was in this very office having a profound discussion with Father Battalini. They both sat and the general spoke.

"What you've discovered is remarkable. Can you tell me how you put all this together?" the general asked.

"It started and evolved as a simple investigation and just picked up speed," Sean said, not wanting to reveal his connection to the CIA agents.

"How did you get connected with the Rockenbachs?" the general asked.

"Alan Rockenbach and I were childhood friends. I bounced some theories off him and he wanted to help. It was simply a coincidence his cousins were law enforcement," Sean said.

The general leaned back and thought for a moment. He asked, "How did you connect with Philipe Laflamme?"

"I don't know who that is?"

"He was one of the men who was shot and taken to the hospital," Pendleton said.

"He wasn't with us. I don't know," Sean said.

Sean hoped the general would believe Laflamme had been investigating as part of his normal activities.

"Who is he?" Sean asked.

"Just someone who took an interest in what you were doing and appeared to have stumbled into the middle of this. I read the report about the assailants. You said they were people trying to keep you from discovering what was in the laboratory. You said you didn't know who they were. I find that difficult to believe, given everything else you were able to accomplish," the general said.

"You're correct, I didn't reveal everything. We didn't know who they were, but we do know they were sent by the Vatican. It appears the church has been silencing anyone investigating UFO crashes the Nazis recovered in the mid and late 1930s. I didn't want that knowledge to be part of the record when I gave the interview to the officer," Sean said.

The general again paused and said, "You know you can never reveal what you found here. This can never come out. Did you take anything?"

"No, I didn't, but I wish I had. The thought this would be quarantined or confiscated was the last thing on my mind. I thought there would be plenty of time to explore what was found. I wasn't thinking straight with all that happened yesterday afternoon," O'Shea said.

"This never happened, do you understand?" the general said.

"*No I don't. This is the greatest discovery in the history of the world. Why would this be covered up?*"

"That's not a question I'm prepared to answer, and it's not a question I choose to ask. This position was established long ago. I wasn't part of that decision process, nor am I part of the current decision-making. I follow orders, and our orders are to remove the contents of the laboratory."

Sean was incredulous. "How can this be happening? This needs to come out. By the way, how did you find out about this and where did you come from?" Sean asked.

"Mr. O'Shea, believe me when I say I understand your frustration and your anger. You realize there are answers I cannot and will not give you. I will tell you we're based in Heidelberg, so we're less than two hours away," the general said.

"I didn't know we still had military bases in Germany. So you're telling me this whole thing didn't happen and I'm not to speak of it. What if I do?" Sean asked.

"You're correct, this is considered a matter of national security. If you're deemed to violate national security, you'll be arrested. Thanks to the Patriot Act, you can be held without due process because you've acted against the interests of the United States. Mr. O'Shea, I don't think you want to miss Liam's and Cassie's weddings and the enjoyment of playing with your grandchildren," the general said.

"*This can't happen in America*," Sean said.

"Mr. O'Shea, this happens more often than you would think. Prior to the Patriot Act, it was more difficult to make someone disappear. Since then it's become standard operating procedure. I admire what you've accomplished, and I would hate to see you make a bad decision affecting the rest of your life," the general said.

Sean marveled at how Pendleton could threaten the rest of his life while being so calm and sympathetic. It was also disconcerting the general knew the names of Sean's kids, and Sean understood this wasn't an idle threat. The general seemed so professional he was almost likable, yet he was threatening Sean's very existence. He didn't know what to say.

"So this whole thing will be covered up?" Sean asked.

"The deaths will be explained as Neo Nazi fanatics attempting to take over Wewelsburg Castle. There have been threats to that end in the past, so it will be accepted as plausible. The curator and security guard were casualties, and a visitor was in the wrong place at the wrong time. The local authorities will be given credit for taking back the castle and killing the perpetrators. The story won't be questioned, and in a month it'll disappear. That's the way we want it, out of the public eye."

"Are you telling me I have no choice at all?"

"Yes, that's exactly what I'm telling you. We're almost done; in fact, we may have everything loaded. When we leave, the castle will be back in the hands of the District of Buren. I'm sure they'll reopen when they appoint a new curator, and it'll be back to business as usual."

"Is this a Roswell and Kecksburg all over again?"

The general smiled. "You know I can't comment," he said. "I think we're finished here, and I hope for your sake and the sake of your family you make the right choice."

"How are you going to control the German citizens?"

271

"That will be handled by representatives of the German government. We have every expectation it will be handled with discretion. Besides, German citizens talking about UFOs without proof or pictures will get zero play in the good old U.S. of A. In case you haven't noticed, Americans know nothing of the Freiburg or Poland UFO crashes even though they had multiple witnesses and are documented. We aren't concerned about what German citizens may say."

The general stood, walked out of the Himmler office and held open the door to the courtyard for Sean to pass. They walked onto the cobblestones without conversation. There were many uniformed men carrying files and handing them off in a mini assembly line as they loaded the trucks. Sean was still standing next to the general when they were approached by a man with a clipboard.

"General, we have everything loaded. Shall we depart for Heidelberg?" the soldier asked.

"Yes, Lieutenant. When you're ready, feel free to get underway."

"General, do you have any issue if I wander around? I won't be back here and I never took it in yesterday," Sean asked.

"I guess it couldn't do any harm. We're packed and ready to go. You may encounter some issues with the District of Buren folks. They're waiting to lock up the place once we leave, but okay by me."

"Thank you. I'll just have a brief look around."

O'Shea didn't waste any time once the general turned his attention elsewhere. He walked around the side of the castle as the troops were moving in the opposite direction. Sean wanted to see the lab before it was closed. He went down into the hole as large lights and batteries were being removed. He could hear trucks starting to pull out of the parking lot and knew he wouldn't have much time to look around. He went into the lab which twenty-four hours ago acted as his tomb for a short time. There were still lights on, but they were about to be turned off. Sean walked through the lab which was now clean and empty. Even the garbage had been removed. The operating room where Laflamme and Alan had lain was empty except for bloodstains on the floor. So much for preserving the crime scene he thought. His pace slowed because he knew there would be nothing to be found.

Without warning, the entire back of the lab went black. The experience was too similar to that of yesterday, so it was exit stage left. He reentered the castle and wandered around to see if anything would occur to him. After ten minutes of conducting a self-guided tour no light bulbs had gone off. His despondency grew when he walked down the hall and saw the extensive amount of dried blood from Alan and Alfred. He entered the curator's office where the yellow tape outlined   the shape of a body surrounded by blood-soaked carpet. Sean surmised the blood may still be wet and shook his head to remove the image. He was leaving the curator's office when he was approached by an official looking gentleman.

"Excuse me, General Pendleton mentioned you'd be in here, and we're ready to close the museum," the representative from District of Buren said.

"That's fine with me. I'm done looking around."

The museum official locked the curator's office without another word, and Sean stepped into the courtyard. It looked different than when he arrived. It was now devoid of vehicles, soldiers, and with no evidence of the mini wall of orange barriers. It again looked as it had yesterday morning when they first arrived.

Sean stopped just before he headed down the access road and turned around. He wanted one last look at the site of the world's greatest find that would never be known. He took it in for about twenty seconds, then had enough. He walked back down and ducked under the yellow tape. There were fewer people hanging around, and he figured when the military vehicles departed it signaled an end to the party. He started his car, did a U-turn and headed toward the hospital.

Chapter 52)

Sean pulled into the hospital parking lot and went into intensive care. He knew he wouldn't be allowed to see either patient unless he found someone from the day before. He was fortunate to find a doctor from the previous night, so he was able to circumvent the normal rules. Since he was involved in the emergency situation, there appeared to be more consideration, but his visits were limited to five minutes each.

He started with Alan, who was sedated but awake. Sean told him it was Battalini who came to their rescue, and Alan already knew of Alfred's demise. Sean told him the U.S. Army had confiscated their entire find and made direct threats relative to the Patriot Act. The nurse entered and ended their time together. Sean was led into Laflamme's room.

Philipe was doing better than Alan. He was upright and his eyes were brighter. Sean gave him the same recap of what had taken place. He also told him of the conversation with General Pendleton and how he indicated he didn't know Laflamme. The agent didn't think the Army would investigate, given they were in a foreign country and just made the haul of the century. He also guessed they would conclude Laflamme was investigating Sean and the Rockenbachs. The Weiler killing in Freiburg, while investigating the same matter, would add validity to that line of thinking.

Sean was about to leave when Laflamme asked for a favor. His car was parked at the bottom of the hill by the castle, and he asked if Sean would bring it to the hospital. Sean said of course and he would do it before he departed for Freiburg.

Laflamme gave Sean a knowing smile. "Did you say the Army took all the evidence?" he said.

"Yes, I walked through the lab and it was cleaned out. They even took the garbage," Sean said.

"Well then, I have a little surprise for you. Remember the artifacts we gave to the lab in Lyon? I have them for you and the report is in the same box. You'll find them in my trunk, under the mat," Laflamme said.

Sean felt like his heart skipped a beat. The last couple of days provided so many of these little adrenaline pops it had become a familiar feeling.

"I'd forgotten all about those. I'll bring your car back to the parking lot and give the keys to the nurse at the front desk. They may not let me see you again, but I'll try. Philipe, you just made my day," Sean said.

Sean got the keys from Laflamme's personal effects and called for a cab. He found Laflamme's car and, holding his breath, opened the trunk and pulled out a shoe box-sized sealed carton. Shutting the trunk, he unlocked the driver's door and ripped open the box before closing his door. The artifacts were covered in bubble wrap, and he removed the report. He scanned until he found what he was looking for.

It read, 'The items presented for testing are fabricated from unknown materials. They possess a tensile strength which could not be measured due to an inability to induce failure. These items represent the strongest materials this laboratory has ever tested. More extensive testing will be required to determine the makeup of these materials, but our expert opinion is these items were fabricated in an unknown fashion.'

Sean held his breath. They now had proof and a lab report to back it up. Sean started the car and drove back to the hospital. He pulled into the hospital's visitor parking lot, locked Laflamme's car, and returned the keys to the intensive care unit.

He wouldn't let the box out of his possession and clutched it as he exited the hospital, feeling reinvigorated despite the warnings from General Pendleton. He at least had something tangible to take home. Pointing the rental car toward Freiburg, he smiled for the first time in thirty-six hours.

***

Sean called Cat and told her things were wrapping up and his plan was to leave for Bend the day after Alfred's funeral. He told her of the warning and of the lab report. As always, she didn't want to push the envelope. Sean felt relieved to have a firm date when he would see Cat and Liam, but wasn't sure how he would handle his knowledge and evidence. He finished his call to Cat, then called Max.

Chapter 53)

Max sounded a little better than the last time they spoke, and Sean filled him in on the fate of their evidence. He also spoke about the warning from the general, the lab report, and the improvement of both Alan and Philipe.

"My, you've been busy. When are you getting back to Freiburg?"

"I'll be back in about two and a half hours."

"Drive safe. You're welcome to join us for dinner. We have a family thing planned."

"Thanks, Max, but I think your family should be together without me hanging around. I can't shake the feeling I'm somehow responsible. Don't say anything; I know what you'll say, but I think it's better if you're all together tonight."

"Okay, I won't push it. What are your plans?"

"I'm heading home the day after the funeral. I have to figure out what to do about all this, and I don't have a clue."

"Drive careful and call me tomorrow."

"I will."

Sean thought about how he was feeling. This was the first time in two weeks he wasn't worried about who was watching and if someone was about to take a shot at him. Even when he thought he was relaxed, the underlying tension hadn't left him, and he was starting to feel like a rag doll. He decided the hardest part was over, and tonight he would eat well, have a nice bottle of wine, and sleep in. That was just what he did.

***

He awoke at ten and moved in slow motion until noon and was back to feeling melancholy. The excitement of getting the lab reports was overshadowed by thinking about Rudolf and Alfred. The loss of the discovery made him wonder why he did all of this in the first place. He went into the hotel restaurant and had two glasses of wine for lunch, a sure sign he was trying to get numb. He took the second glass into the lobby and found a comfortable chair.

He called Max and found there would be a visitation that evening, and the funeral would be at ten the following day.

The visitation was quiet and sad. Everyone came together, and Sean was treated as part of the family. The funeral the next day was similar, with an attempt at celebration falling short.

After the funeral Sean drove to Paderborn to see Alan and Philipe. It was as much to get away from the grief as to see them, although Sean had promised to stop in again before he left for the U.S. They were both appreciative Sean made the effort, even though he was again limited to a five-minute visit.

The family reconvened at Max's home that night, and Sean spent most of the evening with Max. At nine he decided it was time to leave, knowing he still had to pack and had an early and long day ahead of him tomorrow. There were hugs all around. He had grown close to this family, and given the traumas they shared, their relationships intensified in a short time. He promised to call whenever he heard from Battalini and looked forward to seeing them all again.

Sean returned to his hotel and packed. He had an empty feeling in his gut, while at the same time he was eager to get home and see his family. He had accomplished more than he could have ever expected, yet the body count was huge. Two cops and a passerby in Baden-Baden, two cops and *Herr* Schmidt in Villingen, Rudolf Weiler, Alfred, the curator, the security guard and three bad guys. Thirteen people had died and two more were in the hospital, so Sean could pursue his 'Big Project.' If he had it all to do over again, he would shit can the whole thing. As it was, he ended up making a beyond belief discovery that he could never talk about or he would disappear into a black hole never to be seen again. All the good and bad, yet he had nothing to show for it. Sean could only shake his head from side to side. He was tired of thinking about it. He turned the light off and got into his Colombi Hotel bed for the last time.

Chapter 54)

The alarm went off, and Sean was up without hesitation. He was anxious to get home. Sean was in the lobby in twenty minutes, checked out, and left the Beretta in a package for Max at the counter.

At the airport he called Cassie and felt guilty he hadn't been in touch since he saw her in Heidelberg. He'd been concerned she could get involved in his mess, but felt bad for his lack of contact. He was happy to get her on his first call, and their conversation made him feel better. He didn't share the details of his activities, but promised to give her the full story when she came home.

His long trip home would start in Strasbourg, would connect in Paris, then Seattle, and finally arrive in Bend, Oregon. The anticipation of going home created a far different feeling than when he started the trip in Rhinelander. The constant stress and traumatic experiences left Sean wiped out. He would use the travel day to rest, and for once he managed to sleep on an airplane.

The plane touched down at the Bend Redmond Airport at dinner time, and Cat and Liam were waiting. Greeting Sean at the airport had been a tradition when the kids were younger, and it felt great to see them. He gave hugs and didn't want to let go. He knew when they heard the full story Liam would think it was the coolest thing ever, and Cat would be all over him because he hadn't been forthcoming about the peril.

The thirty minute ride to the house was spent catching up on what they'd been doing. The baseball season had started for Liam, and Cat was back on raw foods, with a new kick of drinking copious amounts of alkaline water. She also wanted to tell him all about the latest blue green algae product she found. How wonderful; she really knew how to capture his interest. Sean waited until they were home and bags were put away before he started the story. Cat made tea, and they sat down in the living room. It was time to spin a tale.

"You're going to have some issues with what I'm about to tell you. What you need to realize is I'm home and safe. You're about to hear an amazing tale that I can never tell again."

For the next two hours, Sean told the drama in detail. There were many questions to answer, but by the time he finished they knew the whole story. Cat was unhappy he hadn't been open with her and didn't keep her apprised of the whole situation, even though she knew he had her best interests at heart. Liam thought it was cool his dad was like a secret agent even though Sean told him that was far from the case.

Chapter 55)

Father Battalini was sitting in his office when there was a knock on the door. Three Jesuit Cardinals, members of the inner circle, came into Battalini's office. They looked grim.

"Father Battalini, we need to speak with you."

"What can I do for you?" Battalini asked, stomach muscles tightening, shallow breathing increasing.

Could a surveillance camera have been installed in the Black Pope's office?

"You're aware the Black Pope has passed. We believe he was poisoned. You know the inner workings of the Vatican, and we'd like to know if you know anything about this?"

Battalini wondered if they were setting him up.

"No, I haven't heard anything. I've been on an assignment in Freiburg, Germany for the last week. I didn't return until this morning. I know he had many enemies," Battalini said.

"We have reason to suspect Father Gatto. The Jesuits and Opus Dei don't like each other. In the last few days they had more interaction than usual, and from what we heard, it wasn't pleasant," A cardinal said.

"I would doubt Father Gatto had anything to do with this. I've always known him to be reasonable and easy to work with," Battalini said.

"What did he have you working on?" he was asked.

"I was working on an issue regarding the Alien Theory and was involved in the incident at Wewelsburg Castle yesterday."

"You were involved in that ugly business?"

"Yes. I'm happy to say that everything has been handled and the threat is over."

"You have a knack for solving problems, Father Battalini."

"Thank you, I do my best. Is there any word on a successor to the Black Pope?" Battalini asked.

"No, we haven't had everyone together to finalize it. There are several names we're considering, and we'll go through the process. In the meantime, please conduct business as usual."

"I will, as I always do. Please let me know if I can be of any assistance," Battalini said.

"Thank you Father."

Battalini sat back in his chair and felt relief he wasn't a suspect. It was good they suspected Gatto, but he would make sure Gatto didn't take the fall for the Black Pope's death. In the process he would make a friend with the head of Opus Dei, which would be a good thing.

Late in the day Battalini's phone rang. One of the cardinals who visited him earlier called to inform him there was a new development in the Black Pope's death. He indicated it was urgent, and Battalini's presence was requested in the Black Pope's office. Battalini's alarm went off once again. He stood and started for the door. He stopped and returned to his desk, removed a Beretta and slipped it under his robe. He wasn't sure what he would encounter, but the Vatican was famous for *coup d'états*.

Battalini found himself retracing the steps he made earlier that morning. He approached the secretary's desk, and the assistant looked at him in an odd, knowing way. That increased Battalini's paranoia.

"They're waiting for you Father Battalini," he said.

He didn't like the way that sounded, and touched the butt of the Beretta through his robe, as he twisted the door knob to the former Black Pope's office. The door swung open and he stepped in, but it was empty. He heard voices beyond the office and walked into the living area where there were at least ten cardinals engaged in small talk.

Father Gambini, the oldest of the Cardinals, spoke,

"Father Battalini, please be seated," he said.

Battalini was wary.

"What can I do for this illustrious group?" he said.

"We'll get right to the point. We've chosen a new Superior General and we wanted to make you aware of who he is."

Battalini had a short intake of breath, but it wasn't noticed.

"Father Battalini, we've chosen you, if you would so honor us."

Battalini wasn't sure what he heard. "Did you just ask me to be the Black Pope?" he asked.

The cardinals around the room smiled. It was rare to see Father Battalini be less than his confident self.

"Yes we did. It's yours if you say yes."

"Then by all means, I say yes," Battalini said.

Cardinals from all over the room started congratulating Battalini and began kissing his ring as a symbolic gesture.

"These are your new living quarters if they meet with your approval. You'll be given an unlimited budget to make any changes you wish. The belongings of the previous occupant have been removed, and it has been cleaned. You may move in whenever you wish," Gambini said.

"I'm overwhelmed by your generosity and your confidence in me. I thank you all. I'll do the job to the best of my ability," Battalini said.

"Father, we know you're the only man for the job. Certain fences need to be mended, and we think you have the skills to do so. You're not afraid to do what's necessary, but we think you'll do it with a softer touch than your predecessor. Please let us know if you need anything. An immediate announcement is ready to be released," one of the cardinals said.

With that, they filed out with comments of appreciation. Battalini sat on the sofa and looked out the large picture window overlooking Rome. He'd been so preoccupied it never occurred to him he could be the one selected.

He decided to wait until the next day to move his belongings, but would enjoy the spacious quarters until then. He went through the rooms pondering the changes he would make. He preferred a more rustic, down to earth decor instead of the quasi Las Vegas feel his predecessor preferred.

He finished his brief tour and decided to check out the office. He sat at his new desk and started checking all the high-tech equipment, including the computer that was turned on and operational. He found that to be unusual. He decided this must be his new computer and he would create his own password. That made sense to him.

He wanted to see what software was installed so he started clicking icons until he got to one he didn't recognize. He clicked it, and to his surprise it was a camera system. He had views of any number of locations and started scrolling through the various cameras until he found a familiar scene, the office in which he was now sitting. The Black Pope did have a camera system in the office after all. He clicked on the picture of his new office, and it expanded to the whole screen with date and time stamp options on the right side of the screen. He clicked six-thirty, and suddenly he was looking at himself and listening to the conversation taking place between himself and the Black Pope with a pot of tea positioned in the

282

middle of the desk. His mind jumped to how he could erase the tape, then he realized he was the new Superior General of the Society of Jesus, the most powerful man in the Vatican, and he could pipe this into the email system and would still be untouchable, except, of course, if someone served him special tea.

He was looking at options on the screen and found one stating Views. He clicked it and took a deep breath when he saw this particular segment had been viewed seven times since the Black Pope's demise. The last time was two hours ago. The Cardinals had been aware he was responsible for eliminating the Black Pope and they then named him to be successor. Instead of facing an execution, he became emperor.

How interesting the ways of the Vatican. He knew what they had seen and he could be content with the knowledge he was picked most likely because he had done the deed.

Chapter 56)

Sean stood, he was stiff and tired from his trip. He emptied his pockets on the living room coffee table, including his cell phone, wallet, and his keys.

"I'm going to put on my flannels," he said.

He entered the bedroom's walk-in closet and was naked when his cell phone started ringing in the living room. He grabbed a robe, but knew he would miss the call.

"Cat, grab that, would you?" he asked.

He heard her answer.

"Could you repeat that? One moment please," she said in an oddly formal way.

She came into the bedroom with her hand over the phone. "It's for you. He said he's calling from Rome and said to tell you it's the Black Pope," she said, looking terrified. Sean had just told her about the Black Pope.

Sean's pulse increased. Why would the Black Pope call him at home?

"Hello, this is Sean O'Shea."

"Mr. O'Shea, this is the Black Pope calling from Rome."

Sean thought the voice sounded familiar, but he was confused and quiet.

"Sean, it's Father Battalini," he said.

"Oh my God, you scared my wife half to death. I thought it was the real Black Pope calling and I was thinking what now?" Sean said.

"Sean, for your information, it is the real Black Pope calling. I was asked to assume those responsibilities, and I have accepted. I'm now the Superior General of the Society Of Jesus," Battalini said.

"*Unbelievable. That's great!* I can't tell you how happy I am to hear this news. I just wish Father Schmidt was here to see it."

Battalini was silent for a moment.

"I wanted you to know you have a friend in Rome. Please call on me if you ever need my assistance," he said.

"I do need some advice. The US Army confiscated the contents of the laboratory. They told me, because of the Patriot Act, if I come forward with any announcement I'll disappear. I've just uncovered, through hard work and the sacrifice of many, the greatest find in the history of the world, and I can't do anything about it. I know the release of this discovery is something you'd be against, but I still want your advice."

"Sean, you put me in an impossible position. I would hate to see the worldwide effects if the find became known. On the other hand, I know how you must feel.

"I do have a suggestion. You can't risk going public with this because your government does make people disappear. What you can do is write a novel and do the entire story as a work of fiction. They won't like it, but as a work of fiction you'll be safe. You'll feel your work wasn't in vain, and you can get the word out for people to consider."

"I hadn't thought of that approach, but it's a terrific idea. I can feel this whole thing had some value, and save a little self-respect."

"If you do write a novel, I have a suggestion for the title. Call it the Vatican Protocol. It's what Father Schmidt used to call our solutions to potential problems and would be a fitting tribute."

"Father, you've been my guardian angel and you continue to be," Sean said.

"Sean, you have a friend here. Call any time you need me."

"Thank you, and if I can ever help you, please let me know. Good bye my friend," Sean said.

"Goodbye," Battalini said.

Sean looked at Cat. "It's good to have friends in high places," he said.

***

Father Battalini put down the gold phone. He liked Sean, and he was glad he had been able to help him.

The new Black Pope was also glad he had a friend in General Pendleton.

The End

CPSIA information can be obtained
at www.ICGtesting.com
Printed in the USA
LVOW12s1630010916

502833LV00003B/457/P